Mayfly

by

Michael Nye

ISBN: 978-1-291-93712-1

PublishNation, London
www.publishnation.co.uk

To the Navigators,
who made it all possible.

Chapter 1

"Now, maybe," he thought, as he looked across the river. "Maybe there is some rule, or bye-law that says that I should not be here at all. Somewhere in some dusty office is a book in which is written an edict proclaiming that I should not do what I am about to do. However, in the absence of anybody to inform me of the fact or enforce the said edict, I shall carry on and see what happens."

With the thought in mind, he picked up the rubber hose and slowly squeezed the black rubber primer bulb until he could smell just a feint odour of petrol from the carburettor. Then, leaning over the motor, he flicked the choke lever across and took a firm hold on the starter cord. Two slow pulls with the choke in, another somewhat faster with it out again, then with half choke again and a good swift pull the single cylinder 3.9 horsepower outboard burst into life. The motor was a bit old but very well made and reliable, as long as it was treated with respect. Whilst it ticked over, he set to untying the ropes, carefully placing them within easy reach before getting back aboard. As he stepped onto the thwart, he gave a little push to edge the bow outward before flicking the motor into gear. He was away and, rather than increase speed immediately, he savoured the moment, knowing, that in some small way, life would never be quite the same again.

Where most people of his age hankered after looking cool, mostly by riding mopeds or scooters, he had taken pity on a fifteen foot-six inch plywood boat, not much more than a dinghy, with a small cabin and rather too much water on the inside. Whilst technically it had not sunk it was well on the way to achieving the goal and, without intervention, it would no doubt have done so in a matter of a week or so. Although he felt that one should not feel pity for an inanimate object he nonetheless was stirred into sufficient action as to walk along the riverbank and enquire at an old boatyard as to whom the vessel belonged. A telephone number was written on a piece of paper for him and, as there was a phone box nearby he tried his luck. It was in, and a male voice answered.

"I wonder if you could help me," asked Jim. "Only I have been given your number by Saracen's boatyard as someone that may know something about."

"The Mayfly," came the reply from the other end of the line in a tone of resigned exasperation.

"Did you know it was in a poor state," Jim asked. "And would you mind if I baled it out? If someone doesn't it will sink pretty soon."

"I'd be only too glad if you did, you can have the wretched thing if you want it."

At this remark Jim was rather taken aback, the thought of messing about in boats appealed to him a lot, and had done for as long as he could remember. Now somebody was actually offering him the chance, albeit in jest.

"Look I only offered to help," he said. "There's no need to to go all weird about it."

The voice on the line said, "Who's being funny? Why on earth would you want to empty the river out of a boat unless you had some kind of interest in preserving it? So, I'm offering you the chance. I bought the thing on a whim, and for reasons I don't really want to go into I haven't really been able to do anything more than that. Now I have lost any interest I had in it, so its time for someone else to act on a whim."

"I can't let a total stranger give me a boat," exclaimed Jim. "Its, well, it's more than odd. It's."

"O.K. Then," the voice cut in. "I'll sell it to you. Fifteen pounds and it's yours. If you want the motor as well, it's another tenner. You go back to Saracen's, borrow a bucket, and by the time you have done all that I'll sort things with them."

By the end of the day the deal was done. There was just five pounds left of the thirty that Jim had saved up in order to pay for the Sinclair stereo, in kit form, that he was going to assemble over the Summer, and after some two hours of baling, the Mayfly's cache of river water was back where it belonged and, to Jim's surprise, was making no attempt to return.

That day, to Jim, was as remote as any facts he had gleaned from history lessons, although it did stick in his mind rather better. It was not much more than a month that had passed since the purchase, but in that time the appearance of the Mayfly had undergone a transformation that belied the minute amount of money that Jim had to invest. This was due in part to the fact that Saracen's was very much an old style of boatyard, and the people working there seemed to be as much a part of the fabric of the place

2

as the large weather worn timber buildings that contained the bulk of the business. The yard had stacks of items that may have come in useful but which seldom did. Seldom that is until Jim decided to salvage a small and rather dilapidated boat. Half tins of varnish, tarnished fittings, offcuts of wood and other things, turned up, on almost a daily, basis in a box under the tarpaulin that covered the cockpit. Jim's thanks were generally met with remarks like. "We thought it was being used as a skip mate." Which were then generally followed with advice and quite often a good deal of help and instruction on the particular task he was trying to achieve. One weekend Jim arrived at the yard to find the Mayfly had mysteriously found its way up the slipway, and was waiting, along with half a tin of rather good quality paint, to have its bottom painted. This time he was told that they were testing their gear, and didn't want to wreck anything decent.

Even with the help that he had received, it was a big achievement to have brought the little boat back to life. But here he was heading up river for the first time in his life, and here also was the Mayfly, in use for the first time in over a decade. Jim was savouring the moment, but also wondering what came next. Once the petrol tank was empty he had no money to fill it, so it simply had to get him to his destination. It was unclear too just what that destination would reveal, apart from the more obvious detail that he was to find an island a few miles upstream, and go to one of the two houses on it to talk to someone whom the people at Saracen's thought may have some work that would see him, at least partly, through the Summer.

With the first bridge the scenery changed to something more industrial than the part where the boatyard was. On the right bank there was a wood yard, and on the left an old factory building with a large concrete wharf for barges to deposit their cargoes. This of course was now in a state of slow decay, as river traffic to the factory had long since been transferred to the roads. It was a warm day in the part of the year that you could never be sure if it should be early Summer or late Spring. The weather was mild enough and there was sufficient breeze for the sailing club to be about their business of tacking across the river. Jim remembered the "Sail before steam" maxim that he had read somewhere and kept to a slow speed past the mass of white sails. He could not help feeling that the people in the dinghy race disapproved for no other reason than the fact that he was there.

"It's O.K. I guess," he mused. "Whatever view of me they have is probably wrong, and I have as much right to be here as they do."

He was still pondering as the first obstacle came into view. The locks on this part of the river were quite large, though not as massive as some on other rivers. Big enough though to have a full time keeper to work the hydraulically operated gates and sluices. As he approached, he could see that it was empty and the gates were opening ready for him to enter, so he let the motor slowly tick over until he was called in. Like this the boat would very slowly edge forward against the current and would be controllable. If he were to put the outboard into neutral, the absence of a rudder made any manoeuvre something of a lottery. Eventually the last boat passed out of the lock and he was called in, only to be asked if the boat was his. "Daft question," he thought. "What am I supposed to say? Nope, I nicked it?" He answered that it was, and that it had a current licence, which he'd managed to scrape sufficient cash for from his part time work in a local newsagent. Despite all of that, he still felt he was going to be viewed with a bit of suspicion, but at least he would not need to explain himself to the police. The keeper had disappeared from view, leaving the lock to be operated by an assistant. When the water got to the level at which Jim could see over the concrete edge, he found that he was looking at a pair of highly polished shoes inside of which was the aforementioned lock keeper.

"You're the lad that bought the Mayfly then are you?" He asked.

Jim felt as though he ought to check this in a mirror, or state that in fact he was not, and that he was a much disfigured elephant that had won the thing in a poker game, but politeness got the better of him so he simply smiled and said, "Yup, that's me"

"I just rang Saracens and they said you'd done a lot of work on her. We all thought she'd sink," the man smiled.

"It took me ages, well it seemed like it," Jim replied. "This the first time I've been out in her"

"And the first in over 15 years for the boat, I think," the lock keeper said. "Did you know that the last three owners won her playing poker?" The thought of a disfigured elephant came into Jim's mind and he smiled.

"O.K. Time to start up and move on, I'll see you later no doubt," the keeper added.

As Jim set to the task of bringing the outboard to life he thought to himself, "Maybe, but not today."

In the distance the river split into two channels, one a good deal wider than the other. It was late afternoon, and there was a cool breeze across the water, implying that there may be a late frost, possibly the last of the year.

4

As the island grew closer, he steered towards the narrower of the channels as the roof of a small bungalow came into view. He slowed down again to the tick-over that he had used to take Mayfly into the lock earlier, and looked for the small piece of frontage with a rudimentary landing stage bearing the name. "LlaMedos," this was where he had been told to tie up. As he approached, having passed under a rather ornate little bridge, he checked the last of the speed from his boat by flicking the motor into reverse for a few seconds, before stepping onto the rather shaky looking wooden staging.

"So, you must be the famous Jim Stratton. Nice job you've done on the little Mayfly, she always was a good boat in her day, and there's a lot of years left in her too."

The voice, which at first appeared disembodied belonged to Dave Harris who was shouting down the garden from his kitchen door.

"Well," thought Jim. "He doesn't sound like some posh uncle of two people who may or may not have shot arrows at me, and this is an island not a houseboat so I guess I still have a grip on reality."

"It's me," he shouted back. "Shall I come up"

"You'd better," the reply came. "If I roll down to the river I'd probably fall in. I haven't got the hang of this chair and I don't bloody want to get it either!"

It hadn't occurred to Jim that Dave Harris would be anything other than an able bodied eccentric that may want some work doing round the house. Once the Mayfly was secured to the mooring rings properly he made his way to the small timber bungalow that was one of two built on the equally small island. There had originally been a third between them but that had gone a long time ago.

"I fell over and killed my bloody hip a few weeks ago," Dave said, looking disdainfully at the chair he was sitting in. "It'll get to be O.K. in time but there were things I wanted to do that I can't now do, and in any case I'd probably not have been the right person to do them because my face is too well known."

"Are you some kind of criminal," Jim asked, in a matter of fact way, as though the knowledge didn't really bother him either way. He was pondering the prospect of a life in organised crime when his thoughts were interrupted.

"Who do you bloody think I am? Bloody Scarface! I fell off the doorstep after one too many pints, I wasn't massacred in an all in punch up

5

over the rights to sell illicit cocoa! Bloody hell! Talk about jumping to conclusions!"

"O.K. So what do you want then," Jim again asked. "Shopping? Grass cutting? What? One of the guys at Saracen's said you needed some work done and he knew I needed work."

"You need work and I need a cup of tea" Dave replied. "So come in and lets talk."

It was true, Jim needed money otherwise life looked pretty bleak for him. He hadn't run away from home, well not exactly, he had casually walked off in the direction of the river to "Mess about on that bloody boat!" as his cousin had put it.

In fact home wasn't really home at all, not that he was homeless, more that he was a mildly unwelcome, and slightly unwilling guest. Rather like a character in some Victorian novel he had been forced to read whilst at school, he had nowhere else to stay but with relatives. Neither of his parents were actively dead, and they both still liked him a lot. Unfortunately they no longer liked each other and they had a great deal of enthusiasm for their mutual dislike, so much that, had they chosen to expend the energy of hatred in solving their issues, there would have been none to solve. So there he was, the malevolent brooding castle (Victorian novels had a lot of them) for Jim was a three bedroomed suburban semi, shared with his much older cousin, his cousin's wife and their child. The kid in question was twelve and left no doubt about the absolute contempt in which he held Jim. Enter the love interest (there always was one of those) in the form of a small half sunken clinker built cabin cruiser. That the said love interest was made of plywood is a minor detail, she (most boats seem to be female) had exerted her charm, Jim had decided that life was better this way, and had arranged (or said he had made arrangements) to spend Summer on the water, having chosen her over the brooding mansion. His plan had met with very little opposition, which dissolved totally when he revealed the details of the work he had lined up to pay for his extended break, and which would also give him a greater sense of independence enabling him to stand on his own two feet. Or so he had argued. It was a good job that his plans had not been scrutinised too well as it would soon have been discovered that all of the offers of work were bogus. Jim was not a good liar, but he was pretty proud at having fabricated the lot, and it was only the chance that came via Saracen's that allowed him to take this first step.

Now he was sitting in the kitchen of a wooden bungalow on a small island drinking tea with someone he knew very little about. The knowledge, or rather the lack of it, was not mutual as Dave Harris seemed to know quite a lot about Jim, which was a little worrying to him.

"There's no secrets on the water," Dave said with a smile. "And there's even less that can be kept from me."

"Don't bet on that one," thought Jim, mindful of the fact that, as yet the, only detail he had heard of his own life had stemmed from his first contact with the Mayfly. This, he hoped, meant that the source of the information was Saracen's boatyard and they, so far as he knew, knew nothing of any importance about his home life. It wasn't that he didn't want to discuss it, but he felt that anyone old enough to be either a father or grandfather to him (it was a little difficult to place any number of years on Dave) may be full of advice about going back and sorting things out, or being open or whatever. Basically Jim knew that he was embarked on an adventure of his own making, and that to let too much personal stuff out may end in interviews with social workers, or any number of officials who would, "In his best possible interests," put an end to his plans. Actually he had no plans, but he didn't want anyone putting an end to that either.

Once Dave had got onto himself as a subject Jim felt safer. Dave had worked on the docks further down the river where it was tidal. He had been on tugs, barges and all manner of other vessels, had gone to sea though he wasn't a great adventurer and generally stuck to coastal and estuary waters. This was before he'd embarked on a career that could best be described as a form of journalism. He was retired, may have been married twice (he gave very little detail here) and liked people who liked boats. He had his own craft, a twenty-four foot sailing vessel with a small cabin and no mast, this seeming to be a fairly fundamental omission. It was moored on the other side of the island because the channel in front of the bungalow was too shallow for it. He approved of the way Jim had rescued the Mayfly and had known the original owner who had had the boat built and shipped down from Stromness on Orkney. He thought it great shame that such a well made and good looking craft should have been as mistreated as it had been and was sure the original owner and the builder too would be glad to see it as it now was.

Almost mid sentence Dave stopped. "This isn't really getting to the point though is it? You were told I might have some work for you, and so I do," he said. "There's money to be had but I can't pay much up front.

What I can do is give you a bung for doing a load of shopping for me and getting my boat sorted so that at least I'll know its ready for when I want it which is as soon as I'm out of this bloody wheelchair. That'll keep you in food and fuel for a couple of days, and I have a couple of addresses for you that might get you a bit more."

"Thanks," Jim replied. "I was beginning to wonder how I was going to get any further. I didn't really," he tailed off. It would have been so easy for him to let the whole story go, and now wasn't the time.

"I can get across to the store before it closes and get some supplies in for you, and then I'll make a start on the boat," he said instead.

The small iron footbridge over the channel between the island and the riverbank took the footpath from the island neatly onto a road, and a good stiff walk away was a village shop of the kind that was mostly self service but which still had an old fashioned counter. With the two piles of shopping arranged, the smaller of which was for himself, he waited for someone to appear. The place was so deserted that, had he been less honest, he could have packed the goods up and walked away with them unchallenged. He waited, listening to the steady tick of a large wooden wall clock which had the letters of the words "NO TICK" replacing some of the upper numerals.

"I suppose it was witty in about 1910," said a girl of around Jim's age, who had appeared behind the counter. This stirred him from his daydream and slightly wrong-footed him. In a shop of this type he had expected someone much closer to retirement age, possibly even beyond it, to be in charge.

"I've not seen you round here before," she continued. "Are you a friend of mad Dave then?" she asked.

"I'm not sure he's that mad, and I've only really just met him," Jim replied. "But I'm doing a bit of work for him."

"Shopping for one," the girl smiled. "And let me guess, setting his boat up for the epic voyage?"

"I'm cleaning it up, but I don't know anything about a voyage," Jim said, not quite sure if he was getting just a little irritated by a know it all, and one with perfectly rounded vowels at that.

"You will," the girl continued. "He's a nice old guy really. Dreamer though, and he likes a drink. That's how he did his hip, he was lucky not to break it but he messed up some ligaments so they put him in a chair for a while. He wasn't too pleased about that one!"

8

"He is still singularly unimpressed by it," Jim laughed. "Quite poetic even, well, provided you don't mind a good dose of Middle English in your poetry"

"Where are you staying then? Surely not with mad Dave?"

It had not occurred to Jim at this point that he had not really considered the practicality of anything beyond setting off. Mayfly was in good shape, and could sleep two, but, it having been in a state of semi submersion for so long, anything made of fabric, or answering to the name of upholstery had decomposed beyond redemption, which, due to lack of funds, and foresight, had not been replaced.

"I live on a boat," he said proudly, feeling his answer fitted the question rather well.

"Wow!" The girl clearly sounded impressed, not that it was Jim's intention to impress anyone. "A real boating family," she continued. How many of you are there? Have you lived on a boat all your life?"

"Well, to tell the truth, it's just me, and just since this morning, but that's a start isn't it," Jim replied with a smile.

"Can you wait till I shut up shop," the girl asked. "And I'll walk over with you. I've never been on a houseboat before."

It wasn't that often that anyone had invited themselves so boldly into Jim's life, in fact he could not think of a time when anyone had, and whilst he hadn't warmed to the person minding the shop, he didn't really dislike her either, so he waited, and they walked back across to the island. As they walked, he listened, partly because he never said that much, but also because it was hard to interrupt the flow of speech from the person walking with him. Her name was Amanda Donaldson and she came originally from a smallish village on the south coast, she had been to a posh school but she hated it, and wished she had gone to somewhere ordinary. She was working in the shop on a casual basis to fill time as she had left school early (she never gave a reason for this). She liked all sorts of music except most of the stuff in the charts, didn't eat meat and had tried various religions, currently favouring Buddhism.

"I thought Buddhists didn't go in for yattering all the time," Jim said quietly. The comment wasn't really intended to be heard, but Amanda thought it hilarious.

"You know," Amanda said. "You're quite astute aren't you. That was spot on! I don't think anyone has ever said anything like that to me."

"Probably couldn't get a word in," thought Jim, this time keeping the

9

comment to himself.

"So where is this houseboat," Amanda asked as they approached the Mayfly.

"You're looking at it."

Jim realised that his notion of living on a boat did rather differ from that of Amanda, a realisation underlined by the look of incredulity on her face.

"Well, everybody has to start somewhere," he said.

Whilst Amanda could be opinionated at times, and often rather blunt, she was not impolite. She knew that for reasons best known to himself, Jim had chosen to take up residence on something that was not much more than a large dinghy. It wasn't what Amanda had expected, but she knew that her upbringing had a tendency to make her think that everybody had at least a reasonable amount of money. She could see that Jim was nowhere near as privileged as she had been, and was scratching around for a compliment when Jim interrupted her train of thought.

"Yes," he said. "I know it's a wooden box, but it's my wooden box, and that makes the difference to me. I live in it. As of today."

"And what about tomorrow," Amanda asked politely.

"What about it," Jim smiled. "I'm here now, and this part of my plan has worked."

"And what is the plan?" Amanda was quick with her reply, and genuinely curious.

"Well, you got me there," said Jim. "Thing is, I don't have one. The thought was to do the boat up, it was sort of sunk you see, then, well. Well that's about it."

The conversation was paused by Dave's voice.

"Oi are you going to bring my shopping up this year?"

"Be right up," shouted Jim turning to Amanda, who smiled and said, "You'd better go, I'll drop by later. You don't want mad Dave blowing his stack."

Leaving his bag of shopping under the tarpaulin in the back of Mayfly, Jim crossed the small garden and met his temporary boss at the door of his bungalow.

"I see you met the Duchess," Dave said. "This island attracts oddballs, mostly harmless ones, it is rumoured that we had a proper gangster staying here in the other house once, the one that isn't there any more, but I have my doubts. Anyhow, what are you doing for digs?"

Jim looked blank.

10

"Digs, somewhere to sleep?"

Dave was unimpressed by the concept of Mayfly being a dwelling place, but was happy for Jim to stay moored as he was for as long as required.

"At least come and have a bite at the pub with me. You'd be doing me a favour, it's a bugger to wheel this thing over the bridge," he said.

Some way downriver from the bridge, beyond the tail of the island was a smallish inn that purported to have been there for centuries. It was a bit run down and the clientèle liked to think of themselves as old sea-dog types, even though most of them probably held down respectable jobs in insurance companies and suchlike. The atmosphere of the place was one of cigarette smoke, thudding bass from a jukebox and an over riding smell of stale beer. Dave was obviously well known there, and the cheer that went up as he was wheeled through the door was as much proof as was needed. Nobody asked about Jim's age, and he did not venture to clarify what already seemed taken for granted.

"I'll have a couple of pies and two pints of your best piss when you're ready," Dave shouted to the landlord, who in turn put a thumb up in recognition. Space was made for Dave's wheelchair at one of the low tables that looked almost as old as the pub itself but were more likely the product of M.F.I. than any old world craftsman. Presently the pints of keg bitter arrived, along with the pies which had been heated in their plastic wrappers by a chrome plated appliance on the bar which advertised them as fresh hot snacks.

"Well. Here's to the Mayfly." Dave said, holding up his pint. "Down the hatch lad."

The beer was pretty similar to the stuff that was drunk illicitly behind the toilet block at school, but at least this was cool, and no teacher would put him in detention for what he was doing. The police maybe, but not a teacher. Jim sat back and took in the atmosphere, feeling more at home than he had done in a long time. Dave was occupied in all manner of banter with the crowd, occasionally introducing Jim as either his cousin, his long lost son, even his elder (and much less good looking) brother each time getting a roar of laughter. More beer followed, but thankfully no more pies, Jim had secreted his in an imitation coal scuttle in preference to eating the thing.

"So what do you think of our resident royalty," asked Dave.

"You mean Amanda," Jim replied, almost shouting to be heard.

"That's the one," Dave said. "Plummy accent but she's a good lass, not as rich as you'd think though.   Her family are sort of professional types, but they fell on hard times a few years back.   Her dad ended up working in a small electronics factory.   Had to trade his Jag in for a moped.   They had the bungalow as a sort of holiday home but I think even that's up for sale now."

"I thought that sort looked after their own," Jim shouted across the noise of the jukebox.

"As a rule yes but there's something happened and nobody says what except that they've been left high and dry, the rest is just keeping up appearances.   Or rather it was keeping up appearances, nobody's seen her parents for a long while," Dave replied.   "I'd ask, but the girl has enough on her plate without having to explain her situation to an old git like me."

It hadn't occurred to Jim that Amanda was anything other than the way she came across to him.   Someone who could afford to play at life and not worry too much about the consequences because there would always be a rich mummy and daddy to bail her out should things get tough.

"We'd best head back whilst you can still push me straight," Dave shouted.   "Hi Ho Silver away!"

With that they left the pub, and headed back to the island.   Despite the offer of a sofa and blankets, Jim felt it was important that he spent the first night in his new home, and at around midnight he retired to the, upholstery free, plank bed in the small cabin of Mayfly.

It was at about six in the morning when he woke, cold and with the light of the new day smack in the eyes due to the lack of any covering to the portholes.   Deciding that he was going to live on a boat was, he thought at this point, probably one of the stupidest ideas he had had up to now.   However he wasn't one to back down so, despite feeling that he had slept with a small car parked on top of him, he set about making his breakfast.   A decent fry-up would, he thought, set everything to rights.   In a somewhat rusty olive green tin box that many years ago may have contained sufficient explosives to demolish the island were stored two "Primus" stoves.   They were not made by the celebrated Swedish manufacturer, but were government surplus copies that were pretty similar though more crudely made.   Jim knew the theory of lighting them, and also had heard stories of the volcanic consequences of doing it wrong, so with some trepidation he set about the task.   He had filled both stoves with some paraffin before setting off, and proceeded to fill a small saucer, positioned around the stem of the burner, with methylated spirit which he then lit with a match.   He could just see the the feint blue flame if he shaded the stove from the morning sunlight, and soon the spirit in the saucer started to boil. As soon as the liquid was almost all used up, Jim closed the vent screw on the filler caps and started to pump air in the tanks alternately to pressurise the fuel. After about three strokes of each of the pumps the burners both broke onto a low roar, a further five strokes and it sounded like a small rocket was in the process of being launched. The day had begun, and would look better after fried eggs, fried bread and tomatoes, and a good mug of tea. "The landed gentry can't live any better than this," Jim thought, unashamedly lying to himself.

After the meal came the work of the day, preparing Dave's boat for whatever epic voyage he was about to embark upon. In truth Jim was not the first, nor would he be the last person that undertook the task. Dave Harris was not unlike the previous owner of the Mayfly in that he had big plans into the way of which an obstacle always cropped up at the wrong time. He had made an excellent start along the way by purchasing the wrong boat to do the wrong task. As a sailing craft it looked fine, and would have been a lot better if it had actually been built with more than just a place to have a mast. It was too small for anything but pottering about in an estuary, as an inland craft its fixed keel meant that it drew too much water to go anywhere but a few miles upstream under the power of a none too reliable engine whose Scandinavian manufacturer was clearly not having a good day when its design was finalised. Dave truly liked the craft though, in part because of its quirky design. He probably believed in his plans too, so every now and then he employed someone to keep the craft in readiness for the call to arms. In the short time that he had known him, Jim had come to the view that he could see Dave as a friend but felt a bit sorry that he was deluding himself. Work is work though, and Jim needed money, so he set of to the other side of the island to get the job done, reasoning that, if he hadn't taken it, someone else less scrupulous may have.

"Unknown Destination" was in fact 22 feet in length not 24 as Dave had said, and made of plywood, though not the same type of construction as Mayfly. In a far more logical use of the material, the designers had opted for a double chine hull using single sheets of wood for each surface. This gave the vessel a well groomed appearance, and one copied in a lot of later designs made from fibreglass. The cabin was of varnished wood, and the hull was painted dark blue, some of which needed a bit of a touch up. To Jim, it looked like no more than a couple of days work to render things

13

"All shipshape and Bristol fashion," as Dave had requested repeatedly in the pub the night before.

The first job of the day was to start the motor and get the battery charged, a task that Jim was not relishing one bit. Dave had gone on at length as to how, when he had just bought the boat, he had been brought close to either a heart attack, an apoplexy or, more than likely, both as a result of his efforts to hand crank the machine. After numerous letters to the manufacturer it appeared that it was in fact nigh on impossible to start the motor from cold by hand and that he should purchase the combined generator and starter that they could sell him for twice what it was actually worth. Even with this attached it was no safe bet that the motor would come to life before the battery died. On boarding, Jim switched the isolator on and briefly flicked the navigation lights on to find no light from any of them.

"Great," he thought. "I guess it is time to try my hand starting the thing, after all it can't be that hard."

He was right, it was a hell of a lot harder, in fact it was, so far as he could see, impossible. The generator-cum-starter was permanently connected to the flywheel by two stout rubber belts, and acted as a pretty effective brake, meaning that Jim was unable to get enough speed to get over the compression stroke when time came to let go of the decompression lever. The fact that he also needed a hand free for the wretched lever meant that he only had one hand to crank with, and that at a less than ideal angle too. He figured that if he took the belts off the generator, he may be able to start the thing, but then he would not be able to charge the battery without stopping the motor to put the belts back on, which rather defeated the idea of firing the thing up in the first place.

"Want a hand with that," the voice of Amanda, who had been watching his efforts for no more than a few minutes, eventually got through to him.

"There's not really room for two of us on the handle," Jim replied. "But you could do the lever thing for me."

"I can do better than that," Amanda said. "As long as you don't tell Dave."

"I'll keep the secret to the grave if you know how to start this lump of scrap iron properly," Jim was clearly still out of breath as he answered.

"That I don't know. I don't think even the makers do," Amanda replied, with a slight look of mischief on her face. "But I can do it improperly."

With that she climbed on to the small side deck and lowered herself behind the motor. From her bag she took out a small oil can which she had found in the garden shed at her home, and a tin of old fashioned lighter fuel. On top of the engine there was a small brass cover about the size of an old penny. She lifted it against the spring and put a good three shots of oil down the copper tube that was revealed.

"Now," she said. "I'll hold the lever down and you can turn the infernal machine over slowly a couple of times."

Jim automatically obeyed until Amanda instructed him to stop. Next she put a good squirt of the lighter fuel down the same hole that she had put the oil in.

"Right," She continued. "Swing the thing for all you are worth."

Amid the reek of petrol Jim yet again obeyed and just as he thought that death could well be a better option, Amanda let go of the decompression lever. The motor at last fired, blowing out clouds of soot laden smoke from the exhaust before firing again.

"How did you do that?" Jim asked, slightly incredulously.

"Improperly," Amanda winked. "I can do a lot of things improperly. Now its time for a cup of tea, this thing can rattle its self to death but there's no point in you or I sitting and listening to it. Just leave a note that we are charging the battery, and nobody will bother. It's a bit of an annual ritual anyway, so I think the other side of the island and your magnificent houseboat beckons."

Given that nobody was likely to steal the boat, and that the only prospect of charging the battery was via the engine, it was quite appealing to let the thing pound away on its own for a while so the two set back across the island to a well earned tea break.

"So, how was your first night in the new home?" Amanda asked, as Jim set about coaxing one of the stoves back into life.

"Cold, uncomfortable, and just a bit weird, but sort of good in a way too," Jim replied, with a smile.

"I can't believe that you actually slept on those planks!" Amanda said.

"Well, it was more passed out than slept. It was a long and pretty strange day," Jim replied truthfully.

"And today?"

"Not sure yet, I'd say that you being able to start the diesel that I'd been cranking for what seemed like all of eternity was a bit odd, but somehow it isn't."

"You think I'm some kind of closet diesel fitter then do you?" Amanda laughed.

15

"I don't know much about closets or what people do in them, all I had was an MFI wardrobe. But I could imagine you working on a lawnmower in the dormitory of some old convent school," Jim smiled.

"It was an illicit still not a lawnmower, but you got the convent bit right. I said you were astute didn't I," Amanda said, looking curiously at Jim.

"That you did," he replied. "I expect that motor is just about doing its crust in by now, so I'd better go and get working, or I'll not get paid."

"Me too," Amanda frowned slightly. "Mammon calls. They were none too keen on Mammon at the convent so all in all I'm glad I had to leave."

"Had to?" said Jim quizzically.

"Long story," Amanda smiled. "I'll tell you on some dark and stormy night when there's nothing else better to do."

With that they parted company, Jim to the Unknown Destination, and Amanda to the shop with the "No Tick." clock.

The big clean up wasn't as hard to do as he had thought, mainly consisting of clearing away deceased, insects general dirt, and the mess left by some truly antisocial ducks. By the time he was ready for lunch the little vessel looked almost cherished. There was a lot of metalwork to be shone up in the afternoon, and he would need to raid Dave's shed for any tins of paint that may be of use the next day. Jim stopped the motor, which had been plodding steadily as though it were the most reliable machine ever to have been made, and set off in search of some food. He could have made himself a sandwich, but decided to treat himself to something altogether more sumptuous, remembering that he had actually missed supper the previous night. He was unaware when he set out that the only two establishments within range were the pub that served provender that had probably given the fake coal scuttle severe indigestion, or the shop.

"Well," Amanda said. "We sort of only have butter pies, I got fed a lot of them when I was at the convent school but I never got a taste for the things. I mean, they weren't offensive, just didn't have much in the flavour department that's all. These ones are different though. They are truly absolutely disgusting so I wouldn't waste your money."

"Well, thank you Egon!" Jim laughed. "I'm more of a garden gnome than a gastronome but I want to keep some of my stomach lining intact."

"Tell you what," Amanda smiled. "I'm here on my own today, and I was going to close for lunch soon so why don't you have a bite with me, I can do some soup or something if that's OK."

16

More regarding Jim's mildly surprised expression as it being O.K. than not taking no as an answer, Amanda flipped the cardboard notice on the door to read "Closed," dropped the bolt into the well worn brass plate in the floor and invited him to come through the opening section of the counter.

"It'll have to be from a packet if that's O.K." she added, as he followed her through.

The area at the back of the counter had a door which led through to a small kitchen. There was room for a small table, and a couple of nondescript wooden chairs, so that the owner or whoever serving could take a break from time to time. The stock for the shop was kept in what would have been an upstairs bedrooms had the place remained as a dwelling .

Grasping the initiative Jim asked. "Do you like living on your own, or is it just for the holidays?"

"How did you know?" Amanda replied.

"Well, I. O.K. Dave told me a bit yesterday," Jim confessed.

"And that's all he knows, a bit, the rest is embroidery. I'm fine on my own for now. I can pretend I own the place and make up all kinds of identities as I please," Amanda smiled.

"Is this one of them?" Jim interrupted, wondering why he felt able to ask.

"You should have a chat show, but no, and yes I suppose. For most people that come in I am the nice girl that works in the shop, always polite and always smiling, but," Amanda paused.

"It isn't you?"

"No, not really me at all. Hey, you're prizing far too much out of me! The last thing I'll say on the subject of me is that I don't feel I have to put on any façade for you. You seem straightforward so I hope you are." She smiled again.

"I'm just me," Jim replied. "The all time ordinary and average person. Average height build etc. They turn people out like me in factories and sell them in Woolworths."

"Well I know where to go if I need a tailors dummy. Eat your soup."

After lunch, and a bit more conversation, this time focussed on trivialities Jim arrived back at the island to find Dave had wheeled himself to the footbridge.

"You ready to make a start downriver tomorrow?" he said. "The barge has arrived and they need you to pick something up. And it isn't contraband before you ask, but it *has* to go by water."

"I can go, tomorrow, but I'll have to work till late tonight to finish your boat," Jim replied.

"Then get to it." Dave's voice just mildly abrupt. "I'll catch you there later and bring you a pie."

"The fish will like that," thought Jim. "So, what am I getting myself into?" He said.

"Like I said, it's not contraband, but it is something we need to be a little cautious about. Depends on whether you want to be in on it, or just earn money." Dave replied.

"I think I'd rather know what I am doing and then decide if its all the same to you," Jim frowned.

"Then you'd better push me back home and I'll talk on the way." Dave said.

Jim started pushing as Dave talked, and from the rather garbled story he worked out that commercial use of many waterways was all but dead, that there were people seeking to close many of them and others seeking to stop navigation to turn them into some kind of "Bloody pleasure garden" as Dave so eloquently put it. Either fate was viewed by a surprising number of people as unacceptable, and some were actively trying to do something about the situation. Committees had been formed, bring and buy sales organised, and a lot of half baked schemes entered into. This appeared to be one of them but it was nonetheless pretty interesting, and would pay a small wage too. It seemed that somebody had spotted a loophole in the law, which meant that any waterway that still had commercial traffic would escape closure if it could be proved that the traffic existed. The main problem was that whenever someone tried to get any form of cargo shipped, they could be met with intense opposition from the body that was supposed to be administering the system. So called "Planned maintenance" where vital sections of waterway could be closed without notice, stranding the cargo in the process, were commonplace, as was the padlocking of lock gates. It had even been rumoured that boats had been sabotaged and cargoes spoiled though there was no hard evidence of this.

Somehow (probably in the pub) Dave had met someone who had seen a way around most of the obstacles by sending a small but relatively valuable cargo on a boat that was clearly not designed for commercial use. Jim's boat fitted that bill even if the design was used in the Orkneys as a small fishing vessel (albeit with no cabin and sailing tackle fitted) and therefore was technically a commercial craft. The cargo would consist of a consignment of Soviet made watches which had been imported by sailing barge from a port in France. Due to favourable weather conditions and tides the thing had arrived a day early and time was of the essence to move the cargo on as soon as it had been cleared by customs. If it were discovered that the goods were to be distributed by water (and it was entirely possible that this discovery would be made) then the people in authority would move as swiftly as was possible to thwart the scheme.

All arrangements had been made, and Dave was originally going to borrow a boat to do the job himself. That was before his accident, so when talking to the people from Saracens, some of whom frequented the riverside pub, he found out about Jim. It all seemed too fortuitous to be true. Jim would be paid a reasonable sum for picking the cargo up, and a delivery fee every time he dropped a watch off to a buyer. This would keep him in food, water and fuel if he kept to the schedule. To prove he was using the waterways he would be supplied with an instant camera to record his progress. The photos were to be posted back to Dave along with the signed delivery notes. It all seemed simple so Jim agreed and shook hands on the deal.

The rest of the day was spent cramming as much of the next days work in as he could. He figured that he could spend half a day finishing off when he returned to the island to pick up the camera and film from Dave.

As the promised pie floated off onto the twilight Jim secured the last part of the tarpaulin cover to the back of the Unknown Destination, and returned to the Mayfly for something vaguely edible. It was going to be another early start. It occurred to Jim that he ought really to tell Amanda that he was off in the morning. Quite why, he didn't know, as he had only known her for around a day, but it seemed the polite thing to do. It was late by the time he set off to her temporary home, the "For Sale" board outside seeming pointless as it was so hidden from view. When he got closer, he saw there were no lights on and, not wanting to disturb her or to be considered a weirdo for bashing on the door late at night, he wrote a brief note, which he folded into three and slid carefully through the letterbox.

It was some time after midnight that Amanda woke from a dream that she couldn't really remember the plot of, and set to making herself some hot chocolate. Unfolding the sheet she had found, she rubbed her eyes and read.

Amanda,

Dave has some work for me and I have to set off at 5.30 A.M. to catch
the tide.   All being well I'll be back the day after tomorrow.   Thanks for
the soup.

See you.
Jim.

Chapter 2

The next morning was not at all inviting, especially not at the time Jim had to wake in order to catch the tide. It was one of those damp, slightly misty starts to the day that could leave you convinced that it was in fact the beginning of Autumn. The motor started using exactly the same formula as it did two days previously, and as quietly as was possible, Jim slipped the moorings and slowly edged the Mayfly into the centre of the channel. This was it, another first, he was setting off to do a job of work. He had food, and sufficient fuel for the task in hand. It felt both strange and exciting, the steady note of the motor, the mirror like river in front of him being broken for the fist time by the wake of his boat, the one he had saved and restored to what it now was.

Progress was good and it was not long before he reached the first lock, which was unattended as the keeper was off duty until around nine in the morning. It was permitted to operate the lock by hand but Jim was aware that hand winding the hydraulic pump was a marathon in its self which required muscles that he probably did not possess. As he approached closer he saw that the top gates had been left open, so he continued directly into the lock. He was about to tie up temporarily to one of the bollards so that he could operate the gate mechanism when he heard the familiar hum of the electric pump doing the job for him.

"Kill the engine lad," the keeper said. "And if anyone asks, I am not here, you got that."

"O.K." Jim replied. "And thanks."

"There's people that are on your side but there's too many against so watch your step, particularly at the half tide lock. Be spot on time and give them nothing to pick you up on. Now, no time to chat, but I may see you at the Anchor later in the week."

"As long as he doesn't buy me a bloody pie!" thought Jim.

With the aid of hydraulics the passage was simple and the Mayfly was heading downriver ahead of schedule. Thanks to a phone-call from the lock he had just been through, the keeper of the next knew to expect him so his lead on his expected time grew as he was taken through the obstacle in what must have been a record time.   As he left, the keeper told him to remember what he'd been told about the half-tide.

In the ten minutes he had to wait for the next lock to commence business Jim checked that everything that could be made correct was correct.   Gas was stored properly, as was petrol, licence plate was clearly visible. He had done what he could. The gates opened and, as he was one of two boats descending, there was no conversation with the keeper. Next in line was the lock which he had been warned about.   It was imperative that he got through this so that he could make his rendezvous and get back into the non tidal part of the river at the right part of the cycle. Jim did not fully understand the way this all worked, but he had a time-scale and intended to stick by it precisely.

As he rounded a bend in the channel, it came in site, and even the warning he had received didn't fully prepare him for what was about to happen. He was met at the tie up point to the lock by what he assumed was the keeper and a couple of people who looked official but could well have been traffic wardens.

"Sorry lad but we have to check on boats going through here.   We don't want any accidents you know," the most senior looking of the group said abruptly.

"I've got the tide times and I'll be back before they turn," Jim replied.

"We still have to check, unless you want to have your picnic somewhere else," one of the men said.

"I've arranged to meet my aunt for dinner," Jim lied. "She's old and she loves boats. She was really pleased that I'd done this one up ."

They were not convinced and proceeded to inspect every inch of the little vessel, taking as much time as they could.

"You sure this boat belongs to you?" another of the group asked.

This was it, the question meant they could not find anything and he was prepared for it.   If they thought the boat was stolen they were obviously within their rights to apprehend him.

"If you ring Saracens, they'll vouch for me," Jim replied, knowing that victory was his.

The three men looked at one another and one of them left for the hut on the side of the lock where all the main hydraulics were.   There was a phone inside, and the man came out with an air of disappointment on his face.

"There's nothing for it we'll have to let him through."

The passage through the lock was efficient and Jim was on his way again although he had lost the advantage that he had gained earlier. Whilst time was tight, he would still be able to do the round trip and bypass the half-tide lock on the way back. The thing was a strange concoction of lock weir and bridge, with the lock being only necessary at certain times of the day when the cycle of the tide would cause problems with water levels. Jim had been given instructions on this which he did not fully understand save for the fact that the cargo he was to carry, though not illegal, was best kept from the prying eyes that would be there if he had to use the lock again. This he did understand, and there would be no Saracens to bail him out this time as the barge he was rendezvousing with was going to set sail soon after he had picked up the cargo and, even if they did have any means of communication, they would not be in as strong a position to vouch for the paperwork, as he had already been told that the lock keeper didn't approve of the people who owned the thing.

The motor hummed and the little Mayfly seemed quite at home on the slightly choppier water of the tidal river. The scenery was one of changes, fields, parks and an ever increasing urban feel which eventually became more shabby and industrial. After running for most of the morning he saw an old wooden sailing barge on the left bank which answered the description given by Dave the night before. Swinging the motor round to steer towards it he noticed what almost looked like a sculpture of an old sailor on the front deck. In fact Jim was quite convinced it was made of a rare hardwood until it waved to him.

"You the Stratton lad," it shouted as soon as Mayfly was within voice range.

"That's me," Jim shouted back, as he slowed the motor to tick-over for the final approach.

"Got a box and some paperwork for you lad. Chuck us a rope then fill your tank."

After the Mayfly was made fast Jim did as he was told and filled the fuel tank from one of two cans Dave had put aboard, with the two stroke mixture ready done. Once the box had been handed over, the man that Jim had thought was a sculpture told him that someone with some kind of influence had told some tall stories to the river police, who were dispatching a launch from some miles down-river as soon as an officer became available.

"I'd like to stop and chat," he said. "And we will in better times, but for now just wind that thing as fast as it will go and don't stop for anything until the first proper lock. You'll have to stop there but they're expecting you. Go under the half-tide bridge as far from the lock as you can and don't stop there whatever they geezer shouts at you."

"Am I O.K. once I am back at the island?" Jim asked, beginning to think he must have been crazy to agree to the scheme.

"Aye you should be," the sculpture replied.

With that Jim was cast off and went on his way. The Mayfly was proving to be a remarkably good little boat in a number of ways. She handled beautifully, and the shape of the hull made her slide through the water creating very little wash. This meant the craft was quite efficient, and despite the small size of the motor it was good for a very respectable speed, even against the current. As he rounded the bend leading up to the half-tide lock, his view of it was obscured by a pleasure steamer that was heading downriver with a crowd of noisy party-goers aboard which hopefully meant that the lock keeper would be sufficiently distracted not see him straight away. As per instruction Jim kept as far away from the lock as he could, hearing the greeting of "Bloody yob!" from the keeper as he headed away.

"Heading for friendly territory at last," thought Jim.

The dusk was now falling quite quickly again, and although he had navigation lights (which he had made using plywood and old fish paste jars) it would not be long before he would not be able to see where he was going. On his right hand side he saw what looked like an old entrance to a wharf of some kind, and decided to chance it as a possible night time mooring despite the advice of the man on the barge. As he approached he reduced the motor to as slow a tick-over he could without the thing stopping. A little way up the channel he could see a number of boats tied up so at least he could be sure there was enough water to float. He thought that keeping out of sight of the main channel would probably be sensible so he edged past the line of boats and made fast to a ring in the wall just ahead of them.

While he made his supper he could not help thinking that each day was getting stranger than the next but yet again this made life interesting and even the thought of spending time pending bail in a police cell could only be viewed as another facet to the adventure.

"Anyway, stuff it, it hasn't happened yet," he said aloud to himself.

With another fry up inside him washed down by a mug of tea he was ready to turn in for the night and was that tired that even the uncovered plank bunks of the Mayfly, one of which was now occupied by a small box of Russian watches, seemed luxurious. So luxurious in fact that he overslept, and was awakened by someone banging on the cabin top. Given that he had gone to bed fully clothed, it was not long before he was out of the cabin, ready to tackle the offending noise maker head on.

"Hey lad, sorry to disturb you. You Dave's lad?" said a man of about fifty wearing old jeans, a sweater and a woolly hat.

"Not in any biological sense, but I do know him," Jim replied, wondering just how many people knew Dave.

"Aye well its you, and you'd better keep your head down for a bit at least. People in high places are after you. You'll be alright here though, you're in old Smiler's berth and they know he's away. As long as they don't look too close they won't see you," the man said.

"Thanks but who are *they*?" Jim asked, quite reasonably feeling that he ought to know.

"Just right now its a posh git with a floating gin palace. He's been hovering around the place looking for you. Thinks he's Sherlock bloody Holmes he does."

"He surely can't do anything can he, I mean like he's not going to try and pot me off with a canon is he?" Jim said.

"He would if he bloody could. Piggin' Admiral Brown, but no. What he will do is get the police on to you. He's got friends who know people who know people, if you get the drift."

This was about as reassuring for Jim as finding half a maggot in an apple, and he wasn't quite sure what his next move should be.

"Tell you what," said the man. "We'll distract him a bit and then you can be away when the coast is clear"

With that he was off back to his own boat, a somewhat dilapidated ex-hire cruiser that dated back to the mid fifties, possibly even earlier than that. The motor started and before long the craft was heading out into the main channel. Whatever drama was about to unfold was out of Jim's view, so he set back to preparing his breakfast of fried bread (he had no toaster) onto which he spread some marmalade, washing the concoction down with the obligatory mug of tea.

It was about two hours later that he saw the old centre cockpit cabin cruiser coming slowly back towards its mooring. Jim had busied himself clearing and tidying the Mayfly and generally getting ready for the day ahead, but had been getting rather bored as the morning wore on. When the craft passed the Mayfly to turn in the small basin at the end of the channel the steerer's familiar voice barked down at him.

"I'd get lost if I were you, nothing personal but I told old Admiral Brown that I had seen a boat of your description heading down the river. I didn't lie either, I just didn't say it was yesterday I saw you but then he never asked either. Anyhow you have about an hour's start on him, make the most of it boy." With that he was away down the channel.

The Mayfly was short enough to turn in the width of water it occupied, so Jim lost no time in getting under way. The outboard was as predictable as ever and before too long the familiar lock came into sight and as he approached, the lower set of gates started to open and the keeper waved him in. There were four other boats in the chamber, and the transit through it was carried out with textbook efficiency.

"Good job you made it lad" said the keeper. "I've a horrible feeling that my hydraulics are going to give up on me before too long, which is a real nuisance as there's a river police launch due through in a bit."

"Thanks," Jim said, smiling wryly, though still having the thought in the back of his mind that he may be spending the night in a police cell.

It was mid afternoon when Jim tied up again at the island, to be greeted by Dave.

"You got the box?" he asked.

"Nice to see you too," Jim replied.

"Good. Sorry but we don't have too much time. Take my bike over to the shop to get your provisions, and take the box with you but be quick. I had a call a bit back and they appear to have, well, they fixed the hydraulics if you get my drift. Anyhow its best you aren't here when they do arrive."

"Listen, it is only legally imported watches in the box isn't it?" asked Jim.

"All legal, duty paid, the lot. That won't stop the beggars taking them away on suspicion, then they can keep them until its too late. I'll put a box of paint on your boat and you have brought that if you get what I mean. Mand will see you right. You may have to explain a bit but she's a good sort and she won't drop either of us in it if I read her right."

The bicycle that Dave lent him was about as eccentric as its owner. It bore a famous maker's name on the frame tubing, but Jim had to wonder just how much of it had come from the original production line. The front wheel was so far out of line that on every revolution it rubbed the brake. The back wheel was in better shape though at some point somebody had painted it purple. The three speed hub gear did not work at all and the brakes were little better. In all, dangerous was about the best word to begin describing it, but this did not bother Jim much and he set off towards the village with the box of watches under his arm.

At the shop he found Amanda stacking some cans of soup on the lower shelves by the door, and by the force she was setting them down it was reasonable to assume that she was not having the best of days.

"What's up?" Jim asked, temporarily forgetting the imminent possibility of arrest and permanent incarceration for bringing Communist timepieces into the, so called, "Free" world.

"I'll tell you what's up doc," Amanda snapped angrily. "Thanks to the liquidators, and my folks, I have no home unless I want to live in a grotty flat in bloody Spain! And as if that wasn't all, I am supposed to be happy about it, oh and they only want a decision today. I mean the first I heard about it was this morning for god's sake! I'm not stupid, I knew the place was for sale but."

"Do you want to go?" Jim asked, somewhat nervously. He had not seen the angry Amanda before, and quickly formed the opinion that he did not feel up to having any of this energy come his way.

"No I bloody don't!" Came the answer.

"Then tell them. There's no use doing something you don't want to."

"Simple as that is it!" Amanda looked at him, half still angry, half quizzical.

"If you want to know the truth, yes it is. Something is bound to come up," Jim was now considering the prospect of Convent educated girls being a dead shot with a can of soup. He need not have worried, as all remaining anger was taken out on can and shelf with a force that could have driven a medium sized fence post into the ground in one go.

"It really is that bad?" he added.

"It'll be a bloody sight worse if they don't stand up and fight, I mean they've done nothing," Amanda replied.

"Who?" Jim asked. He was now beginning to make some connections with what he already knew of Amanda's situation but was still at something of a loss.

"Mum and Dad. They've buggered off to Spain because they are in deep shit with the tax people or something. If they had anything as proof then they'd be in the clear but they haven't and I don't even know what it is they are supposed to have done except it involves tax or something and the

Police were getting involved."

"Sounds like someone doesn't like them an awful lot," Jim mused. "But I wouldn't take it too personally, I mean people like that don't really like anybody, probably not even themselves."

Amanda continued, "Oh, and as another little treat. I had a letter from the social services people, because I am not supposed to be living on my own. They want to assess me, whatever that means."

"Oh shit! Do I know what that means," Jim replied. "And trust me you do not want their grubby claws in you."

"How do you know?" Amanda instantly picked up on the simmering anger in Jim's tone.

"That's for later," Jim said. "It's time for me to take you out to lunch and repay you for the soup. There's a tea room or something a couple of miles up the road isn't there?"

"Yes but."

"Look I have to make myself scarce according to Dave, and if you put any more cans on the shelf in the mood you're in you'll damage the foundations, and cause an earthquake somewhere that really doesn't deserve it. Do you mind sitting on the luggage rack?"

"You really know how to treat the ladies don't you," Amanda's face cracked a smile for the first time.

The shop was shut and locked with with the box of watches left on the counter where Jim had put them. The two set off up the road as a police car drove through the village in the direction of the island.

"Life always looks better over beans on toast," Jim smiled.

"What did you mean about the social services?" Amanda asked, forgetting her troubles for the time being. "Have you been in care or in trouble or something."

"Or something about describes it. One way and another I have been moved around and lived with various relatives since my parents got fed up with each other, which is quite a long time ago. In the end I got sick of it and dossed down with some friends from school. That was great until someone told the people in the council that I was too young so it was a choice of more relatives or in care. It stinks."

Jim was about to continue but it was Amanda that spoke first.

"So that's why you chose the boat?"

"It's more it choosing me in a way. I walked past, it was there and, well, if I didn't do anything it'd have sunk. So."

28

"You did something?"

"There's more than that to it, but that about sums it up."

The conversation had drawn to a natural end, and Jim went over to pay the bill. "I've been paid and I still owe you for the soup and starting that chunk of pig-iron that Dave calls an engine," he said in reply to Amanda's glance.

On arrival back at the island in the early evening, Jim found things much as he left them. Apparently the river police had paid Dave a visit, but were told that Jim had been sent on an errand to pick up the said paint (which had actually been languishing under Dave's kitchen sink for a year) from some friends that had some left over. He would have gone himself but he had been disabled through no fault of his own and even though he was, as of about an hour ago, able to get around on elbow crutches he thought the lad would like a bit of an adventure in his boat. Given that they had no proof of anything else they had to take Dave's word for it so they went to. "Piss some other poor beggar off," as Dave, eloquently as ever, put it. He had another box for Jim which contained an instant camera and several packs of film.

"This is the real stuff now lad," he said. "There's a list of addresses in the box, and you get paid every time you deliver an order. You have to take them by water and prove that you have or this will not work. You got that?"

"Seems straightforward enough," Jim replied. "So, I guess I'm properly on my way."

"Aye that's about it," Dave said. "Set off tomorrow if you want, I'll be off the crutches in a week or so, so don't worry about the rest of the Unknown, I'll finish that off. I'll be away later on tomorrow morning so, if I can't see you off, I expect I'll see you at end of trip. Have a few jars for me on the way!"

With that, Dave returned to his home, and Jim set about making his tea. The next day was going to be another one of those momentous ones, the proper beginning. The night seemed to take a long time to pass, partly because the sky was clear, with something close to a full moon which made it both too cold, and too bright. This combined with the thoughts racing through his head kept Jim awake until the early hours, so when he did eventually get to sleep he didn't wake until late. There was a fairly heated argument going on a short distance away, and he could hear Amanda's voice in the midst of it. Climbing out of the boat he could see two people outside of her bungalow, she was in the porch somewhere out of sight. A short walk down the path brought her into view.

"What's up?" he shouted.

The two people, one man dressed in a grey suit, and a woman in a tweed dress, stopped mid sentence and looked in Jim's direction.

"And who might you be?" asked the woman in a manner that was supposed to be assertive but came across as textbook rudeness.

"I might be the Pope, but then again I could also be Genghis Khan. I might be a lot of people and that's quite interesting in a lot of ways," Jim said. "But what really interests me now is who you are and why you have just woken me up?"

"You can ask your bit of skirt that," said the grey suited man. "And whilst you're at it tell her to get out of this property as it no longer belongs to her or her criminal family."

"I could do that," Jim replied. "But I wouldn't get much of an answer. I do probably have a bit of skirt, I think I was polishing the brass-work on my boat with it. Then again I think that was T shirt or did you mean I should consult my bit of shirt and I misheard you. Why do you want me to talk to a piece of textile anyway, are you some kind of religious sect?"

Though Jim often thought of replies such as these, he seldom if ever actually spoke the words, having learnt at school that any form of wit was often replied to with fists or detentions, dependent on who it was addressed to.

"You can't talk to us like that," the woman in tweed said angrily. "Anyway, this is none of your business, we have come to take this girl to the hostel because she can't stay here."

"You could at least let me pack my belongings before I go," Amanda shouted.

"There's no time for that and no room either. You have to come right away," the woman replied abruptly.

A very familiar voice then barked.

"Right you pair of duck turds, If you don't stop harassing my niece I'll have the law on you. She's been keeping an eye on the house so it doesn't get burned to the ground by vandals and this is the way you thank her! Shame on you, now get off my island before I pitch the pair of you in the bloody river!"

In a very theatrical voice Amanda chimed, "Oh Uncle *David*! Thank you for coming so quickly, these two people have been so rude to me and

30

my little brother. Please tell them not to take me away!"

Looking at Dave who was wearing an old pair of leather motorcycle trousers and a grubby string vest, the man in the grey suit, and the woman in tweed must have decided that despite the elbow crutches, Dave actually would be able to land them both in the river without too much trouble, so they turned towards the bridge with the parting shot.

"You haven't heard the last of this!"

About an hour later the three friends were sitting with mugs of tea in Dave's kitchen. Around them were a number of boxes and holdalls containing Amanda's possessions.

"O.K. Buster," she said. "What are we going to do now?"

"I'm going to have to catch my train in a bit, I missed the early one and it looks like its a good job too.. At some point they're going to work out that the version of the family tree we gave them wasn't really that accurate. In other words they meant it when they said they'd be back so if you have anyone you can stay with Mand, I'd suggest you give them a ring. I'll look after your stuff for you. I had a word with couple of the guys from Saracen's whilst I was hobbling back and they said they'd move the rest of your stuff out later this morning, they're just looking at Bill Morris's boat right now. Stick it in my back bedroom, I never use it, oh and lock up when you finish and put the key through the letterbox, I've got a spare." With that Dave was on his feet and, assisted by the crutches he was off to catch a lift to the station.

"Do you think Dave's right?" Amanda asked, more thinking aloud than really asking the question.

"Their sort always are pretty persistent. It's like trying to get chewing gum out of your hair when they get their teeth into you."

"So that means we're both on the run."

"Well," Jim replied after a brief pause. "Strictly speaking I am gainfully employed, transporting watches to customers, and they haven't got a hold on you, not really have they?"

"In a few weeks they wouldn't have but now. Oh god! The watches! They were in the box weren't they!" Amanda remembered the package that Jim had left on the shop counter the day before.

"We'd better go and get them I guess," Jim said. "If we go right now the gits that came looking for you won't have had time to do their paperwork."

Outside the shop was a police car, and inside was a Policeman who was

31

talking to the owner.   Jim and Amanda had seen the vehicle as they approached the village, and made a detour so they could see what was going on from behind a telephone box, which its self was half hidden by shrubs.   Amanda rummaged in her bag, which she was seldom without and produced a pair of folding opera glasses which at first looked like a small cigarette case.   They were not very powerful, but sufficient to see what was going on through the plate glass front window.

"It doesn't look like either of them has noticed the parcel yet," she whispered.   "If I can sneak into the phone box I could tip Marie off, she's owns the place, and I ought to tell her I won't be able to work there.   I mean it's only fair, she is a really nice old dear."

"We're looking for Amanda Donaldson, you wouldn't have seen her today would you?   We know she works here but we'll turn a blind eye if you tell us where she is," said the policeman, just slightly too full of his own importance for Marie's liking.   Marie, who had noticed an unusual package on the counter, but did not want to draw any attention to it replied slowly.

"Now, I'm not sure quite what you would be turning a blind eye to? She's been helping me out because I wasn't so well with the arthritis playing up and all.   I'll employ her If she'll work for me in a few weeks time after her birthday.   Now dear, I'll have to take this phone call.   It's probably my accountant and and I must not keep him waiting must I."

The policeman waited calmly, doing his best to eavesdrop on the phone conversation and heard, "Really, she always was a bad one on bicycles wasn't she.   I hope she wasn't hurt, doesn't sound like she was if she rode off again.   I wonder what she wants in town though.   That Amand, Milly, yes Milly is a silly one isn't she."

"The coast is clear for about half an hour," Amanda said, as she saw the police car disappear up the road.

"Now," Marie spoke firmly, as the pair entered the shop.   "You two both seem to be in a bit of a fix, standing out there trying to be the reincarnation of Sexton Blake or something.   It was all I could do not to pee myself laughing at the pair of you!   Anyhow, you, Jim, old Dave Harris speaks highly of you but you'd forget your own head if it was detachable, and then Mandy! You're so old for your age, but you don't even know you've been born sometimes.   You keep twitching about from one belief to another and you

32

never see what's staring you in the face. If you want to clear your folks name Amanda, you do it, because there's only you that can, and Jim you have been set that task of saving our inland waterways from the mad axe man. You're both barmy and neither of you stand much of a chance singly, but you may do if you look out for each other."

"But," Jim replied. "I um, well, I have only known Amanda for a couple of days."

"Circumstances," Marie said. "It's the way it is, and its not you risking your giblets is it. No of course it isn't, but mind you look out for each other, both of you and things will come right. Well, either that or they won't but they certainly will go pear shaped if you sit on your backsides and do nothing. However proud you may feel, you are each going to need someone that you can trust. Now, I've done a hamper for you, that's my contribution to the adventure, take it, and don't forget this darned box. Have a grand time, post the cards to me, not Dave and I'll see he gets them."

Walking back to the island Jim said, "Is she usually like that? You know, that intense?"

"Not as a rule," Amanda smiled. "But I've always thought there was a bit of the Suffragette to her."

"And are we going to do what she said?" Jim asked.

"To be truthful, I don't think we have much choice. I mean, I have nowhere to go, and, not wanting to be mean or anything, you won't last five minutes on your own. It takes two to shift a work-boat, and that is what it is isn't it. And my giblets are probably as safe with you as anywhere else. It's like you said, something will turn up."

"Surely you have some relatives?" Jim asked.

"None that haven't disowned us, and anyway, I never saw myself as poor orphaned Annie," Amanda replied.

On arrival at the Mayfly Jim set about making ready to go, there being nothing else left to do. There was half a tank of petrol, and one of the cans was still about a quarter full.

"How soon do you think it's going to be before they get back here?" Amanda asked.

"I'm not sure, but from the way Dave was speaking I think we'd best get a move on pretty soon, why?"

"Well, I've been thinking, I mean you don't have much by way of creature comforts here do you, and all my stuff is now in Dave's house,

33

which we still have a key to. I mean it may be a bit risky, but we could take some of the stuff with us, you know, like bedding and cushions and stuff, maybe a radio. I could rifle through everything pretty quickly and it would make life a bit easier wouldn't it."

Jim thought for a moment.

"Yes it would," he said. "But every minute we stay here we could get caught. I get the impression that it isn't to make your life any easier that those guys are after putting you in care, and Christ knows what I've got myself into, but if I'm not wrong it looks like they could now get me for kidnap!"

With a pause and a slight wrinkling of the brow, Amanda said, "You know I hadn't thought of that, there are plenty of my age out working and nobody really bats an eyelid, so why me."

"Because there is someone out there that doesn't want you to clear your folk's name, probably because they would get dropped right in it if you did. They can't get you themselves, I mean it wouldn't look right to have a kidnapper or worse as the chairman of the golf club, so they use their influence to get you into care before you're too old for the system."

"James Alexander Stratton, you have a devious mind, but you forget one thing," replied Amanda playfully. "If they did put me into care they could only keep me there until my birthday, then I could do anything I want, so what good is that to them?"

"If you actually believed that then why are you absconding with someone that you have only met a couple of days ago to live in something that you described as little better than a packing case?"

Amanda had thought that she had scored a playful point by finding Jim's middle name out from Dave whilst the Mayfly was downriver and was surprised that he knew her description which to the best of her knowledge she had only once said to Marie.

"Point taken," she said. "I guess spelling it out like that is, well, like I said, you can be pretty astute sometimes, and that could get irritating. Anyway, just thinking on, the people after me will be looking for me at the bungalow, and they don't know what your boat looks like. If I keep my head down, even if they do come back today we'd see them before they saw us, and I can always hide in a wardrobe in Dave's house if need be. I mean they'd need a warrant to search that and by the time they'd got that we'd be long gone."

This part of the argument seemed solid enough to Jim so he allowed himself to be convinced and the pair set about sorting through the contents of Amanda's former home for anything that could be useful, each item being stacked by the door in readiness for transfer to the Mayfly. Most of the things were packed into old black metal deed boxes of the sort that solicitors use to store documents from long dead people. These had been taken across and stacked neatly in Dave's back room by the people from Saracens who were blissfully unaware that they were actually empty, having been bought at a charity auction some years earlier by Amanda's father because they may have come in useful sometime.

"He was right wasn't he, your dad," Jim said. "They do come in very handy."

"True," Amanda replied. "But they'd both turn fourteen different shades of puce if they knew the circumstances we were using them in."

By the end of the afternoon the Mayfly was probably as well equipped as she ever had been. The cabin had a much more comfortable, almost cosy, appearance, Amanda having furnished it with various quite expensive looking box shaped cushions form the window seats in the bungalow and fitting some rather ornate looking napkins over the brass curtain rods of the cabin portholes. The deed boxes fitted well into the limited space available, they even found one (which technically wasn't a deed box but made in a very similar way) with a hinged front which would serve as storage, and as a wind-shield for the Primus stoves that came with the little boat. Another larger one which bore the gold lettering "Pertaining to the estate of the late William James Heckmondwycke" would serve well as a vermin proof larder.

As they posted Dave's keys through the letterbox as requested Jim commented, "If they dug up that deed box in a few hundred years time they'd think he made his money out of hoarding baked beans or something!"

With a smile Amanda said, "We've spent rather longer than I thought, but it all looks a whole lot better, almost habitable. It's a bit late to set off though isn't it?"

"It is, and they won't be back now, and even if they come back in the morning all we have to do is sit tight with the cover down and they won't know we're even here. Nobody seems to sleep aboard so we should be safe doing that." said Jim.

"This is an occasion of sorts isn't it," Amanda said. "Like one of those times that there was a time before and a time after, and whatever happens we'll both remember today won't we."

Jim looked puzzled as to what was coming next.

"Lets mark the occasion, we're free now, and even if we both get put away for twenty years tomorrow they can't take the here and now from us can they, so lets celebrate with a drink at Dave's local. Nobody from there will shop us."

"O.K but I'm not having one of their pies!" Jim frowned.

"I don't think anybody actually eats those," Amanda replied. "Well Dave might but Dave is Dave and you can see what they've done to him. I think they just retrieve them from where everyone has hidden them, polish them and put them back on display. If we go about half a mile on from the Pub there's Killer Ben's chippy up the road. We could go there and get a big bag of chips and share them on the way back to the pub then wash them down with whatever they sell us."

"Killer Ben's? How appetising do you get salt, vinegar and strychnine?" Walking along the tow-path Jim felt both puzzled and yet reassured. Here he was, the kid from school that nobody talked to unless they had to and he was about to set off to who knows where and a posh girl was going with him. Posh, yet not so posh. Amanda, he thought, could so easily be a spoilt little madam of the kind that was good at everything, or at least that thought she was because her daddy had used his influence to whatever effect he could. In any case she was walking with him and regarding him as trustworthy. All of this was alien to him.

Amanda walked on, leaning slightly forward as though she was walking into a moderate wind although there was none. She was contemplating what was one of the strangest days so far. She had known for a long time that it was coming, but had not had a single idea of how she'd cope with it, so she'd shut it out of her mind and gone on from day to day. Then with a loud bang on the door, things came to a head and she was off on an adventure with someone that she knew virtually nothing about. Twelve months ago she may as well have been on a different planet, one where everything in life is set before you. One where she could now see that she really did not ever want to be a part of again. Times were now strange, and set to get a lot stranger, but she was happy to see what was around the next corner.

The next corner brought Killer Ben's Chip Shop (in reality Benjamin Smith's) and a break in her chain of thought.

"Why the crap is it called Killer Ben's?" asked Jim.

36

"One of the guys serving was heavily into John's Children, and it sort of stuck," Amanda smiled.

The shop was a very old-school type with an Art Deco style fryer in green, cream, black and chrome on the back wall, with with the maker's name "Frank Ford of Halifax" on a little plate underneath the clock. At the front was a marble topped bar with a tiled front..

"Very large chips and a couple of pineapple fritters please," Amanda requested, proffering the right money.

To Jim's surprise the fritters (which were tinned pineapple rings that had been battered and fried) were put in with the chips and given a good covering of salt and vinegar.

"Don't look like that," Amanda said, looking straight at Jim. "We've had enough new experiences today so one extra won't hurt you!"

With that they left the shop, and walked down the road to the tow-path leading to the pub.

"This isn't half bad, like, you wouldn't think it was going to be O.K. but it is," Jim smiled.

"Well there's people will pay a lot for a chunk of pineapple on a gammon steak so why not on chips."

"I just wonder when we'll appear on the wrapper and who will be the villain of the piece," Jim said.

Killer Ben's was one of a slowly diminishing number of chip shops that still used newspaper to wrap chips and Jim had been studying a week old scandal involving a minor back bench politician.

"Oh, I expect that you will. I mean, kidnapping me! And me a poor little innocent convent girl," Amanda teased. "Now drag me into this house of ill repute and ply me with strong drink!"

" Pub shandy do?" Jim joined in the joke. "Two of those and a pie will have anyone under the table!"

"Is that true now?"

"Absolutely, on account of the fact that the pies kill you!" Jim smiled.

"Bloody hell!" was the Landlord's greeting. "What have you done to Dave? Has he been smoking that herbal tobacco from the health shop again!"

"All I did was shave me beard off!" Amanda returned in a mimic of Dave's manner. "Now lets have a couple of shandy's, and the lad is payin'!"

For the rest of the evening Amanda was referred to by everyone as Dave, and she did her best to copy as many of his mannerisms as she could,

37

each time to uproarious laughter. The pair could have easily got drunk on the amount of drinks they were offered but they had to politely refuse most because they knew they needed to be away as early as was possible, and there was the small matter of the fact that neither of them were exactly used to drinking alcohol. Even on the weak shandy they drank, however, they were getting mildly merry by the time they had to make their excuses and go.

As they got up to go the landlord shouted across to them, "We'll see you later Dave! Hope you save the world for freedom lad! And if anyone asks we never saw you!"

"Blimey, you were a hit there," Jim said as they walked towards the island, the night air coming as a contrast to the thick smoke laden atmosphere of the pub. "Looks like it's going to be a bit chilly." he added.

"Shit!"

Jim looked round startled until he saw the reason for Amanda's exclamation. A few hundred yards down the towpath was the end of the footbridge to the island. A police car was parked across the end of the bridge, and two policemen were crossing onto the island.

"There's no prizes for guessing what they have come for," Jim whispered. "Shame we aren't on the Mayfly, we could keep quiet and they'd think we weren't there."

"If you don't mind me saying it Jim. That's not an awful lot of help given that we are standing here, and they are over there!" Amanda was looking at Jim with the slight furrowing between her eyebrows that didn't exactly mean she was annoyed, more that she could be very easily persuaded to be that way.

"What's worse," she said, "Is that they appear to have seen us."

It was true that the policemen on the bridge had paused to speak on the radio and turned back towards the car as Amanda had been speaking.

"That's about all we need!" Jim hissed, as the car engine started, along with the blue lamp and siren.

The pair stepped half heartedly to hide in a nearby hedge that was too small to conceal anything other than a smallish toddler.

"I guess the game is up. I'm sorry," Amanda said. "If only I hadn't had the stupid idea to go off and celebrate! I've given them a reason to get the both of us and you can bet they'll take it."

Jim was about to answer but the police car shot past them, its occupants completely oblivious to the existence of the two suspicious looking

38

characters trying to hide themselves in an undersized privet.

At Dave's local the brawl was in full swing, not too uncommon a thing to happen although the place was a whole lot more respectable after it had fallen out of favour with the local teddy boys. Actually some of them still attended though, due to the onset of children, mortgage, and age, they now looked quite respectable, and normally were. On this occasion the party atmosphere had continued after Jim and Amanda had left, and old rivalries were discovered to be closer to the surface than was previously thought.

"Right you bunch of old gits! You should be ashamed of yourselves!"

This greeting from the police seemed to apply a handbrake to the brawl and ageing Teds could be seen assisting their equally moth-eaten rivals to escape through the lavatory window. The disturbance was quenched before it grew to the epic proportions of the fifties. Names were taken, cautions issued and threats of arrests made, followed by a simple question.

"Has anyone seen two youngsters this evening? We were looking for them when we were pulled off the job by you disgraceful lot. Someone said that they had seen them coming this way from Killer Ben's. They'd have come in a couple of hours back."

The universal answer was that Dave had been in around that time with a relative of some sort and they were off for a couple of weeks fishing or something whilst Dave's tendons mended fully.

Shortly before he closed up for the evening, Ben, who was no killer received a telephone order that was too big to ignore. The various Teds, having agreed that there were good points to all kinds of music, made the decision to cement their new entente cordial by the purchase of a chip supper to end all chip suppers.

"Oh and by the way," the voice making the order continued. "If some coppers come in sniffing round about young Amanda and Jim, tell 'em bugger all, got it! They're in enough of a fix as it is without the bloody law on their tails."

"Say no more," Ben replied. "Your stuff will be ready in about twenty minutes, and as I remember Jim and Mand are on their way by train to the south coast to some festival, or at least, that's what the coppers get from me."

Some time later that evening a police raid was carried out at a quiet camp-site being used by the good people, of various parochial church councils and suchlike, who were attending the first music festival of its kind devoted to the art of hand-bell ringing. Nobody was arrested but a couple of disgruntled pensioners in a camper van were cautioned for

39

threatening to throw the contents of a chemical toilet at or over the police, and or their vehicles. Given that no toilet contents were actually thrown, and that the physical condition of the pensioners indicated that this was not a real possibility, no charges were formally pressed.

"Looks like they've been distracted by something," Jim whispered. "They certainly weren't interested in us."

"Good!" Amanda replied. "I'd hate to have been busted for drinking illicit shandy! Do you think the coast is clear?"

Jim nodded and the two set off in a manner so furtive that, had even the slowest witted policeman on earth been on duty, they could have been arrested on suspicion of just about anything. The pair slowly edged over the footbridge, crouching low enough not to be seen over the parapet, forgetting that it was a railing and they were still on view beneath it. Once on the island they kept close to bushes and trees wherever they could until they got close to the Mayfly. As quietly as he could, Jim unfurled the tarpaulin from the stern until he could get aboard. Amanda followed and they both crouched in the cockpit for a while to make sure they had not been noticed.

"What do we do now?" Amanda asked quietly.

"We could stay here," he replied. "But the coppers could be back at any minute, which is O.K. If we keep very quiet, or we could go up-river a little bit. There's another island in a mile or so, it's smaller than this one but you can tie up there, people do for picnics. Only thing is we may get seen, what do you think?"

"I'd say we go Jim. For one thing, I don't like skulking around hiding from people, and for another, even if the police don't come back tonight you can bet they will tomorrow, and they may have warrants and stuff. How are you at driving this thing in the dark?"

Jim agreed that it would be rather better to move than stay, not being aware of the hue and cry going on near the south coast in their names, so they carefully rolled back the cover and stowed it under the back thwart. There was just about enough light to see where they were going, but they needed to be very careful, as they could easily miss seeing just about any obstacle such as driftwood, which could easily damage the prop. Amanda had packed two large torches from her home, and had them at the ready.

"I thought we could just use them in short bursts if we see anything that looks suspicious." she said.

Once the motor had been started, they slipped the moorings and were under way by the light of Jim's home made navigation lights. With Amanda keeping lookout they needed very little illumination to clear the narrow channel of the island and were soon in the main river. They decided it was a good idea to keep their speed low so as to minimise noise, and any damage they may incur should they be unlucky enough to catch anything in the propeller. In a little over twenty minutes time a dark shape appeared in the middle of the river and Jim reduced the speed still further, Amanda peered out and briefly shone her torch in the direction of it. After the day they had both had, they could have been forgiven for assuming it to be a great white whale but, as expected, it was the island.

"We're looking for a couple of big trees, about twenty feet apart," Jim said. "Dave said that quite big boats tie up between them so we should be O.K. on depth."

"I see them just over there," Amanda replied, and she pointed the torch in the direction of the trees. Jim steered towards them, with Amanda instinctively illuminating the path as she saw fit. A few yards away Jim put the motor into neutral and used what steerage was provided by the outboard to take them the short distance to the bank. Amanda reached out to an overhanging branch and checked the boat's progress allowing Jim to hop ashore with the ropes. Within minutes the Mayfly was tied up safely, and had the advantage of being almost hidden by the overhang from the two old willows. Once the motor was stopped, Jim lit the hurricane lamp which hung just inside the cabin to the left of the door.

"That's it," he said. "I'm off to kill a tree and then we'd better turn in."

"O.K. That's fine for you, but, well," Amanda paused, unsure how to phrase her next question. It had not occurred to Jim or Amanda that the Mayfly was a bit lacking in certain facilities, and it wasn't ever part of his plan to have anyone else with him, let alone a girl that he hardly knew.

"Look," he said. "I'm sorry but, well, weren't you in the Guides or something?"

"I take your point," Amanda replied resignedly. "But I'm also taking a torch. If there's one thing Guides taught me it was not to pee in a nettle patch!"

This somehow broke the ice sufficiently, coupled with the fact that they were both tired out, for them not to become self conscious about sharing the close proximity of the Mayfly's cabin. They both agreed that they could sort the niceties of preparing for the night another day. Having taken their shoes off, they left the rest, took a bunk each and were asleep minutes

41

after the hurricane lamp was extinguished.

Chapter 3

The slow drip of rainwater filtering through trees served as their morning alarm call. Amanda was the first to wake. Jim, who had almost got used to sleeping on the bare board of the bunks was still enjoying the luxury of the new cushions until he he heard her voice.

"My mouth feels like a camel has slept in it!" she said.

"It can't have," Jim replied sleepily. "We'd be overloaded with a camel, are you sure it wasn't a small deer, or maybe a goat?"

"Bog off! I need to pee," Amanda laughed as she moved towards the cabin door. As she was still wearing her day clothes (including her coat) she was able to go ashore to deal with the issue at hand, returning to hear the roar of the Paraffin stove.

"We're going to have to get down to the real stuff today I guess," Jim said. "We can talk over breakfast. I hope you don't mind fried bread and marmalade, it sounds disgusting but it works."

"Right now I'd settle for one of the Anchor's best pies," Amanda smiled. "I'm starving."

The tarpaulin that covered the back of the Mayfly normally just swept down from the cabin top to the back of the boat though there were some poles made of thin steel rods that could support it in a sort of round topped tent shape, similar in a way to the covers of some skiffs. Jim had not as yet used this but it was pretty easy to set up and provided a reasonable degree of cover from the weather. In the bag that contained the tarpaulin were also a pair of side screens made of a much lighter weight of canvas, though Jim had not attached these.

"I don't want to sound melodramatic," Amanda said. "But we are sort of, on the run aren't we?"

"Well, I guess we are, but there's not much we can do about that except not to look too obvious, and not give anyone any reason to do anything stupid. All we can do is what we need to do, kind of get on with it and hope for the best," Jim replied calmly.

"I haven't the first clue where to start on what I have to do," Amanda frowned. "So I suppose we'd better get on with the bit we can do. Where

43

is your first delivery?"

"So far as I know it's about a day away. Probably tomorrow morning," Jim answered whilst looking at the notes Dave had given him.

"That's the plan then," Amanda said. "We can set off in a bit and I'll work out what I need to do as we go. This sort of breakfast is different to bloody cornflakes! Can you go another round?"

"Sure," Jim smiled, pouring the methylated spirit in to relight the stove. "Look, I don't want to stick my nose in where it isn't wanted, but, well, we're in this together you know, so if it's O.K. with you, um, well."

"Thanks," Amanda replied. "We can talk about it when we're on the move, you only got the edited version of me so, well, you know. Thanks, for what it's worth you're probably one of the good guys."

As the burner burst into life again, Jim put a bit more oil in the pan and waited for it to heat before putting in a couple of slices of bread.

"I'll reheat the kettle after, there should be enough water to have another cup of tea if you want, then I'll warm some up if you want a wash," Jim said.

"I'll just have to get the hang of no hot and cold running water, and no bathroom or bog!" Amanda smiled.

"There was a chemical job came with the boat but it was just a bit too disgusting," Jim replied.

Whilst Amanda washed in the confines of the cabin, Jim set about tidying the cockpit. More than ever now, with two aboard, things had to be kept as tidy as possible or life would be pretty intolerable. It was not long before most things were stowed back in their deed boxes, and the area looked a little like some kind of maritime solicitor's office. There was one that was slightly different in shape to the rest, a little taller, and it didn't readily find a place, so Jim placed it at the back on the thwart by the stern and sat on it to think of where it could go. On looking up, he found he could see neatly over the cabin top. Its niche had been found, and a seat to sit on and steer too. The day was beginning to look up.

"I've sort of dressed down a bit," Amanda said, emerging from the cabin. "I don't want to be too noticeable just in case."

"You have a point, it's not like we can run anywhere is it," Jim frowned slightly. "With the weather today you can keep your hood a bit hunched up when we go through the locks, and the staff probably won't ask too much. If they do I can always say you're my sister or something."

With everything stowed it was time so set off. The motor was started, and the Mayfly gently pushed from under the trees. The rain had stopped, so Jim had stowed the covers loosely on top of their canvas bag so that they could dry off, and also be ready should the rain return. They had been under way for about fifteen minutes when Amanda, who had been standing just behind the cabin doors enjoying the moment, turned to face Jim who was perched on the deed box seat.

"It's time I give you a bit more detail isn't it," she said.

"Only what you want to say," Jim replied. "I'm quite happy to take it all on trust."

"Well,"She went on. "On another planet, even on this one I could be the spoilt little rich girl. I suppose I am really, but that part is sort of down the toilet now. I said I left school early, well it's true, but I couldn't have stayed, it was private so when the cash dried up, well I guess you can see where that one goes. I mean I don't mind for me, I hated the place, but someone has stuffed my folks and I don't like it. Problem is that I know virtually nothing of what happened, I was at boarding school, then I wasn't and Dad's Jag wasn't either," she paused and then continued with that slight furrowing Jim had seen before. "We made the best of it for a few months, Dad and Mum both got grotty jobs. Mum cleaned and Dad had an awful job in a transformer factory. The place was really run down, leaking roof, the lot. It looked like we'd pull through somehow but then someone put the frighteners on them and they left for Spain on what money they had left. Yet again I only found out later because I was working out at the island by then. I mean it sounds hard but they had to go right away."

"So why didn't you?" asked Jim.

"I said I would stay back and mind the bungalow but you know what happened there," Amanda replied.

"Won't they wonder where you are?" Jim said.

"I sent them a telegram saying I am staying so they should get the drift," Amanda thought of the note as she answered.

"MUM DAD. STAYING TO CLEAR NAME. SOMEONE HAS TO. LOVE. A."

In a cheap flat in an area often referred to as the "Costa Del Crime" Jean and Edwin Donaldson held the brief message and looked at each other.

After a long silence Edwin commented, "We came here because there was no choice. Amanda will have to see that, and when she does she'll be

45

here. I know we should have fought it, but with what? Everything we could have used as evidence is gone."

Jean added, "I know its true Ed, because it was me that suggested it. It doesn't make it better though."

As a closer to the conversation Edwin said, "When she sees sense she will use the ticket we sent her. She can live with us here and we can all have a good life. What's the alternative? Prison or worse, and for what? We have done nothing wrong, all that is wrong is we have no proof of that."

Back on the Mayfly, Jim was looking puzzled.

"I don't want to push you but what is it they are supposed to have done?" he asked.

"It's O.K." Amanda replied. "Cats out of the bag now. Mum and Dad were both partners in this business that made stuff for offices. Accounting machines and stuff. They'd come up with some kind of security key, or tag thing that made all the stuff more secure. Like if you don't want people reading your books you could copy them to tape and then if they don't have the key code it's almost impossible to get into it. Thing is someone told someone who knew someone, and everything went a bit weird, something to do with the idea being sold exclusively to more than one company. That and some people in the military wanted it too. As I say, I know my folks are straight, they would never screw someone over like that, but there is only my word for it."

"Bastards!" Jim frowned. "Still, something will come up."

"That's all is it?" Amanda replied rather sulkily. This was the first time she'd put the whole débâcle into words and it had not improved with the telling.

"Yes," Jim smiled. "That's about it. The people that did it are bastards, and something will come up. When it does we'll deal with it. Right now there is a lock coming up, so we'll deal with that instead."

There were only a couple of boats waiting, and the lock was set for them, so Jim held the Mayfly almost stationary in the water until called in. Working together with Amanda it was going to be much easier to manage locks and, though she did not have the first clue of what to do, she observed the other boats, and copied the actions of their crews.

"I figured that if I fell in, at least I'm a good swimmer,"she said later.

"Nice to see the old Mayfly back, I thought we'd lost her," the keeper shouted as they left the top of the lock.

The pair waved back, Amanda's spirit having been lifted by the comment and the smooth passage through the lock.

"If we plug on and don't stop for lunch, we could make the Quarry by this evening,"Jim said. "It'd be nice to be well in time for the first drop."

"That's fine by me, It's nice to watch the scenery go by," Amanda replied, by now happy with the thought that something may well turn up. Jim, she thought, could be really annoying with his casual optimism. But, he seemed to have thought this one through. "Surely he hasn't read Dickens, or has he?" she thought.

"Listen," she said. "You made breakfast, so I'll do us some butties for lunch if you're O.K.. with that. I filled a flask with the last of the kettle water so we can make some coffee. If it's all the same to you I think lighting those stoves on the move is probably one of the more creative ways of committing suicide available to mankind."

The Mayfly cut through the water at a steady six knots, just below the speed limit, and at a throttle setting that would not burn petrol too heavily. They would have to stop briefly to fill the fuel tank from one of the cans, but this was easily done whilst waiting for a lock. It was also important that they record their progress using the instant camera. At the third lock of the day Amanda noticed that there was a shop so she bought a newspaper. Just before they left she took a quick snap of Jim holding the paper with the days headline clearly visible. This could now be posted back to Marie at the shop as soon as they saw a convenient postbox.

"What?" Amanda said as she handed a less than hot cup of instant coffee to Jim.

"Sorry," he smiled "I didn't mean to stare, but it was only four or so days ago that I was setting off with a bit of petrol and nothing much else. Now I appear to be, well, I am not sure really."

"A freedom fighter? A smuggler? A kidnapper? Or even some kind of superhero?" Amanda offered.

"Never thought of myself as being out on the edge, it must be the bad company I've been keeping!" Jim replied.

"Thanks a bundle!" Amanda laughed. "Anyway, I bared my soul to you earlier, so how about you tell me about you? I mean you seemed to have the number of those people that came knocking yesterday. How come?"

"Those bastards," Jim spoke with a barely concealed cold anger in his

47

voice. "People like that have been hovering around my life for too bloody long, and trust me, you are well shot if you can keep clear of them. It started when my folks were still together and I was at school. If it wasn't my not wanting to eat the pig food they served as dinners it was my being different to the crowd. I wouldn't mind but I never saw myself as that different, but I guess I must have been. Then when my folks split they could really have a field day. Bastards," he paused then said, "Steer for a bit would you."

Amanda swapped places with Jim who for a while faced forward and remained silent.

"Tell me more later Jim," she said, in a much softer tone than he had previously heard from her.

"There's quite a bit more," he replied, "But."

"But it isn't for now, is it," Amanda looked back at him.

"No, not really. It isn't that I don't trust you," Jim answered quietly.

"Listen," Amanda said, very calmly. "I can see what telling me that has done to you. I shouldn't have asked, not like that, but that's me sometimes. Just a big gob on legs."

"It's a bit heavy," Jim replied. "I'm not screwed up by all that stuff though. It just leaps out and gets me sometimes that's all. I'm still here and all that happened isn't, so screw it," he smiled. "I will tell you the whole story, you've a right to know," he added.

"No I don't but thanks anyway," Amanda thought as she continued to steer the little craft on it's course.

There was a long silence between them after this, a contemplative one and not at all of the sort that happens after an argument. Both Jim and Amanda knew that a re-alignment had happened in the relationship they had to develop if they were going to work together, though neither knew quite why, or in what context it had happened. It was clear that they were stuck with each other by circumstance, and that it would only work if they could get along. This so far had worked, but they were less than a day into an open ended, one would say adventure here, but neither party was even sure of what they had embarked upon. For Jim's part, he had needed some space and Amanda had seen this, he only hoped that he could be sufficiently observant in similar circumstances. As the day wore on, the scenery changed from the semi urban scene they occupied in the morning to fields and woods. Passage through locks was straightforward enough with the two working together, and they made good time. In the mid afternoon Amanda took a break from crewing to nip across to the shop in the lock-house. Seconds after Jim had realised he was actually on his own she was back with a bag full of biscuits and other snack-food treats, together with a couple of bottles of lemonade.

"My treat," she said, as Jim was starting the outboard. "We'll organise hot drinks better tomorrow."

"Pull up a deed box and we can have afternoon tea!" smiled Jim.

Amanda perched herself on one of the food boxes that were kept opposite the stoves. She rummaged in her bag and pulled out a rather rusty looking bottle opener for the pop and set about opening some biscuits to go with it.

"Is there anything you don't have in that bag?" asked Jim.

"A toilet," she replied, with almost perfect timing. "I do wish I had a proper toilet in it."

She handed Jim a bottle and a custard cream which he accepted with a smile. After a while he looked over at Amanda in the same way he had done earlier. She would more than likely have answered his look with the same question as she had before, but for the fact that she had a mouthful of biscuit.

"I think," Jim said. "What I am, and it's odd for me at least, is part of a team."

"Is that bad?" Amanda asked, having washed away the biscuit with lemonade.

"Not if today is anything to go by, no," Jim replied thoughtfully. "It could be a lot worse, but I don't want to put my big foot in it, so please tell me if I do or if I am about to."

"I will if you do the same for me. Deal?" Amanda put her hand out and they shook them almost in a parody of formality. A handshake though it was, and they both silently resolved to stick by the arrangement.

They were approaching the last lock of the day, and had minutes to spare before it closed for the night (which would mean operating it manually). Jim sounded the horn and Amanda waved a green scarf. The keeper acknowledged their presence but waved for them to hurry. Jim wound the throttle fully open and the little boat quickly picked up speed in answer. The wash increased and, if the keeper had wanted to be picky he could have told them off, as they reached about eight and a half knots before Jim dropped back to idle speed for the final run into the chamber.

"She always cut through the water that one," the lock keeper (who had

49

plenty of time as the Mayfly was the only craft passing though) said. "I wasn't going to shut you out, I just wanted to see how well she ran again."

Both Jim and Amanda accepted the compliment with a smile.

"Looking at the map we should be about fifteen minutes until we tie up," Jim said. "Hopefully there will be someone there that knows what we're at and is on our side. I think Dave said they were pretty friendly there, but he doesn't know too much the further out we go."

"He never was, and never will be, the great adventurer you know," Amanda smiled. "But he's a good guy. Better than I'd ever thought," she added, remembering his defence of her on the island.

As the Mayfly ran under the railway bridge they could see the Quarry on the left. There were some landing stages jutting into the water, and Amanda pointed to the least rickety looking one. As Jim closed in Amanda neatly stepped off the thwart with both ropes in her hand. She tied the bow rope first, having looped the stern line through a ring to stop the boat swinging out whilst she was busy. Whilst she made the boat fast, Jim disconnected the fuel tank, closed the vent screw, wrapped the fuel line round the handle and placed the tank in its night time stowage under the centre thwart which crossed the Mayfly a foot or so behind the cabin doors.

"We'd better look for signs of life," Amanda said, pointing to the flat roofed wooden extension that housed some tables. The hotel was clearly having a quiet night so far. They walked around to the front of the building, which faced almost directly onto a small road. It was an unprepossessing structure that looked to be early Victorian in architecture, though neither Jim nor Amanda were experts. What was clear was that it had seen better days. They both went in to what looked like the main entrance and asked at the bar and reception area for the manager, their arrival at the jetty having not been noticed.

"That would be me you're looking for," said the wiry balding man behind the counter in what the pair thought was rather unnecessarily abrupt a manner. "And you've taken your time! I mean first you say you want the work then you say you can't come, then you arrive late! You'd better be good that's all I can say!"

"Hang on," Jim replied. "We."

"There's no time for excuses, come through and get sorted out. I'll switch the stuff on and you can get your music and whatever crap you need," the manager kept the abrasive tone throughout. As Jim and Amanda were led through to the back room (the flat roofed wooden area they had first seen) a card caught Amanda's eye.

"Bloody hell," she whispered to Jim. "They think we're providing entertainment for the evening. Look," she pointed towards the dog eared card which read. "Live Music Tonight."

"What are we going to do, I mean this guy is about to blow his stack, and we shouldn't be upsetting him," Jim replied as quietly as he could.

"Can you play anything?" she asked.

"If it's simple I can knock a tune out on a piano," Jim's stage like whisper was beginning to attract the attention of the manager who was just about to say something when Amanda cut him short.

"We'll just need to sort some numbers out and get straight. Take us about five minutes, ten at the most, if that's O.K," she said.

"It'll have to be," the manager said gruffly. "Stage is over there," he pointed to the corner of the room where a small triangular area was raised by about a foot. It contained an old upright piano, an electric organ that would have looked more at home in a funeral parlour, and something that only very loosely answered the description of a very small and incomplete kit of drums. As he threw the switch four spotlights of the kind used to illuminate clothing shop mannequins lit the area up in all it's seediness. He then left them to get ready.

"You are going to get us killed. No. You have just got us killed, and we were doing so well," Jim hissed.

"Lighten up. I have grade four, and you can play too. I was in the school choir before. Well before. I have a load of sheet music in my personal stuff. I know it was unnecessary, but it's nice to have some familiar things. I'll nip aboard and get it."

"But." Jim faltered.

"Hey, its all pop folk and rock and roll. There's a big wad so we can do something. You go up on the stage and look like you know what you are at, and I'll be back in a couple of minutes."

Amanda left through the back doors before Jim could protest.

"So much for keeping a low bloody profile," he thought as he set about looking professional, or at least attempting to.

As Amanda got off the Mayfly she rolled the tarpaulin over the back of the boat, and secured it, carefully covering the name on the stern (which was facing the river) from any prying eyes.

"Right," Amanda said quietly as she got ready on the stage. "I can either play or sing most of these, so you go through them and find

51

something you can play. Just make sure I know what it is and we should be O.K."

"Or we'll be dead!" retorted Jim who was beginning to wonder if things could get much stranger. "This looks the sort of place where they throw things, probably heavy, sharp, or even both, if they don't like you."

Amanda shrugged in reply, leaving Jim to fumble through the sheet music.

"O.K. I can do this one," he pointed to a tattered manuscript of "Rock and Roll Music."

"Fine. Go for it. I'm ready," whispered Amanda. She looked over to the manager who had re-entered the room and made a thumbs up gesture to him. He replied in the same way, and edged around the room towards them. Once he had stood on the stage, he looked at them and muttered, "Bloody hell! who have we got? Helen bloody Shapiro and the Milky Bar Kid?"

"Introduce us as the navigators," Amanda hissed, as she quickly checked her, hurriedly applied make up in a small mirror.

"But you're not! I mean they aren't," he replied exasperatedly.

"Look, mate," Amanda did her best to sound as assertive as possible without being heard beyond the stage area. "Call it a name change, or to put it another way, it's us or nothing."

They were duly introduced, and Jim banged the first chords out on the upright piano. He had never been formally taught any musical instrument, but always seemed to find his way to a piano wherever he was living and, for a while, entertained one of the families he had been placed with at their tea room until he was told he could do it no more, and was then sent somewhere else because the authorities thought he was being exploited. His style was very much in the long tradition of the pub pianist, being very rhythmic, slightly clumpy, and with a small smattering of bum notes. The style was more than adequate for the current situation. Amanda had the advantage of classical training, and could hit notes perfectly. Her voice was clear loud and confident which was why she had been chosen on many occasions as the soloist in the school choir. She, however, had little time for classical music, and was a closet pop star at heart, despite her saying she didn't like chart music, and had brought her stash of sheet music with her as one of her items that, had she been a guest on Desert Island Discs, she would have chosen as the one luxury that she was allowed. Here was a chance for her to come out of the closet and she was taking it. Towards the end of the evening Jim waved a copy of an old song entitled "Let's Dance" at her. The record had been a hit some years back, and prominently featured loud drumming and an electric organ. He had played a few of these but found them all to respond differently and therefore awkward to play, but there was something about the mood of the night that made him feel he could do justice to the song. Amanda put her thumb up, and Jim pointed to the decomposing drum kit. Amanda shook her head, Jim nodded his and pointed emphatically until she knew she had lost the non verbal exchange, and went to sit at the battered instrument. After a few jabs at the keyboard and bass pedals to get the right sounds, Jim signalled that he was ready. Having found only one drumstick, Amanda had reached out and borrowed the beater from an ornamental dinner gong, and then signalled that she too was about ready. Jim counted her in, and she, remembering the rather loud start to the song, started pounding away with the gong beater.

"Hey baby won't you take a chance, say that you'll let me have this dance."

Jim had used the best of his limited singing voice to support Amanda during the evening but now it was his turn to take the lead, with her joining in on the choruses. Either way the combination was unusual but effective, and went down well with the audience, which, though small at the start of the evening, had grown considerably. As a final number, Amanda went over to the piano, and then to Jim.

"Know this one" she said.

"By bloody heart!" he replied looking at a copy of "March of the Mods"

"Me too. You kick off on the bass and we'll knock 'em all dead." Returning to the piano she counted them both in.

"The Navigators!" shouted the manager over the P.A. amid louder applause than one would have expected considering amount of people there, after the fifteen minute rendition of the instrumental, which had included at least three encores, and saw Amanda swapping from piano to drums and back again. They were taken through to the bar area where the manager, who turned out to be the owner insisted on buying them a drink.

"That was bloody great music, you were worth it even if you were bloody late. I'll sort out the money in a bit, its what we agreed."

"I don't know what we agreed," Jim said, slightly flatly. "On account of the fact that we didn't, which is probably because you didn't book us."

"I did!" the man said, reverting to his rather abrasive tone. "Here it is

53

on the diary!"

"Not us. Them," Jim said. "We just turned up at the right moment. If you want the truth we are not a band, and we haven't performed together before tonight. In fact neither of us even knew if the other could, if you see what I mean."

"And we've missed our tea!" Amanda added. "I'm bloody famished!"

"Oh! Gold plated balls of three kinds of shit! I am so sorry! You're the guys that have a watch for the Judge tomorrow aren't you."

"Yes," chimed both Jim and Amanda.

"And you have never played or sung together before?" the manager looked even more puzzled.

"No," another chime came from Jim and Amanda.

"Well. John Davidson is my name, just call me John. Look, the Judge is usually here around midday so you'll have a bit of time on your hands." John smiled.

"We had a belting run up here," Jim said proudly.

"You must have, but you would have cooked your food and turned in by now I expect. I mean it's made it pretty awkward for you hasn't it," John replied.

"We'll manage," Amanda smiled, still enjoying the buzz of their performance.

"No, I insist," John said. "It's my mistake and you shouldn't suffer for it. You didn't look like Rio Jones and his Hawaiian Seven when I saw you."

"We're about five short," Jim laughed.

"Anyway," John continued. "My bar takings will be doubled by your efforts tonight so, I'll rustle up something from the kitchen, and you can have a room for the night on me. Hows that? In fact, no, I insist, I won't take no for an answer!"

"It's O.K. by us," Amanda replied. "Do you have a pay phone I can use? I promised I'd phone back home today."

"Use the reception phone, you're my guests for the night," John smiled in reply.

"Amanda! Thank god!" Marie blurted down the phone.

"You're an atheist! So that doesn't count for much!" Amanda joked.

"Well, I might change after today!" Marie replied.

"I told John about you and dead stuff," Jim said, when Amanda returned. "So he's doing us both a veggie meal. He said he'd be about twenty minutes."

"Well it looks like that's what I am now," Amanda replied.

"A veggie meal? Twenty minutes?" Jim frowned slightly.

"No. Dead. Apparently I have killed myself by stripping off and jumping into the river. They found my school uniform in a weir all except for the straw boater, I brought that with me, It all still has my name on it. Must have come from that big bag of old rags I left on the jetty. I forgot it was there, and it must have got kicked in when we left," Amanda said.

"Your folks will go mad!" Jim frowned some more.

"I doubt they've heard yet, and Marie is phoning them to let them know. She won't tell the coppers though, not unless they ask. So I guess it will keep them off our backs for a while at least," Amanda smiled.

After they had finished a welcome meal John gave them the keys to room eight.

"You can see your boat from there," he said. "But don't worry, it'll be fine."

Room eight was reasonably well equipped for a small hotel, and was tastefully decorated with a double bed and a small en-suite bathroom.

"Ah," Jim said. "Don't worry. I'll sleep in the chair"

"Don't be so bloody polite!" Amanda laughed. "We'll share the bed. I mean it's not that much closer than we were in the boat last night."

"Isn't that going to make a bad impression?" Jim replied, rather meekly.

Amanda stifled another laugh and said, "Look, the guy's put us in a double room, so whatever we do in here isn't likely to bother him that much is it! And another thing. If anyone does come snooping for us he isn't likely to tell them that it was us that was here, is he. I mean look at it from his point of view, feeding us on alcohol, making us work, and then putting us both in the same room, and us so tender and innocent! I mean. He'd lose his licence, could even end up in clink! I am a convent girl you know!"

The last line, plus the effect of the beer and wine finally got to Jim, who couldn't help, or control laughter. When he could catch sufficient breath, he said, "O.K. O.K. you win, I'll go and get the night things from the Mayfly."

"Talk about a gob on legs," Amanda thought to herself after Jim had left the room. " I mean you have just invited someone you hardly know into

55

bed with you! Bloody idiot! No, that's just the effect of today, or the beer and wine. It's gonna be fine, it bloody well has to be, anyway he won't do anything like that, he's one of the good guys."

She was right too, the moment of doubt was unfounded. Jim was acutely aware of the fragility of their situation, and that there was a pressing case for them to work together. Any pressure or stupidity could mess things up royally and he knew it.

"Well, um, night-night," Amanda said as they both sat rather self-consciously in the bed.

"Ah, yes, good-night. Are you sure you are happy with that side. I mean I don't know which side you usually sleep," Jim replied nervously.

"In the bloody middle like you I expect!" she replied with a slight giggle in her voice, "But we can't both do that, where would it end!"

Jim looked rather startled by her remark.

"Look," she said. "We're here, and well, look I'm not in the habit of sharing beds, well, except at Guide camps and, hang on that doesn't sound too wholesome does it. You know what I mean! I mean, oh bloody hell what do I mean."

"You are safe," Jim cut in. "And that's what *I* mean so let's leave it at that shall we."

There was another of those pauses. Jim had not spoken sharply, but had used a firmer voice than she had yet heard from him, or a different kind of firm. Similar in some ways to when he was speaking about his life earlier in the day, though the tone was different it came from the heart.

"Thanks," she said, breaking the silence. "You played well tonight, you can be a bit of a dark horse can't you."

"About two thirds of the stuff I played pretty much the same tune all through. You can sort of get away with that with rock and roll." Jim smiled.

"What about Let's Dance?" commented Amanda.

"Everyone has their party piece," Jim replied. "And that one's mine. It's still only rock and roll though. No, the evening definitely belongs to you. You knocked their socks off! Bloody brilliant and don't forget it. Now, night-night."

Amanda smiled in the half-light of the room as she drifted off to sleep.

Chapter 4

It was somewhere around nine o'clock when Jim woke, Amanda had got up about ten minutes earlier and was taking a shower in the en-suite, her pyjamas were neatly folded on the bed-cover. She thought Jim deserved such time asleep as he wanted, though she wasn't sure why.

"Anyway, its sort of less embarrassing this way." she thought.

He was getting out of bed when she walked in dressed in a towel, with wet hair.

"I'd have a shower yourself, you don't know when we'll get a chance again," she said. "I've left some stuff ready for you so you go in while I get dressed."

Jim took the advice and was soon enjoying a good wash. The water was pleasantly hot enough, and the room smelt of Amanda, which was a bit odd, not unpleasant but a sort of unexpected intimacy. Amanda answered a polite tap on the door, and was greeted with one of the staff who asked if they would like breakfast in the room. She declined the offer and said they'd be down in about ten minutes if that was O.K.

"You're honoured guests of the boss," the girl replied politely. She was no more than a year older than Amanda, with a beaming smile, added. "So you can do anything you like. By the way, I saw you last night a bit, you should be on Top of the Pops."

"Thanks," Amanda smiled, blushing slightly.

"I hope you had a comfortable night," John said, as they came into the dining room.

"Yes thanks, I slept like the dead," Amanda smiled.

"Which technically you are," Jim whispered as they sat down. "I could get used to this sort of a life," he added in his normal voice. "Shame we have to save your folks, the world, deliver god knows how many watches, oh and a new one, bring you back from the dead!"

"All part of life's rich tapestry!" Amanda laughed. "At least that's what the nuns kept on saying, usually when they were making life hell for us.

We're not going to get that far today are we?"

"Next delivery is not too far," Jim replied. "So we should be there for tonight, then it's a bit of a long haul to the university. I'd better get some fuel soon, I'll see if there's a petrol station handy after breakfast."

"Speaking of which," Amanda interrupted as a full cooked breakfast was served to them by the girl who had knocked on their door earlier.

"Compliments of the management," she said politely. "The boss says you are a charming couple."

Jim would have enlightened her as to the status of their couplehood had Amanda not lightly kicked his shin under the table.

"Ever heard of enjoying the moment," she whispered, after the girl had gone back to the kitchen. "Why burst their bubble for them."

"Well, this beats fried bread and marmalade," Jim replied. "So, yes, lets just enjoy this moment then."

There were at least a couple of hours before the watch customer arrived, so Jim took the fuel cans and tank half a mile down the road to a small petrol station while Amanda set about getting the Mayfly ready for the next run. It was more the need to keep a bit of a low profile than domesticity that made her take this option, but she was happy to familiarise herself with her new home even if it was, as she had ungraciously described it, a glorified packing case. Bringing the comment to mind made her feel somehow disloyal to the little craft which was beginning to exert the same beguiling influence on her as it had on Jim when he first encountered it. The warmth of the varnished wood, the patina of the polished brass-work, the boaty smell. All of these things warmed her to it. She was fascinated by the many details that were so easy to miss, such as the neatness of the cabin door closure the little flaps that you could hinge up from the bunks to make a flat surface across the cabin, the firm closure of the locker doors all so well crafted and altogether far too good to be gambled away in a game of poker or to be left to the elements. She laid the flat of her hand on the pillar-box red painted canvas surface of the cabin top, then, without thinking, stroked it lightly and patted it saying, "You've had hard times haven't you, but you survived and so will Jim and I. I know you're on our side."

"They're like that aren't they," said a voice she didn't recognise. "Boats I mean. They're so much more than what they're made of."

Amanda started. "Oh!" She said. "I didn't see you, um, I'm not in the way am I?"

58

"Not at all." said the voice which belonged to a man Amanda judged to be in his early seventies. He had a kindly bespectacled face and wore a somewhat battered tweed jacket.

"I should introduce myself," he said. "A mutual friend of ours, David Harris, said you were taking over from him, though I thought when he said Jim. Is that short for Jemima perhaps?"

"It isn't, and well, I'm not," Amanda replied slightly flustered. "Jim is getting petrol, he should be back soon, I suppose you're the Judge?."

The man laughed. "That's me, Cut Throat Jake the hanging Judge! So you must be the starlet that sang for everyone yesterday evening, and charmed them all let me say," he replied.

"How did you get the name of the Hanging Judge, um, Jake?" Amanda wanted to keep the subject away from her as much as possible without actually appearing to do so.

"I was a barrister until I retired, a bit like Rumpole if you've heard of him. I always took on the no hope cases, only the ones that I could feel were worthy though. I expect that sounds awfully like playing God, but everyone should have a fair trial, and that doesn't always happen. Oh, and my name is David by the way," he smiled.

"So why Cut Throat Jake?" Amanda asked.

"In my younger days I had a big black beard, and I looked like a pirate and then a daft cartoon became rather too popular in some comic and my fate was sealed amongst my friends. Where I was it seemed that anyone that took on a lot of 'Pro Bono' work was given an evil nickname, and that was about as bad as they could dig up for me. Thankfully it has now been shortened to just 'The Judge'. And here is your partner in crime!" David said.

Jim had appeared with a sack trolley, that he had been lent by John the hotel owner, neatly stacked with two petrol cans, the tank, and a plastic imitation barrel of about two gallons capacity with a tap on the side.

"Oh my! Smugglers cove! You must be Jim," David said.

"Sorry I'm a little late, John kept me talking a bit. He said you'd be down here," Jim replied.

"It's no trouble at all, I have been wasting the time of the charming Jemima here." David smiled as Jim looked over to Amanda who shrugged her shoulders. "Now let me give you a hand with your fuel and we have a little business to attend to."

"John gave us this old Sherry barrel for water," Jim said as they passed the cans from the jetty to Amanda, who stowed them carefully. "Now, we'd better get the watch for you."

"If you are in the business of transport, do you have room for a small package that I would like taken by someone trustworthy and careful to a colleague of mine at the University, if that isn't out of your way." David asked.

"Fine as long as it's not too big," Jim replied.

"It's a very old, rare and quite valuable bottle of brandy and I have been meaning to send it for a while, but I can't bring myself to post it," David replied.

"That's fine, we're going to be there in a couple of days or so. We can pack it carefully down at the bottom of the bow, it'll keep cool there and be safe."

David went back into the Quarry, coming back a few minutes later with a small wooden box which contained the bottle of brandy. The whole transaction including the delivery of the watch took another fifteen minutes, and then David was ready to go to lunch. As he left he turned and said, "She will appreciate you saying kind words Jemima. And she won't let either of you down, I'm sure it'll all come right."

"What's he on about?" Jim asked, matter-of-factly.

"I'm not absolutely sure myself, but, we have just made our first delivery. Things are looking up!" Amanda smiled. "I suppose we'd better set off, I mean it'd be nice to stay for lunch but."

"I know," Jim said. "Or at least I think I do."

They said their farewells, promising to return at some time, and were waved off as though they were the oldest and dearest of old friends. As the Mayfly turned back into the main river and picked up speed, Amanda turned and smiled at Jim.

"You know, I could get used that, but I'd rather be used to this. I mean the hotel was really nice, and I wish I could have taken the toilet with us, but," she tailed off.

"We're a bit behind time, but we should be alright if we keep motoring on like we did yesterday," Jim said, changing the subject. "It's my turn to sort lunch out. Shame we didn't heat any water up for coffee."

The afternoon was bright, with a few clouds that threatened, but never delivered, rain and their progress was steady as the scenery of open country, dotted with large houses and hotels passed them by. Whilst the area was decidedly rural, it had a well coiffured look as though it had its own staff who, armed with brushes and dusters, crept silently by when nobody was looking to maintain the illusion that this was the green and pleasant land mentioned in that school assembly favourite. Occasionally they would pass a village or a small town, even these being polished up to look their best for the chocolate-box photographers. Jim and Amanda took turns of about an hour each on the steering, changing over with what appeared to be a well rehearsed routine that gave the lie to the short time they had spent as a working crew on the river. After some hours Jim broke the silence.

"If it's all the same to you, I'd rather not spend the night in the town," he said. "I thought we could tie up a few miles short and come through on the first lock of the day. We can nip up into the town to deliver the watch and be on our way after that. I know its a bit of a change of plan, but it'd be nice to have some peace and quiet."

Amanda, who had been lost in her own thoughts, started slightly when Jim spoke, almost as though he'd shouted, which he hadn't.

"That's fine by me," she replied. "I didn't much fancy being stuck in a public park overnight."

After another hour or so, on the left bank of the river was a decent looking meadow, that was listed on the map as a public mooring. It was close enough for a quick sprint to the lock the following morning. As a precaution they approached carefully with Amanda keeping an eye on the depth of water. The bank was quite low, just a step off the Mayfly with the ropes and things were secured within a few minutes. With the sound of cooking in the background, Amanda sat for a while thinking of a way to break the silence. Deciding honesty was the best policy, she ventured.

"I haven't upset you or anything have I?" she asked. "Only you have been very quiet today, I mean, I guess I don't know you but, oh shit. I don't want to think I've been a pain or anything like that."

"Nah," Jim smiled briefly. "It's just like I said yesterday. Things sometimes leap out and get me when I'm not looking that's all. Nothing to do with you, I mean, if you want to know the truth, and as daft as it seems, this is sort of the most real home I have had. I've been pushed here there and everywhere, cared for by carers that don't, dumped on relatives who didn't really want me there. The worst is when the buggers from the social get their teeth into you, I mean they never ever let go. I wouldn't mind it if they were actually motivated to help, but most of them are only interested in making themselves look good, that's why I'd have been happy to see

61

those two bastards on the island pushed into the sodding river. It's like whenever I feel settled something or someone comes along and makes a bollocks of it (Pardon the French), like they were about to shit on you and all I could do was be sarcastic to them, and I know what they're like. Then here I am watching the world go by and thinking this is sort of good, like I said, it feels like (even if it isn't) the most real home I have, so I start looking out for periscopes and bloody torpedoes. And then there was yesterday, everyone being so good to us, I mean that never happens to me, even the Judge was a good bloke."

"Oh, he was probably trying to get into my knickers," Amanda interrupted. "But go on."

"Well," he continued. "I sound like I'm being sorry for myself, but that's sort of my life. Inconsequential, I guess. I think that's why I took pity on the Mayfly, I thought, bloody hell I know how you must be feeling. What the crap anyway. It's gone now, I'm here, and like you said earlier on, we should enjoy the moment."

Amanda sat on the thwart next to Jim and put her arm round his shoulder, giving him a sisterly hug.

"Thanks," she said. "I think I know you a bit better now."

They ate their tea in silence, and it was some time after they had washed up and were sitting facing each other across the cockpit that Amanda again broke the silence.

"For what it's worth, you did more than just say a few words to those people on the island," she said

"I did?" Jim replied.

"Yes, you accepted me as I am," Amanda smiled.

"You did the same for me," Jim said.

"Yes but I have invaded your life, and you just went along with it. Look, you've told me probably more than you have told anyone, and I appreciate it that's all," Amanda continued. "I mean I could make a case for life screwing me up, with all the stuff that's happened recently, and it may do, but it hasn't as yet. Even the convent didn't cow my life up like it did some, I mean, I sort of got forewarned of what happened to some of the other girls."

"You weren't, well. You weren't interfered with were you?" there was a distinct tone of embarrassment in Jim's voice.

"I could well have been, some were, but I was armed, well, I still had my skipping rope with me, when it was my turn." Amanda replied.

"Your turn?" Jim frowned.

"That I think you can work out for yourself, its like, well, the talks about being good, usually they happened during a P.E. class so you'd be taken out one at a time for a little chat about what the convent school was about and how you should be good and obedient and all. P.E stuff is, well, you know, whatever turns you on. We'd all been skipping, you know, girls are always supposed to skip. So I went in but I forgot to leave the rope behind. It was one of those ones with the nice wooden handles."

"And?" Jim's frown deepened.

"I fetched him a fourpenny one round the head with the handles. I'd been sort of nervous, and twining the rope in my hand, so," Amanda tailed off.

"Ouch." Jim said flatly.

"Look, what I am saying is I just got on, and, well, nothing was said, and," Amanda stopped mid sentence, for the same reason Jim had the day before, and he knew it. Her eyes had the same glaze that, had she or he have continued on either occasion, could so easily have become tears.

"You make a joke out of everything don't you," he said, not unkindly. "And I throw a moody. Truth is anything that happens, the bad stuff, it all comes and bites your arse in the end, it does for both of us, and the fact is I have no idea how to deal with that, nor have you," there was a long silence before he continued. "Look, we deal with it, don't we. We would do on our own, but. Look I feel better about what happened to me, but worse for what happened to you. That's not the way to put it, look, do you know what I mean. We're here, and."

Amanda looked across at him.

"We've shared," she said, with a hint of a smile. "It's what friends do."

This time it was Jim who put an arm round Amanda's shoulder in exactly the same way, and with the same intent, as she had to him earlier in the evening.

"Let's go for a walk," he said.

The evening was quite warm and not yet dark, so, after being in the confined space of the Mayfly for the afternoon it was a refreshing change. The meadow led onto a path, which eventually led to an old red brick bridge across the river. The bridge had a number of arches with one larger one for boats to pass through, and from the top of this there was a splendid view of the river, and their all important home.

"This thing looks like it's been here for hundreds of years," Amanda

63

thought out loud. "I wonder how many people have either fallen in love here, or killed themselves, and all it does is sit here impassively just soaking everything up."

"I liked history at school, well schools. I went to about seven all told, maybe more, but I sort of stopped counting," Jim looked out into the distance beyond the Mayfly at a church spire. "It puts you in your place. I mean I was never good at it, but you hear of all those numbers and facts. People being killed or living in awful conditions, and it's gone on for hundreds, well, thousands of years."

"It'll go on for a lot more. I know what you mean. We're all pretty insignificant when it comes down to it aren't we. I mean we could turn and walk away from each other, fall in love for ever, or jump in the river. This bridge will still be here," Amanda saw Jim looking at her, he seemed to be deep in thought.

"We are all that we've got though. It all adds up and counts for something in the end. Nothing much gets wasted," he said.

The two stood watching the evening sky for another half hour without speaking until the headlamps and horn of a sports car disturbed their tranquillity, and they set off back to their new found home on the water.

It was just before eight o'clock that the alarm clock went off and Amanda's hand silenced it. The morning was cold, and wet. Clouds had blown in overnight, and looked to be set up for the day with a steady drizzle. They would have known this had they have listened to the radio the previous evening. The spell was not set to last too long and was forecast to be gone by early evening. This, though, meant that they were facing their first seriously wet day. She dressed as best as she could in the confined space, trusting Jim to keep his eyes diverted (which he did) and set about assembling the hoops to hold the tarpaulin high enough to steer the boat under. As there was a bit of a breeze taking the rain into the cockpit she put up one of the side screens and set about lighting the Primus.

"This can't be too much different to the contraption they had at guides, and I've seen Jim light the blessed thing often enough," she thought.

Once the spirit was alight she waited before closing the air valve and pumping briefly. Instead of the low roar she got an orange-yellow flame with sooty smoke and a stench of neat paraffin. Worse than that the flames were not coming from the burner, rather they were spreading just about anywhere they could.

"Bugger!" she said quietly as she opened the air valve again and waited until the inferno had died down, which took less than half a minute, before re-closing it. With a single pump, the burner broke into its familiar low roar. A few more pumps and it was ready for the kettle, which she had filled full so that they could have hot water in the Thermos ready for later on.

"That was a bit of good footwork," said Jim who had been watching from the cabin, ready to get the extinguisher if things got out of hand.

"Thanks. I thought we could have poached egg sandwiches for breakfast then we can eat them under way if we have to," she replied. "But we should be O.K. on time. The alarm clock was a bit fast."

"It's going to be a bugger today if this keeps up," Jim said, looking at the rain. "But we're not on holiday, so we have to keep to schedule I suppose."

With breakfast things stowed, ablutions carried out and two Thermos flasks filled, they rolled both side-screens up, ready for use, and got under way in time for the first lock. It was more awkward to crew in the rain, but the cover didn't affect the handling too badly if the side-screens remained furled, which was a necessity when locking anyway. The rural setting of their nights mooring eventually gave way to the town, not an unpleasant one but not a place that either of them wanted to stay for long. Shortly after a lock they came to a park that fronted onto the river to starboard. This was where they would tie up to deliver the next watch. Jim had the address and directions to an office on the main street, about fifteen minutes walk over the bridge. They locked the cabin and pulled the side-screens down, fastening them at the bottom to keep any rain out. The weather, as promised had followed the forecast, so they were going to be pretty wet by the time they got back despite the waterproofs which comprised no more than a couple of old cycling capes. The delivery was straightforward, the recipient, a local accountant, didn't have much time to spare for talking, so, after posting the progress photo and postal order to Marie, they decided to replenish some of their food supplies at the local shops. Amanda found a health food shop, and picked out various items that Jim had never heard of, mostly dried mixes for savouries and suchlike.

"They aren't the sort of thing I'd would eat every day, but they mostly taste good and they'll keep a long time, you know, as a sort of iron ration if we miss out on shops or run out of money," she said with a smile.

"I've never bothered much about what I eat," Jim replied amiably.

"Except for those bloody pies that Dave had kept thrusting onto me. I'm sort of quite happy to go along with your diet, I mean it keeps things simple and it's probably quite hard to poison yourself with vegetables."

"Tins of beans are probably a good idea, sort of for the same reason," Amanda smiled, realising that Jim wasn't likely to try and make her eat meat.

"Tins of anything make good projectiles if we're laid siege to," Jim laughed. "You can knock a horse over with a well aimed can."

"I'll have to take your word on that," Amanda laughed, suddenly going quiet. "Stop!" she added putting a hand out to halt Jim in his tracks as they were crossing the bridge. "There, look," she added as Jim looked over in the direction of the Mayfly.

"They haven't seen us yet," Amanda said nervously. "And I'm not sure I want them to either. Hang on to the shopping a minute," she rummaged in her bag and brought out the opera glasses she had used at the start of their time together.

"Bugger!" she said, a little too loudly. "It's not much use being bloody dead is it!"

"Who?" Jim asked, rather suspecting the worst. Amanda handed him the glasses.

"Shit!" he said abruptly. "Right that's it, I'm over there and this time I am pushing the bastards in the bloody river. They're not. Well they're just not that's all," he spat the words out without thinking.

"I appreciate the sentiment," Amanda said quite calmly, and in a low voice. "But getting arrested in defence of a damsel in distress is sort of like, well, pretty stupid if you ask me. I mean, at best its sort of counter-productive. Particularly when you'd be seen as the villain that abducted the damsel, that's me by the way, in the first place. Anyway they're probably just chancing it. We need to keep them away, at least for the next three weeks or so. After that *they* can't get me. Maybe a different department can have a pop but they'd need more paperwork. Look Jim, take the shopping back, and tell them you don't know where I am, they can't get you for fibbing because you won't be."

Jim looked back at Amanda without speaking.

"It's a lot to ask, but please trust me. You know what'd happen if I went down there with you, so I have to make myself scarce. I'll see you as soon as I can, I promise. Now, after they've buggered off, just head upriver as we planned O.K. I'm sorry Jim, but I have to go before they look up and see us."

With that, she turned and headed back into the town at brisk walk.

"So," the man in the suit said. "We meet again. Now, perhaps you'll tell us where your bit of skirt is."

"I'm sorry but it is so important that we see her, it is for her own good you know," the woman added, trying, and failing, to sound rather more conciliatory.

Jim was ready with his answer. "Look. As I said a few days back, the only skirt I may have was used for polishing brass-work. I mean, I'm not in the habit of dressing up in women's clothes or anything odd like that."

"You know who we mean lad," the man said, in a slightly more menacing tone. "And we could have you charged if you don't help us."

"With what?" Jim replied "Going on holiday in a boat that I own? What's the penalty for that I wonder?" Jim knew they were just fishing, but also was aware that the longer he kept them talking, the better Amanda's chance of evading them was.

"Are you saying you don't know where the little brat is?" sneered the man.

"You must tell us if you know where she is, she's in a very unstable state of mind, and may even have taken her own life," the woman said, failing in her attempt at sounding concerned.

"Now," Jim replied, the sarcastic tone of voice replaced with one of cool anger. "Let me get this straight. You have come here and the first thing you do is try and intimidate me. You refer to someone that you are supposed to be protecting as either a little brat, a piece of skirt or just by the word 'Her,' then you let on that you don't even know if she's still alive! Some bloody help you two are. Fact is at this moment I haven't a clue where she is, or even if the she in question is the person I think you may mean. If it is the person I think you mean, she isn't and never was my bit of skirt, and wouldn't be anyway because nobody can own people though I bet you think that you can. I know she works, or, if she's gone missing, worked in the village shop, so you may be best asking there. Oh, and if you want my opinion, she never came across to me as a brat either."

"You have to co-operate with us," bleated the woman.

"No," Jim said, even more coldly. "I don't think I do. You have no authority over me at all, so take your clipboards and other crap away from me, then just piss off and let me enjoy the holiday I've been planning since

I rescued this boat."

The words must have hit home, as without speaking any further, the pair turned and walked away. As they did, Jim could just hear the woman's voice as she said, "There's no point talking to him, he's clearly on his own and." Jim didn't hear any more and set half heartedly about moving the Mayfly on. Amanda was now gone, and he didn't know where, when, or even if she'd be back. The adventure of living on a boat now seemed just less colourful than it had done when he set off . The incessant rain didn't help either. The motor at least was reliable as ever and he set off towards the next lock, thinking that for once, it would be nice if, when something good happened, it didn't get snatched away when you are just settling to it. He pressed on, not bothering with lunch. Even though he should have felt hungry, there was a knot in his stomach which was something that often happened when he was upset or angry, and he was extremely angry. In his eyes he could see people far too similar to those that had managed to make large parts of his life a misery setting about doing pretty much the same to someone dear to him. The last thought, made him start slightly.

"Did I just think that," he said to himself. It was true, in the short time he had known Amanda he hadn't really found anything he disliked about her. It was also true that he'd thought she could be a rather irritating person, but that impression was no more than fleeting. He wasn't one to trust easily, but for some reason she wasn't someone he ever felt he could doubt. But she wasn't there any more, and they couldn't look out for each other. Perhaps he shouldn't have let her go, but if they had both gone down to the boat .

"Bollocks!" he shouted at the top of his voice. "Bollocks! Bollocks! Bollocks!"

He stayed silent for the rest of the day ignoring any scenery that went by and moving forward as efficiently as he could.

"At least" he thought to himself. "That's something I can do right."

Keeping to the original plan for the day he tied up by a meadow close to the mouth of a small river, and set about making his tea. He wasn't hungry but thought that missing two meals would be just a bit stupid and imagined Amanda telling him off, which only served to make him feel even more alone. Before anything though, a cup of tea was required. Life always looked better over a cup of tea. At least the rain had cleared and the night wasn't looking too bad. As the stove emitted its familiar sound and smell he waited for the kettle to boil. There were chores he could have done, but

68

he could not be bothered, instead he sat on the deed box he used as a steering seat idly watching the very scruffy looking old lady crossing the bridge at the mouth of the little river, wondering what misfortune had befallen her that left her without a home, taking all her belongings around in a big bag.

As she approached she asked him, "Cor guvner can ya spare a cup o' tea fer me. Oi'd be much 'bliged if ya could guvner."

It had to be the worst of all fake cockney accents he had ever heard and he was too startled to answer.

"Aww cummon guvner oiv bin on me feet these two days, oim diein o' first," she continued.

"Amanda!" Jim's expression changed in a split second.

"Got you going there didn't I," she said. "You made good time, even without me. I thought I might have to walk further downriver. Seems I'm not as indispensable as I'd thought."

"Bloody hell!" Jim beamed, "It's good to see you, I thought you were going into hiding."

"I had a sort of plan, very sketchy though, but tea first," she said.

As the kettle boiled, Jim realised that he had already set things out for two.

"When I saw those two, I had had just one thought in her mind," she said as she warmed her hands on the mug. "We couldn't be seen together by the people that were poking at the Mayfly. I knew I had to do two things. The first was to get away from the town, then I had to throw the bastards off the scent again. I had a bit of money left in my coat so I went to the station and bought a return ticket costing as much as I could afford, then I just got on the train, and got off at the other side."

"Where was that?" asked Jim.

"I haven't a bloody clue," Amanda replied. "It was miles away and that's sort of the point. I still had a bit of change so I went into the town and bought this horrible coat from a charity shop so people were less likely to recognise me, then I phoned the coppers to say I am still alive and going round the festivals, there's a load of them if you know where to look. I then posted them a note, sorry but I pinched one of our stamps. I rang Marie too to tell her what I'm up to, so that her story is straight. After that I put the coat on, muzzed up my hair and set off back again. Oh, and it's good to see you too Jim."

"Those bastards still think you may be, well, deceased. So they

69

obviously still believe a bit of that story," said Jim, who was warmed by Amanda's closing remark, but felt he ought to stick with the subject at hand.

"That's no bad thing," Amanda replied. "I mean any confusion we put in their way sort of keeps them on the hop. I know someone could make a big effort and get us on something but I'm not sure they have either the time or the brains to work out exactly what to throw at us."

"I wouldn't agree with you on the last one," Jim said cautiously. "I've had dealings with that sort before, and as I said, they don't let go, you think they have but they don't, so, for the next three weeks we'll have to keep ahead of the game somehow. At least you've put what looks like a gap between us and them."

"You really don't like them at all do you," Amanda said, almost playfully.

"No," Jim replied firm to the point of being sharp. "No, I don't. And this isn't a game and, even though we have to play it as one, we're playing with fire. Just remember that."

"Hey! Cool off a bit will you!" It was Amanda's turn to be firm. "It's *me* they're after, and if they catch me you don't think I'd ever drop you in it do you? I mean you weren't to know were you. I've walked into pubs with you and nobody asked a thing even though neither of us should have been there. I know I told you my age, but they don't know that, and anyway, I could have lied about it."

"Sorry," Jim kept the firm tone, though less sharp. "That's not good enough. I could have said all that for you. You think I don't know that you wouldn't dump me in the crap? Of course I do, don't ask how, but I sort of knew I could trust you from the first day I met you, which is only a week, but who's counting. Shit! Look. Today you went off and said you'd be back soon, and I knew you meant it, but with those bastards after you. They sent the bloody police after you only a few days ago and we had to give them the slip. I'm not sure you know how dangerous they are."

"Jim? Calm it. I'm O.K." Amanda said

"Yes, you are and I'm glad. Look. Bollocks! You could have been in care by now, and I thought I'd lost a good friend," Jim continued. "Call that selfish but today has been a sack full of shit, and it's rained and I couldn't be bothered to have any lunch. And before you tell me not to feel sorry for myself, I'm not. Just the thought of you being put in some crap-hole! Bollocks!"

70

Amanda was a bit confused by what Jim had just said, partly because of the delivery, but more due to the tone of voice he'd used. It was true that when she left him on the bridge earlier in the day, she did so to have some sport with the people from the department. She'd got away with it, but in the process had hurt Jim, albeit unintentionally (which he knew). His reaction, probably because of his earlier experiences, seemed a bit odd, but brought into focus something she hadn't really thought about. Suddenly it crystallised in her mind. "This is a proper friendship," she thought. "No questions, just it, and the stupidest thing is, I knew it."

"You are right," she said. "None of this is a game, not my situation or yours. You like to think you take each day as it comes, but today caught you on the hop I think. That was my fault, and if it counts for anything, I'm sorry. I should have sat by the bridge and we could have done something better, or at least together, but whatever, it's made both of us think. I'm not trying to excuse myself, I know I hurt you and I was wrong. We'll crack all the stuff we have to do. I don't know how but we'll do it. Yesterday I said we were friends, today I sort of know how it works, well, a bit of it at least."

"And you're right," Jim said calmly. "It is mostly front, I just don't like to think too far ahead or I'll be quaking in my boots all the time."

"Stuff good health, it's time for a bloody big fry-up. I haven't eaten all day either so I'm starving," Amanda smiled.

Jim's face had cleared of the worried look it had worn whilst they were talking.

"Yup," he smiled back. "We can take the whole world on with a good fry-up inside us!"

The meal was certainly large, its lack of finesse being more than made up for in quantity, and it was eaten with the same enthusiasm with which it was created. The pair sat back afterwards watching the mist gradually forming on the river. At that point they both surely felt that they could take anything the world threw at them.

"O.K." Jim said, with a very satisfied smile on his face. "What's for afters?"

"Pig," Amanda laughed.

"Sorry, you can't eat them! It's against your religion or something, and they taste lousy with custard on." Jim laughed.

"I won't even ask how you know that!" Amanda smiled. After a pause she said, "Jim. I suppose I'd better tell you a bit more about me. Just so you know."

"This sounds a bit off," he said jokily. "It's not going to make me sick is it?"

"No," Amanda said firmly. "Be serious for a moment then we can be as daft as we like, but I want to be honest."

"Right, you got my attention. Tell," Jim replied.

"Well, here I am on a boat when I should be at school. Kind of makes me look a rebel, leaving early, sticking two fingers up at the exam system. Fact is, I pandered to that, and it's fake. So am I in a way," Amanda frowned.

Jim looked with a mild furrow to his brow, but he felt too full of good humour (and food) to be worried.

"You never really said except that things went pants for you," he said

"Well the truth is that I am sort of a swat if you want to put it that way. I was moved up a year in primary school, so I did my all exams a year early and I got ten good ones. The fees were paid for the whole year. Then they threw me out!" she smiled.

"Charming" said Jim.

"I ended up at the only school with places, and they would have nothing of my having gone through the exams early, so I was basically just sitting around doing very little, so I packed it in. Nobody was unpleasant to me but there was no reason to be there." Amanda said.

"None of that matters. I knew you were smart," said Jim. "Just means you have pieces of paper to prove it."

"Well it also means that the people from the social have been on to me for a bit longer than I had said. You probably knew one of them was," Amanda frowned.

"The truancy lot," Jim finished her sentence. "I'd kind of worked that one out. Screw the lot of them that's what I say! We'll take them all on and win! Stuff 'em! I don't care!"

Amanda smiled, for some reason she felt so happy that she felt tears forming.

"Tell you what," said Jim. "Let's do the washing up then I'll thrash you at cards by lamplight!"

It was another late night as the two sat in the cabin simply enjoying each other's company. They played various games of cards, the rules of which merged into each other. As they played they talked about any and every subject that came up each finding more out about the other as they went on. Finally the lamp was extinguished and sleep took over very soon after.

Chapter 5

The morning sun edged through the open curtain of one of the portholes straight into Jim's eye as he rolled over and opened it to look at the clock.

"Bloody hell!" he said, blocking the light with his hand.

"I didn't think I looked that bad in the morning," Amanda answered from somewhere in her sleeping bag.

"All I can see is blue spots! Bloody sun! I'll get the kettle on, fancy a fry up for breakfast?" Jim smiled.

"Don't even joke about it!" Amanda mumbled, surfacing slowly. "Did we really eat all that last night?"

"I'm afraid so. I think all I can stand this morning is tea and biccies if you don't mind. It's a bit of a hike, if we want to get off the river today, so we'd best keep things simple," Jim replied.

"Simple is fine by me," Amanda said, shutting the cabin door to get dressed. "I was thinking, I ought to keep a low profile in the locks, in case our friends are still sniffing around. I can still steer and stuff, nobody would really notice who I am at a distance. I mean its unlikely that they'd sit in trees with binoculars."

"You've got a bit of a point there," Jim said. "You've also got those opera glasses, so we could keep an eye out as we approach locks and anywhere else busy. Just thinking too. You know that radio you brought, does it have batteries in it?"

"The Russian thing? No it doesn't, I was meaning to get some, why?" Amanda answered.

"It's one of those they advertise in the papers isn't it?" Jim said. "You know the sort that have so many bands they can even pick up the Martians on a good day."

Amanda looked puzzled then the penny dropped. "You're thinking of getting the police radios on it? And yes, it does do that, I remember when my dad unpacked it. We messed around for a bit, you can get aircraft, police, fire, even the sound from the older television you know, the 405 line ones."

"We'll get it working as soon as we can, it may prove useful," Jim said as he set about breakfast.

Their agreement to be more cautious had now to be put into practice, and it was not going to be that easy to achieve. Had the Mayfly been a larger boat, things would be more straightforward, the possibility of concealment of anything increasing with the available space. To disappear an item the size of Amanda, in the space afforded by the cabin would either require her to be a reasonably skilled contortionist or conjurer. As she was neither of these, it was decided that they would travel as before, but keep watch at all times. When approaching locks or more heavily populated areas, Amanda could retreat to the cabin until the coast was clear. Once they had the radio working, they would do their best to monitor any communications that may be relevant. As soon as they were off the main river, and still some distance from the city they were aiming for, they could probably afford to be a little more relaxed. The canal was much less popular than the river and, if the information Jim had was accurate, you could often travel the whole day without seeing another boat on the move. First though, they would have to head the other way down the canal to the centre of the city to deliver the brandy and another watch. Amanda took the opera glasses out and checked around to satisfy herself that nobody was lurking around. The combination of low magnification but good quality lenses, coupled with Amanda's very good eyesight, meant that they were, at the very least, adequate. The sound of the outboard starting appeared to disturb nobody so, feeling safe from prying eyes, they set off towards their next destination. The weather remained pleasant throughout the day, and they stopped for a while just short of a small town to have lunch, after which Jim briefly went over an old stone bridge to look for a shop that sold batteries. Amanda decided to busy herself around the boat, all the time keeping an eye out for people that she did not want to see. The arrangement, in the event of this, would be for her to start the motor and move on up the river until she was reasonably sure that her pursuers would move on by car to the next lock. When satisfied, she would then double back to pick Jim up from the spot she had set off from. Thankfully this was not necessary and he was soon back.

"I was thinking," he said. "And I'm not so sure we should push on to the University today. We'd get there fairly late, and we'd be right in the middle of town when we do tie up so there'd be nowhere to run if we did."

"Do we need to deliver the stuff today?" queried Amanda.

"Not 'till tomorrow lunchtime, which is a bit of a nuisance. I'd like to

74

be out of the city as soon as we can be.   Shall we try and listen in to the police?" Jim replied.

Amanda got the rather large Russian transistor radio out from a locker at the end of her bunk and put the batteries in.   It had an enormously long telescopic aerial which she extended fully before switching on.   It had not been used for a while, and had last been switched on to listen into a traffic incident on the main road close to her old home.   Tuning it across the band produced some results, mostly snippets of taxi radios, but she did hear a snatch of what sounded like a police car communication.   It made very little sense hearing half a conversation but it was better than nothing.

Whilst they were listening, a police car came over the bridge, pausing before the turn in the road, and heading away from them.

"That was it!" she said triumphantly.   "We've got them!   I saw the guy speaking in the car and heard it here!"

She got a small notebook out and made a note of the radio tuning before switching off and stowing it away.   It made them both feel slightly more secure to know that they had just a little more insight into the activities of people that may be hostile to them.   More immediately important was the fact that the police did not either appear to be searching actively for them, nor did they regard their presence in the Mayfly as suspicious.   They tied up for the night rather earlier than previous evenings, having decided to move on early to be in time for their rendezvous at the university.   During the journey, Amanda had spent a good deal of the travel time just inside the cabin doors, working away with scissors, and the dowdy old coat that she had worn as a disguise the previous day.   Jim had glanced down from time to time and thought occasionally that she was alleviating the boredom of keeping a low profile by exacting her terrible revenge on the garment. Having rearranged her things, she had liberated a stout coated cardboard box, with a tight fitting lid and into this she started stuffing the remnants of the coat.   With the hoops up to take the cover ready for the night, they both lifted the canvas over in what looked like a well rehearsed move.   This was not strictly necessary, but it more than doubled the covered area and they needed all the space they could get.   Jim's curiosity then finally got the better of him.

"O.K.," he said.   "I give up, what were you doing this afternoon?"
Amanda simply replied.   "Hay-box."
"There's no hay in it," Jim queried.
"There doesn't have to be," Amanda smiled.   "I can see you were never

75

a Girl Guide."

Jim raised his eyebrows as she continued.

"If we eat fry-ups every day we are going to turn into pustules, I mean, we'll have so many spots we'd sink the boat if we squeezed them all at once, so I have made this," she said

"I'm not eating your coat!" Jim replied. "I don't know where it's been!"

"We did this once at camp," Amanda returned to the subject. "All you do is put a load of food in a pot and blast on the stove it till it is really hot, put the lid on and shove it in here and it will cook itself during the day. We can do soups and stews and stuff in it, if it works, so we can eat a bit better. Oh, and don't worry about the coat, I got it from a charity shop, and they promised me it had been cleaned, I wasn't going to wear something with things living in it, I do have some standards you know!"

"Right," Jim said, clearly impressed at the feat of improvisation. "We can get some fresh food tomorrow and try it out. Another thing we need to be thinking about though is your problem with your folks. We're going to have to do something about it soon, or, well, you know how things sort of move on. We don't want to have the law sort it out and get it all wrong, then miss the chance."

"It's hard to know where to start," Amanda replied. "I kind of knew very little of Dad's business affairs. I mean, the family are a little on the old fashioned side and never really spoke about things. I only saw the office he worked in once when I was about nine years old. They either had a factory or workshop somewhere too, and there was another company that made things for them but neither were anywhere close to the offices. Dad would visit them periodically and was generally away for a couple of days when he did. Most of the rest is pretty much what I said when we set off."

"I wonder," Jim said thoughtfully. "If we went to a library they may have directories of businesses, we could also look in newspapers to see if there was anything relating to the whole mess up. If the defence people were sniffing around, it may have made the news, if we're lucky, but it could have been hushed up as well. We can live in hope though."

Amanda sat thinking, with the little knot of wrinkles just above her nose that was now becoming a familiar signpost to Jim. Eventually she spoke.

"That's about as good as the hay-box," she smiled. "I have been wondering how to get into this whole mess, but putting where we're going and your thoughts together. The University must have some decent libraries, and they may let members of the public use some. Do we have time tomorrow?"

"Have as much as you like," Jim replied with a smile. "From tomorrow we won't be on the river any more, so we have to do everything for ourselves as far as the locks go. Dave's plan was worked out for just one person and a boat, so he has put in at least half as much time again as we should need."

"Do you know how to work a lock?" Amanda had to ask.

"Well, yes, in principle, but I haven't done one yet. You can handle the Mayfly as well as me so we should be a good team. We'll figure it out. In any case Dave put all of that in his plan as I said. Another thing is we can, if necessary, travel at night on the canal. We can use the Tilley lamp as a headlamp if we have to. It's a hell of a lot brighter than the hurricane lamps."

The evening was fairly clear but not too cold, so they sat in the cockpit just watching the light clouds go by, beginning to relax into what was to become routine for the foreseeable future. The world seemed a wholly different place when viewed from the Mayfly, although there was a lot that mattered, schedules to be kept and wrongs to right, it did all seem slightly disconnected from their former reality. Amanda looked over at Jim, who was staring out across the river, which was rather narrower now than it was where they had set off from, what seemed like years previously. She looked across the meadow which had probably not changed much across the decades, if not the centuries, then she looked up at the stars, unchanged for millennia. This, for now, she thought, was no bad life to lead, and, also for now, she would go wherever it took her. Although she had set herself the task of sorting things out, she felt for once that she didn't really have to. There is a difference to doing something because you want to, or because you are doing someone else a favour instead of simply feeling that your hand has been forced. She, for the first time in over a year, had been able to think objectively about the affairs of her immediate family without the feeling of fear that gripped from behind the knee.

They woke up to a sunny morning, although there was a brisk breeze. The weather forecast on the radio said that it would be a reasonably good day with the possibility of the odd shower. Whilst eating breakfast Amanda scanned across the likely bands on the radio that would pick up police broadcasts but could find nothing of interest.

"When we get near, we're looking for a small footbridge on the right-hand side. I'm not sure if it will be marked, but it's on the map, looks like there's some houses near it," Jim pointed out the location on an old Ordinance Survey map that Dave had given him for the journey.

"Shouldn't that be starboard?" Amanda said with a smile.

"Drink your tea smartarse!" Jim replied, "Then we can get on the move."

With everything stowed away in the deed boxes they were soon moving upriver at a decent pace. The countryside eventually dissolved into the outskirts of town, and it could have been any town. But for a short stretch of frontage that was occupied by some prestigious rowing clubs, the place seemed to have forgotten the river that probably gave it its life in the first place. On one bank a long corrugated iron fence painted a dull green faced the river. Behind it was a terrace of neglected Victorian houses that looked mostly to be occupied by students. The fence was decorated with graffiti comprised mostly of political slogans and various renditions of a tortoise. Not long after the lock, there was a break in the right bank with the footbridge they were looking for. Amanda was the first to spot it, and she pointed it out to Jim, who reduced speed to tick-over as they approached. It was unclear as to whether this was the canal or just a stream and he did not want to run aground or hit an obstruction at speed. Swinging the Mayfly at right-angles to the main river so that the bow was slightly upriver of the entrance, he allowed the current to take him to where he needed to be, before committing himself with a small burst of throttle. The footbridge was much lower than even the last bridge they had gone under on the main river and it almost instantly took them into a different world. The channel was narrow, shallow and choked in parts with reeds and other water plants, around which was a landscape of dereliction. A railway bridge crossed at a level so low that it almost appeared to have been a deliberate hindrance to navigation. Jim kept the speed low as they brushed past reeds in the even narrower channel underneath it. In a short while they were approaching their first canal lock, and, pulling out an item that looked like a very well built handle for a car jack, he handed the steering over to Amanda who, instinctively took the craft in close to the bank so that Jim could jump ashore.

"Here's where we find out how things work !" he said cheerily trying to hide the fact that he had not got the first clue of how to operate the lock. Thankfully it was in their favour, so he was able to open the gate, which Amanda took as a signal to progress into the chamber. She had only encountered the bigger locks of the main river and was confident until she

78

saw the narrow space she was about to enter. She edged nervously forward, not wanting to damage the little boat that was now her home. Even with the motor in neutral there was a small amount of steerage from the shaft which was not circular as with some small outboards, but an elongated fin not unlike an aeroplane wing in profile. Using this and the occasional burst of power she got into the chamber with no major bumps, winning appreciative applause from Jim, who assisted her in getting out onto the side of the lock after she had stopped the motor. The mechanism of the paddles was not too well maintained, but simple, so, apart from the unexpected weight of the gearing, they were able to make it through to the other side with no loss of pride.

"I presume we do a right turn here into the town, and head out later?" Amanda asked as she was setting about starting the outboard.

"Isn't that starboard?" Jim mocked light-heartedly.

"Smartarse!" Amanda smiled as she flicked into forward and took the Mayfly down through the area that the university, and the rest of the town had also forgotten. After some distance, the canal just ended unceremoniously, the wharves and basin that had once been a hive of activity was no longer there, having been filled in many years previously to make a car park. They found a spot to tie up, having checked the bottom for anything that may have been dumped in the water, locked the boat and headed for their appointment, both feeling singularly unimpressed thus far. The town itself was both timeless and rather too full of its own importance.

"It's sort of fascinating but repellent at the same time," Amanda commented.

As they walked, Jim looked at his friend thinking how she was almost totally unnoticeable amid the various groups of students. For himself it was an alien environment, and one in which he did not want to spend too much time even though, to the casual observer, he blended in just as well as she did. Continuing their way up to an old college building to ask the whereabouts of the lecturer for whom the watch was intended Jim heard a squeaky voice shout.

"It's Milly-Molly-Mandy!"

Both Jim and Amanda started and looked round in the direction of the outburst to see a tall thin chestnut haired girl perhaps a year or two older than Jim.

"It *is!* Milly-Molly-Mandy! I don't believe it, how *are* you? Are you checking the place out, and who is *this*?" she said looking towards Jim.

79

"Milly, Molly, *Mandy?*" Jim said, slowly and quizzically. "Who on earth gave you *that* ?"

The voice, the hair, and the gift of a nickname all belonged to Emma Jesmond who had known Amanda when she started at senior school. Because she was there a year early, the people in the higher years took to her, adopting her as a kind of mascot. Now in her second year at the university Emma, though similar in appearance, was sufficiently different for Amanda to take a few moments to recognise. Eventually she spoke.

"Good god its Rocky! Bloody hell, the last time I saw you you were trying to squeeze into a school uniform. Hello Emma! This is Jim. We've known each other for about a week, and we live on a boat. And before you ask. No! We're not. O.K. Right that's the embarrassing bit done, now how has your life been?"

Emma explained that she had got into university with ease, having passed all the necessary exams with top grades. She was studying law, and not really enjoying it that much but it was what her parents wanted her to do, and they were footing the bill so she was making the best of it. She lived in hall of residence which was fine because she wouldn't know one end of a cooking pot from another, and she had a little red sports car which was tremendous fun if she wanted to get away from it all.

"So do tell me." she said in an accent much more distilled into money than Amanda's could ever have been. "What brings you here?"

"Brandy and a Russian watch," Jim replied, with Amanda adding.

"We have to deliver them to a couple of people here and, if possible, I'd like to borrow a library to do some research," Amanda added.

"Well, lets go, now, the watch, that is for?" asked Emma.

"Doctor Ian Meadows, and the Brandy is for another doctor, um. Oh, that's it, Jeremy Simms," Amanda answered as efficiently as she could.

"Well," Emma smiled. "You should be in luck on all grounds. They are both in the law department so we should be able to track them down quite easily. How come you have gifts for them?"

"It's deliveries, it's sort of a working boat and it's sort of our job," Amanda stated nervously.

"That and saving the world," Jim added in a flattish tone.

"So," Emma persisted. "The library? I would guess that is about saving the world? Am I right?"

"Not really," Jim continued the deadpan tone. "That'd be more righting a great injustice. We do a bit of that too when there's a demand for it."

80

"He's a hoot, this guy of yours! Where *did* you find him!" Emma spoke as though Jim was no longer present, so he decided to act the part and kept quiet. "Is it one of those barge things they have on the canal that you are working on?"

"It's a bit shorter than that," Amanda said, deciding not to reveal just how much shorter. "It came from Scotland you know, and Jim belongs to himself, not me, we work together you see. It takes two people to run the boat."

"I'm sure it does," Emma continued probing. "So who is the captain?"

"Well," Amanda did not want to sound a subordinate "It's Jim's boat."

"But it's democratically run," Jim interrupted. "We take votes on every decision, and Amanda provided the fittings so the thing is as much hers as it it mine. Yes, it's a business partnership."

"Ah," Emma pointed out. "But there are just two of you? So who has the casting vote?"

"The cat," Amanda had said the first thing that came into her head.

"Oh how sweet, you have a little cat!" Emma cooed.

"Not as yet, we'd have to vote on it," Amanda replied quickly.

Emma opened her mouth to speak, but couldn't for once think of how to frame a question. After a long silence she said, "Look, lets have lunch together, my treat, I mean I haven't seen you in ages. We can drop this stuff off and then we can go to the library after."

It seemed a good enough plan. They were outside a large dark wood door with the name Dr. J.E.Simms. Amanda looked at Jim.

"If you don't mind dropping the stuff off," she said. "Only I don't want too many people to see me."

Jim nodded, knocked at the door and heard a voice tell him to enter.

"Ah, sit down my boy," said an oldish looking man whose age was indeterminate, though Jim placed him as being close to, or slightly over that at which people retired. "You are the boat people, or at least one of them," the man added. "I think you may be in a bit of a fix too."

Jim looked taken aback. He only wanted to deliver the brandy and get out. The old man sensing this continued, "Now, I am not about to hand you over to the authorities, even though you may well be acting just slightly outside of the law. That is your business, and you must remember that almost all of our better laws have come about because people were prepared to break bad ones. That does of course not mean that everyone should break the law as suits him, but, if, and only if, you feel certain that what you are doing is right, or will cause right to come about then you have my blessing. That is a fine brandy you have brought me! And you have handled it well too and I should reward you above the cost of transport, but I think a tip may well offend your pride because I know you have already been paid for the delivery."

"It's fine," Jim said. "It's what we do."

"That is so," Doctor Simms went on. "But I have been made aware that one or both of you may need help of a legal nature, and as that is *my* job, so, given that money may insult your pride here is my tip." He picked up a piece of letter paper with a printed heading on it, and added a few lines of writing.

"I have put my telephone number on this and you must contact me if you need help. I have all that I need here, save for a bit of interest, so you would be helping me. If you introduce yourself on the phone with some of the words I have written I shall know it's you. Now, you had better go, because your friend will be wondering where you are."

Jim thanked the man as he got up to leave, and received an unusually firm handshake from someone who, whatever his age, did look a little bit frail.

Outside in the corridor, suitably distant from the door Emma returned to her questioning.

"So, why are you so keen not to be noticed? Are you on the run or something? And why is it you and not your, um, friend that can't be seen? It'd be awful fun to be harbouring a criminal!"

At this Amanda spoke sharply, but in a hushed voice.

"Oh, grow up will you!" she said. "Yes, I have to keep a low profile on account of the fact that I am officially dead, and it doesn't do to be seen walking about the place in that condition. Oh, and yes people are after me and if they get me then they will put me into council care, then put two and two together and lock Jim up as well, so at this moment in time it's better off for me to be blooming well dead so far as they are concerned because they don't expect a corpse to be walking down the bloody high street now do they. Before you ask again, neither Jim nor I have done anything wrong, well not really wrong except truancy and a case of technical kidnap could be thrown at us, sort of one each except I don't have to go to school, well I wouldn't do if I was a year older when I did my exams but that's the way it is and I haven't been kidnapped on account of the fact that I am here by my own choice, except, again technically, I'm not old enough to know my own mind. So you can see if we're not careful, the both of us could be down the crapper quicker than a school curry."

"Oh! You poor dear! But I still don't understand why you aren't at school. You just left and that was it." Emma sounded rather concerned.

"How did you know?" asked Amanda.

"My little sister, Tamsin, she was a year below you. She said you just went home at the end of term and never came back, she asked but nobody would say," explained Emma.

"That'd fit," Amanda said flatly. "They never passed any so called gossip at that place did they. Well my Dad went bust, not so much bust as spectacularly bust, and what's worse scandal was associated with it, and none of it was down to him, I'm sure of that. So, along with escaping from the school I went to next, I'll tell you about that another time, I have to find out who did the dirty on Dad. And before you call me a poor dear again, I'm not. I know this sounds awful but this, whatever it is, that I am doing, it's like a new life and I feel alive, in control even though I am not, so don't look at me like I'm some poor waif O.K. I guess I shouldn't have snapped because it is actually all pretty good at the moment."

Emma had no time to reply as Jim came out from Dr Simms' door.

"Sorry for being so long," he said. "But I just had a weird conversation. It was like the guy knew me or something. Anyway, you two look deep in conversation, anything I need to know?"

Emma smiled and said, "Oh! All about you dear! And all *fright*fully bad."

"That's me!" Jim laughed. "Bad to the bone! Now where's the next geezer?"

Ian Meadows' office was in the same building, and Emma led them to it and knocked on the door gently. The watch was handed over and the transaction completed in about half the time it took with Dr Simms and Jim was back in the corridor before Emma and Amanda had spoken about anything other than the weather.

"Right you two," Emma said firmly. "Dinner is on me and I won't take no for an answer. Nobody is going to pay you any attention here because you both look like students. The only thing they'd be interested in is my stash, and that's in the glove-box of my car."

The pub they went to was crowded with people that all looked, as Emma had said, so similar that Jim and Amanda blended in perfectly. Amanda thought to herself that the authorities may be just slightly interested in two people that shouldn't be in a pub, but she dismissed the thought on the grounds that they would no doubt only raid the place if there was any trouble.

"Too many people with influential mummies and daddies to rock the boat," she thought.

With both Jim and Amanda present, the conversation at lunch stayed around generalities and reminiscences from the two school friends. Afterwards Emma and Amanda went to the college library and Jim went off shopping, feeling that the two may work better together without him. Also they were a bit behind time if they wanted to be away from the town by evening.

"O.K." Emma continued an earlier thread of conversation as she and Amanda walked to the library. "You said you felt more alive. That's down to the friend isn't it?"

Amanda was taken aback by the directness of the question.

"No," she said firmly. "Jim is one of the good guys, there's no doubt about that, but it's not really anything to do with him. It's me, I felt just a bit stifled in school, even though I was doing well. I mean that made it sort of more stifling because of the expectation, then the floor fell out and I ended up, well, by a roundabout route, here. I should feel guilty but I don't. I have worked in a shop and lived by myself, and now I live on a boat. Who knows what is going to happen next. It's."

"Exciting?" Emma offered.

"No, not that," Amanda replied. "Exciting is for games and if I get this wrong it could blow back in my face, but yes as well. It's like there's a purpose to what I'm doing."

"Jim knows about this does he?" Emma asked quietly.

"That and more," Amanda smiled. "I think he's guessed a lot too. Now, let's get some research done."

The two spent a couple of hours going through news articles and some old company information that was held there. In some ways it was a disappointing result, but Amanda didn't ever expect to find the solution to everything.

"Tell you what," suggested Emma. "We're not going to unearth any more information today so how about I do a bit more digging and see what I come up with. You can always give me a ring at hall if you want a chat about it."

Amanda agreed to the idea and the two went off in search of the canal and Jim, who was busy attempting to retrieve the Mayfly from the middle of the channel. It must have seemed a tremendous joke to whoever untied the lines and pushed her out into mid-stream, but Jim was not seeing the funny side of it whatsoever. It was still rather early in the season, and not many holidaymakers had discovered the delights of inland waterways anyway. Very few of those that had, had ever ventured down the forgotten end to the town so, unnoticed by anyone, Jim was trying and failing to scoop one of the ropes from the water with a piece of tree branch.

"The little shits!" Amanda exclaimed. "What can they possibly get from doing that!"

"I've been at this for more than half an hour," Jim said angrily. "And got absolutely nowhere. I can't get to it from the other side either."

"Right!" said Amanda "Hold my bag would you Emma," After which she kicked her shoes off and slid neatly into the canal. A couple of strokes got her close enough to grab a line and another kick had her near enough to scramble back, rope in hand, on the bank.

"There," she said proudly.

"What the bloody hell did you do that for?" Jim said, somewhat shocked by her action. "And how are you going to clean up! We don't exactly have a bathroom you know and that canal has god knows what in it. Water is just one of many ingredients," Jim re-tied the lines as he spoke.

"Ah," said a bedraggled but proud Amanda. "I have to say I didn't really think that one through did I."

Emma, who had been watching the spectacle open-mouthed, finally spoke.

"You're bloody mad the pair of you! And as for you," she added looking straight at Amanda. "You're madder than him and he's bloody mad. You can't live on that! It's not a work boat, it's a."

"Packing case," Jim added dryly. "It's been said before, and actually these hulls are quite popular as small fishing boats and with the cabin they get used like taxis between the islands so it owes more to the working boat than you'd think, though mostly for coastal than inland use. Anyway we are working, using it to do so, so it is a work boat, and you can live on it because we do."

"Whatever the situation," Emma interrupted. "Amanda, you need a bath, so come back to hall with me and have a good soak in something clean this time.   I'll put your stuff through one of the machines in the laundry room with some of mine and it'll be done in a couple of hours or so."

Amanda didn't need much convincing, and with a change of clothes, set off back to the college, leaving a trail of, what was only arguably water, behind her. It was more than three hours before she returned looking, and smelling a good deal fresher than she had when she left. It was also getting dark.   Jim had created a hearty vegetable stew the smell of which across the water was more than welcoming. He had lit a hurricane lamp and hung it beneath the hoops, and was busy studying an old guidebook that Dave had included in the bundle before they left.   Hearing her footsteps on the tow-path he looked up and smiled.

"Hi there, that smells rather good," Amanda's voice was cheery. "Sorry it took so long but Emma just won't give up. She was very impressed by your knowledge of boats by the way."

"It's a shame I made most of it up then," Jim replied with a trace of laugh in his voice.

"What! You pig! You even convinced me!" Amanda's tone was one of mock indignation.

"It's true," Jim said. "All that I know about this thing is its made of plywood and it was half sunk when I found it.   They only reason I know it's made in Orkney is the little brass makers plate on the stern post! Dave told me the stuff about fishing so I assume its accurate, but anyway, it's tea time, enjoy."

They shared their experiences of the day over their evening meal agreeing somewhat reluctantly to remain for the night where they were, it being unlikely that they would be able to clear the outskirts of the town before it was pitch dark, and, even with the Tilley lamp it would be hard to spot any items lurking in the water that might damage the Mayfly.

Chapter 6

It was about one in the morning that Jim sat blot upright in his bunk, wide awake but not knowing what had woken him. All seemed quiet but there was something not right, although he wasn't prone to premonitions Jim simply knew but he didn't know what.

"Mand," he hissed. "Mand, there's someone out there." He wasn't sure if he had woken her and sat in the dark listening. Then he heard a scuffling and some muffled voices but could not make out what they were saying.

"Shh," said one to the hushed giggle of the other as the Mayfly moved with a slight jerk in the water. Amanda had slowly woken and was laying still hoping it was just a bad dream.

"Mand, can you hear me?" Jim whispered.

"Yes, what's going on?" she replied quietly.

"I don't know, but I'm going to find out." With that remark, he slowly moved off his bunk trying to disturb the boat as little as possible. He carefully inched the cabin door open and could see two figures silhouetted against the side screen. With the door open he could hear more clearly what was being said.

"Lets see how the other half lives!" giggled a male voice.

Jim felt the anger rise in him and thought about confronting them but, remembering their precarious position, decided to wait and see if they went away. He slithered noiselessly out into the cockpit narrowly missing the slop bucket. There were clearly at least two people out there as he could hear them scrabbling at each end of the screen fastening.

"One. Two. Three," he heard, and then the side-screen was thrown over the hoops in a theatrical gesture that set the two throwers (both having indulged themselves at the college bar rather too much) reeling backwards in an equally stage like manner as they regained their balance. They carefully picked their way back to the boat watching their footing and giggling as they went and oblivious to the figure now standing in the cockpit of the Mayfly.

"Oh my *GOSH!*" said one of the figures. "It's a real life oik! Hey look we've caught ourselves an oik."

The other, thinking that this was the best of all comic remarks replied with, "Let's grab him by the neck and throw him in the drink.   Ha ha! Bloody oiks!"

The first rounded back with, "Drink, wow that's civil of you.   Mine's a pint!   Ha ha!"   Then turning to Jim he said in a slightly slurred, but decidedly posh voice.   "Landlord!   We'll have two pints of your piss!   Ha! And make it your best piss!"

"Certainly sir," Jim replied politely.

As they were tied up in a town and not a rural location, they had to make do with a bucket for facilities rather than the bushes and trees that most walkers and other travellers would use.   This was the so called slop bucket.   It was far from ideal, but it served its purpose and could be left in the cockpit.   It had been Jim's intention to empty it down a road drain early in the morning as he did not think it a good idea to pollute the canal further, however polluted it already may have been.   Together with the general waste from the washing up bowl, there was easily over two pints so Jim obligingly delivered it to his 'customers' with a beautiful high arcing throw which ensured maximum coverage.

"You can have that on the house," he said.   "Now kindly piss off!"

"That's disgusting, what is it?" said one voice to the other, but Jim answered for the second.

"You asked for piss, you got it.   Fair transaction if you ask me."

"Do you *know* who you are talking to!" said the second voice suddenly sobered.   No doubt he was going to point out that he was the son of somebody very important, but he was cut short by the first voice saying, "Come on, he got us fair and square.   Lets get cleaned up before we catch something.   Never know what the oiks and grockles carry!"

With that they left.   Jim lit a hurricane lamp and slipped ashore to check the mooring lines.   The undergraduates had obviously been trying to undo the knots, but lack of light and surfeit of alcohol had rendered the task beyond them.   After checking everything he closed the screen and returned to the cabin finding Amanda sitting up fully awake.

"Good shot," she said.   "Now, get some sleep and I'll keep watch for a couple of hours, then we'll change over.   I'm not letting these people have another shot."

"I can't believe people like that would behave that way," Jim said sleepily.

"Oh," Amanda replied, rather sadly. "I can. Believe me Jim, I can."

The night had been a bit on the cool side and the morning was bright, but this did little to lift the spirits of Jim and Amanda after the disturbances of the early hours. The day's work, for the first time since they set off, seemed more of a chore than something to enjoy or look forward to. It still had to be done though, so they set about the routine of washing and having breakfast, after which things looked a little more promising and they both observed that it was only because they were tired that they felt the way they did. Nothing had really changed.

"Nothing," thought Amanda. It wasn't absolutely true for her though. The previous day when she had been reminiscing with her old school friend there was something nagging at the back of her mind. She was unable to put her finger on it, but it was there during the night's disturbances as well. She sat, with the familiar slight furrowing of the brow, and thought. "Those people went to the same general variety of schools as me, but somehow they looked like they were born to that life. I was but I wasn't, and yet I've done my share of being, well, being a snob or something." Going back over her school days she recalled there being a distance between her and most other pupils which, however minute, was still finite. "Why?" She thought. "Why was that?" When everything was pretty much the same as far as their outward appearance went. Or was it her and there was no distance.

"What's on your mind?" asked Jim.

Amanda thought for a while and said, "Well, those, those bastards out there last night."

"What about them?" Jim replied.

"If things had happened as they should have, well. In a couple of years or so one of them could have been me. You know, spoilt, rich, nothing else better to do," she frowned.

"And daddy bails them out every time they get into trouble?" Jim added tentatively.

"That too," she nodded.

"Not you," Jim replied firmly. "Not ever. You're not like them. You're a different breed."

Amanda looked mildly startled at the observation remembering her father telling her how he had worked his way through electrical, mechanical and then electronic engineering and built what he had himself. She remembered that her mother's family were often a little patronising to

89

her parents, but not to her.

"Bastards!" she thought.

"That lot that caused trouble last night," she said flatly. "They were born to their money. So was I but generations of their lot probably were. My dad started with nothing."

"I was born to mine," Jim added. "Thing is there wasn't nearly as much as they had. But we've had that much for a very long time too."

"But even the president of the United States sometimes must have to stand naked," Amanda replied.

"True enough," Jim said. "And either him, Dylan, or both would smell the same if you throw the bog over them."

"And would I ?" asked Amanda.

"Well," Jim replied contemplatively. "You would, so would I. But they had the money, and I had the bog. So they were the ones that went home smelling like tramps."

"Let's go." Amanda said firmly.

They had to manually turn the Mayfly round as, unlike the river, the canal was very narrow, not much more than the length of the craft. With Amanda holding the bow rope the stern was pushed as far out as was possible by Jim, who then walked it down the tow-path holding and over her head. Once the boat was almost across the canal Jim pulled the stern line towards him, and Amanda walked forward with the bow line until the craft was fully facing the other way. All this done, they both boarded, Jim started the motor and they were on their way. The channel was very narrow in parts and the weed encroached from the edges concealing all manner of rubbish that had been carelessly thrown in. It was not that long before they met an unexpected obstacle in the form of a small road bridge that crossed the canal no more than two feet above the water level. It was in an industrial area and appeared to serve a factory. The worst thing was that there was no visible means of opening it, in fact it looked very much like it was a fixed structure that had replaced an earlier moveable one. As they approached Amanda took a look through her opera glasses but could see nothing but a few of the people from the factory looking back at her.

"I'll have to get ashore if I can." said Jim, looking for a suitable spot amid the weed and debris and finding none. Eventually he carefully nudged the bow into the weed on the tow-path side, and nimbly climbed over the cabin top. Once he was on the bow deck, and had just about committed himself to leaping ashore, a man from the factory went into a

90

gatehouse situated near the obstruction, threw a switch, and the bridge lifted neatly until it was almost perpendicular. By this time the Mayfly was well into the weed and was aground at the bow due to Jim's weight, which meant he had to scramble back to the cockpit before they could move.

"Come on! We ain't got all bleedin' day," shouted one of the men from the factory, adding, "Bleedin' tourists!" for good measure.

Once Jim was in the cockpit, Amanda reversed the motor and they were back in the channel, she then steered forward under the bridge, opening the throttle slightly. As they emerged from the other side there were several wolf-whistles, and a shout of, "Go on darlin', show us your tits!"

A further opening of the throttle allowed the prop to shed any weed it had picked up. Although it was specified by the maker as weed free, it was not absolutely impervious to the stuff, but rarely had to be cleared manually. Their speed soon increased to a decent walking pace, which was the maximum allowed on the canal.

"I guess that whistling wasn't meant for me," Jim said thoughtfully, and, after a pause, adding. "You know, all that stuff we were talking about. It was about class and stuff wasn't it."

"Yes," Amanda replied, wondering what was coming next.

"Well," he continued, "I was sort of seeing what you were getting at, but I wouldn't worry that much."

"I wasn't worried, just thinking that's all," Amanda said.

"Maybe, but, it isn't class is it. It's being different. Sure that is a big part of it because classes are, so are ages and a whole lot of other stuff. That just lets people have the chance of a free pop at someone. There's always a reason," Jim smiled.

"It's how wars start even," Amanda frowned.

"I hadn't thought of that," Jim replied. "But what I was thinking was, well it isn't class is it. It's whether you're an arsehole or not. That's kind of it."

"God," said Amanda, smiling. "The thoughts of James Stratton!"

"It's true," he persisted. "Those geezers last night were, well, arseholes. Posh ones but arseholes. The guys at the factory, just now, they were arseholes too. Not the whole factory, and not all posh people, just some of them. Oh, and arseholes are usually responsible for starting wars too in my book."

After a long pause for thought Amanda said, "Don't philosophers

91

usually live in barrels?"

"Probably," Jim replied. "Mayfly is pretty close to one though, but what do I know."

As they progressed out of the town, the canal became cleaner, and they were soon passing through some pleasant scenery. The first lock they went through had been poorly maintained, the cast iron paddle gear lacking any grease was incredibly stiff. Subsequent ones were in much better shape, though it was obvious that maintenance was very much make-do-and-mend. On one lock there remained one of the boxes that they assumed was for boaters to post their papers to show they had been through. It was still intact enough to be used so, as originally instructed, they wrote out a destination slip, with time and date, and posted into the little blue painted aperture. They decided to stop for lunch in an area of open land not far above one of the locks reasoning that they had plenty of time, and would be able to see anybody approaching. Amanda felt much more at ease, it being unlikely that she would be spotted by anyone. Once they had finished lunch they set about preparing supper, ready to go into the hay-box that Amanda had made which, following their enjoyment of the previous nights meal, was to be another vegetable stew only cooked much slower this time. Jim had put a pan of water on to heat, and they set about peeling and chopping veg for the pot. Neither of them had much of an idea about cookery so they were happy to make things up as they went along, and were so absorbed in their activity that they didn't notice the man approaching on the tow-path.

"That looks a good feast," he said smiling and revealing a rather brown set of teeth. He looked to be in his mid to late seventies at least, but was probably quite a bit younger. He wore an old set of black trousers and a nondescript jacket fastened with a cord. "You been on holiday long?" he added.

Seeing him as no threat, but at the same time feeling slightly annoyed with herself for not seeing him approach, Amanda answered.

"We're not exactly on holiday," she said. "But it's a nice day and we're enjoying it anyway. Are you enjoying your walk?"

The man smiled again and replied, "Well, to be true, I'm like you. Not exactly havin' a walk, it's me job you see. I'm the lengthman for these parts, have been for over forty year."

It hadn't occurred to either Jim or Amanda that he'd be anything other than retired, but he seemed pleasant enough and it was a good day.

"Don't laugh, but we're living and working on this boat," Jim joined in, instinctively trusting the old man.

"Now that be odd," he replied. "Someone said summat about two kids runnin' a work-boat. I think it was one of the bosses, told I to keep an eye out. An' I were expectin' a seventy footer not a little fishing boat."

"We're a little bit shorter than that," Amanda smiled. "By about fifty five feet, but it's all we have."

"You be a might young to be wed, but everyone looks that to me now. An' where are you heading?" he asked.

"Just off north," Jim replied, trying to be as vague as possible, aware that, after all, this was an official of the waterway however nice he appeared.

Spotting this the old man smiled again saying, "I've done my job for longer than any of them there boss men have most bin alive and I've always done me best to keep things right and mended. All they want to do is shut down. 'Tis pitiful, real pitiful, I have to beg for a pound o' nails or a tin o' grease. No, 'tis not them I answer to, 'tis all o' this." He waved his hand in the general direction of the canal and continued. "Forty year an' more I done this job, an' some more learnin' it wi' the last lengthman, an they tell me 'tis all for nothin'. I shan't have it. You do what you do t' keep any trade runnin', an' all I see is someone tryin' t' keep the canal alive. Think I'm lettin on to them as wants it killed you 'ave me all wrong."

Quite taken aback by his assessment, and not sure quite what to say, Amanda asked, "Would you like a cup of tea, we had the kettle nearly boiled so we could do one when the stew goes on."

"That'd be welcome, and thank-you," smiled the man.

"Come aboard if you like," Jim added.

The old man who gave his name as Lou took them up on the invitation and seated himself on the side close to the centre thwart as Amanda, following an almost pre-programmed politeness, set about making three cups of tea, all the time chatting with their new found friend. He was one of nine children and had gone to work for the canal company when he was about fourteen years old, not long after 1910. He had come back to the canal after the great war, which he said he never wanted to remember anything about, and had worked as a lengthman since the 1920's. He'd seen a lot happen and was kept on as an employee either because his wages were stupidly low, or that they had forgotten about him. He remembered pairs of boats regularly plying the route of the canal with various loads, either horse drawn or with motors, but he had to say that he had not come across such a small working boat before. Jim explained how they had come to their current employment, what their main cargo was, and the purpose behind their run. Lou scratched his head.

"Well," he said thoughtfully. "There's many as has tried to get the work boats runnin' again, but the board, as it now is, has always done their best to stop 'em. But here's you doin it right under their noses and all they're doin' is lookin for a pair carryin' fifty ton. Work is work though, an' you got to do it right."

"We can tell where you've been looking after the locks," Amanda replied. "The last few are all nicely greased and much easier to work than the ones where we came in."

"Right enough," Lou smiled proudly. "There's nobody does them, an' they won't let me so they're all goin' to rack an ruin that's what's happenin'. But even with my work you're goin to tear them pretty little hands of yours to pieces if you carry on, and that won't do at all now will it."

Amanda had to admit that working with the rough cast windlass the few times she had tried, having not wanted to be seen as unable to do anything Jim did, had made her hands somewhat sore.

"I'm sure they'll toughen up as we move on," Amanda said confidently, but old Lou was unconvinced. Eventually it was time to tip the stew into the haybox and move on, and whilst washing the pan, Jim offered Lou a lift, reasoning that he was greasing locks, and they had to go through them, so it seemed a good way to work as they were learning so much from him, and were enjoying his company. Lou was delighted by this. He enjoyed the company of younger people but his job was a solitary one, particularly since the canal was now so little used. The three were soon under way, and spent the afternoon working, talking, and even stopping for a tea break which, because of Lou's help they could afford, being well ahead of where they thought they would be. They carried on until the light started to fade, and old Lou had pointed out what he thought was a good place to stop the night. They offered to share their stew with him but he politely declined saying that there'd be a meal waiting for him when he got home. After they had waved him off as one would an old friend Jim and Amanda set about putting the cover up and getting the evening meal ready.

"He was a really nice old guy wasn't he," Amanda said. "But did we tell him too much? I mean he does work for the company or board or whatever it is."

"True enough," Jim replied "But he's not an arsehole so he won't."

"Is that it!" Amanda sounded mildly surprised, startled even, at Jim's seeming innocence. "He's not an arsehole so we tell him the lot!"

"About that," Jim replied. "I mean you told Emma pretty much everything. She was no arsehole either."

"But I know her!" Amanda protested.

"You knew her, a few years back. Anyway, that old guy, he isn't stupid, if he'd have wanted to do something he could have. I mean he popped up out of nowhere, and vanished pretty quickly too for that matter, do you think he'd have made us aware of the fact he was there if he wanted to stop us. He could leave us tied over some scrap iron, lower the pound and hole us if he'd have wanted."

Amanda could have scored a cheap point by suggesting that that was what he may well have done, but she knew as well as Jim did that the old man was what he seemed to be and they were safe where they were. Instead of discussion for its own sake, she moved onto the topic of tea, and the hay-box, which had been stewing all afternoon. On lifting the outer cover, the pot inside was certainly still very hot, and the vegetables seemed to have cooked to being reasonably tender as well. Amanda judged, or guessed, that about ten minutes on the boil would have it done and ready to eat. Jim, whose mind was easily distracted by the idea of food soon lost the thread of their earlier conversation and was full of praise for the invention. The meal was very good by any standard, and they both sat back and enjoyed the rest of the evening after the routine chores had been done. Apart from the odd ripple caused by their movement in the Mayfly, the surface of the canal was mirror like, reflecting the sky and the overhanging trees, and it was hard to think that they were in an environment as man made as any road. The contrast between their location here and that of the previous night could not have been any greater.

Amanda smiled and said, "You know I feel like I was born doing this, and its only been a bit over a week."

Jim didn't answer immediately, being full of food and half asleep. Finally he looked across and, thinking for a moment said, "Yes. It's not bad is it. Leaving all the crap behind and just, well, just being."

"We're not running away from things though," Amanda replied. "Are we?"

"Not running," Jim said thoughtfully. "But walking. Away from some, towards some, and through the rest I guess. But the crap, all the useless

95

stuff. That, we can leave behind us."

Amanda said no more, knowing that Jim had again let a little of himself come to the surface. She felt sure that in time he'd say more, and they'd talk but that this was not the time to have that conversation. Now it was time to sit together as two friends enjoying the evening looking out over the canal into the darkening sky. Not every day would feel like this, she knew that, but this one did, and it was the one that mattered right now. Jim also knew that he'd let his guard down a little further, but it didn't worry him. In the same way he had instantly judged old Lou, so he had with Amanda when he first met her, but his trust had grown over their time on the boat together. His last sentence had unintentionally slipped out, and even he wasn't sure quite what he meant by it, but he could see by the look on Amanda's face that it meant something. He also knew that at some time in the future they would visit the comment again, and that she would remember it word for word. There were times that Jim would have felt threatened by having someone getting any insight of whatever the nature of his revelation was, but, for whatever reason, he was not feeling threatened at all. Just happy, that was it! "Leave all the useless crap behind us," he thought, and smiled at the night sky.

The next day started bright but cool, they had another delivery to make in a town situated on the canal, after which they could move on to a less conspicuous place, to tie up for the night. After the success of the hay-box, they decided to be more adventurous and make themselves a curry for their evening meal, and set about the task along with preparing their breakfast. Although they had no rice to go with it they decided to shop in the town for the missing ingredients together with general items they needed. Their first week had ironed out most of the necessities of life afloat to a workable routine which, although there was room for improvement, was efficient enough to make them feel almost professional about what they were doing. This morning was no different, and they were soon away, with decks mopped, washing done and all other items stowed.

At the second lock they came to they saw old Lou sitting on the balance beam waiting for them. He had set the lock in their favour and opened the gate ready for them. This made the task of lockage much simpler and Amanda thanked him as she walked the Mayfly into the chamber.

"I said yesterday," Lou spoke in a fatherly manner. "That you're goin' to tear them pretty hands of yours to pieces if you're not careful. I know its all different now, I listens to the wireless you know, but why ruin something as good as them if you don't have to that's what I says."

"Don't worry, I'm made of pretty tough stuff," Amanda smiled.

"Well, I hope you don't mind but I brought this along with me for you. It's old but it'll see us both out I reckon," Lou replied.

He had brought an old windlass that he kept by his fireplace, as a memento of the working boats. One of the boaters had given it to him some years back when they had reluctantly retired from the canal and life on a boat. The windlass, with two sockets as per the standard issue ones differed in that it had the sockets in line rather than the simpler side by side arrangement that they had. It was also made better and had a brass sleeve that was free to rotate on the handle to stop the casting rubbing and causing blisters to whoever used it.

"You promise me you'll use this one, and I'll be a lot happier. It's been by the fire for twenty years and more and its about time it were used as it were meant, and by a boater too," he added.

Amanda was not sure if she was more pleased with the gift, the kind thought of the giver, or the fact that he had referred to her as a boater. She was lost for words for a moment.

"Thank-you so much," she almost squeaked. "That's so kind of you, and I'll use it and keep it polished."

Feeling that this wasn't really enough she stepped forward and gave the old man a hug in the same manner as she would her grandparents when they gave her a birthday or Christmas present.

"Thank-you," she said again.

"Steady on lass, or your fella will have me in the canal." Lou said with a wink.

Jim, who had been busy attending to the lock and had missed the conversation, walked back to take the ropes from Amanda.

"I'm sorry but I can't have the lady blistering her hands, that'd never do," said Lou. "That takes care of her hands, now mind you take care of her, she's a rare 'un she is."

"One of a kind," Jim replied, "And thanks, well, thanks," he smiled.

"Now you're not goin' ta be huggin' me too are you?" smiled Lou, "People 'ud talk you knows!"

"Seriously," Jim said. "Thanks, you taught us a lot yesterday, and, well, thanks." Feeling too that this was not enough Jim put his hand out to shake with the old man.

"'Tis good to see folk trying, whatever comes of it," Lou said taking Jim's hand in his and shaking it firmly.

Amanda offered Lou a lift on the Mayfly again, but he was going back the other way to do another job. He thanked her, and was off with a wave of his hand saying he'd probably see them when they were back that way.

"He called me a boater!" Amanda smiled. "A *boater*!"

"And he should know," answered Jim. "He's definitely one of the good guys."

They continued until early afternoon and the next town, a place which had little to distinguish it from many other small towns with some history. A lot of Victorian buildings with a few historical gems set here and there, and another place which had chosen to ignore the canal, which in past times had surely boosted its prosperity. Lou had told them of a boatyard that would let them tie up whilst they went into the place, so Jim went looking for someone to ask whilst Amanda finished tying up. The yard was probably almost as old as the waterway itself, with some of the employees looking as though they had been working there since it first opened for business. He was assured that the Mayfly would be safe, and that there was no charge for their stay. Word had got to them by whatever network of gossip still existed on the canal from its working days, and he was assured that the vessel would be sheltered from any prying eyes whose ever head they may belong to. Thanking them he returned to Amanda who was now ready to go into town. She stopped at the first phone box to ring Marie as arranged, whilst Jim posted another of their progress cards. When the two got back together Amanda was looking decidedly worried.

"Spill the beans," Jim said cheerily. "It can't be that bad can it?"

"I'm not at all sure," Amanda replied. "For some reason the sale of the bungalow on the island has fallen through, and it isn't for sale any more. Marie knows someone that comes into the shop who works in property, and apparently there's some legal reason that it can't be sold, so Mum and Dad are going to be short of a few bob when the vultures have had their share."

"That just buys a bit of time surely. I mean they can't be in that much of a hurry for the cash, it takes ages to sell a house. Anyway if there are any creditors in this country, they'll have the lot before your folks see a brass farthing," Jim said.

"That's not all though," Amanda continued. "The police have been putting the frighteners on Dave, which isn't exactly pleasant or fair. I'm

98

wondering if I should go into a Police station and."

"Give yourself up?" Jim sounded nervous. "No way! You do that and they could make you a ward of court. They can anyway but it's a lot harder if they don't know where you're living. There's not that long before it gets a hell of a lot more difficult for them to touch you so there must be a better way than just giving up. I know it's hard on Dave but he can at least handle himself."

"Not if he's arrested for murdering me," Amanda was now looking rather upset.

"They can't exactly stick that on him." Jim replied. "I mean you phoned them and told them you were alive. Normally they would be happy with that, I mean there's tons of people run off and go round festivals and stuff and nobody seems to care that much about them, so why you."

Amanda shook her head, and Jim could see tears forming in her eyes.

"I don't know," she said quietly. "There has to be something," then, changing the subject, she added. "This is the sort of shit that you have had to put up with isn't it. That's why you say things and then stop halfway before I know what you're on about."

"My life's not been that bad," Jim answered. "You sort of get to sort of expect the crap happening after a while and shut it out of hurting you. I mean, all that's really happened to me is that I have been pushed from pillar to post, so things have been a little disjointed that's all. A lot of people, the arseholes I told you about, you know, the ones that are paid to care but they don't. They seemed to want to read much more into that than there was. I think that was to help them look more important rather than doing anything for me. It's like, they can only hurt me if I let them, and because I trusted a few they did. It was my fault, I should have seen it coming but that's the way it was and I can't do anything about it so sometimes it gets me, but that's just self pity. That's all it is."

"Liar," Amanda said firmly "If it's not that bad then why are you so bothered about it happening to me?"

"You weren't born into it," Jim replied. "Nor was I, but I couldn't stop my folks doing what they did, I was too young so whatever happened I didn't really know life was any different. Well, at least for a while I didn't, and by the time I found out, well, like I told you all the crap sort of washed over me, I guess I felt immune to it. That was stupid in a way because I just let people do things instead of, well in truth I never figured out what the reason was. But I should have done something. Look, stuff it, what I

99

mean is, you can tread in dog-shit and it won't damage you for life, but you don't go and let someone else plough through a pile of the stuff if you can do something about it."

Having recovered her composure Amanda returned to the original subject.

"So do you have any ideas about what we do?" she asked.

"Right now, we deliver the watch, and do the shopping." Jim said. "If we do anything here, we do it right before we leave. The last thing you want is them knowing where you are."

"You've given me an idea," Amanda replied, smiling again.

About an hour later, with watch delivered, and shopping done they headed back to the Mayfly. Amanda stopped, and said. "Right Jim. This sounds stupid but I have to do it. I'm going to buy that Indian cotton skirt in the charity shop. The one we just passed."

"O.K," Jim replied cautiously. "It probably suits you but why is it stupid?"

"Because of what I am going to do next. You'll just have to go with this one," she said, and was gone. Jim waited for a while and was looking at the window of a newsagent when she arrived back wearing the skirt.

"It does suit you," he smiled, "but I'm no judge."

"Now for the really stupid bit," Amanda said. "See that little alley between the shops there. Wait in it and roll your jeans up as close to your knees as you can and neatly as possible when you do. Oh, and take your coat off. You must do this, it's massively important."

"O.K. boss," he said, and went off to do exactly what he was told. Clearly she had a plan, and he felt oddly happy to have been included in it.

The Police station was having a quiet day when a girl walked in, very politely demanding an ink pad. She was doing a school project and should have taken her fingerprints as part of her homework but had forgotten. It was her birthday party later on and she didn't want a detention to spoil it. The officer at the desk was soft hearted and near retirement, so he helped her to make a really good set of fingerprints on some police headed paper. Whilst doing this he asked how come she was not in school uniform and commented on how well the skirt suited her.

"I kind of changed. I had to try this on," she said, making absolutely sure they got a good look at the garment. "It was a birthday present, and it

100

just doesn't go with a school blouse."

After writing her name and a couple of sentences on the paper she handed it to the officer saying clearly, "I'm not in school uniform because I am not at school. My name is Amanda Josephine Donaldson and a lot of people seem to think I am dead, which you can clearly see that I am not. I do not want to be found but I do not want anyone accused of my murder. You will find a matching set of fingerprints in my school project which is in the school library at the address I wrote on the paper. It will be there because it was the best in the year when I did it, and they always keep the best in year projects to show at parents' evenings. I am going now but I won't tell you where except for the fact that I will be safe, and will be in touch with my parents." With that, the girl left. The policeman behind the desk tried to follow, but by the time he had got to the door she was nowhere to be seen.

Jim was beginning to wonder what had happened to Amanda, and whether this was going to be another recurrence of her earlier disappearance, when she appeared at the head of the alley. As she walked past him she placed the shopping bag at his feet and, without a word, was gone. Picking the bag up, he stood in a doorway and watched her as she headed back to the canal, wearing his coat, with the hood up. Some time after the incident, the policeman was still at the desk. He had phoned the description of the girl through, and had been told that someone of that name and appearance was in fact missing, though her school uniform had been washed up at a weir and it was still generally thought that she had drowned either by accident, suicide, or the hand of a third party. There had been a sighting, and someone claiming to be her had phoned in, but the two incidents were generally thought to be the work of a crank. This new evidence would be followed up, and if the fingerprints matched a search could be launched. In the meantime, officers on the beat should be alerted to her description, it being all that could be done. The officer was idly musing on the peculiar event when he heard a loud banging on the station door. The person could easily come in, it was clear that the door was open, but still the banging went on. Thinking that it was probably kids with nothing else better to do he went across to chase them off. Instead of kids though, it was the girl who had asked for the fingerprints. He was sure, same coat, bag, and that skirt, it had to be her. The chances of two people in identical clothes coming to the station was too small to consider. She was already heading off down the road at a fast walking pace and would soon be lost to view. Shouting for someone to come and man the desk, he went off in pursuit. It was clear that she was on her way to the railway station, her intention presumably being to disappear. It was clear in his mind that she was probably unsure of this action and knocked on the police station door for help, but lost her nerve or something like that. She went round a corner and disappeared from view, so the officer sprinted a few steps to catch up. When he rounded the corner she was nowhere to be seen, the only person on the street was a young lad taking some shopping home in a couple of plastic carrier bags.

"Have you seen a girl coming down the road?" the officer asked. "Similar height to you, perhaps an inch or so shorter, with dark wavy hair, a little bit windswept. She was wearing one of those cotton skirts, you know the sort, the ones that hippies wear."

"She's not been down here that I know of," the lad answered truthfully, "But if I see her I'll tell her you're looking for her. Is she in trouble or something?"

"She's a missing person," the officer said. "Or a crank. Let us know if you would though."

"I'll tell her to report to you," repeated the lad. "You could try the station, if I was on the run I'd be on a train." With that he continued on his way.

Amanda stopped by a post box and dropped an envelope in addressed to Emma Jesmond, after doing this she returned to the Mayfly and sat in the cabin waiting for Jim. The Russian radio was beginning to pick up some police signals about the sighting of someone answering her description. It seemed that she had probably got onto a train and they were going to alert the transport police though they would keep an eye out too. Looking out of the porthole she froze. A policeman was talking to the person Jim had been speaking to when they arrived. The conversation was less than a minute but to Amanda it seemed as though they had been in conference for hours. After the policeman had gone, the man seemed to be watching for a long time. He eventually went back into the yard, but to her horror he came over to the Mayfly and tapped on the cabin top.

"It's O.K.," he said. "I know you're in there but the copper don't."

Amanda opened the cabin door.

"Best stay in there," the man continued. "Lou said you're a good 'un. and he knows what's what. You keep your head down though and we ain't seen you."

"Thanks so much," Amanda replied, feeling relieved. "I've done nothing wrong. I hope you believe me."

"Lou said you're a good 'un, and he knows what's what," the man repeated. "If it's good enough for him, then it's good enough for me. Now, Here's your fella. Good luck girl."

"Right, let's go," said Jim. "If anyone had told me that I'd end up being a drag queen in the middle of town, I'd never have believed them."

"Did it work?" Amanda asked.

"Yes it worked. I got chased halfway across the place. In the end I had to dive into someone's back garden and turn back into myself behind their shed. Your coat and skirt are under the potatoes, and your bag is in the other bag" he smiled.

"You'd better have your coat back too." Amanda said. "And thanks, this was probably one of the dafter things I've done but at least it means Dave won't get the third degree."

It was a only short run out of the town, and Amanda was reasonably sure, from information she was able to glean from the radio, that the police were concentrating their searches in entirely the wrong area. Giving a little extra allowance of time she eventually emerged from the cabin.

"I guess that the last place they would imagine anyone doing a quick getaway would be on a canal at four miles per hour," Jim said as she popped her head out of the cabin doors. "But you can't be too careful. I felt a right pillock in that skirt you know."

"If it's any comfort, I'm sure you looked one as well," Amanda laughed.

Even though they knew they were not absolutely safe from pursuit, the two friends still shared the enjoyment of having put one over on the enemy. They reached their tie up point, which had been recommended by one of the people at the boatyard, at around seven o'clock that evening. It was as described, quiet and with a good view of the tow-path in either direction, but sheltered by trees from the nearest road which was two fields away. They had sufficient supplies and fuel to keep them going until at least the next delivery which was due in around three days time, and the canal went through some relatively deserted country in between, all of which boosted their confidence.

"We will still have to be careful," Amanda said, over their celebratory curry. "But if we can keep going for a little longer, I'll be in the clear."

Sounding a note of caution Jim said. "Not entirely, they can still get on your case if they want to, but we'll deal with that if we have to. What we must keep doing is to move on with your stuff. There's all that paperwork you brought back when you went to the university library, we haven't scratched the surface of it yet."

Later in the evening they made a start, but there was very little to find. Mainly Amanda had found snippets of news from local papers, and a few minor documents relating to a court case that involved her fathers company. Nothing really came forward as definitive in providing the first step in what was almost inevitably going to be a long process. There was no important looking person on any train to provide the instant solution of the storybook, and a happy ending was about as likely as any of the many amphibians that populated the canal transforming into royalty when kissed. Before turning in for the night, Amanda sighed.

"You know," she said. "When I said I was going to clear their names I had it in my mind that they'd both be back soon and things would go back to normal. They never will though will they, go back to normal I mean."

Jim thought before answering. "No," he said decisively. "No, I very much doubt they will. It just doesn't happen that way. I mean, when my folks split up I was young and I just thought I'd be away for a week and it'd all be an adventure before. Well, you know the rest. I wish I could say different but."

Amanda cut him short. "It's O.K," she said. "I was being pretty stupid. For one its all the legal stuff which I knew even then took forever, and, well, it just won't, and that's the way it is. At least we've made a start though, and thanks for that."

She blew the hurricane lamp out as a sign that the subject was closed.

"Night Jim," she said.

Chapter 7

The next couple of days were due to be spent on what, in spite of the various interruptions, was now the routine activity of moving their little work boat along the canal to the next delivery. The weather was mostly good with the occasional shower, and the forecast was reasonable. During the traverse of the long summit Amanda was able to set to doing some more research using the paperwork from the university. From what she was able to deduce, it was more likely that any double dealing was not done at the main office, which was close to where she had lived, but at the place that made things for them. It had always seemed rather grand to her that her dad owned an electronics factory and the knowledge of this this had, amongst others, but unbeknown to Amanda, given her quite some kudos at school. She was aware of the fact that money talked but it was not until it ran out that she found just how loudly it did. The fact though was that her father did not own a factory, but ran a relatively small design office. All of the production was carried out by a small firm in the Midlands, owned by a group of partners, one of whom had been at school with her father. The reason she suspected this as the target for dishonesty was partially because it was unknown to her, the mysterious place that her dad went to at times, and that she wished that he didn't have to, but also because she remembered him coming back clearly troubled by his visit on more than one occasion. She had suggested to Jim that they go there and confront the owners but he was not so sure that it was a good idea, reasoning that nobody would take any notice of a couple of teenagers bandying accusations at them. She reluctantly agreed with him, even though she could not think of a better plan. A flight of locks interrupted her train of thought, and she didn't get back to trying to formulate an idea until late in the evening.

"It'd help," said Jim. "If we had an address for the place, then at least if we can't think of anything we could confront the arseholes like you said we should. That is of course if they are arseholes in the first place."

"I'm pretty sure some of them are," Amanda replied. "I remember one of them coming down for a meeting not long after I'd started big school. He was sort of overly posh, fake plummy accent, I mean I know I have a bit of a one but this was really overdone. Anyway I couldn't stand the sight of him, something about the way he looked at me made me feel really uneasy, self conscious, you know."

"He didn't try anything on did he?" Jim asked in horror.

"No," Amanda said firmly. "But I wouldn't have put it past him."

Not much more was said on the subject that evening, instead they went for a walk to clear their heads before finally turning in for the night.

It was about halfway through the afternoon of the next day that Amanda's interest was aroused by something she had caught sight of in her opera glasses. In the distance was a road which crossed the canal at some point, the winding course of the waterway made it a bit difficult to work out quite where, but every now and then she could make out what looked like a person standing by the front of a small car. The magnification offered by the glasses was nowhere near that offered by even a cheap set of binoculars so it was difficult to be sure.

"If only they'd bloody move, then I'd know it wasn't a scarecrow," she said as she took over the steering from Jim so that he could have a look and maybe clarify things.

"It could be a scarecrow," he said. "But it looks to be right on the edge of the field, and there definitely is the nose of a car showing from the hedge. Well, it's more a splodge of red but it's too big to be a flower. Could be a bag or something, you know, one of those fertiliser sacks they use. Doesn't help that every bend we go round it vanishes then comes back into view only it never seems any nearer. I'd keep your head down if I were you Mand."

Jim's inadvertent use of the shortened name implied that, as with the incident when they came onto the canal, he was feeling uneasy about the situation, and this worried Amanda slightly.

"Who do you think it is?" She asked.

"I wouldn't have thought it was the police, the car's the wrong colour, but they'd have radio if it was so you could check it out whilst you're in the cabin. More than likely the bastards from the social have had word of us from someone or they're just trying for a lucky shot. I mean they could have just been following us and waiting their time."

"They wouldn't be that underhand would they?" Amanda replied, already knowing the answer.

"We're in the middle of nowhere," Jim said quietly. "There's a deserted road, and there could be any amount of people hiding behind that bridge.

106

Unless we hurl this thing through it at full throttle they could easily stop us, even if we went at it like that they probably could. Once they've got you, you will have gone voluntarily. Their report will say how you were rescued by them, and they will get promoted."

"That's very cynical Jim," Amanda frowned.

"True though. It hasn't happened to me, but something like that happened to someone I spoke to whilst I was waiting to be assessed once," Jim replied. "One minute he was taking a walk in the country, next he was in the queue with me, waiting to be assessed. Not quite as quick as that but you get the drift."

"That stinks," Amanda said sharply. "But they're not having me, not without a fight."

"Too right they're not," Jim added. "But the best thing you can do is go in the cabin and hide. I doubt if they can see you yet, and unless they have a warrant they can't search my home. At least I hope they can't. There's a patch of weed that I can put the bow into just before the bridge, that'll hold her in so I can get out and keep them talking. If you hear me raise my voice like I am arguing that's your cue to go and hide in the bushes. It's not a good plan but it's all I can think of Mand."

There it was again, if any confirmation were needed that Jim was about as nervous as Amanda now was. They were sitting ducks for this kind of ambush and they knew it, but it didn't help to have it proved so soon. Amanda scanned carefully through the police band but found nothing of any relevance, so she just sat whilst time dragged. Outside Jim kept an eye on the hedge where he thought he had seen a car. Now even with the naked eye he could clearly see the front end of a red vehicle, but the figure wasn't there. There was still a chance that it was a bird watcher or something but anything out of the ordinary was worrying. He slowed the motor to just keep forward motion and steering, and looked again through the opera glasses. The figure was on the top of the bridge waving to him.

"Panic's over," he shouted to Amanda. "You check but I think we're O.K."

"You scared us half to death!" was Amanda's good natured greeting to Emma, who had worked out roughly where they would be, and driven out to see them. "What on earth are you here for?"

"Well. I could hardly bloody phone could I," Emma replied. "Isn't that thing dangerous?" she added as Jim set about lighting the Primus.

"Absolutely, but we like to live on the edge," he said as he pumped it to the familiar sound and put the kettle on. "So. Spill. You haven't come out here for tea in the country have you?"

"Is he always this direct?" Emma asked Amanda.

"Actually no," Amanda replied. "It's quite out of character, but why are you here? Not that it isn't nice to see you."

"I've done a bit of research and I didn't think it would wait until you got back my way. And I like driving anyway. Oh, and whilst on the subject of driving, the coppers now think you are in hiding in a squat on the south coast. I whizzed down there yesterday, or I would have seen you then but that seemed more important. I know some people that set up a sort of commune there, there's loads of stuff going on so I posted it from the middle of the general area."

"Posted what?" Jim asked somewhat bemused.

"Another set of fingerprints, I forgot to tell you I sent a set to Emma," Amanda said.

"Anyway," Emma continued. "I think I struck, well not exactly gold, but maybe copper or aluminium. Something anyway. There was a scandal involving an electronics factory, or rather a director of one that made the locals in the town. We missed it because we were looking at business news, this wasn't. This was a good old fashioned sex scandal, so there was a bit of detail thrown in to make the article more rounded. The company was involved in electronic codes, and had recently had some problem with patents, all they said was that the company name was involved in a row over intellectual property. Anyhow, this guy, one of the directors had been caught by his wife entertaining a couple of schoolgirls, and I don't mean playing the spoons for them either."

"Do you have a photo?" Amanda asked.

"It's that shit you told me about isn't it," Jim interrupted.

Emma's production of the rather grainy photocopy confirmed Jim's statement.

"That's him!" Amanda exclaimed. "That's the bastard that turned my dad over! Fat load of use though. We know he's a pervert, we know where the company is now, but we still don't have anything on him for the stuff he did to my folks."

"Nothing concrete." Emma replied. "But a lot of circumstantial stuff. I mean he claimed the girls told him they were over age, but."

108

"I very much doubt that would have stopped him," Amanda added.

"You're probably right," Emma replied. "But it does mean a case could be put that he was not of good character, and then there's the stuff I dug up about the patents and the like. I found out about one that had your dad's name on it Milly (Emma had always known Amanda by her nickname) but there's no clear proof either way that he had or had not sold the rights to it. That means that either the company was making things under licence, or in other words your dad owned the rights, or your dad had sold the rights to the company and then bought the finished product back."

"That's at least something to go on. It's a shame there's no proof, but thanks anyway," Amanda said.

"Looks like some dodgy footwork's been going on. Like pass the parcel with a turd," Jim added.

"What," Amanda and Emma replied in unison.

"Well," he continued. "Either this guy was nicking the patent and then selling it exclusively to several people at once, then he realises that he's about to get filleted by the law so he's busy doing his best to push the patent back to your old man so he gets the blame instead, or he's claimed that he has the rights to it when he doesn't, and gone on selling it and then dumps the turd on your dad when the law finds out on account of the fact that it would all be in your dad's name then. Either which way he's going to have to hide some pretty meaty evidence somewhere and that's going to be about as easy as putting toothpaste back into the tube with a shovel. I'm sorry but this guy can't have too much by way of brains to go and dink two girls almost in front of his wife, and then claim he had no idea they were under-age when he wasn't even asked if they were which, as it turned out they weren't anyway. I mean is this geezer stupid or what? Cup of tea anyone?"

"That's a colourful way of putting it, but it's all there in the article and I went and missed it! Fancy a job in law Jim?" Emma joked.

"And you hit the nail on the head," Amanda added. "You're training in law and you missed it. If you did, and you're pretty smart, then someone else easily could, or they've been paid to keep quiet. But Jim's right, there's a paper trail leading to all of this. There has to be."

Given that there was no real legal case, although the police had been called it was decided that everyone was there by their own decision, the journalist had done his best to make column inches out of very little. The director in question had not been voted off the board and his wife was now

109

"Standing by him," so it looked as though the whole affair was being, or had already been, brushed under the carpet.

"I can't believe he got away with everything!" Amanda said sharply. "I mean the whole thing stinks, and the slippery git got off scot free!"

Emma, thinking logically said, "Well, the thing is, that he had not actually committed an offence, just picked up the two girls at some pub or park and took them home while the coast was clear. Whilst it is pretty distasteful, particularly because he clearly thought he was outside the law, he wasn't. The fact that he thinks he has got away with things may well make him feel more indestructible so he may not be expecting what he gets from us."

"And what is that?" Jim asked politely.

"It's what we have to work out I guess," Amanda sighed. "It just makes me so furious that we know what he has done, or at least we are pretty damn sure of it, and we still have no solid proof, and that factory can't be too far away."

"It isn't," said Jim, who had been looking though another of Dave's maps. "In fact it is pretty close to a canal, looks like it may actually have had access by an arm or something, but I doubt there'd be much water in it judging by what we have already seen near the university. If we continue our delivery route, and keep ahead of schedule we could spend some time finding things out when we get near. Is there anyone apart from old creep-face that you know there?"

Amanda sat and thought, furrowing her brow slightly.

"I do remember one Christmas we went up there, or at least I think it was probably there. I was about six, or maybe seven," she said. "We were going up to see some relatives in Scotland and we stopped off at this place. It wasn't a hotel, just an old shabby looking brick building. Dad took us in and I remember some of the people there making a big fuss of me, they weren't the bosses, I think they were cleaners or gatekeepers or something, I mean the place was closed for the holiday. Once Dad had finished his business we went off to Scotland and I've never seen the place since. All in all pretty useless I'd say."

"Nothing is ever useless," Jim said, choosing not to explain himself any further. "Look, it's getting late now, and we are pretty well ahead of ourselves so we could stop here and just enjoy the evening. I'm sure we could stretch supper to three. He said pointing to Amanda's invention."

"So," Emma said. "You keep your food in a hat-box."

110

"Not so much keep it as cook it.   If we do a bit of rice and bung some herbs in it'll stretch easily," replied Amanda, rather proudly.

"You know," mused Emma.   "When I knew you at school, you always struck me as the swotty type, in a nice way, you know, someone that would work in an office somewhere and be the person without whom the company would fail, but the sort that nobody really noticed.   Now here you are living on a boat not much bigger than you'd put in the bath, and you seem to feel it is completely unremarkable to cook your evening meal in a cardboard box!   You do look well on it though."

As the evening wore on, Jim lit the hurricane lamps and they chatted and planned until it was finally time for Emma to return to hall of residence.   This at least was her excuse, she knew the main door would be closed and she would probably have to sneak in through a friends window. Amanda had already offered to put her up for the night but she politely declined, not wanting to offend, or to cause undue inconvenience to her friend, and also not really wanting to find out exactly how Amanda proposed to accommodate her.

"She's a good egg," Jim said cheerily as they waved the small red sports car off.   "Absolutely not an arsehole."

"She's changed a lot though," Amanda replied wistfully " I hope she doesn't ever go all respectable.   You know what I mean."

"Not her," Jim smiled.   "I'd guess that she's got enough money to live her life as an eccentric and nobody will bat an eyelid.   I hope she backs a lot of good causes though."

Although he had not spoken much about himself Jim had, over the day, inadvertently revealed a lot about the person he was.   Amanda knew well that the easy-going quiet person most people saw was more of a façade than even he was aware of it being.   Behind this she knew there was a passion, and an intelligence that intrigued her.   His analysis of the newspaper article, which had surprised both her and her friend, both of whom had largely glossed over the sensational in search of hard facts, was now forming the basis of a plan of action.   He had not been fairly treated in his life, and this suddenly snapped into focus in her mind, blotting her own troubles temporarily.   Whilst she had been annoyed by the wrongdoings of the company director, she now found herself absolutely furious about the wrong that had been done to Jim, only a bit of which she knew about.

"How dare *anybody* treat another human being like that!" she thought, having to consciously keep her mouth closed and not speak the words.

Completely misinterpreting the look of upset and sheer anger on her face Jim, in a kind, quiet voice, said, "Hey, look, Amanda. Whatever it is will come right. We'll just work on it until it is." Seeing the puzzled look on her face he added, "We're a team. That's all."

Amanda smiled one of those brief smiles that said far more than its duration implied it could, but her anger did not subside, though she was careful for the rest of the evening not to show it. Her final thought as she drifted into sleep was one of those that stick forever in memory. "Damn them to hell Jim. Damn them to hell. It's over my dead body that they *ever* get to you again. Damn them all to hell. Stuff them!"

The mood had not quite deserted her the next day, and she remained withdrawn for most of it. Not impolite, nor even moody. To Jim it was as though she had been replaced in the night by a very good copy. Everything was running smoothly and they were making good time and would be able to tie up close enough to walk to the small town for their next delivery the following morning, allowing the afternoon to push on a few more miles before dark. Still though Amanda remained unusually quiet.

"You're going to have to tell me," Jim said. "Because I haven't a clue what's up, but I know something is."

Amanda was rather taken aback when he spoke, having thought that she'd successfully kept a lid on her feelings. She was unsure as to whether Jim was either unusually perceptive or that their proximity made them both more aware of atmospheres than would normally have been the case. To Jim, the result of his question was that his friend was standing there and not answering, and he was standing on the tow-path looking foolish. Gathering his thoughts he made an attempt at speaking his mind, though in truth he wasn't too sure what his mind was up to. It may as well have gone on holiday for all the use it was being to him right now.

"Look, Mand," he said. "I can't see you like this. It's not you, but I don't know you well enough to even know that, but it isn't is it?"

"No," she subconsciously noted the shortening of her name.

"Something got to you, was it something I did, or said?" he asked

"No," she frowned.

"Then remember, we're a team. We will make things come right," Jim said.

"Really?" Amanda continued to frown.

"Actually no, we may not, but that's kind of irrelevant right now. Fact is if we cock up royally we will have done it as a team. You're a good person Mand, and I don't know you well enough to know that. Except I do."

"Not an arsehole then," Amanda cracked an almost imperceptible smile.

"No," Jim smiled back.

Amanda said nothing, but her expression spoke on another level to Jim.

"Mand," he said, sounding very unsure of his ground. "I'm O.K. It's in the past. I've said that before. But you obviously care about it more than I do, or it wouldn't have chewed you up."

The thought coming from nowhere, Amanda said, "All of *this* has changed all of *that* hasn't it. I mean, it's digging stuff up for you that you'd probably rather forget."

"A bit I suppose but what of it," Jim replied.

For reasons she was not sure of, Amanda felt close to tears so she kept quiet.

"Look, I can't put it any other way," Jim said, slightly desperate to clear the air. "Whatever this whole experience does to me is going to happen anyway. What if I had gone off on my own? You can't say I'd be the better for it. It's happened like this and right now I'd rather share the experience and whatever happens with you if you don't mind."

"Yes," she said, with a slightly uneven voice. "I mean no I don't mind. Good friends are hard to come by. I just don't want you to get chewed up by all of this stuff. You don't deserve it."

"Nor do you," Jim smiled. "Now let's have a cup of tea, then we'll push on to tie up."

With a hot drink inside them and the atmosphere broken, they continued on much as before, and got to their tie up point about half an hour after they had planned. The area was quiet and they were just discreetly round a bend in the canal that took a very minor road up to what they had thought was a town, but was in fact a village. As the evening was again a pleasant one, they decided to go for a walk, having been in or around the boat now for a few days. The road over the bridge (a typical red brick hump backed variety contemporary with the canal) was narrow, and made its way past open fields to the village. The place was picturesque, but not enough to make the lid of a chocolate box with. There were a few stone cottages, some old brick ones, a few newer houses, church, pub, shop, and that was pretty much it. There must be thousands such places across the country, each of which differs, but is in no way distinguished. They thought about making a call from the phone box but decided against on the reasoning that every time they phoned anywhere something weird happened. This evening they were both happy and intended to stay that way if possible. Having located the address they were to deliver the next watch to (the office of a very small business, that would reopen at ten in the morning), they turned back towards the Mayfly. Within a few yards they were met by the vicar who himself was returning from a function at the village hall.

"Lovely evening," he said. "I haven't seen you two before, are you new to the area."

"We're just visiting really," Amanda replied. "It must be nice to live here though."

"It is, though sometimes I do miss the city, but I can't complain," the vicar said cheerily. "What brings you to these parts?"

"Well, we're sort of working, a kind of project thing that we have to do," Jim answered cagily.

"Oh, I see. Doing research is very rewarding," the vicar continued. "It's so nice to see young people doing constructive things. Are you with your school? Camping somewhere?"

Jim and Amanda looked at each other to find an answer to this question, after a pause Jim raised his eyebrows, Amanda shrugged slightly, and they were silent again.

"Am I prying too much?" the vicar asked politely. "Some people don't like that, but it comes with the job I'm afraid."

"It's not that we don't want to tell you," Amanda said. "We don't want to, well."

"Shock me?" the vicar replied. "I rather doubt that you could do that, I spent many years in the middle of a big city, and, well, I'm sure you know what I mean."

"You're a vicar right?" Jim said.

"Yes," the vicar replied.

"So If we tell you something in confidence, particularly if it isn't that shocking you will keep it that way?" Jim spoke quietly.

"Oh, dear," the vicar said sadly. "This does sound like it might be the makings of a dilemma, you haven't run away from home have you?"

"No," they both replied.

"But you are running away?"

"No," again they both spoke.

114

Jim raised his eyebrows, and said, "In confidence?"

"Yes,"sighed the vicar. "You have my word."

"The fact is," Jim went on. "That we're not running away from anything, more moving slowly towards it. Like sometimes there are problems that you don't want to solve, but you have to because if you don't something bad will happen. I've always thought that you should always try and stop bad things from happening, but that doesn't always make you the flavour of the month does it."

"That is for certain," said the vicar. "You could ask many of the saints about the response they got and it would tally with what you have just said."

"You may as well know who I am," Amanda chipped in. "But don't say anything to anyone unless they ask you about me."

The vicar looked uneasy but nodded his agreement.

"Look," he said. "Come to the vicarage and tell me about it over a cup of tea, then if it is late I will run you back in the car."

"It's O.K," Amanda said. "We're staying pretty close, on a boat in fact, so we'll be fine."

"So," the vicar replied. "You must be the famous Amanda Donaldson? Missing, presumed dead, then reappearing then being assumed dead again. That's one more resurrection than my boss! I read the newspapers you know. But the story went dead when your fingerprints turned up on a piece of notepaper on the south coast somewhere."

"As you can see, I am alive and well," Amanda replied. "I am here by my own choice, and I do not want to be put into care. There are plenty of people that aren't that different to me that the world forgets about, they are the ones, you know the runaways, people that live rough. They need help, well that sort of help, not me."

"Yes," the vicar smiled. "I see you are both intelligent and articulate."

Amanda and Jim went on to explain how they had come to share their journey, and their problems and how they were working on clearing the name of Amanda's father so that her parents could return to the country, and how a simple job of work for Jim had come to mean so much more than he thought it would.

"Well," the vicar spoke slowly. "I should advise you of all kinds of dangers to both your physical selves and to your mortal souls. But you have spoken honestly, and whilst I may worry for you, my worry will achieve nothing. If I were to try and intervene or get those in authority to,

115

it could well make your lives intolerable, and I am not prepared to take that risk. No. You have my word. If asked by anyone in the village (and be sure they will have seen you!) I will say that you are two very good friends of mine that came to have a chat. If you would be good enough to regard me as a friend then I will not be telling lies to my parishioners. Now, it is getting quite dark, you had better go back to your boat, and I may see you in the morning when you return."

"Why did we tell him all of that?" Amanda said as they walked slowly back to the canal, having declined a lift.

"He's a vicar, they do things like that. I think they're trained," Jim replied. "In any case we didn't have much option, I don't like telling lies to vicars, it's sort of bad form I guess."

"Bad form!" Amanda laughed. "Didn't that go out with tea and cucumber sandwiches? I never thought you were so straight laced!"

"I can't help it," Jim protested. "He's a bloody vicar!"

"Can we trust him?" Amanda asked.

"Hard to say, I mean he's a bit of a modern guy, and they can be O.K. but they have a horrible knack of trying to do good, so he could piss it all up by trying to help. Hopefully his brain won't move in too many mysterious ways until it's too late. Anyway you seemed to trust him, after all the stuff that happened to you."

Remembering the incident at school brought a visible chill to Amanda's expression.

"I'm sorry," Jim said, almost immediately "I shouldn't have thrown that at you."

"No, you're right," Amanda frowned. "That was another guy and he wouldn't have helped unless he got something in return, and even then he'd have dumped us in it Whatever he claimed to be he was no man of God. This one, well, he seemed to weigh up the facts, so maybe he's O.K. we'll see."

As they walked back the skies were clouding over, and the rain finally came in the early hours of the morning, at first quite heavy, then steadying to a slow sonorous drizzle of the kind that made everything wet almost by association. The tasks of preparing for the day found almost every inconvenience of life in a confined space parading itself in front of them. Just about everything felt damp, the matches were damp and it took several before they could even get even the smallest spark necessary to ignite the methylated spirit for the stove. The prospect of walking over a mile into

116

the village was not one that appealed in any way whatsoever particularly since the eruption of their paraffin fuelled volcano, its familiar sound having given the luxury of warmth to their little space.

"Bugger it!" said Amanda. "We're having a bloody good fry-up and that's an end to it!"

Jim had absolutely no argument with this and, using a paper spill, lit the second stove to hasten the progress of the feast. The roar of both, brought life to what was about the deadest morning since they set off. The heat from the burners drying things out, and the smell of cooking bringing cheer to their souls and a feeling that they could tackle just about anything. On completion of the meal Jim looked over to Amanda and smiled.

"That was bloody brilliant!" he said. "I'll take anything on now! Any bastard that wants to mess things up for us! Bring 'em here and I'll push them in the bloody canal!"

"There's an awful lot of them, and the canal's shallow enough already," Amanda commented, the offhand remark setting them both laughing far beyond any humour it contained. In another situation, on another day it would have gone unnoticed but here was a time for them to simply enjoy being alive. It neither mattered if it was sunny or snowing, they were there and that was enough. The high spirits managed to survive their putting on of such waterproofs as they had, which, since a visit to the shops, comprised of a transparent plastic mac with a peculiar paisley design printed on it for Amanda, the familiar bright yellow cycling cape for Jim, a rather moth-eaten umbrella of the variety city gents would carry, and some cycle leggings that were so cheaply made as to only be semi waterproof. Placing the watch in its box, in a plastic bag, in a Tupperware box and finally into a straw shopping bag they set off towards the village. After a few hundred yards they began singing as they walked. Neither of them knew who started it, but they sang at the tops of their voices the words of "Follow the yellow-brick road," they continued singing, laughing, and getting quite wet. Anyone passing would have thought they had lost their minds or consumed one of many illicit substances that were readily available at the time.

The tiny office of Planetary Electronic Technologies, a company owned by a somewhat eccentric ex-airforce officer who had turned his attention to building sensitive equipment to measure pollution, had just opened for business. The owner of the concern was typing a letter, a task that he hated almost as much as his perception of future environmental catastrophe, when his concentration was disturbed by two giggling teenagers at the door. He opened it to find Jim and Amanda laughing at what was obviously a private joke. The combination of their ridiculous appearance, and the infectiousness of their laughter set him off laughing too.

"What can I do for you?" he asked as he tried to maintain a straight face.

"Well," Jim said, in an attempt at being serious. "We've brought you a Russian watch."

"From Russia," Amanda, who had meant to say something rather more serious, added.

"It's a good place to get them so I've heard," said the man, keeping a straight face.

They stood for a second then were all laughing at the stupidity of the situation.

"You'd better come in," the man chuckled. "I've been waiting for this, anyway, you are soaked, so dry off, we'll have an early tea break and I'll run you back in the car."

Jim and Amanda were not as wet as they looked, but were a bit cold so they were happy to take up the offer from the man and they were soon sitting round a wood-burner with mugs of coffee chatting like old friends. The man was in his mid to late forties and was called Clive Prentice. He had set the small company up in response to a request from a friend to search out some equipment to measure small levels of chemicals in sea water. Finding nothing that would really do the job required, he had set about designing his own equipment almost as a labour of love. The business was set up to give some credibility to the equipment, and had never made much of a profit.

"In fact," he said. "You two could do some work for me if you would like to."

Knowing that their money from delivery of watches was finite, both Amanda and Jim were interested.

"I have a new machine that is for use in the field, and it could do with a thorough hammering over a period of weeks to see if it works reliably," Mr. Prentice said. "You will need to know how to work it, and I would want you to record the readings as if you were actually using it to gather serious information. The important thing is that you don't treat the box too kindly or I won't know if it can stand up to abuse whilst still giving meaningful

118

readings."

The device itself was about the size of a medium shoe box and was made of thick anodised aluminium. The controls and four small meters were recessed in the top so that they could be covered by the watertight lid which was held in place by sturdy spring catches. It was designed to take simple measurements from water and air to gauge the likely amount of pollutants present in order to ascertain whether more accurate analysis was needed.

"It may seem a bit basic," he said. "But it is the only machine of its kind around, so it is a bit secret and, to me at least, rather valuable. That all means that I'd rather you didn't talk about it to people, particularly those with an interest in hiding the amount of filth that is being poured into our world."

Amanda reassured him saying, "Because of someone nicking my dad's work he's lost everything, so we know what you mean, and we'll keep quiet, you have our word."

"I thought I recognised your face," Mr. Prentice smiled. "Are you Ed Donaldson's daughter?"

Quite taken aback, Amanda almost gasped. "How do you know?" she said.

"Was it the vicar?" Jim added despondently.

"You've met God's superannuated hippie then I suppose, and told him everything too! That man must have the life stories of just about the whole population of the country. But no, it wasn't him. The inquisition wouldn't get him to betray a confidence. No, the truth is simpler than that. Your father did quite a bit of design work for me, and never charged a brass farthing for it. I remember your photo from his desk, I never forget a face you know. And please call me Clive."

"So," Amanda said hopefully, "You probably know what happened?"

"Not the full detail, but it was an awful businesses, and I can't think your father would be involved in any deception. Tell me, how is he?" Clive asked.

"O.K. I think," Amanda replied. "He's in Spain with Mum. They wanted me to go out there but I am the only one left here to clear his name. Well, I was, but Jim is helping. I sort of gatecrashed his adventure."

"Well," Clive said, thoughtfully. "You have an ally in me for what it's worth, and I will start by insisting you take two months pay in advance. Now, do you have a plan?"

119

"We know the place Dad had stuff made," Amanda answered nervously.

"That'd be Carver and Green," Clive replied. "He was a director there, he took a minor shareholding when old man Green went into semi retirement. There were two Carvers, one was O.K. but the other one, I think he was a cousin was a nasty little weasel. If you phoned up and asked for the haemorrhoid you'd get put through to him. I never used them, because all the stuff I do is hand built by me and a couple of local lads that I trained."

"That guy, the weasel, he sounds like the one we should look at," Jim said.

"Very probably," Clive frowned. "He's a nasty piece of work though so watch yourselves, particularly you Amanda."

"I'll pull both his balls off and nail them to the wall if he goes near her," Jim said, opening his mouth without thinking.

"You clearly know about him," Clive replied. "Watch him, and don't let him anywhere near my invention."

It was still raining when they got back to the Mayfly, having promised to post regular reports of the machine to Clive, who had, in turn, promised to arrange future payment to them when the time came. Once any necessary phone numbers were handed over and other arrangements made they were on their way again. Leaving the breakfast stuff in the rain made it easier to wash up, and the flip of a coin on which Jim drew tails, meant that Amanda steered whilst he washed. The boat was a good deal more prone to wind with the cover on at the back, but they would have been soaked without it.

"We should take it down," Jim said. "I mean the guys in the narrowboats went out in all weathers without any cover like this."

"They were a tougher breed to be sure," Amanda smiled, remembering the compliment old Lou had given her. "But we don't have a coal fired range to dry things out on either, and a bit of rain in the bottom of a narrowboat doesn't make a lot of difference." After a short pause she added, "I still feel bloody guilty though."

The rain continued until beyond tie up time, and it seemed as though it had never done anything else and that their permanent state was being damp, and slowly but surely they would turn into mildew. The paraffin stoves, once lit provided sufficient heat to dry the immediate surroundings whilst they cooked their supper and heated water for washing.

"It's odd that Clive knows my dad," Amanda said, in the middle of

120

washing up.   "And that he knew the company, you know, Carver and Green. That sort of helps us a bit."

"I'd like to know a bit more about the danger that the unpleasant Carver poses," Jim sounded a note of caution. "Because we don't want to lose this one for you. Anyway we'd better have first shot at this gadget hadn't we, or we won't get any more pay."

Taking the device from its stowage, Jim removed the lid, inside of which were the two probes, one for air, and the other for water. The probe for water looked a little like a two prong fork, whilst the other was a small cylinder with a miniature fan at one end. With both connected to the box and positioned correctly, Amanda pressed the button labelled "Start cycle." Apart from the fan in the air probe, the box made almost no noise, and the meter needles slowly moved to indicate the level of what would finally be worked out as the combined pollution index.   This involved a mathematical formula that allowed interpretation of the raw data which could then be followed up if the final figure was too high. Originally Clive Prentice said he would do the calculations, and all that Jim and Amanda need do was to record the readings, but Amanda, who had done well in maths was interested in the formula and offered to work it out on the spot, as it would only take her a few minutes and could be done whilst the device was being stowed away.

"There are two things we could do," Jim said, more thinking aloud than conversing. "We either have a definite plan, like they do in the spy films, or we just make a big splat, get out and see what happens. Thing is, either of those could end us up in deep shit so we need a third way, one that does the job but doesn't land us one."

"Bait," Amanda said coldly.   "We know what he likes, it was in the paper."

"NO!" Jim shouted. "Absolutely not! I don't care how we do it, but you don't put yourself in that sort of situation."

"It's his weak spot," Amanda replied. "It may be the only one."

"And if it went wrong? If it got out of hand?" Jim's voice was not to be questioned, so Amanda said nothing.

"If it got out of hand, if he laid a finger on you, I would kill him with my bare hands if that was all I had," Jim said.

This was said with a directness that bypassed normal thought processes and Jim had not realised he was going to say it until he heard the words form his own mouth.

"Jim?" Amanda spoke quietly.

"That stuff," he said. "It always happens when you don't expect it. Someone you trust, or thought you knew better. Then bang, they're at you, and it all happens too quickly and you don't know what to do. It's dangerous, dirty, not something to. It's playing with fire."

"Jim?" Amanda wanted to say more but couldn't.

"It doesn't just happen to girls you know. And not everyone gets away," he replied.

"You?" she said.

"Yes, me," he replied.

Jim looked across at Amanda who was looking wide eyed at him.

"It wasn't all the really bad stuff," he said slowly. "It could have been but they guy got disturbed and I just stayed well away from him after that."

"Who?" Amanda didn't want to pry, but could not help asking.

"Some nameless bastard that was paid to care, but didn't. I got away, but another minute and." He went silent and looking at his feet. After about fifteen minutes of silence Amanda finally spoke.

"I'm sorry," she said, as Jim looked up and smiled a brief smile.

"Thanks," he replied. "For what it's worth you are the only person that knows that."

Amanda lent forward and took Jim's hand and held it for a short while.

"Thanks," she said again.

"When we stop in the basin in the city centre, I'll catch a bus to Carver's and see what I can see," Jim replied, changing the subject rather too suddenly.

"Yes, O.K," Amanda said. "But are you alright?"

"It's the same for both of us," he smiled.

Amanda could see that anything Jim was going to say wouldn't actually tell her if he was alright, and to be fair on him she wouldn't have said much more had he asked the same of her so she let the subject drop. The next few days were going to be hard work, so she focussed on that instead. The section of canal they were now on was a lot wider than they had become so familiar with, and the locks were twice the size, looking to have been rebuilt sometime before the second world war. The mechanisms were smooth but laborious, and she was ever thankful for the much better quality of the windlass that old Lou had given her.

Chapter 8

The following two days were locks, locks, more locks, and a tunnel. Now, Amanda had never said this to Jim but she had a fear of enclosed spaces. She never thought of it as claustrophobia, reasoning that this would have put her off tents (she'd always loved camping with the Guides) and definitely off the Mayfly. No, it was cellars, dark places that she could not see the way out of that terrified her.

"Anyway," she thought. "The Mayfly has a headlamp and navigation lights so we'll be O.K. I think."

All of this was true, but the Mayfly did not have any means of generating power to charge the second-hand car battery that powered them, and this she did not know. She was, however soon to find out as, at their next tie up, Jim went in search of a garage to charge the thing in the hope that it would last the length of the tunnel only to come back from a fruitless search.

"It's not so bad," he said cheerily, and blissfully unaware of Amanda's mounting terror. "We can use the Tilley lamp with a reflector, I made one up out of an old biscuit tin when I was doing the boat up, it made a pretty good floodlight, only thing is someone has to hold it on the cabin top."

Amanda had thought of hiding in the cabin whilst in the tunnel and pretending it was night, but this plan had now been blown away.

"Now," she thought. "That lamp is pretty bright, and it's also not something I like being too near on account of it giving the impression that it is a rather badly designed bomb."

"O.K. That's fine," she smiled nervously.

As the tunnel approached she remembered how time always seemed to go quicker at school when the next lesson was one that you seriously and intensely did not want to attend. P.E. and the prospect of being called away for the little pet talks. Why think of that, it was stupid, this was just a structure that had been in existence for over a century, probably more like two. No bogey men, nothing, just bricks and water. She shut her eyes, swallowed.

"I have been as good a girl as I know how to be," she thought. "And I am sorry if I have nothing bad to tell you but I'm not supposed to lie, not to you am I." The rope was twined round her hand and, after a mumbled phrase that she either did not hear properly, or did not want to, she tensed. Her grip tightened on the coils, and.

"Are you sure you're O.K?" Amanda started as Jim's voice cut through her day-mare.

"You've turned quite pale," he said. "Look, we're going to have to stop before we go through so that we can light the lamps. Why not have a brew too?"

"No," Amanda replied firmly. "I can't be here if I'm useless. It's just stupid, stupid fear, and I'm leaving it behind in there once and for all. And so should you. Now, come on James Alex, we go. Now."

They stopped briefly to prime and light the Tilley lamp, and then set off into the dark. The sound of the little outboard echoed as though a motorbike were racing around the roof which, despite the combined light of the old motorcycle headlamp, and the green/blue glare from the pressure lantern, they really could not see very well. There was, however, enough light to see by, and they maintained a steady pace. Jim did not want to go too fast because he had been warned of the possibility of hitting foreign objects floating below the surface, nor did he want to go any slower for fear of the spark plug fouling with oil from the two-stroke motor running too cool. Soon enough the portal they had entered disappeared and they were as alone as they could be, feeling rather too quickly that this had been the only life they had ever known. Two freshwater troglodytes in their natural environment.

"Can you hear that!" Amanda shouted back to Jim. She had heard and additional beat that did not emanate from their own power plant. Either someone was coming the other way, or they were being caught up. Jim shielded his eyes from the glare of the Tilley lamp and could make out what looked like a candle some way in the distance.

"Boat!" he shouted back, and pointed, wondering what kind of idiot would go through the tunnel using illumination more suited to a birthday cake. It wasn't long before he discovered the candle was in fact a pretty powerful ex-military searchlight that probably started its days on the side of an armoured car, or a small warship. It was incredibly bright when the converted narrowboat passed them. He then wondered what the Mayfly must have looked like to them.

"Holy shit!" he thought. "They probably could hardly have seen us.

Maybe that's how all these foreign objects end up in the water."

The band of light provided by the electric lamp was beginning to fade as they approached the tiny disc of light signalling the other portal's arrival. From disc, to cameo, to miniature it progressively increased and it was then quite soon that they would be back in the real world. Wet from the drizzle of drainage water filtering through the tunnel brickwork, but happy they had achieved something that was really pretty insignificant in the scale of things.

"Right," Jim said. "Now we are stopping for a brew. I was scared shit-less in there and I don't care who knows it!"

"No bed of roses for me either," Amanda replied cheerily. "There's a first time for everything I suppose. Next one will be better. I stink of paraffin! Can you boil a bit extra so I can clean up?"

With little battery power left for the headlamp, and fatigue from the locks prior to the tunnel, they decided to move on after their break only for a short while to find a suitable stopping point ahead of the big push into the city. Neither of the pair were looking forward to this, especially after their experience of their first day on the canal, but it was something that had to be done. There were no less than three watches to deliver, the readings from the monitor to post off and, most importantly, Jim was going to check out Carver's. They reckoned on being tied up for about two days at the basin, which may well have been a welcome change but, for someone that was technically still on the run, any place with a lot of people or in fact any people was a high risk area and this was slap bang in the middle of one of the largest cities in the country. It was no more than an hour before they decided to give up for the night, tying up at a pleasant location amid fields and a few trees. Amanda checked the radio whilst Jim finished preparing the hay-box meal that had been stewing throughout the day.

"Do you think we'll get anywhere with Carvers?" Amanda asked casually.

"Depends on what I find there I guess," Jim said. "It'd be nice if I found all the evidence we need and the guy confessed everything, but we only have the fact that he's known for being unpleasant so I wouldn't hold your breath."

During the night the dream returned to Amanda. She was explaining, telling the truth, and it was still no good. Whatever she said was twisted round to the obvious conclusion that she was not being truthful with herself. And when she asked exactly how she should know the truth in order to tell it everything got worse. The minutes she had spent in the little anteroom stretched into hours with the distortion of the dream. And worse still, where was the skipping rope? She had kept it with her and it was gone, or she had it but couldn't move her arm. Nothing was right, she felt like a character in a book, and yet she knew she had to do something. No. The rope was definitely there, it was there and she would move it, by sheer force of her will. Should she be using her will against the chosen representative of an omnipotent being? If the being were as some stories would have it, then she may be damned for all time, if others held the truth then this was nothing but a charlatan. But still, violence? And then she sensed a move towards her and all reason went. Lashing out with all her strength and shrieking at the very limit of her voice.

"YOU GET OFF OF ME! OFF! DON'T COME NEAR ME! EVER!"

Frozen in time, sitting in a cold sweat, shivering and with tears rolling freely down her face, the next voice she heard was Jim's.

"Jesus! You just scared me half to death!" Then looking over at her he added. "Oh! Christ, I'm sorry. You had one of those dreams didn't you?"

Amanda nodded, drying her eyes on the sleeping bag. "But I'll be alright now," she said, preparing to roll back over in her bunk.

"You won't be," Jim replied. "Trust me on that. Not if you go back to sleep. It'll just grab you again. How long have you had dreams like that?"

Amanda looked across to him.

"Do you?" she asked quietly.

"Pretty much every week or so, only I don't scream," Jim said. "I just tense up and wake up scared stiff, then it eventually goes away for a while. You?"

"I might have, just after. I can't really remember. So this is the first, certainly for a long time."

"It's why you went white at the tunnel isn't it? Something went ping," Jim asked.

Amanda nodded again, and tears had returned to her eyes.

Jim sat on the edge of his bunk, upset at the sight of his best friend being so disturbed, and by things that were not of her making. It was almost pitch dark with a very small amount of moonlight and everything outside was silent. Had he not have been there her scream would have been unheard by any other than nocturnal animals who themselves now were silent having heard what sounded like one of their own being struck down by a predator.   To his surprise, Jim felt the warmth of tears rolling down his own face.   He was about to speak, but could not trust the evenness of his voice should he do so.   It occurred to him that, like the song about the two piano shifters that never actually mentions that it was a piano they were trying to move, he knew what was going on in her nightmare, and what had been flashing through her mind before the tunnel. He now also knew what she meant by them both leaving their stupid fears back in the tunnel, and that she had tried hard, and failed, to do so.

With a somewhat uneven voice he said very quietly, "Amanda.   This has come out of nowhere, and you were right.   It has to be buried."

"Have you been crying Jim?" she asked

"No, well, yes, or not quite," he replied.   "Not like you do when you're a kid and you fall off your bike.   Sort of, I don't know."

"But I do," her voice was steadier than his but still uneven.   "We're neither of us that tough Jim, even though we think we can take the world on and win."

"I've never cried since I was a kid.   And never like that," Jim said.

"No, but you dreamt, and maybe that let the steam off, and you do a moody now and then.   Me, on quiet afternoons the tears sometimes come, and I don't ask why," Amanda said quietly.

The tears had returned with interest.   Jim knew his voice was not to be trusted but now no longer cared.

"Perhaps you should," he said "Perhaps we both should, and now, not later when it is more convenient."

He moved to the cabin door and opened it.   Amanda smelt the spirit, and then saw the flare of the match dying to the purplish blue as the stove heated.

"You have had a bad shock," he said, having regained his composure. "You need some hot sweet tea.   I'll put the kettle on and we're going to talk.   All night and all of tomorrow if that's what it takes.   These two bastards.   They have messed with our minds for far too long, and we've both been stupid enough not to tell anybody."

"Who'd have believed?" Amanda had bunched the sleeping bag round her and was sitting in the cabin doorway.

"True," Jim replied.   "But I will."

"Me too," she smiled, suddenly feeling safer than she ever had.

127

"So. We tell," Jim said calmly. "You can have the lot from me. It's not pleasant, nor that bad as I said, but I want someone to know. Someone to understand it. That's how you've felt too isn't it?"

"It is," Amanda replied. "I wish I didn't act so bloody clever and all knowing at times. That's where all those stupid religions came out of. What a waste of my bloody time! Yes. You can have it all. Chapter and verse then we're even. No. I didn't mean it like that! We tell, then it's all over."

"That's what all the trained people told me but they never solved anything because they were doing a job. They were trained to know, and advise, even to empathise but they were also paid not to feel," Jim said.

"Like I said. Jimmy boy," Amanda smiled again. "We tell *each other,* not the shrink and it stays with us. Then it's gone and nobody else needs to know because we have dealt with it. Nobody pays you not to feel and even if they did, you would and, for a guy, you don't seem to do a bad job of it."

"Thanks," Jim smiled, pouring the tea. "Now let's talk."

As Amanda had said, nobody else needed to know, nor do they. The confidences they shared remained between them to be taken with them when they eventually leave this life. Suffice to say that the two people sat as equals and talked over every detail of the similar wrongs that had been done. Their surprise, shock, self blaming, how they eventually buried it and forgot about it only to have it re-emerge in a peculiarly fermented form at random times throughout their lives. All embarrassment was gone, all taboos lifted as they talked and talked. It was the early hours when they started, so it was beyond dawn when sleep eventually got the better of them, the lamp having been extinguished long before the conversation had ended.

The light wake of a passing pleasure boat slid the kettle off of its perch and sent it clanging to the floor. Both Jim and Amanda woke with a start to find the late morning sun streaming into their eyes through the open cabin door.

"Better?" Jim asked softly.

Amanda nodded in reply. "You?" she said.

"Yes. I think I am," he smiled, his face somehow clearer than it had been in a long time. He too noticed that Amanda wore a less troubled aura. He could not be sure, neither could she, that this wasn't some delusion, or that they were just fooling themselves because they had talked to each other, as two untrained buffoons, that their troubles in that area were now sorted forever. They could never be sure but neither Amanda or Jim ever had nightmares or flashbacks to those times again.

"It's a good day," said Amanda firmly. "I'll do breakfast on the run."

It was late afternoon as they edged into the basin, tired with yet more locks and lack of sleep. As they had predicted it, was not a good place to remain anonymous. Although run down, it was also busy, with boats tied up all over the place, some pleasure craft, some residential and a good few derelict. Amanda pointed to an area near to what looked like some wharf-side cottages, and they aimed for that as a temporary halt, only to be told that it was somebody's mooring and they would have to move. As they scanned the area Amanda noticed someone standing in the back of a converted narrowboat about twenty yards away. She took the steering from Jim neatly flipping the Mayfly away from the wharf edge, and round towards the vessel. The name on the brightly painted traditional rear cabin declared the name of the boat as "Crimson Lake" and the owner's name below it was V. Potter.

"Sorry to bother you," Amanda said to the woman standing in the hatches. "But do you know anywhere that we can tie up for a few days?"

The woman turned towards them, she looked to be about twenty-five or so, tall with very dark hair, her make-up made her look like an oil painting, or one of those photographs you find on the front of magazines.

"You can tie up alongside me if you like my love," she smiled. "Leave a little thing like that by the towpath here and someone would very likely mess with it."

"Thanks," both Amanda and Jim said, almost in unison. This made the woman laugh.

"Do you two always talk like a Greek chorus? Or is it a stage act?" she asked, good naturedly.

Amanda and Jim were not quite sure what to make of the situation, so she went on.

"Don't look so worried, I was only having a joke. I'm Vera by the way, Vera Potter, and I live here so you're more than welcome to tie up to my boat. It's not going anywhere, unless I get evicted. You'll be nice and private there, and nobody will dare touch you. You look like you don't really want people to see you, am I right?" Vera smiled.

"Are we really that furtive looking?" Amanda replied without thinking.

"No but you do look a bit like a pair of runaways." Vera said.

Amanda looked shocked at the accuracy of Vera's assessment.

129

"Hey, don't worry," Vera continued. "You look all happy and that, so who am I to tell you how to live your lives. Live and let live that's my motto."

Amanda was neatening off a couple of stray items and was briefly facing away from Vera, so she used the opportunity to mouth the question silently to Jim. She shrugged lightly and with the familiar wrinkle above the bridge of her nose, her lips made out the word. "Arsehole?"

Jim mouthed the words, "No way."

Satisfied with his assessment of their new, rather talkative friend, Amanda noticed she was now looking puzzled at them.

"You have us bang to rights I'm afraid," Amanda admitted. "I'm Amanda Donaldson, and this is my best friend, his name is Jim Stratton, and thanks for letting us tie up."

Vera smiled. "Right," she said firmly. "Formalities over. You two look bushed, so come up here and have a cup of tea."

With the previous night fast catching up on them, they needed very little persuasion to take Vera up on the offer and, as soon as they had settled the Mayfly in, they stepped up onto the stern of the Crimson Lake, an old working boat, made sometime before the second world war, built mostly out of steel. The hold had been converted into the main living area, but the rear of the boat was still in its traditional state with the boater's cabin almost exactly as it would have been. The engine too was the original oil engine that was common on narrowboats of the time, though Vera admitted she rarely went anywhere and used a small petrol generator to keep the batteries topped up if for some reason she was not able to plug in ashore. There was no proper gangway between the front and rear cabin without using a very narrow door and passing quite close to the engine which occupied a mini cabin of its own, Vera had considered altering things round, but decided she liked the feel of the boat as it was, and didn't want to destroy its history. When the long cabin had been built she had tried as much as she could to keep the line of the boat, and had left the front cratch as it was, with the cabin sides striking a compromise between practicality and the line that the original sheeting would have taken.

"I'll show you round later." She said. "But just for now lets have tea here, its cosy, but it must have been hell for a family to live in it. How long have you two been on holiday then?"

"It's not really a holiday," Jim replied. "We, well we sort of."

"We live on Mayfly," Amanda confessed. "Despite her being not much

130

bigger than a tea chest, well, she's our home."

"Oh!" Vera sounded surprised. "It is a bit small, but you look well on it, well, as I said, you look tired but basically happy and that's the truth."

Vera was generous by nature, and had lived on the narowboat for just over two years, having bought it from her earnings and had it converted by a local person. She fully intended to live on it for the rest of her days, but possibly not in the dingy canal basin which was it's present location.

"I have to earn a little more money yet and then I can move on," she said. "Right now it's sort of convenient for work if you see what I mean."

"What do you do?" Amanda asked. "If it's not too rude a question."

"Well, the question isn't but the answer probably is," Vera smiled, not feeling quite sure of how much to divulge. "It all depends on how you look at life I guess. I mean here am I minding my own business and you two come along. Who am I to judge you? You look cool therefore you are. Like I said live and let live."

"Doesn't bother us what you do," Jim replied, quickly adding. "Well, it doesn't me, Amanda's usually more broad minded so, well, I shouldn't speak for both of us should I."

At that Amanda, tried to control an involuntary laugh and almost choked on her cup of tea.

"Dug yourself into a right one there didn't you!" Vera laughed. "Anyway, I'll tell you before the gossip mongers do, because they always add too much and they know nothing. I'm what you'd call a film maker. I appear in films."

"What, as an extra?" Amanda asked.

"No, look don't get me wrong, I'm not ashamed, but they aren't the ones shown at the big cinemas," Vera said.

Amanda was about to speak but Jim shot a look at her that suggested further questioning was not advisable. He had also turned about the same colour as the name of the boat.

"Look," Vera said. "If you don't want to know me that's fine, there's plenty that won't have anything to do with me. I just do what I do, never drag anyone else into it."

"Sorry," Amanda smiled nervously. "I didn't mean to pry, but it's O.K. We have no authority to tell anybody how to run their lives, and, if you don't mind me speaking for both of us Jim, we're pretty well up to the neck with everyone trying to run ours. It's not that we're running away from parents or anything, we're here sort of by circumstance, but all the same there are people after me, and they'd have no problem with hanging something on Jim too. The big joke is we have done nothing wrong. So we're not into judging, sorry."

"Is she always this gobby?" Vera asked.

"That, I couldn't possibly say," Jim replied with a polite smile.

The three chatted for a long time and then Vera showed them the main area of the boat. It was neatly panelled, with all the things that you would expect in a house, though more neatly distributed, and mostly fitted into their locations. The main sitting room had a small wood burner, comfortable seats, and a portable television. The kitchen was similar to those found in larger caravans with the addition of yet another wood burner. All in all the boat was beautifully fitted and looked extremely comfortable but both Jim and Amanda felt that bit more at home when they got back onto the Mayfly later in the evening.

"Does she do what I think she does?" Amanda asked gingerly, and very quietly. Although it was late, and they were in the confines of the Mayfly's cabin, she felt it would be bad form to be overheard. Jim pondered, Amanda could see the furrows in his brow as he searched for words.

"It sort of depends on what you think she does?" he answered cautiously. "How would I know, I mean, she mentioned films and that was sort of it. They're probably a bit dodgy if that's what you mean. Like, well, you know. The sort of thing that gets advertised alongside the Russian radios sometimes."

"I suppose it doesn't matter. I mean she seems nice, just seems an odd way to make a living," Amanda said.

"There's lots of odd ways to make a living, like delivering Russian watches and testing instruments you know nothing about," Jim smiled. "Like you said, she seems O.K. and if she wants to talk about anything she would do, I mean it's not like she was hiding anything. In any case what's the difference between that and a West End show."

"They're supposed to have artistic merit though aren't they?" Amanda realised how snobby her remark was.

"What's artistic merit anyway?" Jim's answer was quick. "Didn't someone sign a bog once and say it was art. It probably was, but who am I to say. Maybe they do, or will have at some time, and does it matter much if they don't."

132

The conversation drifted rapidly towards sleep, and the lamp was extinguished rather earlier than usual during one of Amanda's more wakeful moments.

Chapter 9

The alarm went off far too early, and Jim felt far from happy about leaving the canal to trek halfway across the city to Carver and Green's factory, but he had promised he would, so was up and dressed as soon as was practical. At around seven-thirty he was away, leaving Amanda wondering what to do with the rest of her day. She still had to be careful about being seen and kept the radio on monitoring the police bands almost continuously to make sure nobody was planning anything. Inspired by the pristine narrowboat they were tied up to, she decided to spruce her own home up as much as she could and it was whilst she was about this housework that Vera emerged.

"Hi!" She said with a smile, she had a cup of coffee with her, and a cigarette on, one of those long posh types that looked sophisticated. It reminded Amanda of a time when one of her friends had brought a pack of French cigarettes back from holiday and handed them round.

"Hi Vera, How are you this morning?" she shouted.

Vera walked to the back of the long cabin and leaned out of what was either a door or a side facing hatch, Amanda did not want to show her ignorance by asking.

"Want a cig?" Vera asked cheerily.

"I don't smoke, but thanks anyway," Amanda said as she remembered the colour of green she was reputed to have turned when she tried one of the French cigarettes offered to her by her friend.

"Where's your fella?" Vera asked.

"He's off to see a factory. He went a couple of hours ago," Amanda replied.

"He trying to get work? I thought you were travelling?" Vera looked puzzled.

"If you've got the time I'll tell you all about it," Amanda said. She felt a bond of trust had rapidly developed and it was nice to talk to someone of the same sex for a change.

"I've all the time in the world my love," Vera smiled. "Can I come down and nose round your home this time?"

134

Across the city, Jim stepped off the bus outside a factory estate that looked like many that he knew of in places he had lived. It was made up of old and less old buildings, mostly built of brick with various prefabricated structures attached. The whole area had a look of despondency about it that crept slowly, like a drowning mist, into Jim's consciousness. Carver and Green's factory stood close to a reedy stretch of water on the other side of which was a similar building, both were at one time part of a busy complex that had been served by the canal. Tied to the wharf on the opposite side was the sunken remains of a narrowboat, now too far decomposed to save. It brought to Jim's mind the likely fate of the Mayfly had he not come upon it that day. Outside of the gate was a vacancy board which offered casual work of a non specific nature. This was too good an offer to refuse, so he went to what passed for a gatehouse and enquired.

Back in the canal basin, Vera had listened to Amanda's account of their adventure and was genuinely shocked by it.

"That's absolutely terrible!" she said. "I mean I'm not an authority on morality, but for goodness sake! That's just plain dishonest. You did right to bugger off even if it does have its associated problems. So, that's why you have the radio on all that walkie talkie stuff? You're a smart girl, keep ahead of the buggers that's what I say. But it ain't no game is it."

"No," Amanda replied solemnly.

"Good job you've got a best friend along with you. How long have you known the fella? Bet it was since you were little nippers eh?" Vera smiled.

"Well, if you want to know the truth," Amanda replied. "It was a couple or so days before we set off. He just sort of turned up in this boat and bought some groceries. We got talking and."

"Now he's your best friend? Don't get me wrong, but you must have judged him right. If he was a bastard he'd have jumped you by now. You know that don't you," Vera's expression showed a depth of concern as she spoke.

"How do you know he hasn't?" Amanda said.

"Because he hasn't has he," Vera replied.

"No," Amanda conceded.

"There you are. If he had, he'd have dumped you by now too. Nope, he's not the type I think. There's all sorts, trust me I've met most, well you do when," Vera tailed off having talked herself into a bit of a corner.

"Vera," Amanda spoke quietly.   "Look, I meant what I said yesterday. I know I have very little experience of anything much really, but I think I'll always believe that we all have a right to be who we are, and that doesn't just always fit what people think we should be.   It's what makes the world bright, and, well I can hear Jim saying this one.   It's when people don't let other people be themselves, that's when everyone gets uptight, and it causes wars and all of that crap."

"God you talk like a macramé pot hanger sometimes," Vera smiled warmly.   "But thanks.   It's good to have friends."

The man behind the counter top at the gatehouse eyed Jim up and down.

"Wiry little bugger ain't you," he said.   "I'll ask the boss if he wants to trial you.   It's only stuff like shifting boxes mind."

"Anything would be welcome," Jim replied politely.   He waited until the man had phoned through to arrange whatever needed to be done.

"Mr Carver will see you now if you want to, or it'll be another week," the man said.   "I'll take you up in a minute when Ray comes to look after the desk."

"Thanks," Jim replied.   "What's Mr Carver like?"

"Not a patch on the old man, and since Mr Donaldson left, well.   I've said too much already lad.   Just keep your head down and work.   If you need the money it'll be right."

"Some recommendation," Jim thought, realising that this was only confirmation of what he knew already.

Mr Carver was a balding man in his late forties, slight of build and with a small moustache that gave him the look of someone who thought their natural calling was of being a lounge lizard.

"So," he said.   "You want to work here. Why?"

"Because I need work," Jim replied.   It sounded plausible even if it wasn't the truth.

"I don't like wisecracks, you'd do well to remember that.   Now, why here," Carver asked.

"There was a board with vacancies advertised so I thought I'd try my luck," Jim spoke almost through gritted teeth.

"Well my lad you're in luck.   Post room needs a runner to take telexes and the like round the offices.   You up for that?   Last little tart left without notice.   Have a day's trial.   If you're useless don't come back."

136

"Thanks," Jim said.

"Thank you Mr Carver!" barked Mr. Carver, sounding like a dictatorial schoolmaster.

"Arsehole," Jim thought, and said. "Sorry, and thank you Mr Carver, you don't know what this opportunity means to me." Then added in thought only, "And you don't do you, you little bastard!"

The post room was a little wooden office populated by a manager, his secretary, and the telex operator.

"You been given a job by Fingers Carver then?" the telex operator said. She was around Vera's age, but did not posses the same easy sense of style.

"I'm on trial," Jim replied.

"So's he," she laughed. "Sorry I'm Bet, you're?"

"Jim. Jim Stratton. Why is he on trial?"

"He's not called fingers for nothing, or haemorrhoid. He was told he had to employ a bloke this time because the last runner made a complaint so he has to take it easy or he'll get it in the neck," Bet replied.

"Should you be telling me all this," Jim said politely.

"Common knowledge." Bet replied. "I mean we all know, and how can you take a message to the haemorrhoid if you don't know who he is."

"Did you know Mr Donaldson?" Jim asked politely. "Only the guy in the gatehouse mentioned his name."

Jim's comment seemed to cause one of those silences in the room, which was only broken by the large grey telex machine kicking its self into life as a message came in.

"This'll be for old fingers himself so you can take it up when its finished printing," Bet said. "Look, old man Donaldson, he was a really nice guy, not here very often, but polite, you know, a real gentleman, sort of old style. Probably around the same age as your dad would be. Carver hates him though, so don't say anything to him about Mr Donaldson or he'll go mental." Bet was turning out to be a mine of information.

"Do you know why he left?" Jim asked, chancing another question.

Again, one of those silences, even the telex machine paused briefly.

"Why are you so interested?" Bet said. "It's trouble, so drop it. That's my advice."

Vera had gone off to do a bit of shopping, leaving Amanda to continue with the spring clean. She was enjoying sprucing the little boat up, and

137

had polished just about everything she could lay hands on when her new friend returned.

"Still on your own then?" Vera smiled..

"I'm afraid so," Amanda replied. "He's probably lost his way somewhere. Still it's given me time to shine our home up. What do you think?"

Vera surveyed the polished wood and brass work, the clean paint, and even the outboard motor which Amanda had shone up with the dregs of a pot of car polish that she had found in Jim's tool box.

"Very nice." she said. "You can have a job as housekeeper for me if you ever get tired of travelling. Now, why not come up and have a spot of lunch. I like company so you'll be doing me a favour."

Amanda, who was tired, quite hungry, and in need of someone to talk to accepted Vera's offer with thanks. She had been quite happy with her own company when she was on the island but had become comfortable with Jim quickly, and enjoyed their conversations a lot. She had not so much missed him during the morning, but found herself wondering what he may be doing, picturing him on the bus, looking at Carvers, all sorts of stupid locations. She was a little uneasy that he had not returned, though some of this was due to the fact that he was due to deliver a couple of the watches that day.

"You like him more than you let on don't you," Vera cut in on her thoughts.

Amanda blushed slightly, saying, "I'm not sure what you mean, I mean he's pretty much my best friend by now, as you know, well, I trust him and everything, and we get on O.K."

"But you don't want to say any more. I get it, I was only teasing," Vera smiled.

"It's not that," Amanda was slightly more pink faced now. "I mean, he's a good guy, and I wouldn't want to mess him about, not that I thought, I mean, we're friends, and it works. I hitched a lift, he's been kind, but I like to think I have put in my fifty percent though."

"Knottygob strikes again!" Vera laughed, and then saw that Amanda was far from amused. "Sorry my love, I really don't mean anything," she added hastily. "You do right, he looks a decent sort, and you're right to be where you are. You don't want to break hearts either of you now do you."

"Of course not!" Amanda replied, almost sharply.

"Well, if its worth anything," Vera said, all humour gone from her voice.

"I'd say you don't want to go lighting fires with the lad if you don't mean it. Strike one with him and it won't want go out, and when it does it'd break him. He's been hurt before, and badly, he won't hurt anyone, he's not the sort but he'll crumble inside all the same, so treat him with care my love."

"How do you know all of this?" Amanda asked.

"Faces my dear. I can see it in them sometimes. I should have been a fortune teller. Maybe I will be when I retire," Vera smiled almost wistfully.

"That's years away though. Shame you can't do it now?" Amanda said, rather innocently.

"Two, maybe three, certainly no more than five, I lie about my age already, but there's not many want thirty year old tits," Vera answered matter of factly.

Amanda's eyes opened in surprise at Vera's frankness, having almost forgotten her actual occupation.

"Don't look so shocked," Vera smiled again. "I know my limitations and I don't want to end up a sad saggy old tart, so I put money by, got this boat and all. I mean there's a lot of villains getting in on the game now, and since the law changed a bit, well, the money is going down the pan soon too I think, so it's retirement city and some proper fun for me."

At clocking off time Jim left for the bus stop, having secured a week's probationary period after which the thorny question of longer term employment may have been broached. As he sat down on the top of the bus he was surprised to find Bet sat beside him.

"Hi," she said. "Sorry I was rude earlier today. Didn't mean to be."

"Think nothing of it," Jim smiled. "I shouldn't pry."

"Someone should," Bet replied gloomily. "Old Carver is a real bastard you know, and he doesn't like anyone talking about Ed Donaldson. There was bad blood between them from the start, but he won the day even though Ed was the better man.."

"Can I trust you?" Jim asked.

"There's a funny question to ask. Why?" Bet looked at Jim quizzically.

"It's no accident I came to Carver's today," Jim replied. "I'm trying to help Mr. Donaldson's daughter, and Mr. Donaldson too, though I have never met him."

"She'd be about your age, maybe a bit younger, I remember him

139

bringing her in to the factory not long after I started, she hid behind him when the telex kicked off. I can't believe I've been there since I left school. So what sort of a fix is she in?" Bet asked.

"None, but her mum and dad are properly stuffed," Jim thought he had already said too much but things had to move on.

It was close to six thirty when he finally appeared on the wharf side next to Vera's boat, finding her and Amanda sitting in the back of the Mayfly with cups of tea.

"Hi stranger!" Amanda called. "Want a cup, we've just brewed up, thought you'd gone walkabout!"

"I got a job at Carver's," Jim said, rather proudly. "That's why I'm a little bit delayed. It was sort of too good an offer to refuse. I'll tell you what though, that guy Carver, nobody likes him."

"I could have guessed that, come down and tell us all about it, then we'll do tea," Amanda replied, looking pleased to see Jim. Vera moved round to let him aboard, whilst Amanda fixed a cup for him.

"What do you think?" she said. "Your pal's not been idle has she."

Jim looked round the Mayfly and was surprised at how good she looked after the spruce up. She was a good looking little craft anyway, but his verdict that it looked like somebody had built an exact replica, only a better one, and swapped them was well received by Amanda.

"Look," Vera said. "You two will have a lot to talk about, so why don't I go off to the chippy and save you cooking, there's nothing like chips from the paper on an evening like this, and I know she doesn't eat meat and stuff Jim, and you don't because of her so I won't offend anyone. I know just the job."

"But we're paying," Amanda insisted. "You have been too kind to us already, so let us treat you for a change."

Whilst Vera was away, Jim filled Amanda in on the details of his day at work. It had been clear from the start that Mr Carver was grossly unpopular with just about everyone. It seemed that he had gained almost total control of the company by some kind of boardroom coup, and was not averse to abusing the power that he had. It would have mitigated some of his poor behaviour had he been a good businessman but the truth was that he had overseen a decline in the company's fortune at a time when other similar businesses were doing rather well. Bet, who had remembered Amanda as a small child had told Jim about Carver's appalling way with women.

140

"He thinks he's bloody Clark Gable or something," she had said.

He would push his attention on anybody he liked the look of and expect them to accept anything he wanted. When his attentions were refused, dismissal often followed, the last person in Jim's new post had made a complaint, but had so far got nowhere with it, though it was strongly advised that the next person in the post be one that he was not likely to make a pass at. His hold on power in the company seemed to be slipping, and would go in favour of Amanda's father had Carver not have pushed him out by engineering some kind of accusation of impropriety. Bet had told Jim that, so far as she was aware, Ed Donaldson was still a minority shareholder and was listed as a director of the company even though his voting rights had somehow been hijacked by Carver. The final piece of information that Jim had gleaned was that the patent that they'd thought was effectively stolen or misappropriated in some way was just that. There were some designs and drawings but Ed Donaldson's invention could not be made to work with the skills present in the company.

"That's a pretty good day's work Jimbo," Amanda smiled. "What are you going to do tomorrow? Stand on a stick and juggle knives?"

"Good trick if you can do it," he laughed. "But I thought I ought to turn up for my second day of work to see if there's anything else I can dig up before old Carver gets wind of me."

"What about the watches?" Amanda asked. "I suppose I'd better."

Vera had appeared on the side, so conversation stopped for food.

"This is a bit odd," she said, "But it sort of works. He does pizza, but not as you'd know it. He fries them!"

She wasn't telling lies either, the frozen pizza slices had been floured, lightly battered and dumped in the fryer until golden brown and looking like triangular fish, albeit slightly flat.

"It's a change from pineapple and chips innit!" Jim smiled.

"Now that has to be a joke!" Vera protested, only to find Amanda backing up the story to the point that she had to give in and believe it even if she wasn't actually quite sure how inscrutable the pair were being. Jim's story of his day's work was recounted, as were Vera's observations on the way Amanda had cleaned up the Mayfly, and the offer of work as a housemaid. Every time the conversation moved on to the next day, Amanda seemed to change the subject, almost as though she did not want to think about it. It wasn't really picked up on in any way though. Jim did notice her unease, but got nowhere when he asked her about it later on in the evening.

"I'm just being a bit daft I suppose, I mean I cleaned the boat out today, and there's not much to do tomorrow that's all.   Night Jim," she said sleepily.

And that was it.   It was the next day, shortly after Jim had departed for work, that Vera put her finger on the issue.

"So, my dear, what's the beef about today?" she said bluntly.   "And don't hide it, I can see it in your face."

"O.K. You win," Amanda needed to tell someone her thoughts.   "He's doing this for me, because I can't or I'll get recognised, but he should be delivering stuff today."

"And something tells me that you don't want to be seen at the moment, am I right?" Vera asked.

"As ever.   I mean, I've nearly been caught twice, I've unwittingly faked my own death, had Jim dress in drag for me.   I'm sort of running dry on ideas, and I don't really want to be seen in a city.   Too many people," Amanda sat looking at the boards in the cockpit of the Mayfly, thinking about scrubbing them clean again.

"And it wouldn't look good if the coppers caught you round and about with me, not unless you dress old.   I don't want the vice squad thinking I've recruited you."

Amanda's eyes opened wide.

"Joke," Vera said quickly.   "I wouldn't, not you.   I mean don't get me wrong, you could make a fortune if you did but you aren't the sort, never could be.   Your face dear, I know, trust me.   Sorry I can't help it."

Amanda smiled.   "You're just plain weird sometimes Vera,"she said.

"So, we dress you up to look like my sister, change your hair, pair of glasses, come aboard and we'll have it so even you don't recognise you."

With the help of a decent blonde wig, make-up, fake glasses and a fake fur coat (Vera hated animals being killed for their fur, and was a good deal closer to Amanda's viewpoint on animal welfare than she let on) Amanda looked like a starlet that had just come off a plane from an exotic location.

"That's amazing," Amanda said as she looked in the mirror.   "You should do make-up for films, I can't believe that this is me."

"Well, I have to pass myself off as not much older than you for those that like that sort of thing, so I guess anything is possible."

Amanda's eyes widened at the matter-of-fact nature of Vera's comment.

"It's the way it is dear, and better me than youngsters.   Like I said there's criminals around now that don't think twice.   There always were, but," she tailed off on the subject.   "Lets go paint the town red, and deliver them watches!"

Because Vera knew her way around the city the deliveries were made more efficiently than if it was Amanda or Jim on their own, so there was time for a leisurely lunch and a slow amble back to the two boats.

"You know," Vera said.   "You'd be a lot less obvious if you didn't react like a startled fawn to anyone you thought may know who you were. Nobody did, and it would be pretty unlikely that you'd get recognised in the city centre even if you had a placard with your name on it.   I mean, think of the amount of runaways there are, they just disappear and, well you see them in squats, sleeping rough, all sorts.   Nobody knows them even though most of them could easily be identified if someone bothered to look."

"Were you a runaway?" Amanda asked.

"Not as such, no, more an early rebel," Vera smiled.   "Some would say I fell in with the wrong crowd, and perhaps I did, but all of life is what you make it, and right now I don't have any regrets."

"What about your folks?   I mean do they know?" Amanda said.

"What about?   My great shame?" Vera smiled and winked.

"Sorry if I'm prying," Amanda replied.

"They probably do know, and I like to think they'd know me well enough to know, if you see what I mean.   But I don't know them, never did.   I've no memories of them though I'm supposed to have been with them as a toddler.   After that, well it was a children's home.   Then I went a bit wild, and now," Vera's voice tailed off again.

"I'm so sorry," Amanda looked almost tearful.

"Hey."   Vera nudged her elbow.   "Life's for the now.   There's nothing I can do about what happened in the past, it's gone.   I got dumped and that was that.   People do that, I have a lot of good friends, and I look forward to what's going to happen and.   Hey who's that?"

Her life story was cut short by the sight of a tallish woman of around her age, though not nearly as glamorous looking.   She was wearing a coarse weave skirt and a twin-set, though no pearls, and had black rimmed glasses. She was sitting on the cast iron bollard that the stern of the Crimson Lake was tied to.   As Amanda and Vera approached she stood and walked towards them.

"Excuse me," she asked timidly.   "But are you Vera Potter?"

"That'd depend on who you are?" Vera spoke rather sternly.

143

"I'm looking for her, or an Amanda Donaldson," the woman said.

"Still depends on who you are my dear," Vera said.

"I'm sorry to bother you, but something awful is going on, I don't want to make any trouble, but."

"O.K. so, I'm Vera, now tell."

"You will know Jim Stratton then?" the woman said.

"I might." Vera replied.

"I hope you do, he needs help and now or very soon. He's been arrested on suspicion of kidnap and, oh dear, Carver has really done it on him. Sorry if I alarmed you, I had to do some asking round to find you or I'd have been quicker here. I'm Bet, Betty Wilton, I work in the post room at Carver and Green."

It was obvious by her manner that she was telling the truth, and also obvious that both she and now Amanda were very upset. The exchange between the two older women had meant that the expression on Amanda's face had been overlooked, now they both saw her tears.

"Oh my god, Amanda, is that you, you were only a little girl when I last saw you."

Amanda pulled the wig from her head, and removed the fake glasses. Her make-up was now streaked with tears but a look of determination had come to her face.

"I don't understand, why are you all dressed up and." Bet asked, only to be cut short abruptly by Amanda, whose voice, unsteady but authoritative was almost a bark.

"Fucking games, that's what," Amanda said. "Just that. Right, Bet? Is it O.K. if I call you that?"

"Sure." Bet would have followed any command at this moment.

"If I get you a phone number can you tell the guy who answers that Jim is in need of legal help, he wrote something to say on the phone so he knows its us. Then go to the Police station where they're holding him and stick there. We'll be there as soon as we can."

Amanda leaped almost the entire width of the narrowboat and gently boarded her own home. Within a couple of minutes she was back, with the phone number, what to say, and her passport.

"Right Bet, I don't know you but we're counting on you. Don't let us down," Amanda's speech was almost manic.

"No worry," Bet said. "He's a good boy, and we'll get him out. I'll do what I can."

"See you later," said Amanda briefly. "Now, Vera, can you clean this crap off me. I need to see a doctor, a good one, and I need to do it right away."

Vera did as asked, clearing the make-up swiftly, leaving Amanda looking as she always had within minutes. They then took a taxi to the doctor that Vera used. The receptionist was a bit obstructive but Vera was insistent and eventually got an emergency appointment booked.

"The quack will be O.K. when we see her, the receptionist is a bit of a dragon but," Vera smiled.

"I'll go in alone if that's all-right with you," Amanda looked solemn.

What seemed like hours but was no more than twenty minutes passed, before Amanda reappeared in the waiting room.

"Let's get right out of here," she said. "That was horrible but I had to do it."

"What have you done?" Vera asked. "Amanda you're worrying me?"

"If that bastard is trying to hang what I think he is on Jim. Well he can't do. Not now. But I can't go to a Police station as me, or, well I've told you all of that haven't I." There were tears in Amanda's eyes, but she was not about to cry.

"If I prove that I haven't then he hasn't. Not to me anyway. And."

"Oh my dear," Vera couldn't say much more but embraced Amanda as a mother would. "You shouldn't have to do that. Not you."

"I've got proof, and a passport, that's proof of who I am. It's in the past Vera, we look forward now. You said that less than an hour ago, so lets get back and you can turn me into someone else again."

About an hour later, Vera and Amanda joined Bet at the police station, Amanda was again unrecognisable, in the same guise as she had gone to the city earlier in the day. Bet got up to meet them as they came in.

"Let's go outside and talk for a minute, it's not private enough in there," she said anxiously.

Walking down the pavement, she told them of how the arrest had come about. Jim had been going about the usual post-room type business and was sent to the top offices with a telex, as often happened. It was for the production manager, not Mr. Carver, but he somehow ended up in Carver's office, and there was some kind of incident. Next they knew Jim was being taken out by the police and that's when she walked out. She had phoned the university as asked, and a Dr. Jeremy Simms was on his way and would be there in around half an hour if his estimate was correct.

"I'm sorry there's not more to tell but it all happened rather quick," she said. "The police say they have him on assault, suspected abduction and, well, it's a bit embarrassing to say what else, though how Carver would know."

"But what about your job?" Amanda asked in a worried tone.

"Screw it, if I get sacked it's about time I moved on anyway. I mean I've been there since I was not much more than your age, so I need time off for good behaviour at the very least."

As she was speaking a bus pulled up at the stop near them, and a girl similar in age to Amanda got off. She walked up to the trio.

"Hi Bet," she said. "Time I joined the party I think."

Bet looked confused.

"Old man Carver has gone too far this time and if he reckons on putting it all on the new lad he can think again," the girl said.

"Oh Liz, he didn't did he?" Bet was visibly shaken.

"He had a damn good try, but the new lad stopped him. Then he went all weird, I mean you know what he's like with accusations and stuff but whoever was on the other end of the phone obviously took his side."

"One of his pals from the bloody lodge I expect," Bet said despondently. "They stick together so Jim could be in deep shit, I hope this guy you've got is good. I suppose I'd better introduce you to Vera and Amanda, but don't call her Amanda in the cop shop O.K. You two, this is Liz Baker who works in the canteen, it was her misfortune to take coffee in to Carver's office this morning."

"Why shouldn't I call you by your name Amanda, don't you like it?" Liz asked.

"Well, It's a long story but I'd rather the coppers didn't know who I am right now, I'll tell you when this is all over. Thanks for coming though," Amanda smiled.

About twenty minutes after they had all returned to the Police station and made themselves as comfortable as they could, Jeremy Simms walked in. As nobody apart from Jim actually knew what he looked like, he walked to reception and politely asked where he may find Jim's friends.

"If you mean Charlotte the harlot, the starlet and the two ugly sisters they're over there," the duty officer pointed in their direction.

"It would pay you not to make judgements so quickly." Mr Simms spoke sharply. "Because you do *not* know who you are talking to, but thank you for the direction."

146

"You'll get arrested too if you talk to me like that you old duffer," retorted the officer.

The party introduced themselves, though Amanda used her second name only and Vera handed a brown envelope to the old man, palming with it a note to inform him that the girl referred to by the officer as the starlet was Amanda but, for obvious reasons, did not want to be known as such. Jeremy took out a pair of brass rimmed spectacles and read the contents of the brown envelope, raising his eyes as he did.

"Someone has a lot of courage, I think," he said as he got up to the counter. "Now, my good man," he spoke with syrupy politeness that bordered on, but did not quite cross the line of, sarcasm. "Could you tell your superiors that Doctor Jeremy Simms, the head of the Faculty of legal studies at a rather famous university is here to discuss the arrest of Mr. James Alexander Stratton. I am a busy man and I do not expect to be kept waiting so hurry up if you please."

"He looked a bit old and frail when he walked in," Vera said. "But I don't think I'd like being on the wrong side of him."

As he was escorted into the bowels of the station he seemed to have grown in stature and strode through the door as though he was fully in charge of the situation. More than an hour went by before an officer came out and asked if Elizabeth Baker would mind going through to make a statement. She said that she would only be too pleased to and walked across the reception area with a spring in her step. After half an hour the duty officer brought the remaining three a tray of tea and biscuits.

"Sorry if I was a bit, well, rude about you. It's my way, I didn't mean anything by it," he said, hoping that his apology would be accepted.

It was getting dark when the door opened into reception and Dr Simms came through escorted by two officers, Liz Baker and Jim, who, although smiling, looked quite shaken by the experience.

Jeremy came over to the waiting group and said, "Jim is free to go now, he was given a very hard time, but I will do my best to ensure that this sort of thing never happens to him again. And you, Miss Potter, you must take my card, and if you need me, it will be my pleasure to help you. Finally you, young Josephine. You are a plucky young lady, and James has as good ally in you as you do in him. Now, it's been a pleasure to have been of assistance, but I must go back to the University before it gets too late." With that he was gone, as though he had disappeared from the spot.

"Let's get the hell out of this place," Jim said. "Thanks for all you've done and thanks Liz you didn't have to come, there's lots that wouldn't, but lets just get out."

Sitting with the group who, on the insistence of Vera, had stopped off at a small restaurant, Jim told the story of what had led up to his temporary incarceration. As had been reported, he had been sent up with a telex for the production manager and on his way back had heard the sound of a scuffle coming from Mr Carver's office. As he approached the door he'd heard a none too happy female voice, which on entry he found belonged to Liz Baker.

"Mr Carver was. Trying it on, a bit too hard," Jim said. "So I sort of tried to get him to stop."

"Carver just told to Jim to get out and mind his own business if he wanted to keep his job," Liz continued the tale. "He could see I was upset, and pulled Carver away in an arm-lock, dragged him to his chair and pushed him down on it."

The two had stood for what seemed like a long time just staring each other out, Jim standing between Carver and Liz. Carver then calmly picked up the telephone and rang someone that he addressed by name simply saying he'd got a bit of trouble that needed sorting.

"Then," Liz continued. "He really went weird as I said. Accused Jim of assault, and then went on about him doing it with someone that he shouldn't do. He really has a dirty mouth that guy. Anyway, I got thrown out as soon as the policeman came in, he didn't even want to talk to me, just took Jim away, it was the guy that looks after the gatehouse that found me sat on a step outside. At first I couldn't tell him, but he's a kind old geezer and very patient, He knew you Amanda, when you came to the place years ago, and he said I couldn't let Mr Carver get away with it. That's why I came."

Jim continued with the story. After he had been taken into custody (he didn't actually remember the formal arrest) he was dumped in a room and questioned for a long time. He was asked about why he had lied, why he's assaulted Mr Carver, and where he had locked Amanda away. They claimed to know a lot more than they actually could have and seemed to be laying the blame for all crime up to and including the great train robbery at his feet. He was at his lowest ebb when an officer came in and told his interrogator that a posse of tarts had come to support him.

"Charmed I'm sure!" Vera laughed.

Not long after that Jeremy Simms came into the interview room and pretty much destroyed any reason for holding him by the use of a few well chosen sentences. The evidence provided by Liz was more than helpful, and after a deal of discussion they could not hold him on anything relating to Amanda either. Her letter from the doctor destroyed their most compelling case, a telegram from her parents giving full permission for her to take a boating holiday with a friend that was known and trusted rather put an end to any chance of a charge of abduction.

Jeremy Simms had said, "This girl is so clearly traumatised by the actions of those whose job it is to protect her that she will not willingly identify herself in person."

The sentence caught the sympathy of the officer in the room, who, hard as he was, was also a family man, and must have thought how he would feel should this be happening to one of his offspring, his change of heart meaning that any possible case was now pretty much dead. There were a number of formalities to go through, but Jim was freed. Before they left for reception, Mr Simms had assured Jim that he would take up the case of anybody that had suffered as a result of the day's events at no cost, and that he would make sure that the decidedly unorthodox process that was used to secure an arrest would be the subject of a police or government inquiry.

"Bloody hell!" Amanda, who was still in disguise, said. "That guy is as sharp as a razor but he's such a softy too. Look I feel so bad about all of this, I mean we'll sail off into the distance, but you two?" She looked at Liz and Bet "Are you going to be alright?"

"I'll see them right my dear. They won't starve," said Vera, who had been looking unusually thoughtful during the monologue. "Bastards like that don't deserve to prosper, and it doesn't look like the people that did this will. If you don't keep, or don't want to keep your jobs, I know people that will give you work of the sort you can do. That and Mr Simms, and you'll be fine."

"But you hardly know us?" Bet said, looking as puzzled as Liz did.

"Maybe not," Vera smiled. "But I didn't know Jim and Amanda until a couple of days ago, now I'm their auntie, they didn't know each other until a couple of weeks ago and they each profess the other to be their best friend. What's time anyway, if they drop the big one we're all toast so we make friends and live while we can. And I'm Vera Potter!"

"She is," Amanda said, smiling under the wig and fake glasses. "But I'm not sure who I am. Mind if I go to the toilet."

Just as Jim commented that she must have fallen in Amanda reappeared,

149

her hair back to it's normal colour, though just a little wilder in style, no glasses, and the thick make-up removed to reveal the face that Jim now knew so well.

"There," she said. "Just so you recognise me next time you see me!"

Later that night, when all was quiet, and the lamp had been extinguished in the cabin of the Mayfly, Jim sat up.

"Mand," he whispered. "Mand? Are you awake?"

Although he was using the abbreviation normally reserved for times of fear he was not afraid, simply using a minimum of sound. Amanda stirred, and sat up, rubbing sleep from her eyes.

"What?" she said.

"Look, Mand," Jim was a little unsure of himself. "Look, I was knackered when I got back here and I sort of dropped off to sleep."

"It's what people generally do when they're tired," Amanda mumbled.

"Well, Look don't go back to sleep. I didn't want to say this in front of the others but I wanted to say it before the end of today," Jim persisted.

"Go on then," Amanda replied, as she too sat up

"That, what you did, getting the letter. I know what the letter said, and what you subjected yourself to. You didn't have to do that. But you just did it without a thought."

"I couldn't let you be hung on a nail like that, not if I could stop it," Amanda replied. "It was the only thing I could think of to do so I did it, that's all. Anyway, it wasn't just one of those stupid things, like me disappearing and not telling you what I was doing, I did think it through," Amanda was slightly more awake now and although her speech was coloured with sleep, it was absolutely lucid. "Bet knew you by name, so did Carver. If he contacted the police, you could bet it was one of his chums from the lodge he spoke to. He'd want as much dirt on you as possible so that any complaint from Liz wouldn't stick. When they turned up the association with me was just a bonus, like green shield stamps. It wouldn't have been that hard for them to find, even though they've no proof of anything."

"But you just did it, I just wanted to say thanks, well, more than that really but I can't think of what to say," Jim said.

"Don't say anything Jimbo, you were arrested because of me anyway, it all evens up."

150

"Whatever you say Mand, but remember. I appreciate what you did, well, a lot more than that. I won't forget it. Not ever."

Nothing further was said that evening, the two dropping off to sleep almost simultaneously allowing their subconscious to unravel the events of the day.

Chapter 10

By the time they had stocked up with fuel and food, and said their farewells to Vera it was mid morning. Amanda had exchanged the address of Marie's shop for a post office box number that Vera used. Then it was time to move on, as the little outboard was ticking over in the slightly uneven manner common to two-stroke motors.

"Bye then." Vera shouted, as Jim flicked the gear to forward and increased the throttle. They were under way again, having opted for a longer route with far less locks and shorter tunnels. Neither Jim nor Amanda had much stomach for a long journey through a deformed underground watercourse, with the added attraction of a malevolent ghost, but both used the logic that the lesser number of locks would cancel out the disadvantage of the longer route, though neither truly believed it.

"It's funny, but it's true what old Lou said," Amanda commented idly. "He said that, on the cut, nobody makes much of a fuss over leaving because they know that they'll see each other again. Sometimes it can be a long time, sometimes short, but when they meet up its like they were just continuing where they left off."

"That and the bush telegraph," Jim added. "You notice people sort of know that you are on the way. I mean I know that Vera was no more of a boater than we are, not born to it, but she seemed to know we were coming, like she was there ready for us. Maybe it's just co-incidence."

They were taking things easy, not wanting to run into any submerged objects, rumours about which seemed to abound. After seeing the state of the canal near Carver's, and from the bus on the journey back, Jim had suggested that their run around the city was no more than a gesture, a longer one better made by someone with a boat made of something a lot harder than plywood. There was no practical purpose to it, as they had not actually got anything to deliver beyond the centre and that had been done the previous day. Also the notion of creeping up on Carver and Green whilst they were unaware had been somewhat scuppered by earlier events.

"I'm really sorry I messed that up," Jim said as he handed the steering over to Amanda. "I know we found a lot out, but there's still nothing we can really do with what we know."

Amanda thought a moment before she spoke, a just perceptible wrinkle forming above her nose. "There's not really a lot you could have done, I mean you couldn't have just left him to have his way could you?"

"I suppose not," Jim replied. "That's the stupid thing though, like after all that anger I had, I thought I'd have flattened the guy, all I did was sit him neatly in his chair and stare at him like a maniac."

"You think Liz would have wanted you to kill him?" Amanda said. "I don't think so, that'd mean she'd have been in a room with two madmen, and you would probably still be behind bars."

"So how do we sort your folks out?" Jim frowned a bit. "I mean that's why I went there."

"Not sure," Amanda said. "But there were two ways, and it looks like we inadvertently did the one we weren't planning on. I mean you have to admit it, we pretty effectively threw a brick into his bowl of soup didn't we."

"True," Jim smiled. "Shame it wasn't real soup and a real brick though."

"It must have been pretty dreadful in the police station though, I mean before Doctor Simms arrived?" Amanda sounded worried but her curiosity had got the better part.

"I've had worse," Jim replied. "They tried to make out that you had told them everything when they found you. I was pretty sure they hadn't, and the stuff they said eventually sort of made it clear they hadn't a clue where you were. Sort of standard form really, no picnic but I'm not going to fall apart, not this time, not even a moody if I can help it."

"Just as long as you know," Amanda cut short her sentence as Jim nodded and smiled.

By evening they were out of the urban sprawl and ready to find a tie up. The run had not been particularly long, but the previous day had taken much more of a toll than they had expected. Their easy routine had come back very quickly after the break in the city and, although they had enjoyed Vera's company, both had to admit that they were enjoying being back on their own again. It was nice too that the pressure on Amanda had lifted slightly with Jeremy Simms' reassurance that they should not be bothered again, though she had made a mental note to keep checking the radio just in case. As they were sitting, digesting their meal, Jim looked through the itinerary that Dave had given him, and spotted something he'd missed.

"There's a festival thing that we're supposed to go to when we get to the next big stop," he said, sounding very slightly disappointed. "Something to do with keeping the canal open in the city, and stopping the developers filling it in."

"Do you think we'll really make a difference?" Amanda asked.

"I don't know.   I can't see that a small boat full of Russian watches would prove very much that transport is still happening.   But I said I'd do Dave's list, so we'll see," Jim replied.

"But we missed a chunk of the stuff we were supposed to do already haven't we?" Amanda asked.

"Well, yes and no," Jim said cautiously.   "I looked on the map, and we did do a loop of the old line on the way in.   We couldn't possibly do the lot, but I'd say we have proved so far as we can that we were there.   Dave did say that we had to use our instincts as to whether it was actually possible to navigate after all."

"You're not really looking forward to the festival though are you?" Amanda had hit the nail on the head.   Jim had to admit that he had absolutely no relish for the event, he liked to keep out of the gaze and didn't like crowds much.

The next day was bright and they made good progress, the countryside greened up, and it almost felt like they were on holiday, though the open ended nature of their venture kept a sense of the almost mundane about their activities.   They lived on a boat, this was their life, and they would continue like this forever.   They both knew that this too was false, but they neither of them chose to think that far ahead.   They hadn't been on the move much more than three or so hours when they saw what looked at first glance to be a floating allotment shed tied at an odd angle to the towpath, a few hundred yards away.

"Sheds on allotments are sort of different to the garden ones," Jim commented.   "People sort of make them out of just about anything that comes to hand, like old bay windows, fence panels, all sorts really."

As they drew closer, they saw that it was some kind of punt shaped vessel, a bit longer and just slightly wider than the Mayfly.   Its superstructure was made up of ornate wood mouldings painted in lurid colours, some of the paint looking like it had been splashed on by a child. There was very little order to anything about it, with windows and hatches seemingly placed at random as though they had been ineptly dealt from a

154

pack of cards. They could see someone at the back sitting by the small outboard, which looked more like a lawnmower engine on a drain pipe than the neatly finished machine that pushed the Mayfly along. Jim slowed the pace as they drew near.

"You O.K," he shouted.

"Motor's dead!" the person at the back replied. "Can you give us a hand?"

"Our turn to help someone out," Jim smiled as he slowed and aimed for a spot just ahead of the moored craft. As they passed, they saw the name of the craft "Chrysophyllax Diver" from the home port of Andromeda. The couple that owned the strange looking boat were a few years older than Jim and Amanda, the man sporting a thin black beard, and the woman having long unruly blonde hair. They both wore colourful clothing and seemed very laid back in their approach to life.

"Just screamed and stopped man. I mean like I thought it was fine but, boom and no go. I'm Rick, and this is Vanessa. Ciao man," Rick smiled.

"I don't know too much about motors myself," Jim replied. "But Amanda is pretty magic at starting Scandinavian diesels."

"Some claim to fame that is," Amanda laughed. "But we'll try and help."

Vanessa told them that they had decided to drop out of university and live life at a slower pace. The rat race was not for them, and she had bought their boat as a part finished conversion of a military surplus pontoon. It leaked quite a lot from the top, though the hull, which was aluminium was at least watertight. They were going to chill out, enjoying what came their way and that was as far as their plan went. The motor was straightforward enough, there was no gear shifter, you just started the thing, went forwards and that was it. The fuel was supplied from a small tank that was attached to the cylinder block, and starting it was achieved by a piece of rope with a knot in one end wrapped round a pulley on the flywheel. All was simple except nothing would budge. That was how they had been for nearly an hour, and the engine block was still almost too hot to touch.

"At a guess I'd say that you have picked something up that has stopped the cooling water going round," Jim hoped to sound like he knew what he was talking about. "The thing is frying hot so the best thing is to let it cool off for a bit longer before we try anything."

"Cue a cup of tea!" Amanda asked brightly. "We were going to stop for lunch anyway in a bit so we may as well have a break a bit early. We normally have lunch on the run but we forgot to get anything ready."

"Jeez!" Rick said. "You sound like an old married couple! All tea and sandwiches and stuff!"

"You'd not think she was seventy-five! And all her own teeth too," Jim laughed. "Been together these sixty years last whenever it was, and hey!"

Amanda had thrown a handful of used teabags in Jim's direction as he was speaking, and scored a direct hit on the back of his head.

"That's it Donaldson!" he laughed. "You get keel hauled. Well you would if we had a proper keel!" With that remark he returned the tea bags in the same manner but, Amanda ducked and they went neatly into the canal with a satisfying plop.

"Don't mind Rick, he's always political and stuff." Vanessa spoke with a soft voice. "You're young to be on holiday together though. How did you get your parent's permission. Mummy and Daddy are still pretty sore about Rick and me, but we're doing our own thing now."

One of the gleaming paraffin stoves on the Mayfly was now emitting its familiar sound and Amanda was trying to think of a believable way to explain their situation. Finding none she simply said, "You probably wouldn't believe us if we told you. But we're not on holiday, this is a working boat, we deliver stuff to people, sort of like a mini narrowboat, but without the coal."

"Like we don't do money man, its like too much of a hassle," Rick said.

Jim rather wondered that, if they didn't do money as he'd just been told, quite how they planned on paying for fuel and food, but he was too polite to comment. With tea and sandwiches finished, the motor on Rick and Vanessa's boat seemed cool enough to approach and Jim started by tipping it out of the water to check the cooling pump intake. Sure enough it was well and truly blocked by a combination of plastic bag and weed, probably picked up on the run out of the city. Amanda held the motor, there being no obvious lock position on it, whilst Jim poked around with the end of an attachment on his penknife (the use for which he had never been properly sure of) eventually freeing the obstruction and holding a messy clump of natural and man made material up as a sort of trophy.

"We could make a nice salad out of that!" he said, getting a contrived grimace from Amanda in reply. Moving the motor back to its normal position he noticed that a few drops of fuel had leaked from the tank. He had forgotten to close the vent and the tank being a part of the motor, tipped with it. Before long, however, it had evaporated without trace so no harm was done. On checking, the flywheel was still pretty solidly stuck so, taking a spanner, Jim removed the spark plug and sprayed some penetrating oil into the cylinder.

"Jim," Amanda said in a thoughtful tone. "Shouldn't that petrol have left a bit of an oil film when it went in the water?"

She was right, even the motor of the Mayfly could leave the odd droplet on the surface of the water if they accidentally flooded the carburettor. They'd found that it was soon mopped up by dropping a piece of toilet paper on the surface of the water, which, when scooped out, retained any oil that may have caused pollution. The mix of oil to petrol on their motor was fifty to one as opposed to ten to one on the rather older machine that powered the Chrysophyllax Diver. In other words ten percent of the fuel was actually two stroke oil and should have left its mark on both the tank and in the water.

"Amanda's right. Did you put oil in last time you filled up?" Jim asked.

"Does it need an oil change man?" Rick said, looking puzzled.

It transpired that the boat had been prepared for them complete with two cans of fuel which must have been mixed for them, and when these had run out they had refilled them at a petrol station some distance from the canal. Clearly the tank was full of neat petrol, which had compounded the problem caused by the lack of coolant. The penetrating oil had done its job though and the flywheel now moved fairly freely. Jim sprayed a little more oil in the cylinder and replaced the spark plug. After disconnecting the fuel pipe and draining the tank back into one of the cans, he refilled it with the correct petrol and oil mix and set about starting. The choke and throttle arrangement were rather different to the Mayfly's twist grip and flick-switch, but after a few pulls, it came back to life, and sent a stream of water plopping into the canal from the edge of the cylinder head.

"Wow!" Vanessa squeaked gleefully. "You are so clever, I mean. Wow!"

"Yeah, thanks man." Rick added laconically. "You want to run with us a while?"

Given that there wasn't much of an option Jim smiled and let them get a head start so that he could see if they got into any difficulty. Once the Mayfly was tidied and back under way the Chrysophyllax Diver was a good long way in the distance, but clearly visible.

"Fucking halfwits!" Amanda scowled. "I mean, what kind of idiots are

157

they."

"Probably rich ones," Jim chipped in. "They sound like they haven't really been going for long, but mummy and daddy can bail them out if they cock up badly."

"Is that how you see me?" Amanda didn't really know why she'd turned on Jim like this, but he was still calm.

"I might have done," he said, honestly. "If I hadn't got to know you, but you couldn't be like that, not really, so I'd have been judging you harshly."

Amanda thought, and replied in her view of honesty. "That, that woolly headed. That apparition. Oh bloody hell, all that religion and stuff. She could have been me!"

"Not in a hundred years," Jim assured her. "You never really bought into it, I mean you looked for sure, but you read the books too. They just look at the pictures. We all have to find our way, and you're as entitled as the next to do that. People do all sorts, box, join a band. They think they've dropped out, you studied other religions, and chose not to eat meat."

"And you rescued a boat?" Amanda looked Jim full in the eye.

"So that I could walk away from the life I had. Well, more sail than walk, but, yes. I didn't like what I had, so I went looking, and then I found the Mayfly," Jim smiled.

"That's almost like you believe in destiny?" Amanda said

"That or co-incidence. Doesn't really matter, I sailed into the sunset I guess," Jim replied.

"And is that any better than what you had?" Amanda asked.

Jim slowed the throttle as they were catching up with the underpowered and ungainly pontoon. He looked at Amanda, catching the expression on her face and for the briefest of moments more, directly into her hazel brown eyes, seeing an openness that made him pause for thought. He drew breath and released it, finding the words he inhaled again and said.

"If you want the truth. Yes, It's a hell of a lot better, I can't think of anywhere I'd rather be to be honest," he said.

Amanda was going to say something, but thought for a little too long and couldn't find the right words, so Jim continued his train of thought.

"It'd be nice to have a bathroom of course, but here is O.K. I suppose it must be by choice because I could pack up and go back to where I was, but."

There he stopped, he wanted to say more but he didn't want to at the same time. Also they were approaching a small flight of locks, which they had decided to polish off before the evening stop. Although it was not as necessary now to avoid towns, both Jim and Amanda preferred the quieter moorings. It should have been easier with twice the hands on the flight, but time seemed to pass excruciatingly slowly. Where the Mayfly was nimble and always seemed to know what was wanted, the pontoon base of the Chrysophyllax Diver was unwieldy and slow which, coupled to the almost terminal ineptitude of the steerer, made each entry to a lock like some kind of giant game of water-tiddlywinks. At least the fact that, more out of politeness than forethought, Amanda and Jim had suggested Rick and Vanessa go ahead meant that none of the bumps and scrapes were administered to the Mayfly. In total they took about four times as long to get through the flight than they would have done by themselves, and at the end they were about twice as tired. Along with an ungainly boat and an unbelievable lack of ability, Rick and Vanessa seemed more than willing to let Jim and Amanda do all the work on the locks, and even a bit of crewing of their own boat. As the Chrysophyllax Diver left the last lock in a haze of blueish smoke, Vanessa, who was steering waved them on to pass.

"We'll catch you up at the tie up if that's alright with you!" she shouted as they passed. "You probably know a much better spot than we do"

Amanda smiled and nodded politely then turned away to face Jim.

"Jesus!" she exclaimed when the distance between them had taken them out of earshot. "We're going to have a tea party with two characters that wouldn't look out of place with the Mad Hatter!"

After about an hours run they decided to stop, and prepare their evening meal. They had almost forgotten that a hay-box curry had been brewing for most of the day. All that was needed was the final heat up and the rice, which they both set about attending to. Amanda had lost her fear of the aged stoves and become as good at lighting and maintaining them as Jim, who had improved in his ability to prepare food, and they somehow came to enjoy the mealtime routine a lot.

"I'd have thought the plastic hippies would have got here by now," Jim said, smiling. With his words the feint patter of their motor became audible just before the pontoon rounded a bend. "I spoke too soon," he added.

"Do you think we should ask them to tea?" Although she'd made it clear that, for her own reasons, she wasn't at all keen on their travelling

159

companions, her sense of doing the right thing had crept up on her, and she was just a little house-proud too.

"I suppose it would be a bit mean to stuff ourselves full of curry whilst they haven't even started preparing food.   If we wait and see, we can stretch it if we have to."   Jim was aware of how much they had been helped and felt that this was a way of putting something back.

The Chrysophyllax Diver eventually hit the bank with a bit of a thud a few feet behind the Mayfly, and then proceeded to swing out into the canal as Vanessa found the hard way that, having stopped the motor too early, there was no steering.   Amanda stepped carefully ashore with the boat-hook from the Mayfly's cabin top and, leaning out about halfway down Rick and Vanessa's boat, managed to get enough of a hold to pull it back to the bank.   After helping them secure their mooring ropes she made the offer of supper.

"We've plenty if you want to join us," she smiled somewhat falsely. "As long as you don't mind there being no meat."

Vanessa was thrilled by the invitation, and accepted for both of them.

"You're such professionals at this," she beamed.   "I mean, how did you cook whilst on the run?"

There followed a detailed description of the principle of the hay-box and how to plan ahead with meals.   Vanessa listened intently whilst Amanda spoke and prepared the rice.   Jim was busy extending the curry with some onion and a few vegetables that would cook quickly, whilst Rick was nowhere to be seen.   Vanessa wasn't an unpleasant person, just a bit woolly minded, and Amanda was beginning to feel just a trifle guilty at her earlier harsh judgement of her.   She hailed from the home counties, had a father that worked in the city and a mother who was very big in the local social scene.   She had gone to a 'Red Brick' university as her grades were not good enough to get into one of the really old ones and it was there that she had met Rick at a political meeting.

"It was all about anarchy, and freedom," she said with equal enthusiasm and ignorance of most of the facts.   "The stuff they were teaching at the University was so, so old.   When I heard the stuff at the meeting I thought, well, wow."

Amanda was trying to get a hold of any philosophy behind Vanessa's conversion, but could find nothing, whilst Jim cooked the curry.

"It was all so, so nothing I suppose, so I left and decided to live on a boat, and this was so dinky.   I got it all painted up and then Rick said we

160

should just leave all our cares behind, be free. Love, life, everything, just, well, just be totally free as birds."

"Well," Jim said. "You can add hay-box curry to the list of new experiences if you like. Where's your fella?"

Rick must have sensed the imminence of the meal, and had come out from the cabin of the pontoon, having changed his clothes to suit the mood, choosing the guise of the political folk singer for the evening.

"That was really good man!" he proclaimed after the meal. "You two are so *married!* I just can't believe it!"

"Don't be so unkind," Vanessa pouted from behind her mug of tea. "They can be whatever they want to be just like us, we're all free."

"But we've all got to be, you know, out there! I mean really out there if we want to make a difference. Don't you two feel that?" Rick, though he spoke with what sounded like conviction, actually seemed to make a good deal less sense than his partner, and she was none too eloquent.

"I've walked away from a life that I didn't like," Jim replied calmly. "And into one that I do. That's made a difference. There's other stuff too but that's a bit private."

"Man!" Rick exclaimed. "Private! That's just bourgeois thinking, right out of the middle class man. There's no private out here! Let it hang man, free your burden, free your love!"

"He is right Jim," Vanessa added. "You shouldn't hold anything back, it poisons you, and it's what's wrong with everything. I mean just feel the wind in your face and let it all go!"

"He meant he didn't want to talk about things to do with me that I might not want to talk about as well," Amanda tried speaking in Jim's defence. "Call it respect if you want."

"But that's it man," Rick chimed in again. "You got to lose all that goody two shoes girl guide brown owl stuff. I mean it's so old and dead. Free yourself before its too late. Anyway, no mind, you did dinner, how about some afters!"

Rick pulled out something that resembled a cheap fabric pencil case, and proceeded to assemble a large roll up cigarette from three papers.

"I think I'll pass on that," Jim said, not impolitely but firmly.

"Hey man, you don't know what you're missing, I mean you got to try this stuff man!" Rick protested.

161

"I think freedom means we can derive intense pleasure from just about anything doesn't it?" Amanda queried.

"The chick's got the right idea man," Rick's use of the word 'man' had gone beyond the irritating stage, and was even abrading Vanessa's good nature.

"Too right I have, man," Amanda replied in a very slightly mocking tone. "So Jimbo, let's go and *do*, what we enjoy the most!"

Jim's eyes opened wide as Amanda added, "Washing up! It always makes me go weak at the knees!"

Vanessa thought the verbal manoeuvre was so clever and giggled like a schoolgirl for rather too long as Jim set about heating some water. While cleaning the pots and plates, they watched Rick and Vanessa become more and more stupid in their behaviour as the substance they smoked took hold. Eventually everything they had used in sharing their supper was clean and neatly stowed as it had to be given the size of their living space, with no help from their two guests, and they decided to treat themselves to a cup of tea. Out of politeness Amanda offered Rick and Vanessa a cup, but wasn't sure what the garbled answer was beyond it being the most witty utterance of the century in both their eyes.

"I think we'll take that as a no shall we," Jim said dryly.

"Hey man!" Rick giggled. "You just do what you gotta do. Like hang loose man! The chick needs more than tea man!"

"Don't be cruel," Vanessa chirped. "He's only young, so sweet. A sweetie sweetie." Her words dissolved into juvenile laughter again and became indecipherable.

"I *think* I'm going to puke," Amanda whispered. "I really want to pitch the pair of them in the bloody cut!"

"Have a cup of tea," Jim smiled.

It wasn't the answer to all but it was the best he could offer. It wasn't, he thought, that either Rick or Vanessa were bad people, more that they seemed to be peculiarly artificial in the way they acted. It was as though they had read about dropping out, or seen an article in a Sunday supplement and made a sort of pastiche out of it. That in itself would have been tolerable but he could see that Amanda was as fed up, if not more so, than himself due to the superior attitude they seemed to be facing. Either Rick was preaching, or Vanessa was patronising, or both were both. Either way it was very tiresome. They sat for a long while in the back of the Mayfly whilst the pair from the pontoon got sillier and sillier on the bank.

162

Eventually they seemed to have gone quiet.

"I think they've gone to sleep," Amanda said quietly. "And it's probably about time we do too."

There was no sign of either Rick or his partner, and neither Amanda nor Jim were sure where they were, having lost interest in them, as they'd had to look on whilst their travelling companions became completely stoned. They assumed that, as the chill of the evening drew in, their friends had returned to their boat and crashed out in whatever stupor they had induced.

"Right," Jim said. "Time to find a tree," saying this he hopped ashore and disappeared from view. He was about to answer the call of nature when he heard some movement in the bushes behind him. Turning round he found Vanessa standing a few yards away. She was wearing some concoction made of a bright tie-dyed cotton that was translucent, and in good light probably transparent too.

"Hi," she greeted him casually, "It's a lovely evening, and you are so uptight. It's such a shame. I want to make it up to you."

"I'm fine," Jim replied rather nervously. "No need to worry."

"Oh but I do. We do. We want you both to be so free, as free as us, part of the new dawn. Atlantis returning and everything," Vanessa said.

"Really, well, that's, well it sounds quite nice but Atlantis is supposed to be at the bottom of some ocean, not a canal," Jim answered flatly.

"Oh come on. Dance in the moonlight," she half sang as she pirouetted and reached to take his hand, which he pulled back.

"Jim, Jim, Jim, you've never been stoned before, and you need to be so free. Have you ever made love under the stars? It's wonderful," she continued speaking what Jim had decided earlier on was total nonsense.

"Right, no, not done that one," Jim deliberately sounded like he was checking items on a list.

"Oh and we should, we all should, let's do it together, all of us!" Vanessa answered, not taking the hint.

"Well, I suppose I'd better go and tell Amanda or she won't know will she, now how about you go back to Rick just for now," Jim smiled politely.

With that he was gone at speed, having not done what he originally set out to do. He was back on the Mayfly in less than a minute and had all the covers down and tight in record time.

"Mind if I use the bucket tonight," he said.

"That's some kind of greeting! And welcome back to you Jim," Amanda replied, "What's up, no suitable vegetation?"

163

"You wouldn't believe me if I told you," Jim whispered in a slightly flustered tone. "Maybe you would, I mean they're totally out of it. You know what she just offered."

Amanda sat quietly as he recounted the tale, listening attentively in the lamplight to his hushed voice with a sombre expression on her face. Eventually it all got too much for her and she exploded with laughter, tears rolling down her face.

"But it's serious, I mean they wanted us all to, well, you know, together! Swapping around and everything!" Jim protested.

That just fuelled Amanda's laughter. Eventually she calmed down enough to speak.

"God, I wish I could have seen your face!" she laughed.

That set Jim off, and they then both fuelled each other's mirth until they were quite out of breath and they heard the sound of footsteps and Rick's familiar voice, slightly hushed.

"Man," he said. "They're having their own sort of party in there," then more footsteps and a loud splash as he stepped neatly off the bank, having not been looking where he was going.

"Ricky, Ricky! I'll help you," Vanessa's voice squealed, followed by another splash as she fell in from the stern of the Chrysophyllax Diver.

"Now you don't have to pitch them in," Jim said calmly.

"But they're too dumb to get out, so we've got to do *that* for them too," Amanda sighed. "I draw the line at wiping their backsides for them though. You can do that Jimbo."

Amanda groped around her locker for her swimsuit and put it on as Jim looked away. She climbed out onto the bank and dived in to catch first Vanessa who clearly could not swim, whilst Jim who had stripped down to underwear rescued Rick who could but only just.

"Right you two," he said. "Get dry or die of cold that's your bloody choice, but I'd suggest you get dry."

They meekly obeyed him and he and Amanda saw them tucked into their bunk before returning to the Mayfly to wash the canal from them. It was very late when they finished and they had used up a lot of fresh water in the process but both felt the better for it.

Waking up the next morning Vanessa had a revolting taste in her mouth, a headache, and she smelt something decidedly unsavoury in the cabin of the Chrysophyllax Diver, something that did not originate anywhere near Andromeda, something that was actually her and her partner.   She had dried herself off, as instructed.   Then she'd gone to sleep soon after Amanda had left them.   Their clothes still lay sodden on the cabin floor giving the whole boat an atmosphere like a stagnant school changing room. Normally she'd have taken a shower or a long bath, with those cubes that were advertised on the television, then a quick trip to the college launderette and the job would have been done.   In the middle of a field, some miles away from any such facility she had little idea of what to do. Rick eventually stirred to see his "chick" sitting on one of the bench seats by their galley table with her head in her hands.

"What's up doll?" he asked.   "I mean you look like you need a lift.   Or you could come back here and."

"Don't be so stupid." Vanessa spoke in a sharper voice than he had so far heard.   "We both stink like a tramps bottom."

"Oh man, was that some kind of a night!   Were we wasted or what.   I mean like flying high with the birds man," Rick said happily.

"Oh shut up!   We got stoned and made fools of ourselves!   That's what we did, and then we nearly drowned," Vanessa replied even more sharply.

"Hey, doll, I'd have saved you, no worries," Rick reassured her, slightly reinventing history as he did.

Amanda was washing her swimsuit, and Jim's underpants nonchalantly in a bowl of fairly clean canal water, with a bar of household soap.   She had decided that there was not enough fresh water to do the job properly and found the canal water was pretty clear in the mornings before boats had churned it up, not that there were that many boats around.   That morning she had decided to put the theory to the test and, using the electronic monitor that they were testing, found that it was indeed pretty clean.   Clean enough to wash clothes at any rate.   Jim was preparing a hearty breakfast as a bit of a treat after the previous evening reasoning that Amanda was the true hero of the hour as she was the first in to the rescue, and he wasn't nearly as good a swimmer as her.   The fact that he would also benefit from the treat was a long way secondary in his thoughts.   The washing was flapping across the back hoop of the cover and they were finishing their third round of fried bread and marmalade as Vanessa walked towards them. She looked a shadow of the person that was offering rather too much the previous evening, and seemed quite crestfallen.   Her hair, that was so free the day before seemed to have matted together and lost a lot of its lustre, also her clothing was much less flamboyant than the previous day, just a tie-dye t-shirt and faded jeans did the job.

"Hi," Amanda greeted her, "Want some fried bread and marmalade?"

The offer instilled a similar fear in her as hers had to Jim the night before, though she didn't run away.

"Look," she said. "I doubt you even want to know me today. I'm really sorry if I was an idiot. I feel so stupid."

"Don't worry," Amanda smiled brightly. "Jim told me about it. Look it's no big deal, you were a bit out of it that's all. At least have a cup of tea. How's Rick by the way?"

Vanessa accepted the offer of tea, and sat with Amanda at the back of the Mayfly whilst Jim poured it out.

Not mentioning how her companion was she said, "Thanks Amanda for pulling me out of the canal last night, and you too Jim, and for fixing the motor, and the lovely meal. You're both very kind."

"People have been good to us," Jim replied. "So it's just passing it on, don't worry about it."

"That's what karma is, isn't it. I mean really that's it." Vanessa smiled. "I'm so stupid, you know I get these ideas and then, off I go. I don't ever plan anything, not like you have, I mean this must have taken months to arrange."

Amanda couldn't help laughing a little.

"If you want to know the truth, we're what would be called runaways, well actually I'm a stowaway too, except there's no room in here *to* stow away so it was easier to just hitch a ride," she smiled.

"But how are you so organised?" Vanessa was rather puzzled.

"Girl Guides, be prepared and all that," Amanda replied. "It comes in handy sometimes. But there's a load of stuff we both need to do, you wouldn't believe the half of it. We're sort of helping each other out that's sort of about it really."

"This isn't for me." Vanessa sighed. "I've ripped my dress on the wretched motor yesterday, nearly ruined the thing too, then. Well you know all the rest."

"It can't be that bad," Jim tried to cheer her up. "I mean you've not been going long."

"No, but I feel bad. I need to go back and actually do something that is me," Vanessa frowned.

"What about Rick?" Amanda asked. "I mean you're together."

Vanessa looked down at her feet.

"No," she said. "No I don't think we are. Not like you two. Sex is fun but it isn't all of everything, not anything really. He's got plenty of others around, it was all open anyway, that bit was true, but. Oh look I shouldn't. I am so sorry."

"I'm not sure what you're trying to say," Amanda said. "But don't read things that aren't there. Jim is my best friend, that's what you see, nothing else."

Had Vanessa have been listening which she wasn't, having lapsed into her own thoughts, she may have come to the conclusion that Amanda was labouring the point just a little to much to be truly convincing.

"I feel awful asking you, but can you help me down those locks. I'll be alright after that if I'm careful. Then I can get back to the mooring and sort things from there," Vanessa asked in a soft tone that neither Amanda nor Jim could refuse, even if it would lose most of the day's progress.

"Are you sure that's what you want to do?" Jim replied. "I mean, we can make up time, but shouldn't you talk it through with Rick at least."

Vanessa now looked slightly sheepish.

"He has gone off to find a road and catch a bus. He wants to do the big trail to India and everywhere. I think the boat was too limiting for him, or I was. He said I was too straight laced. Too like, well I don't mean to be rude but, too like you," she looked at Amanda as she spoke.

"Bloody hell, I've never been a catalyst before!" Amanda spoke before thinking. "I'm sorry," she added, but Vanessa was smiling at the comment.

"It's true you know. I saw you and thought, that should be what I'm like, only I was so stoned that everything seemed so funny. Then I almost drowned and it didn't seem so funny any more, everything swung the other way, and it was sort of horrible."

"Life's too short to be out of your tree for any of it," Jim said, rather firmly. "Even the shit, well, especially that, you need your wits about you if you're in the shit don't you."

"Are you sure you can get back on your own after the locks?" Amanda asked politely, only to be met with a blank look by Vanessa, who did not want to admit that she didn't even know how to start the motor.

"There's only one thing for it then," Jim said resignedly. "We'll have to take her back ourselves."

"But that'll take days!" Vanessa protested. "You haven't that amount of time to spare."

"It'll take about a day if we work hard at it," Amanda said. "Jim, you go ahead, I'll take Vanessa back then I can catch a train or something and meet you tonight. It'll be late so leave a lamp on so I know where you are and don't get on the wrong bloody boat!"

"No! You cant! It's unfair on you." Vanessa really didn't want to be a burden, but underneath this she also knew that she was well and truly stuck if she didn't take the offer up.

"I insist on driving you back," Vanessa said, as they waved Jim off in the Mayfly, having arranged their meeting point. "I'm a lot better in a car than on a boat, I promise," she smiled.

"Thanks," Amanda replied. "Now let's get away," she added whilst winding the knotted cord round the motor pulley.

With the little outboard at full throttle the pontoon could do about three miles an hour which wasn't good, but there were very few locks and only one tunnel in their path, so the task wasn't impossible, but wouldn't be that easy either. Although ungainly compared to Mayfly, the Chrysophyllax Diver wasn't as bad as Amanda had feared, and it did have some good points, most notably it had a lot more room, and you could stand up straight in the cabin. It wasn't home though and, as Jim disappeared round the shallow bend Amanda felt slightly sad that she'd offered her help. Vanessa reappeared from the cabin with two mugs of tea and a packet of biscuits.

"Right," said Amanda authoritatively "You keep on the Diver as much as you can and I'll do most of the lock-wheeling. We can go quicker like that. I wish I'd brought my windlass but, yours shouldn't be too bad. Then we'll take it in turns to steer, an hour each. There's not a lot of time spare if we are going to do it in a day but that's how it is. Oh, and thanks for the tea!"

Vanessa had been staring slightly open mouthed at this little speech, and after a while said, "How do you do it? I mean you're like my mum, except she's not a bit like you but you're younger than me."

"It's a long story, but I've sort of had to get on with doing things for myself that's all. Like I said. Girl Guides and stuff," Amanda replied.

That was the limit of her revelations for a while as the locks soon loomed. She had hoped that Vanessa would be able to manage the steering better than she did, but their progress was far better than when she was partnered by Rick. The routine that worked best was for Vanessa to cut the motor before the lock and tow the boat in by hand, leaving Amanda to do the hard work. In the meantime, Jim made his slower than usual progress in the opposite direction. It was a pleasant enough day, and he didn't mind the fact that Amanda wasn't there, mainly because her temporary exit from the scene was due to a totally different set of circumstances and he knew she would be back that evening. Left to his own thoughts he found, each time he mused on a subject, whether a tree, the state of the canal, or just a general thought on life he always seemed to end up comparing his own conclusion with a speculation about what Amanda would say on the subject. Although he never really considered the social order of things, he saw that she and Vanessa should have more in common than he actually had with Amanda. Vanessa, he thought, was much more typical of her class than his travelling companion. Maybe it was just that he knew Amanda better, or for whatever reason, but he couldn't see Vanessa referring to anyone of his class (there was that niggling word again) as a best friend, or even an acquaintance. Even her proposition the night before, had he taken her up on it, would not have rendered them any closer in terms of actually knowing each other. Amanda, however, he thought, was different, not necessarily better, but yes, better. She was, well, she meant something to him. Best friends do, but he had never had a girl as a best friend, not that that should matter. He let the thought linger perhaps for too long, but used no words in his head to describe his feelings and carried on the duties of the day, silently, and as efficiently as he could, until the agreed tie up point. It was near enough to a road bridge, but still quiet enough to be inconspicuous. Although there was less of a necessity now to hide, it had become a sort of second nature to keep a low profile.

The erratic progress of the Chrysophyllax Diver continued through what was a reasonably pleasant afternoon, with the sun breaking through sufficiently to be cheery but not so much as to overheat the crew. Whilst Vanessa had not the slightest idea at the start, in Amanda's opinion, of how to handle a boat, she was a very quick learner, and was soon able to cope with the workings of the motor, including the all important fuel mixture. At the high concentration of oil in the petrol this was best prepared just before filling the tank. Fear of the seize-up that had happened together with the problem of spark plug fouling made her perhaps a little too keen to get it just right, but just right is what she managed each time and they had no issues throughout the day with reliability. She had the good sense to tie her hair up to prevent accidents with the exposed flywheel, which had already devoured a large chunk of a floaty skirt that she had been wearing the day before. The two settled down to an easy routine, which reminded Amanda of the way she and Jim had coped in the early days of learning to work together. It wasn't the same, but close enough to make her pause for thought occasionally. Vanessa, who had always been perceptive regarding atmospheres to the point of her parents sometimes thinking she was a psychic, picked up on this with a casual comment to her young mentor.

"Penny for your thoughts?" she smiled.

Amanda almost startled, looked up but said nothing.

"You've been staring into space for nearly ten minutes, but you look sort of pensive, not sad, do you want to tell me?" Vanessa persisted.

The little furrow above Amanda's nose that Jim would have taken as a signal of deep thought was missed by Vanessa, who waited until her friend broke the silence.

"I thought I'd hate this. I mean, I was really dreading it. I had to do it, I mean you'd have drowned or killed yourself in some kind of spectacular or disgusting way if you'd gone by yourself. No offence but you would have and I didn't really want to come, but I did. But I'm not hating it at all."

Vanessa smiled. "I suppose I asked for that really didn't I," she said. "I was rather awful yesterday, and I am terribly sorry as you know, and you've already saved my life once, now you seem to be doing it again, and you are probably right. I mean it's only that my skirt snuffed the motor out that it didn't mangle my legs or something. But I'm glad you are not hating being here, I wouldn't want you to be doing that when you're helping me out so much. So, why?"

"I don't know," Amanda replied thoughtfully. "The fact is, I am actually enjoying this a bit, but I feel, well, a bit disloyal. Not in too bad a way, but it's nice to talk to you, like it was with Vera but, we were all there together. This is, well."

"You miss your home?" Vanessa asked.

"Probably. I mean it's daft, to miss a chunk of wood, but, yes, I do, already," Amanda smiled.

Vanessa hadn't meant the Mayfly, and was puzzled as to how this could be home. Surely this was just a schoolgirl adventure, running away only to be caught later.

"But I thought you missed your family," she said. "I did at first, when I ran away."

170

"Jim has no family as such. He's been passed around the place, and mine," Amanda tailed off.

"So." Vanessa launched the sixty-four thousand dollar question. "Tell me about Jim, what does he mean to you."

"Everyone seems interested in that one," Amanda tried to side-step the question but failed.

"Well, two of you, on a boat together." Vanessa's interrogation continued with, what from anyone else would have been a piercing stare, but from her, was simply a look that asked you to reveal your soul in a way which could not be refused.

"That too, but, what he means to me? To be honest it's out of my range to think of it. We are what we are, if we is the right word. I am me and he is Jim and we sort of get along, and that's about it," Amanda frowned slightly.

"So why the long look into the distance. If he was never coming back, I mean what then?" Vanessa asked calmly.

When someone frightened Amanda as a child, or there was a thunderstorm approaching, she felt an odd sensation, almost tension behind her knees. It isn't an uncommon feeling and may well be caused by a release of adrenalin or some other bodily substance into the bloodstream. She felt this now, though only just perceptibly, but there for sure. Again she swerved the issue.

"Why ever would he not come back, anyway it's me going away from him at the moment, not the other way round," she said.

"But I shan't be seeing Rick again, and I am not really awfully worried. So why?" Vanessa's answer was rather quick.

"You are a bit like a terrier aren't you," Amanda smiled.

"I expect I am, but you saved my life, and I would like you to be happy," Vanessa replied.

"And I am," Amanda said firmly.

"So, are you going to tell me?"

Amanda was silenced for a while, and continued to steer the pontoon along the canal. She could feel Vanessa's gaze though and it unnerved her somewhat.

"I'd like to tell you the definitive truth," she said. "But I really don't know what that is. So much of everything just happens, there's no script, and for the short time I have known him things just keep happening to us. Like having to run for it, Jim getting arrested, us meeting you, this. It all

171

just happens.   Jim won't leg it, nor will I, so I trust the guy, and he trusts me I think.   I mean I haven't asked him or anything but."

And here again Amanda cut herself short, not wanting to reveal the confidences that they had shared over the past days.   If she had mentioned these, no doubt Vanessa would have worked the truth from her and she did not want to betray a trust.

"You know each other a lot more than I knew Rick," Vanessa replied, almost mournfully.   "That's something.   It's so different, almost alien to me," she paused to gather her thoughts.   "When I was with him, it was everything to me, but it wasn't me although it seemed like my life.   Now I have just walked away and I feel nothing.   You haven't even asked anything of each other have you."

"I asked Jim to dress up as me!" Amanda said with a laugh in her voice. "That was pretty big."

"Did he?" Vanessa asked.

"Well, yes, of course he did, but it just happened," Amanda smiled again.   "Like I said.   Things do, well they do to us anyway."

This led to various tales of their escapades so far, with Vanessa reminiscing about her days at boarding school and finally had the desired effect of pushing the subject away from how Amanda felt about Jim.   It took the subject away from the spoken domain anyway.   The question still begged an answer, but Amanda lacked any kind of experience to frame it. In a quieter moment, she thought to herself, "Things happen, that's all."

And things did happen.   It was well after dark that the battery finally gave up and the headlamp dimmed to a glow that made it dangerous to keep moving.   Worse than that, they were just about in the middle of nowhere so far as could be seen.   Amanda, who was steering screwed her eyes up in the last of the failing light and, slowing the motor as far as she could, took the Chrysophyllax Diver close enough to the bank to make a jump for it with the ropes in her hand.

"This is going to have to do, we'll hit something if we go on, I mean it'd be alright if there was moonlight, but without anything we're stuffed," she said despondently.

"What about Jim?   Won't he worry?" Vanessa's face was barely discernible in the gloom.

"He'd worry a damn sight more if I have an accident.   We can't be far away from where we're going, so I'll just have to make time up tomorrow. It's not ideal but it'll have to do.   No offence meant," Amanda said.

It was a tall order to take the boat back over two days run in less than half that time, and they had almost made it, but Vanessa was ready to accept her helper's judgement and stop. She would have been willing to stop as soon as darkness had fallen, and had been happy for Amanda to steer in the failing light too. They had eaten on the run so there was nothing much left to do except turn in for the night. They were both exhausted after the non stop run and were more than ready for sleep.

"I'm not sure how we manage this." Vanessa said sheepishly. "But there's only the one bed, I think the seats may be meant to be two more but."

She looked over at Amanda who had spread out on one of the bench seats in the front of the cabin and saw that she was already sound asleep so she took the blanket from her double bunk and placed it over her.

Jim stared out into the pitch dark, he had waited a long time for Amanda to turn up before having his tea but hunger eventually got the better of him. He was pretty sure that progress of the Chrysophyllax Diver had obviously not gone as planned, so he decided to stay put until she turned up.

"This," he thought. "Is what it would have been like."

He felt relaxed and for a time almost enjoyed the solitude, then a pang of disloyalty caught him unawares. It had been his intention to sail off into the distance, and leave all his troubles behind, an impossible notion at best but he had sailed off with another person instead. The night was calm and moonless, the only illumination coming from some distant street lighting, the air was fresh but not cold enough to worry about so he just sat, and looked out across the canal until eventually he decided it was time to sleep.

Chapter 11

The sun was just beginning to come through the curtains as the smell of toast and wood smoke wafted across the room to the sofa on which he slept.   Other members of the commune had stirred earlier, knowing that they should get their new guest off to school. He had turned up in the back yard of their squat some weeks previously and had emphatically pleaded with them not to give him back to the home that he had left, bringing with him a vinyl holdall with what looked to be all his worldly possessions in it. They thought at the time that he would only stay the one night but it seemed that wherever he had been staying had not taken the trouble to inform anybody that he was missing.   The lad, who had told them he was ten years old, was pleasant enough and and he seemed to fit in well with the comings and goings of the commune.   Although the members were against most things to do with the establishment, they also felt a curious responsibility towards the newcomer, making them want to do their best for him at al times.   So they fed him, kept his school uniform clean, ensured he did his homework and tried as best they could to entertain him in the evenings without the help of a television. He in turn was not too bad at the piano and was able to join in their music when they all sat round to share songs.   Slowly sleep left him and the smell of breakfast took over the rest of the job of waking.   He sat up blinking in the sunlight and smiled.   This was what it must feel like to fall on his feet.   The previous people who were supposed to care for him hadn't really.   It wasn't so much that they were deliberately cruel, they just had no time for him, never spoke or corrected him and sometimes forgot to feed him.   He often came home from school to find doors locked and nobody in until quite late. Eventually it happened, one day he just didn't get up and nobody bothered to wake him.   On hearing the last person leave he packed his bag and left for a new life.   The general idea was good, but that was all it was, an idea. There was no plan behind it so he wandered aimlessly throughout the day and would have returned to what hadn't ever been home, despite the authorities having listed it as such, except for the fact that he was by then quite lost.   He tried the back gate of an old and derelict looking house and wandered into the yard at the same time as a tall girl dressed in Indian cloth with a shock of unkempt black hair tied under a bright headscarf came out of the back door. She was calm and not frightened by the intruder, mainly because she didn't see him as such.

"Hello," she said calmly. "I'm Miranda, welcome to our commune and who are you?"

He didn't like telling lies and so used a name that was his but not the one he commonly used.

"I'm Alec," he said nervously.

"Well, come in Alec and have something to eat," Miranda replied. "It looks like you've been on the road some time."

Back in the present, he had seated himself with the others and was enjoying home made bread toasted on the wood fired range, and a mug of tea before what was becoming the usual trip to school on the back of Paul's ageing Panther motorcycle. Things happen though, and a loud crashing bang on the door signified a police raid, and the end of the commune that had done nothing but good to him.

In a different place the same sun, coupled with the vague aroma of lawns being mowed at school towards the end of summer term, brought Amanda to wakefulness. It was morning, and the surroundings were not what she expected at all. The confines of the small cabin of the Mayfly had been distorted, opposite her was a set of glass fronted drawers containing entirely the wrong labels for the foodstuffs they contained. Then she remembered, the tea and coffee were kept along with the sugar in the drawer marked "Men's Singlets," and the cutlery in the one labelled "Shirts." She set about lighting the gas and making a cup of tea for herself and her travelling companion. Although somewhat dreamlike due to the eccentricity of the interior, this was reality and she was in the cabin of the Chrysophyllax Diver.

"So you are awake?" Vanessa shouted over the engine noise. "I thought I should get going, I mean you have to get back and I have to do this alone next time so I just went for it."

"Tea?" Amanda shouted. "I'll be up with it in a bit."

Vanessa was dressed in old jeans and a sweater, with her hair tied back under a scarf. She had watched Amanda throughout the previous day and learned the knack of starting the motor, in theory at the very least. On her first attempt she gave a terrific pull to the cord and the thing started on half choke. It almost stopped soon after but she released the lever just in time. She felt quite proud at the success, which came at the expense of an elbow banged on the cabin door when the starter cord came away from the pulley, but was surprised that this had not woken Amanda. Knowing how much work the girl had put in the day before and feeling that she should have pulled her weight some more, she let Amanda sleep.

"Blimey, we're nearly back!" Amanda exclaimed as she brought two mugs of tea and a packet of chocolate biscuits through the door.

"I see you've found my stash!" Vanessa laughed. "Rick told me that they were bourgeois so I hid them!"

Soon they were approaching a line of moored boats, some of which had the distinct look that they had been in the same place for a long time. Vanessa steered the Chrysophyllax Diver towards a gap between two ex work-boats that had been altered in a similar, if less well engineered way, as Vera's Crimson Lake was. At just the right moment she swung the motor round to bring the pontoon into a turn and stopped it. With both ropes in her hand she neatly hopped ashore and checked the forward motion with the bow line whilst closing the gap between boat and bank with the stern one.

"There," she said. "Not bad if I do say it myself! I think I shall live here and commute to college, then I can have some peace in the evenings."

On finally waking Jim found that this was no police raid, instead it was a publican, who had walked down the canal with his dog on his usual constitutional. Before setting out he had received a phone call and, having found the intended recipient, wanted to divulge the information he had.

"Your name Jim?" he asked as Jim put his head through the cabin door. As he didn't immediately reply, the man went on.

"Amanda says you may as well go on until lunch, and she'll meet you up at the next village. She said you'll know where she means."

"Right," Jim answered, still not quite out of the sense of unreality created by his dream. "Thanks, she must have taken longer than she thought."

"Aye, playing nursemaid to the beatniks or whatever they called themselves," the man on the towpath laughed.

"She was, but only the one," Jim replied. "I'm not sure what happened

176

to Rick, but she needed help, and we couldn't leave her, well, Amanda couldn't."

"Aye she's a good 'un that lass of yours. Now good day, I have to be gettin' on." With that he was away up the towpath with his terrier fast on his heels.

"How on earth does everyone know everything, wherever we go!" Jim thought as he set about preparing for the day. He made a special effort to keep everything neat and tidy, not wanting to show himself up when Amanda returned. And there was the one they always seemed to get wrong, his train of thought continued as he worked. Amanda was not *his* lass nor could she ever be. That said, there was no reason to let her down either, so the necessary routine was gone through, and the Mayfly was on her way in what must have been close to record time. The run over a few miles of canal was pleasant, with the early sun clouded slightly since he woke, though there was no threat of rain. His recollection of the dream was not unpleasant, though he wished he could get in touch with the group of people that were so kind to him when they really didn't have to be. Once the police had raided the squat he had never seen nor heard of them, they were never mentioned, except by the counsellor who seemed to have a keener than healthy interest in any wrongs they may have done him than any benefits he may have derived from his stay.

"Wrongs?" He remembered saying. "What do you count as wrong? Home made bread? Getting me to school on time? Making sure my homework was done?"

Of course nobody believed him, he was only young and couldn't possibly be telling the truth. On consideration, he thought, they probably weren't that interested in truth, just wanted some information about his so called captors. Miranda and Paul were one of about four couples that lived in the house, all of whom were never anything other than kind to him. He had pleaded to go back and have them, all of them, as guardians but apparently they were a bad example to someone so impressionable. So they sent him to a children's home for a while where the abuse that haunted his nightmares and clouded his moods for years afterwards took place. His thoughts rounded back to Amanda, as the village came into sight with its narrow waisted brick bridge, and canal-side pub, which looked as good a place as any to tie up.

177

Vanessa's old VW minibus trundled along the lanes quite amicably, it was noisy, and pretty well devoid of any form of luxury but it was fairly reliable, or so Vanessa said.   Amanda was enjoying the view across the fields as sleep eventually got the better of her again.   The previous day had been long and she was still pretty tired even though she didn't really want Vanessa to know.   Had she stayed awake she would, as Vanessa did, have herd a sound similar to the Mayfly hitting an underwater obstruction as sometimes happened, only rather a lot louder.   The lagging of a thick coat and two sweaters plus scarf and seat belt saved her from anything much more than a good shaking, and she remained asleep.   One persons discarded pop bottle though had come rather too close to ending two young lives on a sunny, but cool morning in early Summer.   Vanessa had responded as well as was possible to the sudden loss of the front nearside tyre, but was in some pain from what would later be diagnosed as two suspected cracked ribs.   She was able to move away from her companion, who she had landed on when the vehicle clipped a pothole in the road surface some yards further on from the offending bottle, finally snatching the steering wheel from her hand and landing them almost on their side in the ditch.   No windows were broken and there was no smell of petrol which, although no guarantee of safety, was at least reassuring.   The old minibus had managed to stop short of overbalancing and was sitting with two wheels in the ditch at an angle of about 45 degrees, Vanessa slowly opened the driver side door, and clambered out to see what could be done. There was nobody about, except for a tractor about two fields away.

"Amanda," she said softly.   "Amanda, can you hear me?"

After a pause that was more painful to Vanessa than her ribs, Amanda opened an eye.

"I knew I had a slanted view on life, but this is a bit much even for me," she said looking at the road from an entirely new angle.   "You're lousy at parking this thing, I'd stick to the boat if I was you!"

"Listen," Vanessa said quietly, trying to be calm.   "We've run off the road.   I think we hit something in the gutter or something broke.   Are you O.K.?   I think you got knocked out."

"For someone that's just been in a car crash, I'd say I wasn't too bad at all," Amanda smiled in reply.

"I'm going to climb out and try and get help."   Vanessa said, will you be alright for a minute?"

Amanda gave her assurances and Vanessa scrambled fully out of the

178

vehicle to attract the attention of the tractor driver. Somewhat puzzled at the situation, and unsure even if she was still asleep and dreaming, she felt around to see if there were any signs of her having been hit by anything. Deciding that she was neither asleep, nor dead, she too clambered out of the old minibus to see what could be seen.

It was getting later than Jim had thought it should, so he went up to the pub, reasoning that they would more than likely know his business as well as, if not better than he did, to ask if there were any hold ups. The landlady soon answered the door to tell him in no uncertain terms that it was not opening time for some while, and he should not bother her. Although she seemed rather fierce he stood his ground and asked if she had heard anything of Amanda and Vanessa.

"Aye," she replied. "I'd heard some lasses in an old van had run into the ditch a way back, right mess its made."

Taken aback, Jim almost shouted, "No! Are they alright? I mean how bad a mess is the van? I've got to get to them!"

"Hold your horses," she said in a slightly kinder voice. "And what could you do if you did run all the way there. I heard it and I heard they were bein' looked after so don't fret too much. I think one took a knock or two but she'll mend."

"What about the other one? I mean I don't want either hurt, but," Jim blurted.

"Aye and you're soft on one. You've had a shock lad, I'm sorry I said it like that, I didn't know it was you at first. Now come in and you can sit and wait. You shouldn't be alone, not if you're soft on one of the lasses. I'll see if I can find anything out, mean time you need a drink even if it isn't openin' time." With that she poured him some whisky and added a good measure of ginger ale to it.

"Now, sit and sip that slowly, I'll go see what I can see."

All Jim could see at that moment was the alternative outcome to the incident.

"Soft on one," he thought. "Does it always have to come down to that, and especially when things are being taken away from you. I mean I was happy and when I'm happy," he sipped the drink as instructed and then thought again, only more clearly.

"Surely everything has two sides," he continued the thread, almost but not quite talking to himself. "I mean Miranda and the folks back at the squat accepted me, and they got on with me. I was as happy to be there as they were to have me there, and they must have got a lot of shit from the arseholes that broke the place up, even more for the so called kidnap of me!"

Another sip and he returned to the matter at hand, what had happened to Vanessa and Amanda, his thoughts cleared on that one too.

"I really mean nothing in this, they have had the accident and here am I thinking of *my* loss when I have no right or claim on the word. Amanda would be well pissed off if she'd got herself killed, except she'd be." Another big sip to keep the thought at bay.

"No. She said that one of them had taken a bit of a knock that's all. Be sensible!"

Jim's thoughts raced as the whisky took the desired effect, the landlady had known, almost instinctively how much to give him, so that he would not be harmed but would be able to lose himself in what ultimately became futile musings on just about any subject he fixed on. She had not made him drunk, but mellow, mellow enough to rest for a while. He was left to sleep through the lunchtime opening, which was not a busy one, and nobody disturbed him as his dreams switched between the squat, and his current life as a boat dweller, sometimes merging into one reality that was, on waking, just about completely unfathomable. It was after closing time that he woke, to be confronted with a pub lunch, cooked for him by the the same landlady that he had viewed as some kind of military dictator-in-waiting on first meeting.

"There lad, get that inside you, I know your lady-friend won't have any truck with meat so I've done my best for you with what I had. Nothing wrong with a good meat pie that's what I say, but it takes all sorts, and I don't want to be the one that's causing you to upset her," she said with a smile.

"Thanks, um," Jim said cautiously. "Let me know what I owe you won't you,."

"I'll not be wanting your money son, you've had a shock, and it's often worse for the ones that have to wait and see what happens than them that's got the troubles in the first place," she replied still smiling.

"Well, thanks again," Jim smiled, wanting to ask how so many people knew so much about the pair, but knowing he would not get much by way of an answer. So he satisfied himself with practicality.

"I don't suppose you know what's going on with them do you?" he asked tentatively.

"I'd heard that Jim Long, who farms a way down the road saw the van go into the ditch, I think he'd have pulled it back out again for them. He's a bit of a stickler though, so he won't have them drive it until he's looked at it, and he won't want them moving on until the doc's seen to them."

And so it was. Jim Long, a man in his mid forties saw the van abruptly stop, and was in the process of turning to take a better look when he had seen Vanessa waving. The damage to the old vehicle didn't look to be much more than an extra twist to the already twisted front bumper, and of course a badly shredded front tyre, but he would have none of them just changing the wheel and continuing.

"Nah," he said through his cigarette. "Won't do, that won't. Steerin' might have got a knock too. I'll jack it an' have it right by tomorrow for you if it is buggered. I can get a cheap tyre if you want."

"That's very kind of you," Vanessa smiled, beginning to feel more of the pain from her brief contact with the steering wheel. "Let me know what it all costs and I'll pay you straight away."

"I'll do that, and I'll take you to Doc Williams too. You can get another car but you can't get a new you you knows," Jim added.

"I'm really not that bad," Vanessa lied. "And Amanda actually slept through it," she added, telling the truth.

"We'll let Doc Williams see what's to do. You've hit something in the car, was you driving?"

"Well, yes I was, but it isn't bad, I did have a belt on," Vanessa admitted.

"Then you clipped the wheel. I done that once and cracked three ribs, bloody painful it were too. And your mate, slept through it? Sure she weren't knocked cold? Doc'll sort you out without fuss, we all trust him round here, and he'll not talk to anyone about nothin' if you're, well, whatever. What I see is two lasses and a mishap, so let's do the right thing," Jim said reassuringly.

The Doc, as he had been referred to was close to retirement, and very much the last of his kind, running his small practice from the next village. His thin white hair, fraying tweed jacket, and horn-rimmed round glasses made him look like a character from a television drama set in the thirties. He had seen many people from birth through to having their own family,

181

and some sadly to their eventual departure.   Despite his age he was thorough, and used his accumulated knowledge where equipment and the obvious reluctance of the two patients to go to a hospital prevailed.   The two had eventually agreed to see him partly because of the insistence of their rescuer, but mostly because Vanessa was a bit worried about her ribs which were becoming more and more painful.   Eventually though, both were discharged as having escaped anything more serious than a couple of bruises.   If Vanessa's ribs were cracked it was the sort of damage that nothing much other than rest would cure, and this she was instructed to do. The Doc had poked and prodded around any area that could have been a cause of Amanda being knocked out, and found no sign of any impact, and had to agree that she must have been well asleep at the time.   The man was so pleasant, and well mannered that Amanda felt really bad about giving a false name, still being worried about anyone from back home that may yet be after her.

Back at the Mayfly, Jim sat and waited, he was glad of the company and the atmosphere of the pub earlier on, but now he felt the need to be alone, and in a familiar environment.   The home that had been his shared residence for no more than a few weeks was now one that he found more comfortable being in than any.   It was that time between late afternoon and early evening, and he was setting about preparing a cup of tea, still hoping that Amanda would be back for an evening meal.   His attention was distracted by the familiar patter of an air cooled Volkswagen engine, one that he had heard described as similar to a bag of bolts trapped in a vacuum cleaner.   Looking up he saw two familiar faces in the front, as the vehicle, pulled into the pub car park.   The farmer had managed to fix the damage, which was only minor, whilst the two were at the doctors.   Jim put an arm up to wave recognition and then wrote the letter "T" in the air to which the reply was an emphatic thumbs up from both occupants of the vehicle. Gauging that Amanda would probably not want a big fuss, he set about making three cups of tea, and finding some biscuits, allowing the pair in the VW minibus to come across at their own speed.

"You two O.K?" he asked as they came into earshot.

"You heard then?"   Amanda saw the mix of worry and relief blended like poorly applied make-up on Jim's face.

"Everyone knows everything on the canals," he replied through slightly

182

raised eyebrows.

"Just like me to be in a car crash and sleep through it!" Amanda smiled. "Vanessa's a bit sore but the Doc reckons she'll mend in a few days so all in all we were dead lucky. Even the minibus only got a bent bumper."

"Looking at it." added Vanessa, "It was pretty bent before we set off, I think it may have actually straightened it a bit. I am sorry for running off the road like that though."

"Don't be daft," Amanda mock-scolded. "You heard what Jim the farmer said. You had the front tyre ripped to pieces, and you did well not to up-end us fully in the ditch, but what would I know. I was asleep!"

Tea and biscuits were shared with much conversation about the afternoon's events until it was time for Vanessa to head back to her chosen home, the Chrysophyllax Diver. Amanda made her promise to phone the pub on arrival, almost sounding motherly or even grandmotherly in her tone. They promised to keep in touch by whatever means, exchanged such addresses as they had, and the VW clattered out of the car park to head back to the city, a journey of not much more than an hour.

"We'd better phone Marie at the shop you know," Jim said quietly. "She may hear you've had a crash and then everyone would worry unnecessarily."

Amanda agreed and they set off across the lawn to use the pay phone in the pub entrance. As they walked, Jim said in a contemplative tone, "Look, I know it's going to be a bit late, but do you mind setting off for a tie up a couple of miles off. I mean it's nice being with people, but, I think I'd just like to be a bit quieter this evening. I'll do us a good something for tea even if it is late."

"I know what you mean," Amanda replied. "It's been a bit of an odd few days with those two, I'd like to unscramble my mind a bit too."

Jim left Amanda once she was on the phone so that he could set about getting the Mayfly ready to move, having made the excuse to the landlady that they needed all the time they could get, on account of their being behind schedule by over a day. She had agreed to let them know as soon as Vanessa called, so that they could set off straight after. There was not really much to do, he topped the tank up, checked the lights, filled the big lamp in case the battery failed before they reached the tie up, and then all was set. He saw Amanda coming back across the lawn, having missed the fact that she had been on the phone for some time. He did, however, notice the furrow between her eyes, that familiar look of either puzzlement or the precursor to fear. This, he was pretty sure, was puzzlement, and his observation was proved correct when Amanda greeted him with.

"That was one of the strangest phone calls that I have ever had," she said.

"I thought you looked a bit off," he replied. "What's to do?"

"Well, for a start Marie wasn't too pleased about the crump in the minibus, but she eventually promised to play it down when she spoke to my folks. No, the main thing seems to be that there are all kinds of people, you know, men in suits and posh cars, keeping turning up at the island," Amanda frowned.

"Any idea why?" Jim asked.

"Not too sure as yet but they now definitely can't sell the little bungalow, so it's just there and nobody knows what to do about it. Worrying thing though is that there's a lot of geezers want to talk to me, which could spell trouble if I don't keep, my head down for the next few days. Even if I do for that matter," Amanda replied despondently.

"Surely they can't touch you after your birthday?" Jim said, knowing that this was almost certainly not true.

"I wouldn't be so sure, Marie said to tread carefully and watch my back. There's something going on with my mum and dad too, well something that affects them. Marie reckons they may be off the hook if things go right," Amanda smiled.

"Surely that's good news isn't it?" Jim said.

"It would be but again she reckons that situation isn't safe either, she said the affair was far from over. There were some decidedly unpleasant guys turned up at the island a few days ago looking for my folks, and Dave had a bit of a run in with them. He warned her that they may come looking for me, but neither she nor Dave have a clue who they are," Amanda frowned again.

"Did you tell her all that stuff about the factory and the arrest? It may have something to do with things?" Jim asked.

"I said a bit but I'm not sure she knew what I was on about. We need to do a bit more."

"We still have a good half hour before Vanessa is even likely to phone. Maybe someone like Clive Prentice would have a bit of an idea what's going on?" Jim suggested.

They were lucky to find the man still working, and he was glad to hear from them.

184

"The box hasn't packed up yet has it?" he asked. "Oh, and I'll have to sort out how to pay you at some point when the two months is up won't I."

"No," Amanda replied. "It's nothing like that, we just need a bit of advice. We sort of created a bit of a stink at Carver and Green and it looks like there may be some other things happening as a result of it. People have been round the bungalow on the island. Not very nice ones either so far as I know."

"It'd be just like the little weasel to try and sort things by less than legal means, but he isn't going to have a clue where you are, not if he's looking down south, that's if it is him, so you're safe for now I'd say, but Marie, it is Marie isn't it, is right, you'd best watch your back, and I know I'm being selfish but don't let him get wind of the box you have. Listen, can you ring me back in a day or so and I'll try and find out what the bum-boil is up to," Clive said.

Amanda thanked him then she and Jim set back across the lawn to the Mayfly.

"It's going to be quite like old times," Jim smiled.

"Why are you looking so happy, this could be serious!" Amanda scolded.

"And it hasn't been all along? We beat one lot, and so we'll beat this git too, if he's even involved. Has it occurred to you that it may just be the company that thought they'd bought the bungalow trying things on? Nope, we'll keep the flag flying," he smiled again.

"You're nuts, you are! Stark staring nuts!" Amanda smiled, and the two finished crossing the lawn in silence.

The run to the next tie up was rather a longer distance than Jim had estimated, but the battery had recently been charged and they both secretly enjoyed moving in the dark. The headlamp wasn't that bright, but adequate to see by, and there was no need on a canal for the convention of traditional navigation lights, so they stayed in the box they were stored in to economise on power. Vanessa had taken rather longer than planned to reach her destination, admitting a spate of very cautious driving along the country lanes, but had not been so late as to worry either Jim or Amanda who, despite the unsettling news they'd had earlier, were in high spirits. As Amanda steered Jim set about preparing the ingredients for the meal that he had promised as soon as they had tied up. The canal took on a different look after nightfall, the water ahead was mirror like, returning surprisingly quickly to the same state after their passing.

"Someone at Saracen's told me it was a very well designed hull," Jim mentioned, when Amanda commented on the lack of wake. "That's probably why we run on so little fuel I guess," he added.

Rounding a shallow curve, the headlamp picked out a clear part of the bank that looked suitable for the night. Amanda pointed, and Jim got a torch to shine directly down into the canal to gauge the depth as they slowly approached. A little closer and he probed the area carefully with the back of the mop to check for any sharp objects, and finding none he put a thumb up to signal it was all O.K. With all made fast for the night the promised fry up became ever more welcome.

As Jim worked away at the cooking, Amanda looked over to him and, speaking without thinking, said, "Have you ever thought of trying to find Miranda and the people that took you in?"

She only knew part of the story from one of their late night conversations, and would normally have been a bit more cautious about such a question as she knew Jim had suffered in the past. Her question related directly to such a period, and she really did not want to upset him, but she'd asked, and it was out now. The answer soon came.

"I have thought about it, and tried once or twice, but they were kind of moved on by the coppers and the council after they had supposedly kidnapped me. I mean, being as I was pretty much the cause of their trouble I wonder if they'd even want to see me again," he said.

"They don't sound the sort of people that would hold a grudge, and the police would have raided the place anyway, it wasn't because not you. If the people at the commune had been less caring they could have turned you away as being too much of a risk. No, I expect they'd like to know," Amanda replied.

"Bit immaterial really though isn't it. It was all a long time ago and I don't even know if they'd have stayed together. They were the real deal though," Jim smiled at the memory.

"Not like Rick and Vanessa?" Amanda said.

"No way like them. I mean I know Vanessa turned out to be an O.K. person but."

"Well, you could have got lucky with her you know!" Amanda winked.

"Depends what you mean by luck," Jim said, rather coldly. "I think you'd have a different definition to me. Anyway, tea's ready so let's stuff our faces!"

Amanda was handed a plate with all manner of food on it, all of which

186

smelled good, making her feel more hungry than she properly was.

As she started on the feast she thought, and again almost spoke, "We'll see what we can do about them, if they can be found, I'll find 'em for you Jimbo."

With all measurements made and Clive's box stowed where it would not easily be found, they both looked at each other. The first to speak was Amanda.

"Hang the washing up!" she smiled. "We can do it while we're on the run tomorrow, let's just get some rest."

Jim agreed with her, as the next few days were going to be hard work. They had lost nearly two days and had to be at the gathering, that was planned in another city which was still quite a way to the north, at a set time. It was true that Jim could quite happily have missed the event altogether, but he'd promised to keep to the set schedule and did not want to let Dave Harris, or the organisation that was funding the carriage of watches by water, down.

Chapter 12

There was little time for conversation as they moved forward faster than they had yet managed, gaining more than two hours on their normal daily mileage, but both had plenty of time to think as they worked the locks or steered. The weather had turned somewhat morose, with cloud and intermittent drizzle that threatened, but never achieved, much more. The weather itself was tolerable, but it turned the stone and concrete of the lock sides and foot-ways very slippery and treacherous. They could have taken one of two quicker routes than the one they had settled for, but this would have involved either a brief coastal run, which neither of them fancied, or crossing the wide, and rather busy river in the city. The latter was discussed at length, but they were not even sure that they would be able to access the parts of the city they needed to due to the unknown state of the waterway by the docks. So they went the long way round to gain access via the north, which would take them to the gathering with the added advantage that they would be navigating the stretch of canal that people were trying to preserve, the only down side being the need for extra vigilance for any underwater obstructions that may have endangered the plywood hull of the Mayfly. As they moved forward Jim noticed that Amanda became rather quiet, putting it down at first to a combination of delayed shock from the accident, and hard work making her tired, but after a couple of days he was worried enough to ask. It was not so much that she was abrupt in speaking, but that sort of difference that only someone close may notice. The animation in her expression was less, smiles of recognition, though warm, were brief, and he saw that furrow now and again just above her nose. On a long pound, whilst she was steering, and he was making lunch he finally put voice to his concerns.

"O.K. Buster, what's eating you?" he asked. Not subtle, but it raised a smile.

Amanda thought a while, eventually answering, "It's like, well, you seem to cope with things changing without notice, I guess because you've had to. Like you can be so laid back sometimes about stuff, unless it's something that ruffles your fur."

"That's about me though, I hope I haven't," Jim said nervously

"No! Don't be daft, you haven't done anything, it's just that I thought I could hack this, and, well, most of it I can, but just right now. Well. Things would have been a bit different, a lot different if things hadn't happened."

"You want your old life back?" Jim asked.

"Well. Yes, but no, but bits of it, like, well. I can't really say without sounding like a spoilt brat." Amanda's voice tailed off.

"Say," Jim said firmly.

"Look, I don't really know, but it's like some things. Well, it's like time can go past and then suddenly you retire and you just leave the company and not go back," Amanda frowned.

"But you're nowhere near retirement yet?" Jim tried to work out what his friend was trying to say before he continued, finally realising that a big day was approaching for her, and it would be the first one spent without her family.

"Look Mand, you are no spoilt brat, no way," he said. "Just don't be sad about things that's all. We've this do to go to, the festival thing. If you want the truth I'd rather eat shit, but we promised so we go. Then time is our own. We have to get across country before the next delivery and that's nearly a week's run on it's own, maybe more. Hopefully we can pick up a few deliveries from the do as well, we need the cash." It wasn't all he wanted to say but was the best he could manage.

Amanda smiled, albeit briefly, and her expression was still a bit wistful, but it was a start.

"You're not too keen on crowds are you," she observed with a degree of accuracy.

"There's different kinds of crowd, somehow I don't really feel too good about this one, but I'm probably wrong so don't read too much into what I just said. Fact is we have to be there and probably take part in something. I sort of find that a bit unnerving that's all," Jim smiled.

Over the next few days the summer finally started feeling like the season it was supposed to be. The sun made even the more moribund industrial parts they passed through take on a more optimistic look. Weeds that had self seeded in gutters and brickwork flowered in a riot of disorganised colour, as though a vertical garden had been planted by an abstract expressionist. Stone bridges warmed in colour once dry, and slowly the optimism began to pervade all things, lifting both Jim's and

189

Amanda's mood until both found themselves actually looking forward to the forthcoming festival. Their progress had been sufficient to more than make up for lost time so they were able, over the two days before the event, to take life at a slower pace once again. The canal had more traffic than they had yet experienced due to others making for the same place, but it was far from crowded, and they satisfied themselves with the odd wave of recognition and an exchange of comments on the weather where necessary. Eventually they were heading, along with a varied selection of vessels, ranging from full size ex-working narrowboats to those similar in size to, and smaller than the, Mayfly, creating queues at locks, something they had not seen since the river.

"Well, this is it," Jim said nervously. "I guess somebody will be expecting us."

"That's if Dave bothered to tell them it is us and not him," Amanda smiled. "They may run us out of town if you don't look like him."

"We're not exactly a stereotypical working boat though are we," Jim observed. "I mean not like those seventy foot monsters."

"No, but you said the Mayfly was based on a work boat hull?" Amanda said.

"You know that I embellished that just a little though don't you!" Jim smiled wryly.

"So what's wrong with a little, well, bullshit. I mean, if it's for a good cause," Amanda smiled, more warmly than Jim had seen for a while. "We'll be alright here Jimbo, I'll protect your virtue!"

It was just past midday when they arrived at the broad area of water at the top of a flight of locks that took the waterway down and eventually into the dock complex. Several boats were already there, some tied two and three deep. The hope of getting any space on or close to the tow path was neither desirable nor possible, and they settled for an offer of attaching their lines close to the front of a narrow boat that was still in its original guise, many there having been converted for dwelling, cruising, or both. There was quite a step up to get off despite the fact that the vessel had been partially loaded with old concrete railway sleepers so that it looked more like a working boat, but at least they had some degree of privacy should they have wanted it. The owners were a pleasant enough couple in their mid thirties who had purchased it at an auction a couple of years previously and had no particular plans in mind, and not enough money to carry them to completion even if they had. Events were slowly kicking off, with the main day being the Saturday, and the general atmosphere seemed quite convivial.

"Let's go and explore," Jim said, in as positive a voice as he could muster.

After locking up, they scrambled across the bow of the narrowboat to get ashore and, deciding first to get any formalities out of the way they went looking for the person or persons in charge. Somebody pointed them to a converted or purpose built narrowboat of about forty feet in length, the owner of which was about to do some exploring himself. He was a man of similar age to Dave Harris but entirely more respectable looking, though friendly enough when approached.

"I was told to expect someone," he said cheerily. "On a work boat too. I believe you have a watch for me?."

"We do," Jim said proudly "One of many hand made ones imported from the Soviet Union."

"That'll be you, then. I expected you to be somewhat older," the man replied.

"We would have been," Amanda explained. "But Dave hurt his hip and couldn't make the trip so you get us instead, but we are a work boat. That is to say we have been working on a boat even if it's not a big one."

"Now I am intrigued," the man smiled. "I was expecting another narrowboat but I suppose it would take an awful lot of watches to fill one."

"We're from the Mayfly, over there," Jim pointed. It's not really a canal type boat, they use them for fishing off the coast of Scotland and the Orkneys."

"They have more guts than me then," the man replied. "And you say that your journey so far is entirely funded by your work with the little boat?"

"Well," Jim said. "Apart from the five pounds that I had, and anything Amanda brought with her when we started, sort of yes, I guess so. Not all cargo, I mean we did sing for our suppers once, and we are helping with some research for someone else, but the boat is what we have. Sort of our home and our living."

"You mean you really do it? Not just a weekend thing?" The man looked puzzled.

Amanda chipped in, "There's a lot that isn't what it seems but, as Jim

191

said, we neither of us have any other home than the Mayfly at the moment, and we have been running for a bit longer now than most people would have as a holiday so it's kind of by accident that we ended up doing this but there isn't anything else for us to do if you see what I mean."

"I'm not sure that I do see," the man frowned. "Are you running away from something?"

"Not as such," Jim rejoined the conversation. "We're taking life as it comes, and solving any issues as they present themselves, but we have to eat, so we work, and it's fine to do that in my book specially if the work is enjoyable. That sounds bad because I know the original boat crews had an awful life, but I can't change that. I can only live this one."

"Bloody hell," Amanda said, sounding rather surprised. "That was a bit profound, have you been drinking canal water again!"

The comment derailed what seemed to be becoming a bit of an interrogation and allowed the pair to find out what, if anything, was required of them.

"It would be interesting," the man said. "If you would be willing to come up and talk about your experiences. Maybe I can ask the theatre company to tag something on and talk with you at the end of a performance or something. Oh, and I'll see if I can drum up a bit more business for you carrying parcels if you like."

They both thanked him and set off looking around the site. There were numerous activities going on with various emergent canal preservation groups represented, some with stalls, some just displaying banners and flags from their boats. Slowly the carnival spirit took hold of the pair.

"We'll be O.K. after all, I think," Jim smiled. "Tell you what, I'm starved, lets go and get something off of a stall, spoil ourselves."

Although the main part of event was on the Saturday and Sunday, there were a good few people offering food with all profits going to their particular waterway of choice and it was not long before they had found one that specialised in vegetarian food at which they both treated themselves to a concoction of curried vegetables loosely assembled into a large bun. Unusual it was, but it was as good as it smelt when they approached the stall. It was well into the middle of the afternoon when they got back on board the Mayfly, and with a kettle on for tea, set about sprucing the little vessel up for the weekend's events. They were not long into the task when they heard a voice.

"Hi, I'm Tamsin from the theatre company, are you Jim and Amanda?"

"That's us," Amanda shouted back whilst tipping a bucket of grubby water into the canal. "It's O.K.," she added. "It's just deck moppings, muck from the canal being returned to its rightful place. We don't do pollution here."

Tamsin smiled. "Can I come aboard?" she asked.

As they sat down round mugs of tea, the three talked about their experiences and how they came to do what they were doing. It was surprising for each as to how much common chance had played a role in their being where they were.

"Look," Tamsin said tentatively. "The guy in charge of this, I forgot his name."

"We forgot to ask it," smiled Jim, who had moved well away from his earlier view of the event, and seemed quite relaxed.

"Well, whatever," Tamsin continued. "The big guy wants you to talk at the end of one of our performances that's if you and we don't mind, and we don't."

"We're O.K. with it," Amanda replied.

"Well, thing is," Tamsin now had an enthusiasm in her voice. "We all thought it may be a bit of fun to actually include you in a performance, kind of improvise it. I mean all of our stuff is based in truth, and comes from study of the experiences of working canal folk, and well, you are on the canal and you are working, and from what I have heard it's not a middle class hobby thing either."

"Bloody hell!" Amanda blurted. "Sorry. I never thought I was a Thespian! What do you think Jim?"

"I don't mind if you don't. It'd be less of a shocker than the stuff we did at the Quarry," he replied.

"That seems like it was in another lifetime," Amanda added wistfully. "But we did alright."

"Is that when you sang for your suppers?" Tamsin quizzed. "I heard about it from the guy that seems to be in charge. That reminds me, we'd have to pay you if that's O.K. I mean we have to pay all of our actors, it's like a part of our funding contract and that makes me seem such a fraud compared with you."

"Don't think about it," Amanda chirped. "Anyone offering us money is in our good books, you're in a different game to us, and you're trying to get the message across too. If someone funds you for it as well as your ticket sales then you'd be daft not to take the cash."

"So that's sorted," Tamsin smiled. "We'll write you in to a scene then we can talk through things. I'll be back later on if that's O.K. We have to move pretty quick because we perform tomorrow afternoon. Look, why don't you finish up what you are doing here, you know, what I disturbed you from, then come down to our boat and we can go through things then."

With this agreed, Jim and Amanda set to cleaning up every part of the Mayfly until it shone like an antique sideboard. Brass-work was all mirror like, ropes coiled like giant table mats, even the deed boxes were cleaned and any rust spots touched up with some black nail polish that Amanda had in her bag, but which she had never yet found a use for.

"I tried it once," she said. "But it just looked like I'd jammed my finger in a door so I put it in my bag and sort of forgot it."

When finished the little vessel bore no resemblance, except in general shape, to the piece of wood that Jim had taken pity on what seemed such a long time back. The hooped cover was fitted ready for the evening, and tied with a neatness they never usually had time for. The final touch was Amanda sweeping the canvas free of dust to give it a beautifully groomed appearance.

"We've done the old girl proud," Jim smiled. "Now let's go and see what the theatre people have in store for us."

The boat occupied by the Tamsin and the rest of the group was an old steel work-boat onto which a plywood cabin had been fitted, covering the hold. Due to lack of money, the lateral bracing chains were still in place, requiring people to climb over or duck under them. It looked comfortable though, if a bit crowded with all the things they had with them. Tamsin greeted the pair and introduced them to the other four people in the company and then they got down to work.

"We thought that the easiest thing for you two would be to appear as yourselves, you seem to look the part without having to try much," she said.

"Not sure how to take that one," Amanda muttered to Jim, who winked in acknowledgement.

"I meant it as a compliment," Tamsin hastily added. "What I meant was that you haven't made a point of trying to be traditional in either dress or choice of boat, it all looks like it was born out of necessity rather than design, which is pretty much how all the stuff with the working boats came about. So you two are the real deal so far as we can see, therefore why alter the truth."

194

"So what do we do?" Jim asked. "I mean being ourselves is O.K. What did you have in mind though?"

Here another of the cast spoke introducing himself as George. "We do a bit about the way everything is eventually meant to go by road, which is like Armageddon waiting to happen. Like why don't even the railways get a proper look in. You kind of fit in as a good illustration of how this canal kept profitable for much longer than others. It was a lot of local traffic that certainly helped, and that would be what a small boat on a lock free stretch would be really good at."

The part was honed down to a limited script with the provision for improvisation, which the whole group liked doing.

"Reacting to the situation we find ourselves in is a real buzz," Tamsin said.

"Some of the ones we have had to react to have been downright scary," Jim added, letting his voice speak a thought he'd have rather kept private.

"You two had trouble?" said another member who didn't give a name.

"You could say that," Amanda replied. "But that's a story for another place and time. I guess we need to read through or something."

There wasn't really that much to learn, just a few lines that meshed into the performance, which was mostly worked around songs and stories, theirs being just another to add to the list. The flow of performance was generally pretty loose, but centred round the waterways still having their role in the bigger picture, as Tamsin put it.

"You two have sung for your suppers so I am told? Would you mind joining in on some of the songs too? They're pretty simple," she added just as things were winding up.

Amanda and Jim were happy to join in and were given the words to some of the songs, quickly scribbled on old file paper.

"Come back a bit later if you can and we can have a bit of a sing together," said an unidentified cast member.

All was agreed, and they set off back to the neatly spruced Mayfly for supper, which had been slowly maturing in the hay-box all day. The two had settled in to the festival and were now actually looking forward to the next day, though Amanda still had a small touch of the wistful about her expression.

Jim was up early the next morning, saying he wanted to get some more

195

two stroke oil before the festival got under way.   They had stayed up too late the previous night with the theatre company and Amanda was quite happy to let him sneak off on his own to do the chore, even if it did seem a bit like obsessive attention to detail.   This allowed her to have a bit more of a rest before she had to stir herself into action.   It was almost an hour before he did return with a shopping bag and the gallon can of two stroke oil of the special variety required for their motor.   Carefully boarding the Mayfly he stowed some of the shopping, and then quietly set about preparing for breakfast.   Amanda, who had spent a leisurely amount of time washing and dressing popped her head through the cabin door.

"And I was going to do breakfast in bed for you today!"   Jim smiled. "Happy Birthday funny face!"

Amanda's eyes opened wide in surprise.   She was about to ask when Jim interrupted her.

"When I last spoke to Marie, she reminded me, but the penny had already dropped," he said.

"Oh, and we sorted out forwarding some post so there's a wad of stuff for you from the post office, and, well, um.   There's this too."   Jim thrust an envelope and a small package into Amanda's hand.

"That's from me," he said, with a tinge of embarrassment in his voice.

As Jim set to do the breakfast Amanda opened the card, and present.   It was a small wristwatch.

"It's not a Russian one," Jim said.   "That'd be too much like work.   Just a Timex I'm afraid, but I hope it's O.K."

Amanda leant over and gave him a small kiss on the cheek.

"Thanks Jim," she said warmly.   "This isn't where I thought I'd be spending this birthday, but, thinking on, there's no other place that'd be quite the same."

The pack that Jim had picked up from the post office contained cards from all the relatives, Dave at the island, and, most important, one from her parents.   She knew they wouldn't forget her, but the confirmation was more than welcome.   They had included a book token as a gift, together with a promise of a proper present when circumstances allowed.   As Jim finished preparing breakfast, Amanda found various ways of putting the cards up, thinking that it was a shame to leave them in a stack when people had gone to so much trouble sending them.   Sitting down to admire her work, she wound and put on the watch that her friend had given her.   Smiling, she looked up to see Tamsin.

196

"Hey!" she said. "Happy Birthday to you, why didn't you say?"

"How do you know it's not me?" Jim said with a wink.

"Well, unless you are hiding something, you aren't anyone's niece or daughter are you?" Tamsin replied.

"Um, dunno, I'd have to look. Want a cup of tea?" Jim smiled.

"No thanks, you two need some time together, but don't forget the run through, about eleven o'clock O.K." With that she left them to their own company.

After breakfast they had to go off and make the delivery of the watches to the organiser, as part of the opening which was due at about ten o'clock. This was pretty straightforward, and they were introduced as evidence that the canals were still fit for their original purpose. Whilst it was a bit embarrassing, the effect was that quite a number of small packages were entrusted to them for delivery after the gathering had drawn to a close. Their route was no secret and had in part been arranged by the same organisation as the festival so it was relatively easy to accommodate the extra work. The event was soon in full swing with what looked like close on two hundred boats present, and it had attracted the local press and television, all of which helped the cause. As the pair wandered through the stalls and chatted with people they lost track of time, and it was gone quarter past eleven when they made a dash for the theatre group's boat. Puffed as they arrived, they apologised in such a school like manner that the people on the boat couldn't help laughing.

"Hey," said one of the members. "All timings, but the time of the show are relative! Let's get on and then we'll see you later."

The run through went well, Jim and Amanda's part seemed to have been dovetailed neatly into the second half of the performance, with them joining in on the songs from their arrival on stage until the end. After an hour they all felt as though they had done enough so Jim and Amanda went for another wander round the stalls in search of the purveyor of the strange curry concoction of the previous day, having firmly promised to be back at the boat at least half an hour before the performance which was due to go on at half past three.

"I wonder what it must have been like to be born to working on a boat?" Amanda speculated idly. "I mean it looks dreadful from our perspective, but."

"I've wondered that too," Jim said. "I mean they didn't really have any option, but it was probably better than a lot of jobs, like down mines and stuff. To talk to those that are left you wouldn't think it was so bad though so I don't really know. Maybe we'll find that one out one day."

"There's a lot to find out," Amanda thought, then said. "It's O.K. for the here and now though, and that's all that anyone has or has had."

Jim looked at her, her comment disjointed from the thought that provoked it had puzzled him. Amanda smiled.

"Hey, don't mind me Jimbo, I'm happy so lets do damage to one of those curry thingies," she said.

Not thinking further Jim put his arm round Amanda's shoulder and the two went off to the stall, the thought never actually making it through to consciousness in either of them that this was comfortable and in some way new.

Time for the performance was soon upon them and they arrived exactly to the minute. There were not many props to take, and costumes were simple so the set up time was short. A small crowd had gathered, programmes were on sale, and, as the audience almost instinctively went quiet, it was time for the introduction.

"Let us take you on a slow journey across the landscape of our country." Paul spoke in a town crier's voice. "We will meet new people, and we will find out good and bad things."

"And for today only!" Tamsin had come onto stage from the left "We have with us not one, but two guest stars of whom you will know more later!"

"God that's us!" Amanda whispered to Jim.

The first half covered a lot of history in a light hearted way and things were rapidly brought to the present at the beginning of the second half, a pointed song crafted by the group, called "Road to Ruin" was sung, followed by Graham, the person who Jim and Amanda only knew by sight, running onto the stage.

"NO! NO! You can't sing *that* about progress," He shouted. "This is the only way in the modern day!"

"That's our cue," Amanda hissed, and the two shambled slowly on stage as though they had wandered in by accident.

"Err, what do you mean?" Jim asked politely, but clearly enough to be heard.

"Why!" Graham continued. "It's young people! My favourite sort of people !" Then cupping his hands in a mock whisper to the audience said, "So easily led." and loud again. "Welcome friends to the new age of progress. Are you ready to go forward?"

"Not if it means going over a cliff!" Amanda shouted scornfully.

"But nobody earns money from these ditches any more?" Graham protested. "So why keep them?"

"So Mister Roadbuilder!" Tamsin chirped. "You have come face to face with progress! Progress! Nay Enterprise. Meet the boaters of tomorrow!"

The section continued with a stylised version of Jim and Amanda's voyage and the part they were playing in the rebirth of the canal system.

"But!" Graham blurted. "But, BUT, BUT!"

"But what?" Jim asked in his polite voice.

"But it'll NEVER work!" whined Graham.

"So how come it does?" Amanda asked. "But then who cares about you, when we can sing songs."

Two old canal songs preceded the final part of the performance, with a finale of more music with the almost traditional audience participation. At the end, Tamsin came to centre stage and introduced the cast finishing on the special guests.

"Now!" she added, rather loudly. "We have just one song left in us, and you must all join in. And I mean ALL of you!"

Jim and Amanda looked at each other unaware that there was a song at the end, and hoping they knew, or could pick it up.

"Today is a special day for one of our guest stars!" Tamsin spoke in her best town crier voice this time. " So let's all sing Happy Birthday to our friend Amanda Donaldson."

As she spoke both Jim and Amanda were pushed to the front of the stage next to Tamsin.

"I sort of wanted to disappear," Amanda said, as they sat with two mugs of tea back on the Mayfly. "But then again, I wouldn't have missed that for anything. You know, the whole lot, not just the birthday thing."

"Bit like the Quarry," Jim added. "It's kind of weird, I mean we keep a low profile, then."

"Splat!" Amanda smiled. "It's a good day today. One I'll remember for a long time. Forever I think."

"Nearly forgot!" Jim said. "Bloody hell! Shut your eyes! No! Go get the theatre people here now!"

"With eyes shut or open?" Amanda asked.

"Open, I don't want you falling in. Just go get them, they should be here too," Jim smiled.

Amanda was nonplussed by Jim's manic behaviour and meekly went over to the theatre group's boat. They were unwinding from the performance, but responded to the urgency of Amanda's request.

"What's up?" Tamsin asked.

"No idea," Amanda replied "Jim does this sort of thing now and again, well, no he doesn't. This is all a bit odd but could you come?"

On arrival at the Mayfly, they found Jim in the cockpit looking pretty much as he had done earlier. It was a bit of a tight fit but, with some sitting on the side of the adjacent narrowboat and others in the cockpit of Jim and Amanda's little craft they all waited. Then, as if performing a conjuring trick, Jim opened a deed box and produced from it a birthday cake complete with the appropriate number of candles. The early evening was calm enough for them to be lit outdoors and Amanda was called upon to do the honours and blow the lot out to another rendition of "Happy Birthday To You."

"That's it," Graham said. "You know this city was built on foundations of music, and you two should come and do a bit of revelling tonight! Sorry, not taking no for an answer."

"Then take some cake instead," Amanda laughed.

The evening air in the city was warm, and it surprised Amanda how unused to it she was after such a short time on a boat. They had taken a bus to the centre, and gone down several side streets, guided mainly by Graham who had lived in the area until his early teens. Eventually they arrived at a rather uninviting looking doorway with some very inviting sounds emanating from it. Following the group in, Jim saw Graham in conversation with one of the doormen. After a short wait they were beckoned forward, and allowed into the club.

"I went to school with the guy," Graham said. "And he's turning a blind eye. They got a liquor licence this year so strictly you shouldn't be here, but we'll be O.K."

The place was low ceilinged and claustrophobic, but it also possessed an abundance of atmosphere, as though many stars had first performed and many had been discovered under it's roof.   There were more famous clubs in the city but Graham was of the opinion that this was one of the best on account of the proprietors never having sold out.   If the music was anything to go by, his opinion was to be heeded.   It was loud and raw, but new.   Words and chords hit the walls and bounced back until, on finally lodging themselves in the eardrums, they could have energised the dead.

"Sorry Jim, but this makes me want to dance," Amanda shouted over the din.   "I know you're not that demonstrative but."

"So," Jim shouted back.   "Let's dance.   This is your night."

And dance they did for almost the whole night, pausing only to have a drink (Graham had promised they would stay on soft drinks) now and then. Their energy and enthusiasm got to the rest of the group, who, though tired from the performance, joined in the party until they were exhausted and sat at a nearby table.

"Jesus!" Tamsin shouted.   "Those two are raving nuts!   They won't be able to walk in the morning!"

"Pound says they'll wake up without any ill effects whatsoever," George howled back.

Had she taken the bet, Tamsin would have lost.   Both Jim and Amanda were greeting the new morning, which was bright and promised a proper Summer's day ahead, with something similar to a traditional English breakfast.

"That night was bloody brilliant," Amanda beamed, having lost any trace of the wistful that had dogged her expression for the previous week. "I could have danced all night"

"You sound like Eliza Doolittle!" Jim laughed, so Amanda threw the dishcloth at him.

"It was good though.   That was real music, good stuff, like the stuff they keep at the back of the shop," he added.

"What time did we get back?" Amanda asked.

"Somewhere between late and bloody late, not too late though or we'd still be on our way back and our breakfast would have gone cold," Jim replied.

"Daft git!" Amanda smiled.   "Shame we are all going our separate ways soon all the same."

"Travelling is what we do best though, and we won't be going till this afternoon or Monday if you'd rather, I think quite a few are staying on 'till then anyway because there'll be less traffic so we can stay the extra night if you like. I mean it's not as though we'll get far today anyway," Jim said.

Amanda agreed that there was little point in setting off in the middle of the afternoon, only to cover a few miles and tie up somewhere they weren't happy with, when they could get up early on the Monday and get a whole day in. Their stopping points for the next couple of days were on the same route as they had taken into the city, after which they were to head off eastwards across the country before returning via a circuitous route to return the electronic measuring device they were testing. This would get them into more familiar water, but beyond this point they had no further idea of where they would go.

"It'd be nice if we could keep going as long as possible," said Jim. "I mean that was my original idea, like to wander around and see where it got me."

"You had this really well planned didn't you Jimbo!" Amanda smiled.

"Point taken," Jim said. "But I figured that if I'd managed to get the boat right, then the rest would somehow fall into place, and it sort of has up to now, I mean we're here. Anyway, I don't see that your plans were much better. You were doing a runner really, nothing much more."

"True, so we're even. Well, I'm up for keeping on and seeing where it takes us too, if you can put up with me," Amanda smiled.

"Not really a case of that now," Jim spoke thoughtfully. "So far as I see it the Mayfly really is as much yours as she's mine now."

He hadn't meant to go that far with the comment but once spoken he was entirely happy with what he'd said. Although it was he that had put the initial work into getting the boat back into good repair, it was Amanda that had provided a lot of the things that they relied on for their daily life. She had looked after and defended the little craft, and now he could not see it without his best friend in, or close to it. Amanda was taken aback by the cool delivery of the remark, which seemed to have come from nowhere in the conversation. He's said something similar before as a throwaway remark to her friend Emma, but this time she knew it had substance. The familiar furrow appeared and then disappeared as she thought about what he had said. The Mayfly, which she had once compared to a packing case was now a place that she regarded as home. Even if she thought of the home that she had lived in, it was in the past, her folks home, Mum and

202

Dad's house, but no longer hers. It was her thought, but she knew also how much of himself Jim had invested in the little craft, yet he had just clearly said that she had, either by design, or inadvertently, put the same sort of investment in, and deserved the recognition he'd just given her. She had not felt like a guest since the very early days, in fact Jim had not really regarded her as being anything other than there, so it was hard to determine where she stood. The thing was, she had never felt the need to ask questions either of herself or Jim, so now, when it was spelt out to her she just sat wide eyed and said nothing.

"You look like you've just sat in a pool of duck poo," Jim broke the silence.

"I can't quite get round what I'm thinking Jim, but well, it's almost like we're sort of part of the boat, like she owns us almost. Like you rescued her, and somehow she dragged me aboard, like she has a bit of a hold on us. Does that make any sense?" Amanda said.

"No, but nothing much does. It was there, and I guess I felt a bit like she needed help. I mean, it would be firewood by now if."

"Oh! Jim! Don't say that," Amanda had tears forming as she spoke.

"Sorry, but that may have been the case only it wasn't," Jim replied quickly. "So we're here. That's where we are so far."

Again, Amanda's reply was checked by her thoughts. How could she suddenly have felt such a strong emotion for something that in reality was no more than an assemblage of plywood and copper rivets.

Eventually she answered. "It is, and thanks," she smiled warmly.

Chapter 13

Monday had come all too soon, and the daily routine returned to the Mayfly as though they had never done anything else in their lives. Travel with the theatre company was easy going, and they often shared the locks with one or two other small boats. The theatre company had a booking in the next town, which was where Jim and Amanda were turning off to go cross country, a journey that their friends could not make easily due to the length of their boat. Because of the economy of time in running two boats together properly, their journey time was reduced by half a day, leaving them with a free afternoon to do some shopping in the town before moving on. Addresses were exchanged, and the usual promises to keep in touch made before the outboard was kicked into life, leaving Jim and Amanda on their own again. The run was set to take them through very depressed areas, as well as some of the most beautiful countryside that the north had on offer, the weather was now fully worth calling summer and the pair were in high spirits.

"Hey we made the local papers!" Amanda shouted over the engine note. "They did a whole two pages on the rally, and, oh my god!"

"What?" Jim looked worried.

"They put a photo of the end of the performance. You know, when they all sang happy birthday? We're both in it!" Amanda replied.

"One to cut out and keep then," Jim smiled. "It was a good do."

"There's an odd article here about some hippies," Amanda continued. "That were about to be evicted from an old farmhouse on the moor-tops. Listen to this! The landowner had given them permission to stay almost rent free. He felt they'd been kicked around from pillar to post enough, but someone complained that the house had been empty too long so it wasn't allowed."

"That's about what you'd expect from arseholes in the council," Jim said with more than a bit of feeling.

"They won, or rather the landowner did, by about a month. The house had been empty for a long time, and another few weeks they'd have been out, but they won. They look really nice people too, not that you can tell from a photo that size," Amanda held the paper up for Jim to see.

"Blood and sand! Let me have a closer look!" Jim handed the steering to Amanda as she passed him the paper.

He sat down and read the article several times over before speaking again.

"Mand?" he said. This wasn't the frightened use of the abbreviation.

"Yes? What," she replied.

"Well, the names don't match, it says they are Carlina and Aaron, but I'd put a pound on it," Jim said.

"What?" Amanda frowned.

"Remember when we were talking , you know about those dreams when we were helping Vanessa out." Jim looked across at her as he spoke.

"You mean you think that's, who was it?   Miranda and Paul?" Amanda's brow was a bit furrowed.

"Well, the guy has grown a bit more of a beard, but if that isn't Miranda, then it's her sister, and I'd recognise that motorbike anywhere," Jim smiled. "It's good to know they made it."

Nothing much more was said on the subject either that day, or the next, but Amanda's curiosity was aroused about the couple that had helped her best friend when he most needed it. Somehow this almost wasn't for Jim but for her, she felt the need to thank them. There wasn't much to go on, and a phone call to the paper didn't throw much by way of information out as they would not, quite rightly, give the address of the community. It was late afternoon that Amanda made the discovery of a big clue in the photograph. All that had grabbed her attention previously was the faces that Jim had pointed to, any other information had been overlooked. In the background there was what looked like the parapet of a canal bridge, with what could have been the end of a balance beam just intruding into the frame. That and a small pylon line was about as much as there was, which coupled with the name "Bank Top" really gave little to go on. But to Amanda it was something. They tied up near a mill in a stone built area of one of the many towns they would pass through. At least one of the mills still looked to be using steam power, which would have roused more curiosity in Amanda had she had the time to notice. Jim had taken a peculiar interest in the area and wanted to walk around, so they agreed to split up, so that Amanda could get some shopping in. She also needed to call at the local library, though Jim was unaware of this desire. He wandered around the industrial area, knowing the little Mayfly was safely tied close to the hut of a watchman who told him he'd keep an eye out. As, in Jim's opinion, the guy was no arsehole, Amanda had agreed to buy him a tin of ready rubbed as a thank-you. The mill and its associated buildings were in varying states of repair, though all well past their best, but all fascinating. Possibly, in another life he may have taken pity on the whole area as he had done with the boat. He walked and dreamt of what the place must have been like at its peak, knowing too that, like the canals, nothing would either last or stay the same.

At the library in the centre of the town, Amanda was in deep conversation with an aged librarian as to local place names and landmarks. He remarked that in an area full of hills and banks, each hill had a top, as did each bank. Though not as common as "Mount Pleasant" on an ordinance survey map, Bank Top featured several times on many of them. The fact that there was a canal near, and possibly a lock, plus the pylon line would make it easier to spot, and the projected distance from the city, that made the item newsworthy would help too. It wasn't too long before the search had been narrowed down to two two and a half inch scale maps that contained similar information. Studying carefully Amanda made the decision that the second map had the information she wanted. She had been good at geography in school and was able to read ascending and descending contours along with other features relatively easily. Looking at one house in particular, no more than a small rectangle on the map, she could see that it had the correct angle to the pylon line and canal. Better still it had the lock in the right place too. Next problem was how to get there. The lock gate that she saw was of canal, not river origin, but not the one they were on, and neither was it an easy diversion, it would mean them doubling back on themselves which would take too much time and fuel. Their current route, however would take them fairly close, which she found awfully tempting. So much so that she decided to make an excuse to go walking by herself when the time was right. She didn't want to lie to Jim, but thought a little economy of truth would shelter him from any harm, should her venture go awry in any way.

It was after a particularly good run that, finding themselves so far ahead of their schedule, they both decided to take a bit of time out to avoid being far to early for their next delivery. Amanda took the chance to put her plan into action, suggesting that she took a bit of a walk whilst he attended to

206

some necessary chores.

"I'll be fine," she smiled. "I just want to have a little time to myself, no offence."

"Enjoy yourself, but keep the bridge in sight if you can," Jim suggested.

"I'll try," she replied with a smile. "Just not too hard that's all," She added under her breath.

Taking the photocopy of the map from her bag, she followed along the lane, turning left onto a minor road, about half a mile down which was a bus stop. The next bus would be in about twenty minutes according to the timetable in the library. She smiled, looking at the neat Timex wristwatch that she had been given, feeling a slight pang of guilt at her little deception. The bus ride was no more than fifteen minutes, the request stop being just over the arch of the bridge, which, if her map reading was correct, would have a footpath marked somewhere which led across the land close to Bank Top.

"You're going to look a right twit if you've got this wrong," Amanda thought to yourself. "In fact," she added silently. "You are a twit, but you're here now so what the hell."

With that thought in mind, she knocked at what was commonly used as the front door, but was in fact the back of the building. It was a while before anybody answered, as most people that knew the place came and went as they pleased, there being no occasion when the door had been locked since the house had been re-occupied. Just as she was becoming impatient enough to consider knocking again, this time a bit louder, she heard some activity from behind the sturdy oak door, and instantly thought of running as fast as she could in any direction.

"It's just nerves," she thought. "Wait, count to three and bloody well calm down."

When the door opened, it had been Amanda's intention to speak first, and as quickly as possible, to explain what was more than likely a fools errand, but she simply stood tongue-tied, scrabbling in her mind for even a polite greeting, and a comment on the weather."

"I've seen your face in the paper haven't I," the woman that answered the door said "Hi, I'm Miranda."

"Not Carlina?" Amanda asked.

"No, that was just us having some sport with the papers," she smiled. "We do that sometimes you know. It never does to give too much away."

"And how is Alec?" she smiled again.

207

"Well, he's fine, only his name is actually Jim, if it's who I think you think. I hope you don't mind my coming, but," Amanda stopped, rather unsure of what to say next.

"It's O.K." Miranda replied. "He'll have been protecting himself, we all have to do that at times too. I have often wondered what happened to him. Look, come in, there's probably a lot to talk about and Paul will be back soon. He's going to want to catch up too. So where is the guy?"

"Well," Amanda hesitated. "He doesn't exactly know I'm here. I said I wanted to have a walk whilst he cleaned and greased the motor, not that we don't do that together, but well. I didn't know, and nor did he, know that is, well, he didn't exactly say but I can read him a bit, and there was a bit of."

"We got busted," Miranda laughed. "It happens. The men in suits wanted us out, so they had someone dump enough dope to kill a horse behind a cupboard then the coppers raided us. The fact that we were possible kidnappers and child molesters into the bargain was nothing more than the cherry on the cake. So no ill feeling. It wasn't his fault, they would have done it anyway. Sad though, we really liked him."

Their conversation was stopped by the slow thump of a 1951 Panther motorbike and side-car.

"Here's Paul, I expect you need to get back at some point so how about we give you a lift and surprise your fella! That must have been some long walk though," Miranda said.

"I went on a bus. Oh and he's not my. Don't you need to lock up?" Amanda quickly changed tack and asked, somewhat naively, only to be told that there were seven other people living at the house, which was pretty big, and a few more in the outbuildings meaning that it was rarely locked.

"The way I see it,"Miranda smiled. "If the coppers want to do a raid, they at least won't go breaking the doors down."

"Hey!" a bearded man in his mid thirties said. "It's the girl from the paper. I thought we might see you."

"Why?" Amanda was a bit startled.

"Well, if that wasn't our Alec I'd pull my beard out and eat it, even if he does call himself Jim now. And you look like you'd do that sort of thing that's all. Kind of determined," Paul smiled. "Know anyone that drives a black Jag?" he added.

"Blimey," Amanda now smiled "All that from a photo! No, I don't know anyone with a Jag, not any more, should I?"

"He was parked a way up the road when I came in. He's not staking us out, they usually do that from the lock with big binoculars. Get a better view from there, and there's a good little café along the road from it." Paul spoke matter of factly.

"And you don't mind?" Amanda's eyes had widened.

"Well, yes of course we mind, but we know when they're there. I mean they're not awfully bright you know. If we miss them the guy in the café lets us know. Tells us what they've had for lunch too sometimes, so it's a sort of fair trade in a way," Paul smiled.

"Time to get the young lady home I think," Miranda said. "You'd better do the side-car my love, the back of that thing isn't for the uninitiated."

Paul set off in the opposite direction to the parked Jaguar so as the person in it did not see them pass. The road went in a slow loop until it pointed back towards the canal and the Mayfly.

Jim had just about finished tidying up after the routine maintenance, and was beginning to wonder when Amanda would return, when he heard a sound that took him back to a dream he had had earlier. The smell of fresh bread, the house, and of course the motorbike. The motorbike and side-car that had just crossed the bridge and parked up in a small area near a field gate. He waved to Amanda as she came down the towpath and then to the two people that were following her. Jim got out onto the path and ran a short way to meet them.

"Never thought you'd see us again I'll bet!" Miranda said as she hugged him like a long lost son. Paul patted him soundly on the back, and just said, "Hi bud." It was almost as though no time had elapsed since they were last together. Amanda just stood and enjoyed their moment until they were ready to talk.

"He needn't think I didn't see him because I did," Paul said as the Jaguar slipped quietly over the hump backed canal bridge. "Got my eye on you buddy and don't you forget it," he shouted at the parapet.

"Just some arsehole out to poke his nose in on us. They do, maybe this one hasn't found the café yet," Miranda said.

"Now I know where you got your method of assessing people from Jimbo," Amanda laughed. "Do you use the same criteria as Jim?"

"Well," Miranda replied. "The way we see it people are either arseholes, or they aren't. It's sort of simple. And the guy in the Jag."

209

"Arsehole," Amanda smiled. "You do!"

"Thing is," Jim added, "So do you now. You never did before, but I guess it's infectious."

The group of friends set about mugs of tea and reminiscences, making arrangements for a proper visit to the community in the near future. Though Paul and Miranda were only there for just over an hour, Jim was more than delighted to have been re-united with them.

"Thanks Amanda," he smiled, as he waved the couple off. "I really appreciate that," he added, instinctively putting his arm around her shoulder and half hugging her.

"They seem really nice people," Amanda replied. "I can sort of see you there when you were younger. I think you'd like what they've got now though.

"So." Miranda looked at Paul firmly across the big kitchen table at Bank Top. "That guy in the Jag really got to you. Why?"

Paul's brow furrowed, and he went across to the range, a nondescript cast iron thing that was built in as part of the fireplace, and re-filled the teapot from a kettle that would not have looked out of place in an antique shop.

"Because the bastard wasn't looking at us," he said, with some anger in his voice. "I could live with them prying on us, even from down the lane, but he wasn't or he'd have taken the time to follow us back."

"You think he's after our Alec? I mean Jim, I'll have to get my head around that." Miranda looked worried as she spoke. Paul had a knack of summing up situations that bordered on to the psychic.

"That or his friend," Paul said. "More likely her, didn't you detect she was, or rather has been, keeping an eye over her shoulder. You know, watching her back. And Alec, Jim, he's had some bad deals along the way, it's written all over his face." Paul frowned as he poured the tea.

"Even I saw that," Miranda's face fell slightly. "It was good to see them, but it makes me so angry that. I mean, we looked after the little guy when he needed it then they raided us and he's gone. He was just staying with us because the placement the suits gave him was crap. We could have sorted something even if it meant a load of forms. Now who knows what has happened to the guy because we weren't there."

"Amanda happened to him," Paul replied with a smile. "He has a very

210

good friend there I'd say, but I think."

"You've never stopped either have you," Miranda was again looking directly at her partner warm heartedly, but with a stare that could read the contents of any man's soul.

"No," he studied the grain of the kitchen table as though he was about to write a masters thesis on the subject.

Back on the Mayfly, Jim was enjoying another cup of tea with Amanda.

"It'll be nice to see them properly at the weekend," he said. "Thanks for sorting that one too. I had no idea, and I wouldn't have had the guts."

"There must be a load of catching up though," Amanda wanted to talk but wasn't quite sure what to say.

"I wasn't there that long though. I mean only about a month or so I don't really remember, you don't count. Like if you asked how long we've been travelling now, I haven't a clue," Jim smiled.

"Things would have been different if," Amanda said.

Jim cut her short. "They may well have been, but they aren't and if I learnt anything from that time, it was to enjoy what you have. You don't know when it gets taken from you. It's nice to see them, but I can't go back in time, so we take it from here. But thanks, I really never thought I'd see them again."

With the comment, he leaned over and kissed the top of Amanda's head lightly. She smiled, content that she had done the right thing. They both sat silent for a while and watched the light of a pair of headlamps cross the bridge, briefly illuminating the trees before disappearing into the night. It was a warm one, and neither of them were that tired, having had a short day on account of Jim being convinced by Amanda that he wanted to do the work on the motor that afternoon, followed by the brief reunion. Eventually it was Amanda that broke the silence, wanting to move away from thoughts that were there but not tangible enough to identify.

"Do you know how long those two have been together?" she said, a little clumsily.

"Probably forever," Jim stared along the length of the canal watching the small movements on the surface. "Some people are, they just don't know it. Some never will be I guess, not however much they try."

"That's a bit deep," Amanda replied.

"Just saying that's all. There were others in the house, maybe they'll see us sometime, but it was Miranda that first spoke to me, so I sort of saw her and Paul as. Well, it's daft, but I guess they must have seen the same, so maybe that's a forever thing," Jim's voice was more placid that Amanda had heard it before.

"All of that is a bit of a mystery to me," Amanda looked at her feet, she hadn't really meant it to come out that way, and now she felt that she had lied. "Well, no it's not. Not really," she continued trying to put the thoughts that had now become slightly more focussed into words. "I don't know, not for certain, but I guess things just do become straightforward sometimes, like you don't have to think. Do you know what I mean."

"It didn't make any sense whatsoever, but I do know what you mean," Jim looked over to her.

"This, is," Amanda thought carefully about what she was about to say, the furrow appearing and vanishing as her thoughts clouded and cleared.

"It," she said.

"It?"Jim's face looked so serious by the light of the stars.

"It," Amanda firmed up on her thoughts, and moved on before she lost her thread, and her courage. "This is it, Jim. It's what I want."

Jim opened his mouth to speak.

"No Jim, let me continue," Amanda's voice was a combination of firmness and fear. "This, all of it, it's me, now, my life is here, and with you, if you want me to put it that way."

Jim looked at her face, the furrows coming and going, the hazel brown eyes piercing his soul.

"Jim," she said calmly. "This may mess things up, even ruin them, but, look, this boat has been owned by a couple before, I want it to be like that again."

Jim was as frozen to the spot as Amanda was. She had the feeling at the back of her knees that fear of a big dog often brought her when she was a child. But she had to push on now.

"Us," she said. The feeling that had started as a kind of fear, had moved its axis, she knew what it was, but did not want her mind to be governed by it.

"You and me?" Jim answered softly.

"Yes Jim, and now. This is our time. We leave everything as it is, and we go into the cabin. We put the flaps between the bunks together and we," she stalled. Knowing as far as she was able that it was her mind that

212

had put her on this track, and it was her reasoning that had caused her to be feeling the way she now did. She briefly shut her eyes to gather her thoughts together. Jim's eyes were wide. This had come from nowhere, but he knew that she was taking his innermost feelings and stating the same from her point of view. He suddenly knew what his feelings for her were. His realisation was not clouded by hormones, as the suddenness of the turn in conversation had been like an electric shock to his system, and it would take time for anything to function normally.

"Things make sense Mand. You've always made sense of stuff," he said nervously. "What now?"

"We make love Jim. That's what we do. We go into the cabin and make love. And that's what it will be isn't it."

"Yes," he said, almost inaudibly.

"And I am as sure as you are Jim. What you said earlier sealed it. Some people are together, and some are not. I just think we are that's all."

She reached over and touched Jim's face, as she did so he instinctively put his hand behind her neck to gently draw her close to him. Although not expert, their first proper kiss told both what they needed to know.

As the morning sun through the porthole caught Jim's eye he realised that he wasn't in his bunk. In fact, where he was he should have been on the bottom boards of the cabin, it was hard for him to call it either a floor or a deck. Either way he was not on it but above it. Clearing the last of the sleep from his eyes he found Amanda next to him in the two sleeping bags which had been zipped into one double. She was as naked as he was himself. On the bottom shelf of the cupboard was the mysterious box that had been given to Amanda by Vera Potter some weeks back. She had been told not to open it until the time was right. The muzz of sleep now slowly left his brain and the new day came into sharp focus, as did the dreamlike memory of what had happened the previous night. The slow move into the cabin, losing the bashfulness of undressing then, well, then.

The combination of Amanda having thought things out, and the rush of surprise as Jim realised what had built between them had produced an equilibrium. Their bodies were somehow in tune with each other, and with their surroundings. The sympathetic motion of their home felt as though it too was letting its approval be known, and the ripples in the canal caused by the craft's gentle movement told any in the heavens who needed to know, that all was as it should be. Jim ran his hand lightly down Amanda's side, stopping at the waist, as if to make sure it really was her there. She felt warm and soft to touch, and responded by, moving gently across the bunk to make fuller contact with him. She rubbed the sleep from her eyes then put her arm around her partner.

"Morning Jimbo," she said, with the warmest smile he had ever seen. "Here," she added, as she moved still closer.

It was more than an hour later that the two emerged into the sunlight of what was still relatively early morning. The day was bright, the sky was clear, and they were both very different people.

"Don't go lighting fires with the lad if you don't mean it." Vera's words came into Amanda's head as she watched Jim lighting the methylated spirit.

"Well," she thought. "I lit the fire Vera, and I'm not putting it out, not ever."

All of the previous night came back to her. The look on Jim's face as she spoke. Her feeling of relief as she finally showed herself to him, his gentleness when gentleness was required, feeling and responding to another as though the person was a part of her, of him moving with her as one entity. Of waking up and finding that it was no dream, but making sure by reprising and rekindling the tenderness of the previous night.

"The last thing I would ever do is hurt this person," she thought, and, as she did, as sometimes happens, the negative voice came in.

"What if he feels trapped?" it said. Not so much as a downward spiral but thoughts rolled round, as though her head was stirring trouble for its own sake. The train of thought was cut short by softest touch of the back of Jim's hand, lightly stroking the furrow that so often gave her thoughts away.

"You have absolutely no idea how many times I have wanted to do that." Jim said, as he slowly smoothed the area just above her nose. "You look so sad and serious when you do that, and when I see those wrinkles, well, I've never had the nerve."

Amanda smiled, remembering childhood when the words "Cheer up chicken." were attached to the smoothing of the same little furrow when she had been worried or frightened.

"I," she said, but was cut short by Jim.

"My turn this morning," he said, smiling. "Look I'm not sure what just

214

got to you, but I know you'd never hurt me, and I won't hurt you. I'm glad you spoke your mind yesterday. For what it's worth you spoke most of mine too."

Amanda could see Jim was finding it hard to put his thoughts into words and was about to speak when he regained his composure.

"Amanda, what you said, last night, you said that this is our time."

"Yes," she looked intently at Jim.

"Well, it is, this is our time, and I want that time to go on and on. That's all," Jim smiled.

Amanda's brown eyes stared into Jim's though it was Jim that was seeing Amanda's soul.

"If you want it in the language of films, I love you Amanda Donaldson. I have done for some time, though I didn't know it," he said, meaning every word.

"Jim," Amanda spoke very quietly.

"Yes?" It was his turn to look back at her.

"What you said yesterday about Miranda and Paul. That some people are," she said.

"Is that us?" Jim filled in the blank for her.

"Is it?" she asked.

"Some people are, but they just don't know it," Jim smiled. "I hope so Mand, I really do. And if you want the truth, then, yes, it's what I felt yesterday when you spoke, and I feel the same this morning. I really can't see a time when I'd stop either."

Amanda looked at the thwart she was sitting on.

"When you said that yesterday, that's when I knew. I mean I guess I knew, like we all know but don't admit, or it's kind of stuck in the pipeline somewhere. But I knew, and I knew it was time to say," she replied.

The whistle of the kettle took their minds to making the rest of breakfast, but the train of thought stayed with Amanda who, with a mouth still part full of fried bread and marmalade said, "I love you too Jim Stratton, film talk or no, I won't let you down."

The conviction behind the words was clear, but the sound, obscured by the breakfast, made them sound ludicrous.

"Now," Jim said in a mockingly stern voice. "Didn't your mother ever teach you not to speak with your mouth full." The second half of his sentence was spoken after he had deliberately taken rather too big a bite of his breakfast. When they had both finished laughing, Jim having almost

215

choked as he made the joke, he added.

"This *is* our time Mand, it just *is*. That's all"

And from the day, it looked like it certainly was. The bright dawn was followed by some of the best weather that year, hot but not stifling, with a light breeze. The little boat cut through the water as well as ever it had, but it seemed to be doing better, and it's occupants behaved as though they had not a care in the world, which at this point, of course, they had not. As with all things new, there was an energetic spirit that pervaded every aspect of the day. What was drudge before was now a joy, what was previously regarded as a mishap was just a bit of a laugh. So they went, making about the same progress as always, but feeling as though they were covering more miles with ease.

"We'll be doing a stop for a watch delivery in the next town, and there are a couple of packages from the rally to deliver," Amanda said, looking at the diary. "And I suppose I ought to check the radio."

"Aye aye cap'n," Jim mocked a salute as they went under a bridge.

Amanda smiled and waved to the man standing on it, but he didn't appear to notice her. She thought for a moment about the job he probably had, reasoning that it was not agricultural as he was too smartly dressed. That left a brush salesman or an insurance man. Flipping a coin in her head she decided that he was probably a brush salesman. The next couple of locks brought them to their temporary stop, and they secured the craft to some convenient bollards.

"Doesn't look that nice an area here," Jim said. "Should one of us wait with the boat?"

"If we're quick it should be alright I'd have."

"Mind yer boat mister?" Amanda was cut short by what looked like a twelve year old boy.

"How much?" Jim asked resignedly.

"Half a quid and I'll get me mates round too," the urchin replied.

"I'd haggle but I'm in too good a mood," Jim smiled. "Half a quid it is, half now and the rest when I get back. And cola all round as a bonus."

"Cold ones?" the lad asked.

"Frozen bloody solid if you want!" Jim smiled. "Stripe me and I'll land the lot of you in there," he pointed to a particularly grimy area of weed and rubbish.

"You'd 'ave ta catch us first, and you don't know."

Jim cut him short. "One thing I do know, is everyone knows everything

216

when on the cut. Here's half the cash, the rest when I get back," he said. "Play silly buggers and you're in it."

"Yer a hard bugger you are. But it's a deal," the lad smiled, and called his friends for back up.

About an hour later the couple arrived back to find that the lad, who's name was Amos, had indeed kept his part of the deal. Four of them were having an improvised kick around on the tow path, and half time was called as they approached.

"Right," Jim said. "It's still floating. So it's time to settle up. There's no surprises for us on board is there, rats or anything."

"No mate," Amos replied. "But there was this posh geezer. Tried to chase us off he did but we didn't go see."

"Posh geezer eh," Amanda said. "I don't like them much. Tell me about him."

"Well he talked like you, like dead posh, no offence missus, but you ain't like him," Amos replied.

"Why not?" Amanda was curious to know.

Amos pondered. "Well he was, well he was a shite-hawk, and you in't. That's sort of it. Drove a big posh car, that's how we lost him, kicked the ball at his posh bloody door."

"They've earned their money, and a bonus," Jim smiled, still feeling on top of the world. "And they've chased a shite-hawk off. Tell you what. I'm doubling your pay, but don't tell anyone else I'm a soft touch or." He pointed to the area of grime he'd threatened them with earlier.

"See!" said Amos to Amanda with a cheeky look in his eye. "Hard bastard he is. He in't goin' to have a shite-hawk for 'is bird."

With that, Jim paid up and handed over a bag full of cans. "Thanks, he said. Good job well done." Then he set about preparing to move on.

"Is that your boat missus," Amos asked politely.

"Well, it's sort of Jim's really, but he said I own it as much as he does now, which is really nice of him," Amanda had been rather nervous of leaving the Mayfly in the care of Amos, but had warmed to the lad. Scruffy he was, but it seemed he had a good heart, and was, underneath the bravado, an intelligent young man in the making.

"You rich then?" Amos persisted. "Live in a big house?"

"To tell the truth this is all we have in the world," Amanda replied. "It's our home. Jim found it half sunk and repaired it. I think it cost him about twenty quid or something."

"Cor! You got a clever fella missus. An 'ee's got a looker in you if yer don't mind me sayin." Even with bravado, Amos blushed slightly at the last remark.

"How much have you overpaid Amos Jim?" Amanda laughed.

They were soon under way, and the gaggle of kids followed them along the towpath until a factory yard got in the way. They waved the little boat off until it had all but disappeared, and then went back to their game.

"I guess you'd say Amos is no arsehole then Jimbo?" Amanda smiled. "But what do you make of the geezer in the car?"

"Right about the first one," Jim said. "The other one, well, I'm not sure we've seen the last of him, but we've dealt with worse, I think Amos had him pretty well sized up though. But today is our day, so if anyone wants to make trouble let them. We'll knock seven bells out of the lot and dump them in the canal."

A lot of northern towns nestle in valleys, or convenient spots surrounded by hills or open country so it was not long before the landscape of brick, stone and dereliction gave way to fields again. The weather was beautiful and they were ahead of time, their next delivery only being a few miles away, but not due until the next day. Even if they had turned up early there would be nobody in to take the package. Jim wanted to tie up well away from civilisation, and as far from a road as he could, wanting only the company of his partner that evening. Amanda pointed a space that was shaded by a couple of trees, and which looked ideal. On closer inspection, there was plenty of water, so they decided to tie up for an early stop to enjoy the rest of the day.

"One other thing Amos was right about too," Jim said, catching Amanda's attention as she was preparing a cup of tea. "I have got what he called a looker in you, if you don't mind my saying it as well."

"Knock it off," Amanda laughed, facing the stove she was in the process of lighting. The compliment was not lost though, even if Jim only saw the smile of satisfaction as a distorted reflection in the brass of the tank. For all the time they had been on the boat together, he had not really looked at Amanda, she was a friend, but you look at friends as friends. This was different, suddenly the person that he had been sharing a cabin with for a number of weeks was what he could only describe to himself as beautiful. Not in the way of a catwalk model, but possessing a natural grace, a face which without make-up was the face he wanted to see in every portrait in every art gallery.

"That," he thought "Would make the places worth visiting."

Waking up next to her in the morning, there she was, with her hair in a mess, but still, she was beautiful. There, smelling of paraffin and methylated spirit, with sooty fingers, hunched as an improvised wind-shield she was still beautiful. More than that, he knew he could trust her in a way that transcended the word to make the thought of considering it almost some kind of betrayal. He knew she was there, and would be there, and that he wanted that today and every day of the rest of his life. The stove broke into its familiar sound and Amanda turned to meet his gaze. As she caught the intensity of his concentration, she too looked back at him, trying to read his thoughts. She had never seen such an expression before and, although knowing it was nothing bad, she had not got a clue as to what was going on in his head. Eventually he spoke.

"Not sure how I missed that," his words were more for himself than to be heard. "But, you're beautiful, that's all."

"I think you're allowed to say that now," Amanda smiled kindly. "Even if you'd thought it before it could have queered the pitch a bit I guess. For what it's worth you're not so bad yourself matey. And don't think I've not been getting my eyeful of you today because I have. And yes, I missed that one too."

Jim blushed to an almost crimson hue at her remark.

"There's going to be a lot of little things that aren't as they were before aren't there Mand," he said somewhat seriously. "But I'm looking forward to each and every one as it comes."

"Me too Jimbo, me too," she smiled back at him.

The whistle from the kettle set the brewing of tea into operation and conversation ceased for a while. There should have been a lot to be said, but so much was taken in non verbal communication. Amanda knew, without having to ask, without the need of Vera telling her, that Jim was there for the long haul. Jim knew there was a lot about Amanda that was a mystery to him, but at the same time anything he did discover was no surprise to him either. It was now the two of them that sat staring at the length of canal behind their home. Jim put his arm around Amanda's waist, and she responded similarly. Much later on they would make love again in the tiny cabin, and fall asleep in each other's arms to wake again in the same state as soon as the sun was up.

219

Chapter 14

It was Friday, and they had been as far north as they would go. The canal now wound its way in a south easterly direction towards their weekend rendezvous with Miranda and Paul. They had been given details of a waterside pub, that the couple liked to visit on their rare days out from Bank Top, and it would be approaching lunchtime when they tied up there. The weather had held fair for the whole week, and did not show any sign of clouding over. Even if it had been pouring with rain, sleet, hail, or snow even, it is doubtful as to whether either Jim or Amanda would have been bothered much, or even noticed it. They were happy and nothing was going to burst that bubble for them. Rounding the corner, a low, stone built building sat at a right-angle to the water. A sign proclaimed that there was good food, moorings and accommodation available.

"That's it!" Amanda pointed. "Wonder if they'll be there yet?"

"Not sure what they said they'd do, but, hang on. I'd recognise that thing anywhere," Jim smiled.

In front of the pub was a red Panther motorcycle combination looking as though it had been half lovingly restored and half left to rot. Not having noticed them yet, the owners of the vehicle sat in the pub garden, simply enjoying the late morning sun. Their peace was disturbed by the sound of an old motor horn.

"Oh God!" Amanda blurted out. "They're going to know! Aren't they!"

"What's to hide Mand," Jim smiled. "There's nothing to worry about with them. We were friends when we left, now we're, well. What we are I guess. Give them a wave and we'll head for the tie up."

"Landlord says if you put the boat under the big willow, nobody can see her." Paul shouted from the pub garden. "He'll be out to sort things when you tie up."

Jim put his thumb up to show he had heard.

"Sort what out?" Amanda frowned. "Are we going to get charged?"

Jim shrugged his shoulders as they made for the tree. It had obviously been there for many years, and had grown well over the channel, hanging like a huge curtain almost down to the water. A larger boat than theirs usually tied up there but the owners were on holiday in it so the space was free.

"Hey there you two!" Miranda greeted them. "Paul's gone off to get Joe, then we can have lunch. It's on us, I insist." She was going to tell them about the pub, and how Joe, the landlord had come to be one of their friends, and had supported their efforts to stay in the farmhouse they now occupied, but she decided there was some more important news.

"Have you two got something to tell me?" she asked, looking at Jim's hand, which was inadvertently clasped in Amanda's.

"As long as you don't want too much detail," Amanda said before she'd thought not to say it.

"Well, I'll be! Paul!" Miranda shouted, Jim remembering just how loud her voice could be. "Get yourself over here and take a look at these two!"

Paul hurried back across the lawn.

"Joe'll be across in a moment," he said. "He's just got to."

"Never mind if he's got to clean the toilets with his own head!" Miranda pointed to Jim and Amanda, who were still holding hands. "Look!" she added.

"So," Paul said quietly. "You two worked it out at last. Good on you," he smiled.

"It's a celebration lunch now," Miranda said, with a distinct note of cheer in her voice. "You two look good together. I thought that when I saw you, but I didn't dare hope. Look Paul, lets get lunch ordered, Joe can sort this evening out later can't he?"

"This evening?" Jim looked puzzled.

"We couldn't phone you to ask, but we'd like to invite you to the house for a night, if you can leave your home?" Miranda smiled. "It'll be safe here, and we'll run you back on the bike tomorrow. Please say you'll come. It can't ever be like old times, I mean you're grown up now, but it's like, well, Amanda, I hope you don't mind me saying, but it's like you brought a son I thought was lost forever back to me. For that matter, I hope you don't mind me saying that Jim. I mean you were only with us such a short time."

"On the Mayfly the other day," Jim replied slowly. "Didn't I say something like that to you Amanda."

"Something. I wasn't sure that's what you meant," Amanda said, "But I

221

do now, and I'm glad I was part of it."

"So you'll come?" Miranda asked again.

"We'd love to. Not that I should speak for Jim, but." Looking over at her partner she saw him smiling at her getting tongue tied.

"We would," he said, "And thanks. It was a happy time at that squat, and I got the best marks I ever got in school there too. For what it's worth, I wouldn't have minded parents like you at all."

That sealed, lunch was ordered, during which more talking than eating was done. Amanda had been right when she had suggested there would be a lot to catch up on. Joe, the landlord eventually came over to sort out the mooring so that the couple would be sure that their home was in good hands.

"I'll put old Jake over there in his kennel, give him a ten foot chain. He'll see things alright," he said with a smile. "I'll bring him over to meet you."

Jake was an Alsatian dog, past middle age, if dogs have such a thing, and looked to be the sort that would survive a nuclear strike. It looked rather like the theory may well have been tested on him, but he seemed amiable enough with his owner.

"Right," Joe said, taking the animal to sniff each of the occupants of the garden table. "Friends Jake, friends. You got that?"

The dog barked once as if to say he understood. Joe then took him over to the willow, under which the Mayfly was tied.

"Jake," he said firmly, pointing to the little boat. "Guard that. It's theirs. Got it?"

The dog again barked once, and set himself on a comfortable piece of lawn for a well earned rest.

"Is that it?" Jim asked.

"That's it," Joe replied with a smile. "You can all come and go as you please. He'll not bother you."

"What about anyone else?" Amanda asked gingerly.

"Oh, he'll eat them," Joe smiled. "Not a pretty sight, but it usually puts most people off."

"That dog's been with Joe for a lot of years," Paul said. "They're both as mad as one another. So let's get on, you've no worries with him there."

Amanda packed a few things into a shopping bag, took the readings from the monitor, placing it, after she was done, in another bag to take with her, and all was ready. Jim tied the side screen down and slightly reluctantly left the little boat in the charge of Jake, who seemed to have settled to his task happily enough. Sitting in the side-car on the way to the farmhouse brought memories flooding back to Jim. Suddenly he was on the way to school, then going out on a run around to cheer him up, then off to the rather surreal parents evening, where Paul and Miranda were praised for their helping to motivate him. Amanda, sat behind, left him to his thoughts, spending her time looking at the changing scenery. Soon they were bouncing up a very rough track which led to the house. The bike seemed as at home on this terrain as it had been on the surfaced roads and country lanes, it's big, lazy and slow revving motor seeming to have endless power. As they arrived in the yard, there were a couple of other people cutting firewood and stacking it in a neat pile in one of the outhouses. As one of them looked up, Jim recognised the face, but couldn't as yet put a name to it.

"Bloody hell, it's Alec!" The man shouted, and ran across to the side-car. "How are you doin' me old pal! Remember me? The guy with the banjo. I've got another one now, since the coppers bashed my head in with the last!"

"Jesus! It's mad Dave!" Jim smiled. "I know another Dave now too, and he's about as nuts as you were!"

"Can't be! Man that ain't possible! I invented nuts I did," Dave laughed. "Who's this?"

Amanda was carefully extricating herself from the side-car, whilst trying not to laugh too much in case she looked like a schoolgirl with the giggles.

"I'm Amanda," she said, slightly formally. "Amanda Donaldson. I'm Jim's," there she stopped, she wasn't quite sure how to introduce herself further than that, but there was no matter, as Mad Dave chipped in.

"Any friend of Alec is O.K. with us girl, come and have some tea," he smiled.

The house was occupied by most of the people from the old squat, plus a few new faces, all of whom seemed to be aware of who Jim was, even if they did keep calling him Alec, and how he had been kidnapped and stolen from them by the Police. As they stood in the doorway, the familiar smell of baking bread hit Jim and he was back again to the day he first walked in on the old place. Without really thinking he turned to Amanda and kissed her.

"Thanks," he said. "Thanks Mand."

The place, where seconds previously general day to day chat filled the air, was suddenly quiet. There were quite a few in the big kitchen when suddenly two strangers were more or less propelled through the door by an unseen hand.

"It's O.K." Dave announced. "They ain't burglars, well the posh bird might be! But she won't burgle us. It's Alec, although I think it's actually Jim isn't it?"

"Posh! Bird!" Amanda squeaked, in mock indignation. "Want to wear another banjo do you!"

"Dangerous too. You picked a right one there Al, Jim. Crap! I'll never get this right," Dave laughed.

Paul and Miranda, having pushed the motorbike and side-car into another outbuilding, now came through into the kitchen. Miranda held a hand up, and spoke loudly.

"Can we get everyone together," she said.

Most people were close by and it wasn't long before there were about twelve in the room in addition to the new couple.

"This is Amanda and Jim," she said. "A lot of you remember Alec. Well this is him. He came to us for shelter some years back, and now, thanks to Amanda here, we've found him again. His real name is Jim, but he wasn't telling lies because Alexander, or Alec is his second name. And lets face it we all tell porkies sometimes. He's brought Amanda with him, and she's as much one of us as Jim is, if that's O.K. with all of you. Do we need to take a vote."

Mad Dave shouted, "Yes, all in favour raise your hand." It was Dave's joke, but the unanimous result made Amanda feel more on the inside of things than she had done anywhere.

"Is this what it was like?" Amanda asked, as they were enjoying tea with fresh baked bread and home made jam.

"Sort of similar," Jim replied. "I think this is what they'd wanted. The squat was in the town so they weren't as, well, as like this as they are now."

"And it wasn't allowed, so they got busted. For what!" Amanda's face clouded.

"Hey my dear," Miranda smiled. She had caught a bit of the conversation. "Shit happens my love. We're here, Jim found you, and you found us. It all comes round. Now, I've set the bathroom out for you, why not go and pamper yourself whilst we get a few things ready."

Feeling just a little overwhelmed, Amanda was happy to have a little time to herself, and to let Jim be Jim, or Alec, or whatever amalgam of the two he chose to be. A girl, not an awful lot older than she was, who gave her name as Claire showed Amanda to one of the bathrooms. She hadn't been in the original squat, but had joined the group some time after the raid, when they were looking for somewhere more permanent. She got some towels from a large cupboard on the landing, and set them down on the bathroom stool, putting a bar of their home made soap on top of the stack.

"It's a bit of an odd shape," she said. "But it's all pure, and there's no dead animals in it."

The bathroom had been installed by members of the commune, and, though not high luxury, was rather nice. It was an eclectic mix of end of line fittings procured on price rather than style, but they had been assembled with more care than the average builder would use so that the overall feel was quirky, but solid.

Downstairs, Miranda had cornered Jim.

"As long as the two of you are sure," she said, her tone was one of a concerned mother.

"We can talk, and tell each other things. You know, sort of, well, just things that's all," Jim was a bit at a loss for words, but knowing full well that Amanda would know exactly what he meant. "It was Amanda's idea to find you. She does things like that, you know, knowing me better than I do. It was a bit weird at first, but, well, I knew she cared, almost from the first day."

"You're really sold on her aren't you," Miranda smiled.

"Yes," Jim blushed slightly. "I love her."

"And?" Miranda looked into his eyes.

Jim looked back. "I do know the meaning of what I've just said," he added. The rest was between him and his partner.

"I won't interrogate you any more. Let's show you round, and sort your room out," Miranda got up and Jim followed, picking up their hastily packed bags.

The house was huge, it had been the main building for an influential farmer whose descendants had not been anywhere near as prudent as he. Much of the farm had been incorporated into neighbouring ones, leaving the house and its outbuildings redundant, and surrounded by a few acres of scrubby pasture that was generally thought to be no good to anyone. Although not in a tumbled down condition, the place was in a severe state of disrepair when the commune found it. The landowner was sympathetic to their way of life, and didn't really want to see the house crumble any further, but couldn't afford to maintain it either.   As the place was too inaccessible to be saleable, and not of any immediate use, beyond being a landmark, he was happy to allow the people to renovate it in exchange for a peppercorn rent.   The commune had to put a lot of work in after they arrived, and their first winter was dismal but, unbowed, they continued through and created the homely place that Jim now saw.   The land too had been worked, and they grew a lot of their own food, supplementing their income by working on farms in the area when required.   The case that caused their near eviction was assembled by one person that did not like their lifestyle, and who, for whatever spurious moral or religious reason, saw fit to cause them as much trouble as possible.   Ultimately the community won, but it had been a tense time, and where effort was diverted to fighting their cause, it was not directed to their home, so there was a great deal of work to do before the winter set in.   Spirits were high though, so it looked, to Jim at least, as though nothing on earth could stop them. As they rounded the top of a flight of stairs, Amanda popped her head round the bathroom door.   She'd had a long, and surprisingly luxurious bath, but, having been ushered away so neatly, had forgotten to take any change of clothes in with her.

"Hi my love," Miranda smiled.   "You may as well come along and I'll show you your room.   I expect you'd like a dunk too Jim, so."   She opened the same cupboard as Claire had.   "Here's a towel.   There'll be plenty of hot water."

"The soap is brilliant," Amanda smiled as Jim was gently nudged in the direction that she had just come from.

"You're keen on us being clean aren't you," she added.

"Well, I like people to feel at home, and you never do unless you've had a bath there.   That's what I've always thought," Miranda replied.   "Now my love, will this do you?"

She pushed open a bedroom door, revealing yet another eccentric interior.   Similar to the bathroom, any serviceable piece of furniture had been used regardless of style, and the walls painted in four separate colours. There was a very comfortable looking double bed in the far corner.

"It's brilliant," Amanda replied, her interest being attracted first to each individual item, and then to the effect of all of them.   It was a bit of an assault on the senses, but in a joyous way.

"And Jim?" she asked somewhat nervously.

"Well, that one's up to you my love."   Miranda was suddenly looking

226

thoughtful. "We've plenty of rooms, but."

"If it's O.K. with you, we're sort of a couple now," Amanda said, blushing brighter than the colour scheme of her room and adding, "Well, there's no sort of about it if you want the truth."

"I'll leave his bag here too then." Miranda placed Jim's bag on an old wartime utility chair next to a Victorian wash stand. "Would you like me to brush out that beautiful hair of yours?" she asked.

Apart from Jim and her parents, nobody had ever called her hair beautiful. Amanda thought it average if a bit unruly, so before thinking she agreed, forgetting that she was still only dressed in a towel. As she gently brushed, Miranda spoke.

"You seem to be good for Jim," she said. "Good for each other I think too."

"He's a good person." The sound of conviction was clear in Amanda's voice.

"That he is," Miranda said. "I wish we'd known him longer. I do"

"Look," Amanda said, summoning up some courage to be as frank as possible. "What turned this all on its head, between last time you saw us and now. What did it was something Jim said about you and Paul. Well, not directly but."

"Go on my love, I'm listening," Miranda replied calmly.

"He said that some people have been together forever, something like that, only they don't always know it, but some never can be, and they don't know that either. Like I guess he meant that they can try as hard as they like but, nothing." Amanda frowned slightly.

"Two sides of a coin," Miranda added.

"I guess so," Amanda went on. "But it was that. It wasn't directed at me, it was about you, but there was something that had been nagging, you know, rattling round my head for days, weeks. I don't know even when it started, but it was there and it got out that evening," Amanda said, looking at the floor.

Miranda paused from brushing, and, looking into a distance beyond the bounds of the room, said softly.

"And from then it all changed. I know what you mean my love. I know," she smiled.

"It has done, and everything is the same, except that it isn't," Amanda paused, whilst Miranda, who appeared to be deep in thought, resumed the steady, calming, brushing of her hair.

"Suddenly," she continued. "There I was, remembering the times when I got," she screwed her face up at the memory. "You probably don't know what happened to me."

"I don't, but It wasn't good was it," Miranda replied.

"No," Amanda looked at the floor.

"Jim got the same treatment? I can work that one out," Miranda frowned.

"Pretty much at the same time, could even have been the same day, certainly the same time of day," Amanda said as tears formed in her eyes.

"Don't go on if it hurts my love," Miranda spoke calmly.

"It's O.K. Thing is, we were, it happened. And it was only distance," Amanda regained her thread. "Anyway. My mind was jumping around and, well, there it was, some people are, and we'd shared things before we knew each other, sort of synergy I think, and I felt it, larger than life, we were meant to be. So I spoke my mind, and it *was* my mind talking, not, well, you know. And what follows, well, I haven't a clue, but I'll happily take the lot as it comes. Good or bad."

Miranda restarted brushing, and carefully arranging Amanda's hair.

"Look," she said. "I'm not Jim's mother, though I wouldn't have minded being, and I have no claim on him other than friendship, but all of these things are bonds. You've been honest with me, and it's my turn now. You don't need my approval, but, for what it's worth, you have it, and I'd like you to feel welcome here whenever you want to come and see us, and for however long you want. The bond of friendship is a hard one to find. I hope we have found that too. There, your hair is nice, let it finish drying and it'll really shine. You get yourself dressed, and I'll see you downstairs."

Amanda sat for some time, just thinking about the conversation, about the co-incidence of Jim taking shelter in the yard of what looked like a derelict building, and then, years later, all of this. When studying literature, she had dismissed such happenings as mere tools to make a sentimental plot in what was only really a newspaper series move on. But there it was, things like that were happening to her.

"You decent in there?" Jim knocked on the door as he spoke.

Amanda, still almost in a trance like state, went over and let him in.

"Hi Jimbo. I'd better get dressed," she smiled.

She rummaged in her bag, and picked out a loose fitting dress with a floral print which she had bought from a market some weeks before meeting Jim.   A further search brought a colourful woven belt, and the necessary underwear.   Without a hint of embarrassment she slipped out of the towel, and began dressing.

"I stuck a few decent things in there for you too Jim," she said, pointing across to the other bag.

Downstairs, the rest of the commune were in party mood, the joy from Miranda and Paul at the discovery of their friend having permeated though them like water in a sponge.   All was being done without a thought for organisation, yet all was coming together as though it had been planned months in advance.   Food was cooked, home made wine and ale retrieved from the cellar, and placed close to the door, ready for use, but still in a cool place.   Then, almost with perfect timing, Jim and Amanda made their entrance.   They had, of course, simply come down the stairs after their baths, totally oblivious to what they were walking in on.   As the two rounded into the big kitchen, Mad Dave picked up a steel wok and hit the base hard with a wooden spoon.   The sound was like the one at the start of so many films, only louder.

"Pray welcome!" he shouted in a mock formality "The best pub piano player in the district, and his dangerous partner! I give you Jim, or Alec if you prefer, and Amanda! Raise your glasses and toast our friends both old and new!"

"Blood and sand!" Jim whispered.

Amanda looked at his expression and couldn't help laughing, saying later that he couldn't have looked more surprised if someone had stuck a bomb up his arse.   Feeling that he should say something, Jim looked round, and, mustering such thoughts as he had, drew breath ready.

"Thank you," he said.   "Thank you all.   I wasn't with you long, and, well, it's bloody good to be here now, because I know you made it."

At this, Amanda, suddenly filled with the spirit of the day, exclaimed, "Yes! You made it! And right now it's great to be alive, and here!"   She looked marginally embarrassed by her outburst, but was still smiling when Dave chipped in.

"There she's as mad as the rest of us!" he smiled.   "Come and sit, or dance, we're having a party!"

Almost as if he'd cued it, one of the newer members of the commune stood up and started playing a fast blues inspired tune on the mouth organ, he was almost immediately joined by three other members who picked various instruments from their places leant on the wall.   The house was alive, and the party was set to go on into the night. Jim was coaxed to the piano, and Amanda, joined him, to sing some of the songs they had done back at the Quarry some weeks back. Food and drink was passed around, prepared in a manner that could not have been bettered by professional caterers. Later on some space was made for those who wanted to dance, all to the music of the members of the commune, with additions by Jim and Amanda, who when not playing music, danced to it into the small hours. Amid the general noise, Dave arrived at the back door, having slipped out unnoticed. Paul, who had been standing close to the door, just enjoying the atmosphere, looked at Dave and raised his eyebrows slightly.

"Those two need nothing to get high on," he smiled

"Just air matey, just air," Dave replied. "They got the real thing they have, and you can't put it in a tin and smoke it."

"Hows, um," Paul tipped his head to the door.

"Bugger's still there," Dave frowned.

"He isn't one of the usual lot, I've checked at the café. So I don't think he's after us," Paul replied.

"We should fix him if he's after." Dave nodded towards Jim and Amanda, who were sitting with each other, sharing a plate of food. "They don't deserve."

"No," Paul said firmly. "They don't, but we'll have to be a bit subtle. They're safe here, and so is their boat where it is, so we bide our time. Something will turn up."

Nothing more was said on the subject that evening, and nothing happened to spoil the day. It was about three in the morning when Jim and Amanda eventually landed back in their room.

"God!" Amanda gasped. "They know how to throw a party!"

"They do, always did I think. I remember one they had when I was at the squat," Jim replied, idly watching the tail lights of a car disappear along the lane. Shutting the world out with the curtains, he added in a falsetto sing song voice. "I could have danced all night!"

"We did matey! We did," Amanda flopped back on the bed. "Time to turn in pal, before *you* turn into Eliza."

It was gone ten the next morning before they woke, feeling strangely refreshed after the nights revelling. Most of the house was up and about, and as they arrived down to the smells of a hearty breakfast, they were ushered into the kitchen by Claire, who Amanda had met the night before.

"Hi guys," she smiled. "You two sure know how to party. I wish you could stay with us."

"We'll be back, lots of times if you'll have us," Amanda said cheerily. "It is a great place you have here."

"It is, and you're welcome any time," Claire replied. "Now, come and have something to eat. Mad Dave has gone off with Paul on the bike, but they said they'd be back in an hour, that was a while ago, so just tuck in."

"So, now we know something he doesn't," Dave said as he was standing with Paul across the road, from one of the town's two hotels that would be regarded as worth staying in by a man with a relatively new Jaguar. "Now let's find out who he is."

They had followed a trail left by the Jaguar created by a plastic bag of left over white emulsion paint that Dave had thoughtfully placed in front of the vehicle's back wheel whilst some of the revellers created a bit of a distraction for the driver the previous night. Beyond a slight pop as the bag burst, spreading paint over the bottom of the car and the back wheel, the driver was oblivious to what had been done. As the car sped down the road, it left a trail for long enough for Paul and Dave to know which way it had gone when it had got to the main road. Some simple deduction took them to first one, and then the other of the two hotels the town boasted, in the car park of which was the offending machine. Some splatter from the paint which was visible around the wheel arch, gave them the proof they needed that it was the same vehicle. It was reasonable to assume that the driver would not rise until relatively late, given that he had been outside the commune until the early hours, so, guessing that whoever it was would make the assumption that the revellers would also have a late morning, Paul and Dave had set off to follow the trail early, leaving two other members to clear the paint up before the Jaguar arrived again.

"So, your turn, what do we do now?" Dave scratched his head.

"Well, we could brass it out at the front I guess," Paul mused. "Or we could go to the tradesman's entrance. I always think you find a better class of people at the tradesman's entrance."

Before long the pair had charmed their way round one of the maids (the hotel proprietors still called them chambermaids) and started on the subject of the owner of the Jaguar.

"We don't like him," she said with some conviction. "He's never a good word to say, and he seems all furtive, you know like he's some kind of spy or something.   My mate was working the switchboard, she overheard him talking to someone, all hushed voices, like he thinks he's James Bond or something. That, and you don't go into his room when he's there, dirty old git. Bloody hands everywhere, I tell you, I near belted him one the other day.   Then he behaves like we should be all respectful.   I look forward to him going. Toffee nosed lecherous little git. Anyways that's my troubles, what can I do for you?"

"We're always on the lookout for a bit of casual work."   Neither Dave not Paul liked telling lies, and this wasn't one as such.   "Do your bosses ever need gardeners or anything?"

"Well," the maid replied.   "They're not in right now, else I wouldn't be standing here gassing with you two.   I can ask, or you could come back in the middle of the week."

"Thanks," Paul said politely.   "We'll get back as soon as we can."

Whilst Jim and Amanda were being given the shortened lecture on the finer points of the Panther motorcycle by Paul.   Mad Dave sat at the kitchen table with Miranda and a few of the others, letting them know the situation before going back out to meet their friends.   It was a sunny morning, with just the lightest of breezes.   English Summer on it's very best behaviour.

"The way he's eulogising about that thing, almost makes you forget what he calls it when it won't start in winter," Miranda laughed.   "Still he's got their attention, so what did you two find?"

"Well."   Dave replied, looking as Jim and Amanda listened intently to Paul.   "We don't have a name, but he's a nasty piece of work that's for sure."

Miranda looked thoughtful as Dave described the morning's sortie, her brow furrowing slightly as she took each item in.   After Dave had finished, she remained silent, trying to piece some things together in her mind.

"So, they, it must be they because he was sorting stuff on the phone. You're right though Dave, there isn't much to go on, but there's something nagging in my head.   The bloke you described, he sounds familiar.   I know there's too many like him around, but this one.   I've heard of him, either from Amanda or Alec, I mean Jim," she said

"So," said Dave, coldly.   "He's after them then.   That can't be allowed."

"No," Claire chipped in.   "No it can't.   Because it's not whether they're

232

after Jim and Amanda, or us."

Miranda looked across the table to Claire, who looked, wide eyed, back at them.

"You two look like a pair of tom cats circling each other!" The familiar bounce was back in Dave's voice. "Neither of you want to say it, but Claire's got it, if I'm not wrong. Just say it girl, Miranda's thinking the same, then we can have a little meeting."

Claire looked nervous, but spoke her mind.

"They are us," she said firmly. "So if that shit is going after Jim and Amanda, he's after us as well." Miranda looked puzzled but Claire went on. "It would be too easy for some of us to think, like who is this Saint Alec when he turns up. But we don't do that do we. You welcomed me without asking questions. I've never felt anything other than an equal even though I've not been here anywhere near as long as the rest of you. And that's about it really."

Miranda smiled as her friend spoke.

"I know they will go away, but they are still part of us," Claire added.

"You want them as part of the community?" Miranda asked.

"I would, I mean, they sort of are, but we should say it in the open," Claire replied. "It's clear they have their own path too, but that shouldn't conflict. I mean it's not as if we have hard and fast rules, but they are part of all of this and they should know it's here for them. Jim was before I was, so it sort of makes sense."

"If any sense is needed," Dave added. "I don't have much of it but you have my vote."

"What goes round." Miranda thought out loud, adding, "Let's talk with the tribe, and thanks Claire, I was too close to this to think straight. The bastard is after them, he's after us too, you're spot on."

A few minutes later, Paul walked into the kitchen which was now full of people. Claire was the first to speak.

"We've been having a talk Paul. And we'd like to make a collective decision," she said

"About?" Paul looked uneasy.

"About Jim and Amanda. I suggested they be a proper part of all of this. We wanted to wait for you so we could decide," she replied.

"So, let's," Paul smiled.

Shortly after the decision was made, it was also decided to have a picnic, and it was during this that Miranda nudged Claire to speak. She

233

was naturally quite shy, but had gained a lot of confidence since joining the commune. She liked being there for the feeling that, whilst anything went, nothing ever felt that radical in spite of the fact that most of it was. The whole notion of a bunch of people just making things up as they went along, sharing things and all the stuff that went with their existence was, to an outsider, both absurd and unworkable, yet it worked, and had done for a long time. There were no rules, no governing body, and no work rotas, but things still got done. Claire looked around at the gathering, as they sat round a big table cloth on the edge of one of their small pastures. Some of the people noticed she may want to say something, and fell silent. This eventually pervaded the group and Claire looked round.

"I feel like I should tap a glass or ring a small gong," she said. "But you are all listening so. Look, I'd like to ask if Amanda and Jim would like to consider themselves part of this community like, on the same footing as we all are. We all know you have to do your own thing too, it's important that we all do that, but we'd like you to know that you have a family with us. If you want us that is. That's sort of all really."

Amanda looked to her partner and could see the tears slowly forming. Stroking his head lightly, she took a deep breath and then shut her eyes briefly to clear her mind. All attention was on the couple now.

"Most people that know me," she spoke in a slightly faltering voice. "Pretty much all in fact know I'm not often lost for words. But you lot are full of surprises, and this one's just knocked me over. I turn up a few days ago, and." Jim put his arm on her shoulder, she could see he had something to say.

"I can't put it into words either," he added. "But thanks, as you come to know me you will realise what today means to me. And, yes, we do have stuff to do, but we'll keep in touch, and we'll be back if you'll have us. I don't know how it all works out but it will," his voice tailed off, so Mad Dave took on the mantle of speaker.

"Let's raise a glass again to one new, and one old member of the family here."

Back at the pub, the little Mayfly was much as it had been when they left it. Their time at Bank Top seemed to have gone by in minutes, but they were also happy to be back in their home, however cramped it was. Joe had mentioned Jake kicking up "One hell of a racket." not long after they had left, but there was no further incident, and all seemed as it should be. Jake greeted Jim and Amanda, as though they had been away for years rather than overnight, and it was hard to believe that he could be fierce in any way.

"It's what they're like," Jim commented, later in the evening. "Alsations, very much a one person dog. He liked us because his owner told him we were friends. Even with all that display when we got back, if Joe had told him to kill us, well would you have stuck around?"

The weather was pleasant, so after a round of drinks, which Miranda, Jim, and Claire insisted upon, they had moved a couple of miles along the canal to more open country, to enjoy the peace. Claire had wanted to see the couple off, and to see their home so that she could picture them in it. She'd managed to squeeze into the side-car with Jim and Amanda for the run.

"I did mean what I said back there," Jim continued. "I want to stay in touch, and go back there. Not to live, but, they're sort of, well family. Mine don't want me, they've made that plain enough, and Bank Top do."

"That's a bit harsh if you don't mind me saying," Amanda looked worried. "Your folks must care about you."

"Mum and Dad," Jim thought before continuing the sentence. "They're O.K. when I see them, but they could have let me live with one of them, you'd have thought that, but. Shit, look you know all that crap. Bank Top reminds me of a happy home, brings back memories that I don't really have but that doesn't matter. It's, well. It's family."

Amanda looked down. "It's the same for me Jimbo," she replied ponderously "Up until recently, well, you know how secure it all was, except for all the shit that happened that my folks knew nothing about. Then it all went, gone, and I'm on my own as much as you."

"And now we're not," Jim added.

"No, you're right. There's us, and Bank Top. Does this make them my in-laws?" she said.

"Only if we're married. I mean, crap, that sounds like we're doing something we should be ashamed of, except we're not are we," Jim replied.

"I know what you mean. We are what we are Jim, no worries."

"I guess they'll have to be outlaws then," he smiled.

"Yes." Amanda laughed. "Outlaws. Mad Dave would like that. I mean in-laws have a pretty poor track record on the whole."

They talked a lot about the commune, and its people in the following

235

days, sometimes speculating on what they'd be doing, and others musing on how, after such a brief time they felt they'd always known them. Summer was well and truly in command of the weather, and the couple almost forgot they were actually working. The canal here was quiet, and they could go for hours, almost all day sometimes without seeing a boat on the move. It couldn't last, they knew that, they were heading for industry and coal, a lot of it, but for now everything was right. On the approach to a medium sized flight of locks, Jim decided to go ahead to set things for Amanda to make the slow descent into industry and eventually another city. Stepping off at a bridge-hole, he paced swiftly towards the lock. The speed limit here was, as for all canals, four miles an hour, but there was no hurry, so it wasn't long before Jim was quite a bit ahead. The flight was around a shallow bend which was obscured by another bridge. As Amanda steered the Mayfly round, she saw the first lock was not ready, and no sign of Jim. Seeing too that the lock gates were chained shut, she reasoned that he'd probably gone back to tell her and they must have crossed under the bridge and missed each other, though she wasn't quite sure how. It was not hard to turn in the width of the canal, which close to the lock, had reasonable depth on both sides. She'd not noticed that all the time she was being watched by a man in a grey suit, who shouted across to her as she was about to retrace the short distance to the bridge.

"You looking for someone?" he asked.

"Yes," her reply was obvious. "He's just a bit taller than me and," she was cut short in her description by his words.

"Jim Stratton," the man shouted.

"Yes. How do you know," Amanda replied.

"Because, you little tart, we've been looking for the pair of you, and if you want him to stay in one piece, you come with me."

"What do you mean?" Amanda shouted.

"I mean we've got the little bastard, and if you behave he won't get hurt too much."

Thinking quickly, Amanda tried to buy some time.

"Look, I can't stop here, there's not enough water," she lied. "I can tie up just after the bridge." With that she put the engine into gear and flicked the choke on. The motor responded by spluttering and then stopping amid a haze of blueish smoke.

"Damn!" she shouted, and started pulling furiously at the starter cord. This pulled far too much petrol into the outboard and it simply refused to

236

start.

"Get a move on you little brat!" the man shouted.

"It's flooded, it sometimes happens," Amanda said. "Jim's told me about it. I'll get the thing going in a bit." Knowing that this was the best she could do, she flicked the choke off again and set about restarting the motor.

"You'd better," the man replied. "Look, I'm not standing here all day. If you aren't through that bridge soon. Well you'd better be."

"Where else do you think I'm going?" Amanda shrieked back petulantly. "And I want to see Jim before I go through the bridge. Bring him round to the front so I can see him."

She continued her show of trying to start the motor, knowing full well that it would start as soon as the deliberate flooding had evaporated. Eventually the man lost his patience and left.

"We'll have the little bastard for you to see," he shouted as he walked off.

Five minutes later the motor started as easily as it did when new, and she edged her way down the canal thinking her next move. As she approached the bridge, she could see three men and Jim, who was being held in an arm lock of some kind. She opened the throttle aiming to take the bridge well above the speed limit, hoping that the increase in the minimal wake that the Mayfly threw out would not be noticed. As she started to close with the group a glint of metal caught her eye in the sun. They were holding a knife to Jim's throat. Taking care to hit the bridge-hole centrally she cut the speed to tick over and, once under the arch pointed the vessel to a large hawthorn bush, some way along the far bank. With fingers crossed, she picked her windlass up and, trembling in every joint, stepped onto the towpath. She could hear Jim's voice protesting that he wasn't moving until he saw her, and that they could cut his throat if they pleased. He too was stalling. The Mayfly obediently puttered across the canal and lodged its self in the bush, causing no damage to either vessel or vegetation. Presently, she thought, the earlier flooding of the carburettor and the very low throttle setting would cause the spark plug to oil up, and the motor would then stop.

"This is our time," she thought. "And nobody is taking it from us." With that in her mind, two paces took her to the edge of the arch.

"The little cow has gone to the other bank!" the man holding Jim shouted.

Seconds later though, Amanda rounded the bend in the towpath that took it under the bridge, and swung her windlass as hard as she could at the arm

237

that was holding a knife.

"Jesus Christ! She's busted my bleeding arm!" the man screamed.

Whether or not this was true, the knife dropped into some long grass by the canal and Jim followed up the windlass blow with an elbow backwards into his captors stomach.

"Shit, you said these were a pair of kids on the run not bleeding animals," the man gasped.

Transfixed on the spot at the sight of what she had just done, Amanda felt an arm grip her around the throat. There was no knife this time, but the grip was near strangulation.

"Right! You little whore! Game is over, you're coming with me!" the unidentified voice said.

Jim who was bleeding from a small cut under his chin, where the knife had caught him, gathered his senses and went to help Amanda, who, on recovering hers, issued a sharp blow with the windlass, making solid contact with the knee of her attacker, and elbowed him in the stomach for good measure. Jim, having rounded the bend in the towpath briefly saw a face he recognised, as the man doubled up in reaction to Amanda's elbow. She was ready again with the windlass, but Jim simply pushed the man backwards into the canal.

"That's for calling Amanda a whore," he shouted.

The man who had been holding Jim at knife point had by now recovered and, nursing a badly bruised, but not broken, arm came to join the fray. It was unfortunate for him that he stumbled slightly on a protruding stone, allowing Amanda to trip him still further and land him in the canal.

"That's for assaulting Jim, you can rot in fucking hell you little weasels!" she shrieked "Now stay in the water or I'll kill the pair of you, and don't think I don't mean it." she brandished her windlass at them, her face red with anger.

"You little brat!" protested the man that had attacked Amanda.

"I'd keep quiet if I were you," Jim said firmly. "You'd better meet the arsehole that has messed up your family's life. This is Mr Carver."

Amanda, still full of rage lunged forward, aiming another blow with her windlass, but Jim held her back.

"The shit isn't worth it," he said, turning his attention to the two men steeping in the canal. "But you can tell us what your game is, and that's before we let you out of the water," he added.

It was a warm day, and not too unusual a sight for about twelve motorbikes to be winding along the lanes of the area. Some time earlier in the day Paul at Bank Top had a message from the café that someone from one of the hotels in town needed to speak to him, so, using the payphone there, he took the opportunity to return the call.

"Look," the maid said, having been lucky enough to be doing reception duty. "I don't care what this costs me but your friends might be in some kind of danger. The geezer that was staying here is off in search of them and he's got two heavies with him. I think they've got a pretty good idea of where they are too."

The news wasn't entirely unexpected. Both Paul (proud owner of the Panther) and Mad Dave (owner of a BSA Super Rocket) did repair and tuning work for an amiable local biker gang. They were not Hell's Angels, but liked to look the part, and were up for assisting the pair in their venture. After a zigzag route, that took them across each of the canal bridges, they had found what they were looking for, Paul having done the necessary arithmetic to work out their mileage. The Jaguar that was parked at the hotel, and outside bank top, was in a lay by near a bridge over the canal. The man in the car was, however, not the one that had been watching them the previous weekend. When the sound of their engines had died down they could hear what could only be called a disturbance of the peace going on beneath their feet. Paul propped his trusty machine on its stand, having detached the side-car that morning.

Tapping on the window of the Jaguar he asked the driver. "Hey bud, you know anything about what's going on."

"If I did I'm not telling scum like you anything," the driver replied gruffly.

"Now now," Mad Dave added. "My pal is only being polite. I mean you won't mind us having a look then, you know, like as the good citizens we are. We'll leave you in the hands of these gentlemen." he waved his hand in the direction of the rest of the gang. "Though, to be truthful, I can't vouch for them all being of very good breeding. I mean one of them rides a Honda. A Honda! I tell you!"

The bikers played to image and wandered round the vehicle, some sitting on the wing, and all doing their best to look downright menacing. Underneath the bridge it was Dave who first witnessed the situation.

"Blood and sand!" he exclaimed. "Come and look at this Paul. I told you the girl was dangerous, and I'll say one other thing. I'm not ever, ever upsetting you Amanda!"

239

"You can say it in prison if you want. I'm pressing charges, and you have no evidence," spouted Mr Carver.

"Jim's blood on one end of the knife, and the prints on the other are a bit of a give-away you little fucking turd!" Amanda bellowed, still red faced. "It's attempted fucking murder you'll go down for, or conspiracy to it. Hanging's too good for you, you, you, shit, arsehole, fuck brained little piece of turd!"

Tears then came flooding, and Dave put a comforting arm around her. As he did so the two, who were still in the canal made a move to get out.

"I wouldn't do that if I were you," Paul said meekly, then whistled. Three of the ugliest members of the gang joined the group at the bridge.

"Could you make sure these guys don't get out until they have washed behind the ears. I'm going to call the police. Now that's something I never thought I'd say with a straight face. Jim, did you see where the knife fell?" Paul asked. Jim nodded that he had.

"Well, show Dave, but nobody is to touch the thing until the coppers turn up. It all hinges on that," Paul added.

Dave walked slowly, still comforting Amanda, to where Jim was standing next to the weapon.

"Don't look at it my love," he said softly, and gently stroking her hair added. "You need your man now, and he needs you. Leave the rest to us."

Without a word Amanda took Jim in her arms, and held him tightly.

"I'm O.K," he said. "It was only a nick, he just caught me a little when you clouted him."

In a muffled tone, with her head firmly against his chest, she replied, "He was going to kill you Jim. He was going to kill you."

"I doubt if he really had the balls to do it," Jim replied reassuringly, doing his best to hide his own shock at the turn of events. "But either way, you stopped him, and Carver is finished for good now."

"You're still bleeding," Amanda's muffled voice said. "He hurt you," she cried openly.

"And you stopped him," Jim repeated softly. "You stopped him."

The police were not long in arriving and, though at first rather suspicious of the gang of bikers, they listened attentively to their story. The scene under the bridge was much the same as it had been when Paul left. Carver and his henchman were still standing in the canal being watched over by the trio of bikers. Jim and Amanda were a few yards away comforting each other, and Dave, who had found the spot where the knife landed was standing guard over it. Although this was not really necessary he had nothing much else to do and, having taken in the situation, wanted some time to himself to get over the thought of what could have happened.

"There's sufficient blood on that to tie the one end to whoever the blood belongs to, and you say the attacker wasn't wearing any form of glove?" the policeman queried Dave.

"You should ask Jim and Amanda, but tread lightly mate," he replied. "Neither of the guys in the water had gloves and it was the big geezer that had the knife."

"Bleeding amateurs!" the policeman said as he looked under the bridge. "I think they've soaked up enough for the time being lads. You can let them out now, if we need to we'll chuck them back later"

"Are you really going to take the word of these vandals, runaways, and freak farmers over me!" Carver protested.

"Well," the policeman stroked his chin. "Everybody gets a fair say, but I doubt if the lad nicked himself shaving with a hunting knife so there has to be something behind all of this."

A search of the Jaguar uncovered various drafts, and a final letter that was addressed to Mr E.Donaldson, care of the shop that Amanda had been working at when she met Jim for the first time. This and the knife, together with allegations of impropriety still under investigation from earlier in the year were enough to place the three under arrest. The radio confirmed that the maid at the hotel had also been in touch with the police, having found various suspicious items in the room she had been told to clear out. The policeman now walked over to Jim and Amanda.

In as soft a voice as he could muster he asked, "I'm afraid I'll have to ask you to make a statement. I know this has been a shocking time for you, but we don't want these people to get away with this."

"Nor do we," Amanda replied firmly. "That man has ruined my family. I can't prove it but."

"If he's done anything else that's criminal, we'll find it," the policeman said. "I can't imagine he was just after kidnapping you, well, he wouldn't do it this way if that was the case. And the letter in the car is pretty damning. I'm afraid I may to have to ask your friend to give a sample of blood so we can tie things up about the knife."

Amanda screwed her face up trying, and failing, to avoid tears. Jim answered for her.

"Do what you have to," he said. "But I don't want to be away from my home too long."

"It's O.K. we'll take you back. And where is it you live," asked the policeman.

"Just over there," Amanda replied. "Oh god!" She squeaked. "I left it to, no!"

Without a further word, she had dived into the canal and was swimming strongly over to the Mayfly, which was still amiably nestled in the hawthorn. As soon as she was on the boat, she set about changing the fouled spark plug and within five minutes, the motor was running and the boat reversing in a neat arc to line up with the bridge. A further five had it tied neatly to a convenient bollard near to where the knife had lain.

"This is our home," Amanda said, still dripping wet. "It isn't much, but we love it. I've been running away too long, and now I suppose you want me to be normal."

"Normal means entirely different things to different people," the policeman replied. "Your mate here has been telling me about you. You're O.K. stick with it girl," he smiled. "You go and get dry and we'll sort things out here."

As the nick on Jim's chin was still bleeding, it was decided that he should take a trip to outpatients to have it cleaned up. A W.P.C. was called to look after Amanda, and take a statement from her on the way to the hospital. She and two colleagues arrived in a van almost as quickly as the first two policemen had. The arrested men were taken away with two policemen accompanying them, and the Jaguar was driven back by the third. Paul and Dave promised to look after the Mayfly until they returned. A few of the biker gang decided to accompany Jim and Amanda to the hospital, because they felt it was somehow the right thing to do. Some hours later the couple were back in their home. Jim had narrowly escaped the need for stitches, and had a large plaster on his chin, which he was instructed to leave there for a few days, and to call at any outpatients department if he felt there was any sign of infection. With statements completed and arrangements in place for contact to be made should it need be there was no further need for their immediate presence.

"The bastard's finished now," Jim said as he looked out across the canal.

"You know," Amanda spoke dreamily, as though the day hadn't really happened. "Old Lou did say that that windlass had probably been used many times to defend a maid's honour, or to sort out a dispute. I hope he won't mind."

"You used it to save my life, whether or not the guy would really have done it, you weren't to know were you. You do seem to be making a habit of jumping in the canal though," Jim said.

Amanda smiled for the first time since the ordeal.

"That bit," she admitted. "I hadn't worked out, but hey, swimming is one thing I can do well so I swam. Now lets get out of here. I want to put a couple of miles between here and us if we can before tea. The place sort of freaks me out a bit."

Chapter 15

"But the letter clearly said that there would be trouble if we came back," Jean pointed to the unsigned document that arrived earlier in the day. "We should have taken her with us."

"She should have done what she was told," Edwin replied. "We sent her a ticket and made every arrangement. She knew we had to go straight away. She should have followed not got a half baked idea in her head, I mean you just can't mess with these people."

"However did it come this far. I mean how did we get involved. Why or how did that evil man get on the board. And now he can threaten us because," Jean stopped abruptly, unable to bring the threat that had been made, into words.

"We weren't planning on coming back, at least not for a long time, he says that if we co-operate no harm will come to her," Edwin tried to sound reassuring but was interrupted by the telephone.

"That's probably them," he sighed, a deep furrow across his forehead.

"Hi dad. It's me." The sound of his daughter's voice left Edwin lost for words.

"Dad? Are you there?" Amanda asked.

"Where are you, what do they want us to do, let me know because whatever it is," he was cut short by the voice of Amanda.

"I am free, I wasn't kidnapped, and Carver has been arrested," she said.

"For what?" Edwin asked.

"If you want to know the truth, there were quite a few things. He was already being investigated for trying to force himself on some of the girls at his work, then there's conspiracy to kidnap, and conspiracy to murder," Amanda stopped sharply.

"Murder!" Edwin replied.

"Yes, but not me. They wanted to kidnap me. One of his men held a knife to Jim," she bit her lip as she spoke, and closed her eyes tight to stop any tears.

"Jim? Who is Jim?" Edwin asked.

"He's my best friend. I thought I'd told you about him via Marie. You

244

sent that telegram back, remember." Amanda said.

"Marie just mentioned the name, we assumed it was Jemima, from school. I don't like the sound of this," Edwin tried to sound paternal. "You aren't seeing too much of this Jim are you?"

"Sorry dad, but that's not the question. He was willing to have his throat cut for me, and he damn near did. The question is when are you going to come back and fight your corner," Amanda replied.

"But we can't. You should come over here for your own safety. I insist on that now," her father frowned deeply.

"It was you that left. I chose to stay and fight Dad. And I have fought, so has Jim. He doesn't know you, and he didn't have to do anything but he has. And so have I," Amanda said.

"You have to come over here on the next available flight," Edwin insisted.

"No Dad. You must come back here, and finish the fight."

"You can't tell your own father what to do!"

"No. That's true, but I can ask," Amanda answered him, rather sharply.

The phone call ended soon after that exchange. Jean had tried to persuade her daughter too, but failed. Eventually the poor line quality had the last say by cutting them off mid sentence.

"They just won't bloody listen," Amanda had tears rolling down her face as she spoke. "They just won't bloody well listen."

Jim looked at the floor not knowing quite what he should say.

"You take a knife for them, you get arrested for them and they still don't get it," she said.

"For you," Jim found his voice again. "It was for you. Not them. Maybe it should have been but I only know you."

They stood by the phone, which was in the foyer of a small hotel. The police had found out that a letter setting out terms and conditions had already been sent to Spain and had made contact with the Mayfly by sending a junior constable along the towpath on a bicycle. Having found them, a call was arranged to be put through to the hotel. Somebody had obviously decided that it it may be upsetting for Amanda to have to talk from a police station. As they stood talking, the phone went off several times with bookings and suchlike but eventually the receptionist passed it over to Amanda who, on hearing the voice on the other end, instantly passed it on to Jim.

"Mandy!" It was Jean, her mother. "I can't leave it like this, please come back."

245

"Look, you probably don't want to talk to me now," Jim replied. "But Amanda passed the phone to me like it was a bomb or something."

"I want my daughter!" Jean protested.

"I'll pass you over in a second. But just think from her point of view for a moment," Jim said

"How dare you!" Jean interrupted. "How dare you think you know my daughter better than I do."

"I wouldn't pretend that I did. But she already knows me better than anybody," Jim said calmly. "Because I trust her. She's a special person. That's all I really do know about her, but those two things are enough."

"You leave my daughter alone, you've got her into enough trouble," Jean replied angrily.

"No. I'm not buying that," Jim concealed the fury that was building. "You left the country, and now you're in a prison of your own making. Maybe it's sunny, and you can go to the shops, but you're still in a prison because you feel you can't come back."

Jean tried to cut in but Jim kept talking.

"Over here. If you'd got clapped in irons and sent to the nick, the both of you, they wouldn't put Amanda in as well. And you want to know the big joke here. You didn't do anything, you're innocent, and you've put yourselves away. Now you want to sentence your own daughter to the same as you. And all because you're too scared to come back and kick the crap out of whoever did this to you. Sorry but if you don't like that, it's the truth as I see it, now here's your daughter."

Amanda spent a long time listening to her mother and said very little in response. The look on her face was one of resignation rather than any form of upset or anger. The voice chirped away like those heard in comedy films, and Jim had very little idea of the exact words, but the general gist was pretty obvious. Eventually the voice fell silent, but still Amanda did not reply. She stared into the middle distance for a long time. Her mother knew she was still there by the slight sound of her breath on the receiver.

"It's all different now Mum," Amanda said. "I'm sorry but it is. It's you that must come back. That's really all I can say. I do love you both and I miss you horribly, but that's not why you should come back,"

The silence then continued for some time.

"We couldn't just come. Things don't work like that, but we want to know you are safe," Jean replied.

"I am. And I know nothing happens quickly, but at least think about it," Amanda said.

"Alright Mandy. I promise that your father and I will talk about this, but that's all I can promise," Jean said resignedly.

"That's all I can ask," Amanda smiled.

"I wish I could make you change your mind about coming here. But you won't will you," Jean said.

"No," Amanda replied.

"Then be good, and be careful. You are a special person. Your friend was right about that bit," Her mother's voice was a good deal calmer as she spoke.

"I will, and thanks. 'Bye Mum. I hope to see you soon."

Amanda carefully replaced the receiver and continued staring blankly into the reception area. After some time Jim put a comforting arm around her shoulder.

"Come and sit down," he said. "This has been horrible for you, and I'm sorry for what I said."

Amanda moved her head, looked into Jim's eyes and spoke in the softest voice he had heard from her.

"Don't be. You spoke from the heart. Mum will get it eventually," she said.

"I'm sorry to but in," the receptionist said, having come over and stood by them. "But you look like you could both do with a cup of coffee."

The pair thanked her and she returned with a tray laden with cups, coffee pot and biscuits.

"You take as long as you like," she said. "The police told us what happened to you. Awful. I hope he gets put away in a dark dungeon forever."

Amanda smiled.

"I'll leave you two to talk then," the receptionist added, and returned to her post.

Jim and Amanda didn't actually say very much at all, and drank their coffee in silence, each with their own thoughts. It was Amanda who spoke first, pouring a second cup for herself and Jim from the well filled pot.

"It's true," she said quietly, but decisively. "It's all different now." A tear slowly tracked down her right cheek. "All the time on the island, I was expecting things to go back to normal like I said. All the stuff that we did before. I was looking forward to it." She closed her eyes for a

247

moment and on opening them, continued. "But it never can be can it."

"No," Jim replied. "Never. I'd be lying to say otherwise. I said that before, and nothing has changed, well except."

"Even without you it wouldn't have," Amanda said.

"You can't unscramble an egg," Jim smiled wistfully.

"True. And I'm not sad, not really. It's just that I hadn't thought about it much since, well, that's all. Now I do, it's all like a memory, something that happened to someone else," Amanda replied.

Jim knew too well the feelings that she was experiencing, there having been so many abrupt changes in his short life. But he had no words of comfort for her other than that which he had already said. After some minutes, he did speak again though.

"I'm not sad either Mand. Not even when I had the knife on my throat. Things have changed, so let's just see where it gets us."

She smiled, her face clearing of the look of worry.

"Yep Jimbo. Let's go face the world again," she said.

As they arrived back at the canal, the police constable, who was not much older than Jim, greeted them. He had been set to look after the boat so that Jim and Amanda could go directly to the hotel.

"I've always dreamed of just taking a long journey into the unknown," he said. "How did you two manage it?"

"Long story," Amanda smiled. "Would you like a cup of tea whilst we tell you some of it."

"I shouldn't," he replied. "But what the hell. It's a nice day."

With the kettle beginning to sing the couple did their best to tell their story, leaving out anything that may have appeared dubious in the eyes of the law. It was good in the telling, and the constable listened with interest.

"I sort of followed in the family footsteps, but I'd rather not be a copper if you want the truth. We're not that popular at the moment," he said.

"Like anything, a good policeman is," Jim cut himself short before saying what was on his mind.

"Rare," added the constable. "You don't have to say it. I've seen the file on you, and you have every right to mistrust the lot of us."

"It must be hard though," Amanda interjected. "Following orders and all. I mean you could be told to arrest us for no reason, and you'd have to."

The constable blushed slightly. " I guess so," he replied cautiously. "But we have to be here. I mean."

"You seem O.K," Jim interrupted. "And whatever your view on law and order, a good policeman is better than a bad one."

"Thanks," the constable smiled. "I do my best, but there are some as are on the make."

The whistle of the kettle cut him short as tea was made, and biscuits brought out of a deed box.

"These things are good for keeping mice out of old paperwork, and they're bloody brilliant to keep food in too," Amanda declared. "They do look a bit odd out of context like this though," she added.

The conversation covered a number of subjects, and was in full swing when the constable's superior officer came along the towpath in search of him.

"Please tell me he's not going to say what's all this 'ere 'ere 'ere," Amanda joked, leaving the constable trying to conceal laughter as he addressed the officer.

"Err," he giggled under his breath. "Can I call it community relations?"

"Can I call it community relations *sir!*" his superior replied. "And only if you two have a spare cup of tea for me?"

About half an hour later, the Police and ex fugitives parted company, to the onlooker at least, as best of friends. Amanda started the outboard and they were soon under way, their intention to be close to, but not in, the city. The plan after that was to do a long run and tie up somewhere pleasant, to work out the next stage of their itinerary.

"That was a bit odd," Amanda mused. "I mean we wouldn't have told all that to the coppers earlier."

"No, but then we didn't know they had it all on file anyway, which is a little bit worrying if you want the truth of it. I mean why have a file on us?" Jim replied cautiously.

"I thought that too. I noticed you were about as cagey with some of the stuff you were saying as well," Amanda replied.

"Yup. Only tell them what they know already, even if they were friendly. A bit like teachers I guess. You know, the trendy guy that wants to be one of the gang," Jim smiled.

The city was their last delivery of a watch until they returned south, where there was one for a wealthy person in the "Square Mile" who was one of the backers of the scheme, and the remaining one for Dave Harris. Most of the parcels that had been given to them to deliver were now with their recipients, and there was something of a big hole looming in their finances. The pay for taking readings on Clive Prentice's machine was not quite enough to keep them in food and fuel for the return trip.

"We can economise on petrol by just towing the thing," Amanda suggested. "And whilst the weather is warm we can do less hot meals, that'll save a bit. I mean as long as we can eat we'll be O.K. everything else is paid for."

"I'd like a bit in reserve though," Jim replied cautiously. "Repairs and stuff. I mean we've been lucky up to now."

"I wonder if there are any short term jobs going, you know, like a week picking fruit or something. We're ahead of ourselves now, despite all the setbacks. Well, not so much ahead, but we go a lot quicker than we ever thought we could."

"No harm in looking I suppose," Jim smiled. "We might get lucky."

What did turn up was sheer scale. The waterways they had traversed so far were relatively small, even the river that they started off on was small by comparison with what now faced them. Hand towing at a sleepy pace was out of the question and they shared the water with full size commercial traffic. The little motor could rev freely here as there were higher speed limits, but this meant that they would use more fuel if they wanted to keep up and not miss too many locks. The thought of stopping anywhere to enjoy a summer job was not going to be possible at least for the next week or more. It was refreshing for the pair to see proper cargo being taken by water, but it was also a bit frightening comparing the relative hugeness of the barges with their meagre little craft. Still, they had been earning their living from the water and felt justified in continuing unashamed at what they were doing. Where time permitted, some of the people working the larger craft talked to them, at first thinking they were holidaymakers. Their explanation of their presence often was met with surprise, and sometimes derision, but more often they were encouraged to stick with it. The traverse of the wider waterways was less physically tiring due to manning of the locks, but they worked long hours which seemed to more than compensate for the lack of physical effort. They were also spending an awful lot of time on the Mayfly. On narrower canals they could hop off at bridges and go walking, often one of the pair would walk to a shop that was close to the canal, and meet at the next lock. Here they could not avoid each others company even if they had wanted to. It was during the big traverse that Jim noticed, yet again, Amanda's mood had changed.

250

When asked if he had upset her he was told not to be stupid, and it was just one of those things. He knew, from what she had told him when they shared some confidences, that there were going to be certain days that she was likely to be shorter tempered than others, but this didn't seem to fit the pattern.

"O.K. Donaldson," he thought. "You figured out what I needed, now it's my turn to do it for you."

With that as his starting point, he sat and thought, he steered and thought, and eventually decided on a plan. At first the ideas were sketchy, but it eventually looked like something he may get a result from. He now knew he'd have to go back to Carver and Green's factory before all of this was over. They were making good progress, possibly up to twice the distance they would normally expect to cover in the time, but it was still some days before they, at last, entered the narrower water that they had previously known, and now, due to lack of money, they would have to tow the boat by hand for at least some of the time. The situation was not as bad as they had thought, but it still wasn't too good. There was cash enough to buy food, and a small amount of fuel, but the reserve that Jim would have liked was not going to be there for some time, if at all. Thankfully the Mayfly was not a heavy craft, and the fin like shape of the motor shaft allowed it to be used as a rudder, albeit a somewhat ineffective one. Amanda had sat down one day and calculated their finances, almost to the last penny, and had worked out that one or two weeks work would resolve things reasonably well if they could get it. There was time to go to village shops and post offices to look at the small ads, and this made life more interesting than it had been. The countryside was pleasant, though there were quite a lot of locks, all of which now had to be worked manually. As evening came, the pair decided to turn in relatively early, a day's towing and lock-wheeling having taken its toll on them. The area was pleasant, and they had a good view across some fields which were slowly coming ready for harvest. The sunset behind the trees that bordered the far side of the field would have inspired Turner or Claude Monet had they have been alive to appreciate it. Instead they inspired, in no less valid a manner, a tired couple as they drank mugs of tea.

"This is going to stay with me for the rest of my life," Amanda thought out loud.

Jim, who was sitting at her side, put an arm round her and smiled.

"We're not running from anyone now," she added, "And it hasn't gone

251

stale."

"It won't do," Jim replied. "It's a brilliant sunset though. I've never been anywhere but this country but I doubt you'd get better anywhere."

"I have, and you don't. Different, but not better," Amanda smiled.

Jim noticed tears slowly running down her face, but had the answer before he asked.

"Mum and Dad should be seeing this, or one like it. I want them back," Amanda spoke softly, and her voice was steady. "Don't worry Jim. We're here, and that counts for something, the rest will just have to do what it does I suppose."

The sun slowly sank behind the trees as the first of the stars became faintly visible in the darkening sky. The air was warm, so they sat until late, just watching nature from the back of their little home. The next day was warmer still and progress was made at a little over two miles an hour, excluding any interruptions where they took time to explain to anyone showing concern that their motor was not damaged in any way and that they were simply saving on fuel. Though slow, they were making steady progress, and they were enjoying the late Summer sun, which seemed to get warmer with each hour. The next day continued the trend. This was the kind of weather that led, like the slow progress of a loaded carriage on a roller-coaster towards the summit, to a release of energy, with a lot of accompanying noise. It had mustered a good deal of energy by the third day, and slowly the high peaks of cumulonimbus clouds began to replace the blue skies of previous days. The temperature however, kept rising, until it was almost impossible to tow even the light little Mayfly. The peak had come, and there was only one way. First an almost indiscernible rumble, then a few heavy spots of rain. Amanda, who was steering, left the boat to Jim to control with the tow ropes as she pulled out the cover. The first lightning bolt hit a tree about two fields away, it may as well have been two feet away for the sound it made. Then came some more rain, Jim remembered the drenching from school showers, only this was magnified tenfold on them. He pulled on the bow line to bring the boat in to the bank, making it fast temporarily on a convenient mileage post then he got aboard as quickly as possible. The second and third blots followed, their explosiveness forcing the pair to duck even though there was nothing to duck away from. The cover was quickly retrieved from its night time storage, and assembled with as much speed as they could muster. Despite the hurry the pair were soaked through before the cover provided any shelter, and the wind, which whipped up was forcing a lot of the rain through the gaps in the side screens. Lightning and thunder were upon them with no time to count distance, and the whole effect was terrifying, even though neither of them were frightened of storms. A tree, much closer than the previous one, was hit with a deafening crash.

"That's it," Jim shouted above the sound of rain beating on any available surface. "We're getting out of here. There has to be a bridge ahead that we can hide under until this dies down."

Amanda put her thumbs up, and set about starting the motor, whilst Jim slipped the moorings. When he stepped back through the screen he was, if that were possible, even wetter than before. A quick push with the pole had them in mid stream and Amanda put the motor in gear. It was hard to see through the driving rain, and hard to steer in the wind, but she did her best and kept the craft reasonably straight.

"It's like we've just arrived in Hell!" she shouted as more thunder added to the noise of rain and motor.

There was a bridge in the distance and, responding to the sight, Amanda increased speed slightly screwing her eyelids into slits to see through the almost impenetrable rain. There was another blinding flash ahead of them, and for a moment she could see nothing. Jim, who had briefly gone into the cabin to change clothes, Amanda having insisted on this as he was by far the wettest, came out at the sound.

"What the! Shit, put us in reverse, Mand, now!" he shouted.

Amanda blinked a moment, then flicked the lever straight across the gears, checking the forward progress within a few seconds.

"Shit!" Jim repeated. "That was too close."

Amanda now saw the bough that had crashed into the canal so close ahead of them that it could easily have landed directly on them. Mayfly had answered the command though, and stopped somewhere around its own length from the obstruction and had now started edging backwards, and was allowed to retreat a few hundred yards. Putting the motor in forward gear again, Amanda nudged the bow towards a clump of reeds on the opposite side to the towpath. The ground sloped up from here, and there were no trees close to the edge on this side, and nothing that could hit them if it fell from the other side.

"This is going to have to do," she said, stopping the motor as she spoke. "We should be safe from lightning here because of the high bank."

The storm continued for just over an hour after which the air was a lot clearer, though there was still a feeling that nature may not yet have finished showing off. The immediate problem now was that the canal was blocked by a rather large amount of wood, which they had no way of moving.

"Looks like half the bloody tree went in," Jim said, as he surveyed the scene. "It could be days before anybody does anything about it."

"There must be something we can do," Amanda replied forlornly. "First thing though, is to get the boat sorted and change out of the wet stuff."

The storm had blown water everywhere, and the mud from the towpath was also pretty well distributed around the back of the vessel. Cleaning up took the better part of an hour after which they both changed all their clothes, neither of them having any garment on them that wasn't well and truly rained upon. Once ready, they pushed the boat out of the reeds with the pole, with sufficient force to allow it to drift back to the towpath side, where they tied up so that they could survey the blockage at close quarters. Jim's initial assessment was about right, maybe not half, but a very large piece of tree now blocked the canal almost for the full width, leaving nothing wide or deep enough for navigation. The obstruction would have to be moved, but they couldn't move it by themselves, and it was unlikely in the extreme that the powers in charge of the canal would do anything much about it for some time. On Amanda's suggestion, having seen a farmhouse which looked as though it was adjacent to the lane that crossed the canal, they went off towards the bridge in search of help. The house was quite run down, and the farm looked to be doing nothing more than ticking over, though there were some signs that renovation was in progress. The door was answered by the farmer, who had taken shelter in the kitchen when the storm broke. He was a little abrupt at first, but at least was willing to listen to Jim's description of the incident.

"Lucky it didn't get you," he said when Jim had finished. "It's on my land and all," he added. "And them waterways bods will be sure to want their pound of flesh if I leave it there. If it were theirs they'd leave it to rot before touching it."

"Can we help you move it?" Amanda asked. "We could go across the canal in the boat and saw some bits off to make it easier to pull out."

About half an hour later they were crossing the field in a trailer, pulled by a small Ferguson tractor, with various implements in the hope of dismantling and removing the obstruction as effectively as they could.

Jim's agility and ability with the saw enabled quite a lot of the top growth to be cut away, and put on the trailer, whilst Amanda's light and cautious touch at the tiller of the Mayfly, made it easy for Jim to get where he wanted to be. The farmer then cut as much of the branch as was possible with his chainsaw, leaving about half of it still in the canal. This was pulled out by the tractor with chains, across a sheet of corrugated iron that he'd used as a ramp. Once it was on his land, he chopped it into more manageable portions for loading onto the trailer. Jim and Amanda tied the Mayfly up more securely and left her to dry out whilst they went back with the farmer to help unload into an area of one of the barns for storage as firewood. Jim noticed a concrete foundation, and a load of what could have been mistaken for scrap metal outside of the main farmyard and asked what it was.

"It should be another barn," the farmer replied despondently. "Except the labour never turned up to build it, and I can't do it on my own. Too small a job you see. Nobody wants to know."

"We'll help," Amanda seized the chance. "Any work would help us right now."

"You'd not know how," the farmer replied slightly patronisingly, but Amanda was ready.

"We didn't know how to earn our living from the boat until we had to," she said proudly. "And Jim repaired the Mayfly. She was almost sunk when he first saw her, and you saw how good he was chopping the tree up."

Jim smiled, but said nothing.

"You young 'uns," the farmer smiled. "You think you can do anything."

"It's a case of having to," Jim replied. "We'll work on the barn if you'll let us, and you can pay us what you think we're worth even if that's nothing. But we'll see the bloody thing built if you want it."

"That's fighting talk you know," the farmer gave in. "Right enough. You come back in the morning, and we work on the barn. If it gets done and you're not all talk I'll pay you the going rate, and there may be more jobs to do after that, if you're good workers."

The need for money, and the desire not to be proved wrong helped in the making of eager workers. The following morning Amanda studied the detailed instructions that came with the prefabricated building, whilst Jim and the farmer set about sorting the muddle of parts out. Once they knew what they were looking at, the assembly was straightforward enough. Amanda joined in, with some enthusiasm for the task, proving herself every bit as able as her partner despite her total lack of any experience. It was not long before the framework was bolted together ready for cladding, and the whole task was completed within the week. As barns go, it was a bit on the small side, but the couple reasoned that any outbuilding may well be referred to as a barn, particularly when the conversation included novices such as themselves, who knew little or nothing about farming. Another week saw more concrete laid to provide easier access to the building, and a number of small repair and painting jobs. The relationship between them and the farmer was, although good humoured, very much as boss and hired labour. He was not a bad person, but one of few words, and with little time for those he perceived as time wasters. He was happy with the work that they had done, and paid them well for it, and would probably have offered them more had they had the time to stay. There was an urgency in Jim to move on though, and it was something that Amanda did not quite understand even though it fitted in with her desire to keep going as well.

"I'm not sure I'll be able to stay anywhere too long after this," she commented as they set off past the site of the fallen tree that they had moved just over two weeks previously. They now had sufficient cash to keep them in fuel and food for some time, and the payment due for their work with Clive Prentice's invention came in equally handy. The weather had improved again, with sun and a cooling breeze. Jim smiled agreement at her comment, happy to be on the move, but also anxious for other things to progress as well.

In Spain, Amanda's parents had just arrived back from shopping, and were sitting on the small balcony of their flat.

"We maybe shouldn't have been quite so hasty," Edwin said thoughtfully, as he sat looking at the town. "But with hindsight it is easy to plan things better. No. We did the right thing, and although it left Amanda to follow, which she did not do, it could have been a lot worse for her had we stayed."

Since the phone call from Amanda, they had been a lot more contemplative of their situation.

"Now Carver is out of the picture, surely we should try and do something," Jean replied.

"He is, but he's done the damage, and what he did goes beyond him now. I'm not sure that anything we have could combat that. Besides

256

which, he's been put away for a completely different reason, which is nothing to do with us really," Edwin frowned.

"Amanda won't come here though, except by force, and I am bothered about what's going on with this Jim that she's taken up with," there was a note of disdain in Jean's voice as she spoke.

"Yes. There's an opportunist if ever I saw one. Amanda will see through him though surely, then she'll come. I don't think we should have trusted that shopkeeper friend of yours as much as we did, she seems to have her own agenda on life." Ed frowned again.

That was true enough. Marie had been sparing with the truth which, in her opinion, was to protect Amanda as much a she could. When the people turned up at the island she had had to think quickly, suspecting as she did that they were not as genuine as their paperwork suggested. She had made light of Amanda's disappearance as a bit of teenage amateur dramatics, and vouched that she was safe and having a holiday with others of her age on the river. To Amanda, she had said that her parents were more than happy for her to enjoy some time with friends though the actual truth was they were rather less than happy, but prepared to tolerate the situation in the hope that she would join them in Spain after her vacation. There was no reason to Marie as to why she should pass on anything more in either direction. Jim was within a year or so of Amanda in age, and they were enjoying their time together. Her judgement of Jim was that he was to be trusted, and her knowledge of Amanda told her the same. That her parents were not overjoyed by her taking a holiday without them vetting the situation first was something of a red herring to Marie. She had been asked to act in loco parentis and this is what she had done. If she was satisfied then so should they be, or they should be there to state otherwise. Anyhow the decision had to be made on the spot and she had made it. Then there was the small matter of the bungalow on the island. She had been led to believe that it was to be sold, and that the estate agents would handle things. Nobody had told her that it was being sold with Amanda still in residence. It seemed to her that this was something of a case of indecent haste, to put things mildly. Then a rather curt phone call from the estate agents telling her not to waste their time put her wise to the fact that there were some restrictive covenants as to usage, which when added to the terms of a will that requested it be handed down to the first born of whichever family inherited on the occasion of their coming of age whomsoever that may have been or would be. Each bit of paperwork seemed to have conspired to make the place unsaleable. She had tried to inform Amanda of this, but she didn't fully understand the implications herself, and so did not want to mislead a girl who already had enough to deal with. It was no half truth to say that it did not look like it was possible for anyone to sell the place, but the extra detail was omitted. They would return soon enough and Amanda, as the only member of the family present, would have to sort it out with a solicitor then.

On familiar territory once again, Jim and Amanda were relaxed about what was awaiting them, and were able to plan their movements with some degree of accuracy, retracing their steps to the canal basin in the middle of the city. The odd looking Chrysophyllax Diver was safe in its mooring with no sign of habitation. Amanda half thought about stopping early, but there was a kind of urgency about Jim to get to the basin as quickly as possible. Figuring it was only a relatively short journey by bus, or minibus, they posted a note under the canvas cover and weighted it with a small water can before continuing on their way. Crimson Lake, Vera Potter's fine narrowboat was still sitting majestically at it's mooring as they entered the basin the next day, looking much the same as it had done earlier in the Summer. The hatches at the back were open, and Amanda could see a feint wisp of smoke rising from them. It was still too warm for the range to be fired up, so it had to be Vera enjoying a quiet cigarette in the small traditional cabin. This was confirmed when, on hearing the patter of the outboard, Vera popped out of the hatches to greet them.

"Hey!" she shouted and waved. "It's good to see you, are you still," she ran two fingers across the cabin top like a little pair of legs scuttling for cover.

"Not any more," Amanda replied, as they drew up. "But it'd still be nice if we can tie up next to you for a day or so. A lot has happened since we last met, and it'd be nice to catch up."

"It would too my dears. And you tie up for as long as you like. My but you look well, caught the sun a bit. And you do the boat stuff so smoothly now! You'll be putting me to shame when I eventually move this old thing. I'll put the kettle on and we can have a right old gossip."

As Amanda ducked down to shut the motor off, Vera surveyed the couple.

"So, my dears, how did it all happen?" she asked, slightly starchily.

258

"There's no denying it, it's all over your faces, so, come on, tell all to your auntie Vera."

There was a somewhat embarrassed silence, which Jim broke saying, "Hey, I only do what I am told you know."

Amanda's mind flashed back to the conversation after they had met Jim's surrogate family for the first time. Had she really said that! She blushed slightly, then elbowed Jim lightly in the ribs trying, and eventually failing, to contain laughter, which immediately infected her partner.

Vera didn't help by adding, "It's a good job that someone had the sense to say something or your heads would have both exploded by now."

Amanda carefully climbed aboard the Crimson Lake whilst Jim briefly tidied and locked the cabin of the Mayfly. As they entered the cabin, Amanda's face suddenly turned serious.

"I know what I have done Vera, and it was me. Jim never pushed anything," she said solemnly. "And I thought hard about what you said to me. I won't ever knowingly hurt him."

"Nor will he you my dear," Vera replied, with a kindly smile. "I trust your judgement, and that goes for your fella too. Not that it means much, but you have my blessing."

"Have I walked in on something I shouldn't hear?" Jim smiled, as he entered the back cabin.

"Nothing you don't already know," Vera smiled back. "Now sit down and tell me how you got that scar."

Amanda winced at the reminder, but was ready to add to the sparse detail that Jim gave about the attempted kidnap. She knew what she had done, she knew too that she had acted out of sheer gut instinct. He was the one that had to stand with. She couldn't think about that. It could so easily have gone wrong, and Jim would be dead now if it had. All of these thoughts swirled in her head as she spoke, and again she felt too close to tears for comfort.

"He just stood there," she repeated. "He mouthed for me not to stop, but."

"Like a lemon," Jim added. "Like a stupid bloody lemon."

"I'd rather you stood like a lemon than become a sliced one Jim," Amanda said calmly. "You big daft twit. You stood there and didn't get yourself killed. Maybe he didn't have the guts to actually do it but if you'd made a move," she stopped mid speech.

"I could so easily have made it worse," she added, the submerged

259

memory of the day coming back. "I just lashed out, I didn't think. He could have killed you, and for what."

"You're both a pair of lemons if you go on like that," Vera spoke matter-of-factly, concealing her dread at the talk of knives. "You each did what seemed right, and you came through. That's really all that counts. There's something else though, and I'm guessing it's unfinished business from last time you were here."

Jim knew that Vera had realised his intentions, even if Amanda wasn't quite sure of what he was thinking.

"You need your folks nearer than bloody Spain so we'll have to force things a little bit. Carver and Green will be less hostile, as they are well shot of that little turd that was in charge, and they should know it by now. Thing is you can't just go in making demands or asking favours, they need coaxing otherwise all they'll want to do is sweep things under the carpet. A plan is what we need," Vera said.

"It sticks in my throat," Jim replied. "But do you think we could do a deal with Carver, to let him off the hook if he co-operates?"

"No!" Amanda shouted. "No way. He was in it, he tried to kill you, and I won't forgive him. He pays for what he has done in full. Hanging is too good for him!"

"Then it's plan B," Vera sighed. "We have to work some little bit of subterfuge. I could call in a favour or two, but we need a little more to go on. I mean neither of you could turn up at the factory, they'd know you even in disguise. They don't know me though, but I could do with."

Vera was interrupted by someone on the towpath waving.

"Is this someone chasing you?" Vera asked.

"Bloody hell!" Amanda smiled. "Vanessa! Come here before our auntie shoots you!"

"She's a bit weird but mostly harmless," Jim whispered.

Vera was mid plan, and did not really want to be interrupted, but this was obviously a friend, and some more catching up was in order, also, nobody at Carver and Green would know *that* face. The afternoon and evening took on a party atmosphere, and Vera, who loved company, enjoyed it as much as the other three friends. Stories and news were shared. The infamous Rick had been chucked off of his course when he tried to rejoin it, and had decided, as he'd earlier bragged, to do the "Hippie trail" but had got a bad dose of indigestion in France, and gave up on that. Someone had found out that he was living in what he called a garret in

Paris, though the truth was that he had charmed his way into the desirable flat (and bed) of a Parisian socialite who had a soft spot for undiscovered artists and would presumably remain there until such time as he was found out. Vera too told some carefully edited stories of some of the fraudsters and conmen she had encountered in her life. On her insistence the four friends were all treated to a meal out, at which still more stories and gossip were shared.

"You do have some strange friends!" Vanessa giggled as they slowly made their way back to the canal basin.

"They must have, they know you!" laughed Vera who had overheard the comment.

"Oh my God!" Vanessa squeaked. "You must be psychic! You don't know just *how* weird I was when I met these two!"

Suddenly Vera's face went serious, she had had an idea.

"Look," she said. "Would you be willing to assist us in something for a good cause?"

Vanessa pondered for a moment, and accepted. She did not want to let her friends down, and felt she owed Jim and Amanda for their help earlier on. Whether this was for them, Vera, or someone else, it seemed the right thing to do. Fresh coffee was made on the Crimson Lake and the party carried on into the early hours. Realising that she had stayed far too late, Vanessa was contemplating either driving back or sleeping in the minibus when Vera made the decision for her.

"It's too bloody late for you to go halfway across the county, why not stop over on the Lake. I've plenty of room," she smiled.

The next morning was bright, but there was a slight chill to the air as a small reminder that seasons do eventually change. Jim and Amanda were up and about first, and had spruced the Mayfly up well before there were any signs of life from the narrowboat. After breakfast, which Vera had insisted on preparing for them, Jim was going to phone Dr. Simms, to see if he was willing to help again. As time was now plentiful, they were in no hurry and, if their judgement of the old lawyer was correct, Jeremy Simms would not appreciate too early a call from them. It was around eleven o'clock that Jim made contact, having been allowed to use the telephone at the office of a car dealer that Vera knew.

"Yes," Jeremy said. "I did receive your letter, and I had been doing

261

some research into the subject for my own interest, the name did crop up in an article some time ago."

"Is there anything that we can do. I mean I just want Amanda's folks to come back, she misses them a lot," Jim said earnestly.

"I'm sure she does," replied the doctor   "I am aware of your circumstances, and that you have become hardened to them, though I am sure it still smarts for you rather more than you choose to reveal.   Young Amanda though, you are right to try and convince her parents to return or she will be hurt badly.   Whilst you are a devoted friend, and your part in her life can be filled by nobody else, the same is the case for her parents. So, yes I can, and will only be too delighted to help, but there are some things you have to find a way to do for yourself."

"Whatever it takes," Jim spoke firmly.

"Well," the doctor continued.   "The situation with Carver and Green is quite interesting, if my research is correct, and, let me tell you sonny, it seldom has been incorrect.   They seem to have dragged their feet about any paperwork concerning the case of Edwin Donaldson's fall from grace, and because of this he appears to still be a director of that company.   What is also interesting is that the younger Mr Carver is not!   Although he took on the role after his father's partial retirement he seems to have been on some kind of probation despite him wielding so much influence.   Now, given that he has rather blotted his copybook, I rather doubt that anybody would be mindful to allow him any directorial freedom.   In fact it may not be legally possible for him to be a director for some time."

"Why is that?" Jim asked.

"It would seem that all of this thing with the agreement and the so-called tax fraud was something of what you would call a trumped up charge.   Most of the paperwork that I could find relating to this puts your friend's father beyond reproach, and any that does lay blame at his door appears to either be a fabrication or a forgery."

"Christ!" Jim replied.

"I have to say I did not find any documents with the Messiah's signature on them, but those that I did find may as well have had, so infantile was their execution."

"That's amazing, so they're in the clear," Jim smiled as he spoke.

"Well. Morally they are as white as a new handkerchief, but legally we need a burden of proof.   Before you interrupt me again or invoke another deity, let me explain."

Jim couldn't help laughing at the comment.

"We all have friends that will do us a favour do we not," Jeremy said.

"Yes," Jim replied.

"And such is the case with me. Whilst I know of the existence of documentation that would exonerate the Donaldsons completely, I am unable as yet to reveal the source of the information that I have in any court of law."

"Why?" Jim asked.

"I knew you would ask that, and I draw you to a conversation we had when we met at the University. The brandy is truly excellent by the way. But you do remember what I said do you not?"

"I think so," Jim said.

"Well, I view that this is for the greater good, even if the means by which I got the information, was, well, you have no doubt heard the term 'The old School Tie'."

"Yes," Jim said.

"Well, though I am no longer too proud of the fact, I was privileged enough to attend one of our country's better public schools, as did a number of people who now hold positions of power and influence. I like to think I hold one of those myself."

"I see what you mean. So, what do I have to do," Jim asked.

"Well, James my boy, you must find a way to convince those that have a more orthodox right to the information that I have revealed, that it is in their best interest to allow you access to it. You must do so in such a way that only alludes to the content. If they think you have seen it, they may well want to pursue *you* through the courts, and they may have the funds and grounds to do so. So tread carefully. It is a big responsibility for you."

"Bloody hell," Jim could not help himself.

"That is not another deity. Well maybe it is to some, but yes, you have summed the situation up well. Think, plan and do. When you have, then we can go ahead. Good luck my son," Jeremy said.

Even if Vera and Vanessa hadn't noticed, and she was pretty sure they had, Amanda knew that Jim was troubled when he returned. There had been a lot of talk of how they would carry out a plan that would finally sort any issues out, but Amanda could see that it was all talk, of the kind that

263

she had read in so many girls' story books when she was in primary school. The look on Jim's face as she caught sight of it brought home the actual gravity of things. She walked a short distance along the towpath to meet him.

"It's the real world again isn't it Jim," she said softly.

"It is Mand," he replied, using the shortened form of her name with the tone of voice that she had not heard for some time. "It is exactly that."

"Let's walk a bit, and talk," Amanda took his hand gently. "We're going to do this."

"We have to convince someone that his son is a cheat. He probably knows it but you know what they say about blood and water," Jim said, and followed by telling Amanda the details of the phone conversation and, as she listened, he saw her brow furrow on more than one occasion.

"We set a foot wrong and we could be in major trouble. These people seem to be pretty ruthless, and they'll know about the side of life that Vera is in. They're the sort that would watch her films and stuff. They're not stupid," Jim held Amanda's hand tightly as he spoke.

"I trust you Jim," she said "And whatever happens as a result, at least we will have tried. Let's go and talk to the others."

Vera had busied herself making lunch with the help of Vanessa, and was almost ready when she saw Jim and Amanda approaching.

"Looks pretty heavy," Vanessa said as she saw them. "I think I may have to make a phone call. I have friends in the rugby club that may be able to."

"Not too smart a thing to do dear," Vera cut her short. "We'd only get ourselves into trouble going at it that way. Keep it on the back burner though, just in case."

Vanessa smiled and greeted the couple as they boarded the Crimson Lake.

"So it's back to the factory then?" Vera asked rhetorically. "If you want to get in you can't just walk up there this time. You know that."

"It's exactly what I was going to do," Jim said firmly.

"But," Vera replied. "They won't let you in. We need to do this by stealth, catch them off guard and."

This time it was Jim that cut her short.

"It's what we did before, and it's what they'd expect. Do anything that strikes them weird and they'll be on to us. No, it has to be played straight."

"I should come with you," Amanda said quietly.

"I figured I could phone the switchboard and get an appointment," he continued, uncharacteristically ignoring Amanda's comment. "Hopefully someone will remember me and get me in. I can try."

Jim's voice had a dark tone to it, Amanda remembered it from some of his descriptions of the worse parts of his past.

"I shouldn't have bothered you with all of this Vera, I'm sorry," he continued.

Later in the afternoon, Jim phoned the factory, and was lucky to get through to Bet, who arranged a meeting for the next Monday, as Mr Carver senior was away on a short holiday. He had a list of appointments for the afternoon, but the morning was free, and likely to remain so. Realising that this was probably not a meeting that Mr Carver would particularly want to attend, she was more than slightly vague about the name of the visitor.

"Why just you?" Amanda asked, whilst Vera and Vanessa were out shopping. "Why not me too."

"No real reason, but you have enough bad memories of the place, and it may all turn sour. I don't know, just a feeling that's all," Jim stared across the canal basin.

Amanda didn't press the argument. Jim, she thought, must have a degree of intuition, and he was absolutely right about her not wanting to go anywhere near the factory.

"No." she thought, "There's a few days before the meeting, and nothing can happen until then so we spend them just enjoying life."

Jim noticed her smile, and could see it wasn't forced. Amanda's face was always animated, and it was hard for her to hide her feelings from those that knew her well. Jim simply sat looking back at her, letting the warmth of her mood infect him. They were still sitting together, saying nothing half an hour later when their two friends returned, Amanda jumped when she heard Vanessa's voice.

"There are some really good shops around here, I could have spent a fortune but I'm trying to be good. I was a bit bad though because I bought some new jeans, and shoes," she said.

Vera added in a motherly tone, "So, you have a plan then."

"Yes," Jim said, smiling. "Of sorts, but a plan. But right now we can't do anything about it, so lets just enjoy a long weekend. That is if the two of you have nothing on?"

Chapter 16

Monday morning was wet, and cold. The rain had started at about three in the morning and had fallen either as a heavy shower, or steady drizzle since. The hooped cover at the back of the Mayfly did a good job of shedding the water into the canal but everything seemed damp. This was yet another omen of the change of season that was becoming imminent. Amanda, stirred from the huddle of sleeping bag and human that occupied the centre of the cabin.

"Boaters, the real ones," she said sleepily. "Had to put up with weather like this all through the winter. It's still rubbish though."

With that she put her head against Jim's warm back and slept for a little longer. There was no need to be up with the day, as Jim's appointment was mid-morning. They woke, dressed slowly and set to making breakfast at about a quarter to nine. Amanda had offered him any treat he wanted for breakfast, and he had opted for their almost traditional fried bread and marmalade, with plenty of tea. He said it reminded him of all the good things that had so far come out of their journey together, and in any case, however disgusting it sounded, he liked it. All of this was in his mind as he got out of the taxi, a luxury that Amanda had insisted upon, just outside Carver and Green's factory.

"I had been expecting this," Mr Carver Senior said as Jim entered his office, the same one that had been occupied earlier by the younger Carver. "Perhaps you will tell me why you have come, and why now?" he continued.

"I've come to try and sort some stuff out," Jim stated nervously.

"Stuff!" Carver almost mocked. "Is that what you call it these days. You want money? For me to buy your silence?"

"No," Jim said, having gained some confidence seeing that he had not even needed to hint that he knew anything.

"But everybody has a price," Mr Carver looked stern. "And I do have money, a lot of it."

"Well," retorted Jim. "I do have a price, but I don't want your money, any of it."

"Then what *do* you want?" Carver now looked half way between worry and anger.

"I want *you* to do the right thing. Not for me, but for you, and for a very close friend of mine," Jim said firmly.

"For me?" Carver frowned.

"Yes," Jim came back instantly "You know what happened to me a while back?"

"Sadly, yes I do, and it was unforgivable. I see it has scarred you," Carver replied.

"Nothing is unforgivable. And the scar will fade in time. Thing is, nobody does something that desperate, or stupid, unless there is something to hide," Jim's tone was now firm and confident.

"That's astute of you," Carver looked him in the eye. "Now tell me what you want."

"You know about what happened to one of your directors. Mr Edwin Donaldson," Jim said.

"Yes. But he is nothing to do with us now," Carver replied.

"He is still a director, check your paperwork if you don't believe me, it can be seen at Companies House too. And the Mr Carver that arranged this, is not," Jim pointed to the red mark that was left from the knife attack as he spoke.

"But that is only paperwork," Carver said hastily.

"Yes, but it is legally binding paperwork, and there is more of it. A paper-chase that could lead to allegations of fraud and all sorts of financial crap hitting you personally," Jim replied calmly.

"If you are trying to blackmail me?" the man frowned.

Jim cut Carver short. "I am not. In fact I am here to help," he said.

"I don't need help, you impertinent little boy," Carver suddenly sounded very much like his son.

"You do, and all you have to do is the right thing. Because of your company's actions under the direction of Mr Carver junior, the parents of a totally innocent person have been forced to leave the country when they themselves are also innocent. The documents relating to tax, and transfer of ownership of patents contain very poorly forged signatures," Jim said calmly.

"You are remarkably well informed," Carver growled.

"Not that well, but well enough. Look at it this way. Here I am. I am young, and poorly educated if you want to know the truth, but I can see that

267

if all this blows up, and it will do, then it will attach scandal to the company that you built. Your creation, your mark on the landscape, your attempt at changing anything will go down the toilet. So will any hope for the parents of a very good friend of mine. You don't deserve that and neither does she," Jim replied, exhaling and briefly looking at the floor.

"Where did you get this information. If you have stolen it you risk prison." Carver's attempt a threat was half hearted at best.

"So," Jim smiled. "I go to prison. We may even share a cell. What would I get? If I took the blame for any wrongdoing in finding the information I'd get about six months, and even that would probably not be in a proper prison. I may even get bound over. Whatever, six months, a year. What's that at my age. Now this next bit I have looked up, and I have had it checked. If all this blew up, you, yes YOU! could be looking at five years minimum. Check yourself if you don't believe me."

Carver's expression changed. "Listen," he said in a much calmer tone. "I know there has been some unpleasantness, and you say that my money will not set things right. So what will?" he asked.

"You know Edwin Donaldson. You know he is a good person. I have never met him and he probably hates me. But he is Amanda's father, and she misses her parents. They should be here not in Spain. If they came back and fought, the case would be proven but they are afraid of the consequences. I would guess that some kind of threats were made that neither Amanda or I know about. It's all a pile of shit when it comes down to it," Jim said.

"So you want me to help you by incriminating a family member?" Carver now looked both old and upset.

"Not necessarily. If you'll pardon me for saying it, he's done a pretty good job of that himself, I can't alter what he did, and I can't change the evidence that the police took. I can't unwrite the draft of the blackmail letter he sent to Amanda's parents. The basics are that all of the financial wrongdoings could be unravelled and Amanda's folks could be back here. Your son does not need all that crap landing on him as well, even if he does deserve it. I don't know how, but there must be a way. If it lands on you, I'll still be touring the country with the love of my life, maybe I'll do six months in an open prison, but we'll make it. Amanda wouldn't judge me on that one. And we'll probably end up in Spain with her folks from time to time for visits, it wouldn't be ideal, but it would work. Thing is, what happens to you? Even if I don't go spouting my mouth off, the people that are in the know will still investigate at some time," Jim had slightly lost the thread of what he was saying and fell silent.

"You care deeply about this girl don't you," Carver said thoughtfully.

"Yes," Jim replied, flatly.

"There are better ways of impressing a girl you know," Carver half joked.

"That isn't the reason and you know it." Jim said.

"So you would risk prison for her?" Carver replied.

"You know the answer to that," Jim maintained the flat, calm tone of voice.

"I can't promise anything here and now in the way of sorting everything out, but I do give my word that I will investigate the whole affair. If such paperwork exists, then we have a copy of it, or there will be signs of a cover up. You are right that my son is not the most efficient manager, but he is still my son. Whatever is there will be found and acted upon, that I promise. As with all things it will take time. Whether this brings Amanda's parents back to this country is not something I would be prepared to place a bet on, but you are right, she should have them close to her." Carver replied.

Jim stood up. "You've given me enough time, and thanks. I didn't know what to expect. Do what you have to do, and we'll keep moving," he said.

He shook hands with the old man, and handed him a piece of paper with addresses on it if the need for further contact arose. As Jim left the factory, he saw a trio of faces he knew well.

"We thought you may need some moral support, or cheerleaders," Amanda said, as she took his hand. "How did it go?"

"I had half hoped that the old man would just give in," Jim spoke slowly.

"But that only happens in fiction," Amanda finished the sentence.

"It's not made things any worse, so that has to be good. I'm starving, is there a café round here?" Jim smiled again.

Mr Carver senior sat in his office for an hour after Jim left, before calling his secretary in to cancel his meetings for the rest of the week. He knew what his son was capable of, but thought the opportunity of the senior role in the company would keep him steady. Clearly it had not done, and it was down to him to limit the damage done without putting him in any worse trouble than he already was in. The worst part of the meeting was the realisation that, even without proof, he knew that Jim was telling the truth.   The honesty of his manner could relatively easily have been fabricated, but it was the detail.   Everything fitted to the style in which the junior Mr Carver operated.   It had always seemed odd to him that Ed Donaldson would either dishonestly, or unwittingly commit fraud.   He was too honest, and too methodical, his only fault was that he was also too trusting, and it was that feature that Carver junior would have looked for and exploited.   But proof had to be had.   Unlike Ed Donaldson, the senior Mr Carver did not put trust at the centre of things until he knew he could trust.   After another hour he walked into the archive room with his secretary, and set about his research.   Bet was seconded from telephone and general office duties to assist his secretary, her first job being to go around the factory and gather any remaining documentation relating to his son.   The threat of dismissal if any concealment were discovered was there but not necessary.   Nobody had time for the Junior, and all were happy to co operate with the senior Mr Carver.

The café wasn't posh but it was warm and out of the weather, which had not improved since Jim set off for the meeting.   It was one of many such places that were slowly being eroded by American chains offering the delights of many different kinds of burger, all of which tasted the same and had the nutritional value of the packaging.   The Formica on the tables was chipped at the edges but clean, the atmosphere was thick with the smell of cooking, and noisy with the clank of crockery.   Egg, beans and chips with mugs of tea were ordered, and the four sat down to wait for its arrival. Suddenly the day, which Jim had been dreading, seemed to be turning out alright.   He sat back in his chair and smiled contentedly.

"It's not so bad, all of this," he said, merely voicing his thoughts.   "Not so bad at all."

"Have you been smoking the tea-leaves again Jimbo," Amanda smiled as she spoke.   "I mean we can't have you cheerful, it's bloody raining."

Jim whistled "Singing in the rain" and then just smiled some more.

"It just wasn't as bad as I thought it would be that's all," he added.

Their food, well cooked on white plates with matching large utilitarian mugs full of steaming tea, was set neatly down by the waitress, who smiled at the four strangers and then paused.

"Hang on.   I know you!" she said.   "You were the lad that punched the

270

boss!"

Jim had only briefly met Liz and the white coat she wore as a waitress had thrown Amanda and Vera off the scent of her identity, but eventually the penny dropped.

"I'm well out of that place," she added. "Far nicer doing this, at least if someone has a grope they can wear their dinner! Enjoy yours, and thanks for what you did, the bugger deserves what he gets."

"Come and see us, we're hard to miss. Down at the old canal basin in the middle of the city." Vera, who was now truly in party mood, replied.

It would have continued too, but for the scene they were presented with as they arrived back at the canal basin. The three young friends could see Vera's face drop as soon as they came in sight of the water.

"What's up?" Amanda asked. "Can we help?"

"No dear, but you have to go. Now I'm afraid," her voice was hollow with fear.

"Not a chance of it," Jim said firmly. "You helped us."

"This isn't a bloody kids game,"Vera snapped. "This is the real world, the dirty one where people get hurt and nobody cares."

Two police cars sat on the wharf and numerous officers were rifling through the immaculate narrowboat that was Vera's home as though they were frenzied thieves.

"And?" Jim said, leaving it at that. They were facing a very different Vera to the one they knew.

"Vera," Amanda spoke placidly, but firmly. "Whatever it is, we won't leave you to face it alone. You told us what you do for a living, it didn't bother us then and it doesn't now. But it obviously bothers them. We've had enough shit thrown at us to know that you don't look that frightened unless someone is threatening you. Now tell us what's up."

"Well," Vera replied, with a bit more of her old character coming back to her voice. "It's the bloody vice squad. I should have known it, I'd heard there was a new broom at the top."

"And the arsehole doesn't like you," Jim said.

"That's about it. The down side of all of this stuff is that people think they own you, and they cut up rough if you don't toe the line," she replied.

"You'd better come with me," Vanessa said quietly. Everyone had almost forgotten she was there. "I don't expect that you want them quizzing you right now."

"But," Vera hesitated.

271

"But nothing. Go with Vanessa," Jim said authoritatively. "We know where to find you. Give us your keys and we'll sort it."

Vera meekly obeyed. She wasn't in the mood to be insulted all night by the new broom or any of his minions. Seconds after she turned back up the alley that they had entered the basin by, Jim strode forcefully across the cobbles, directly into the melee of blue uniform that was slowly wrecking the beautiful vessel.

"HEY!" he bellowed at the top of his voice. "I suppose you have a warrant do you."

The officer in charge confronted him.

"I'm looking for an old slag called Vera Potter and I believe this boat is hers," he said.

"Do I look like my name is Vera?" Jim shouted. "Now leave my home alone. It took the owner bloody years to get it right and you fucking well ruin it in minutes."

"Who the hell are you," the officer shouted. "This thing is crawling with her stuff."

"Where is your warrant?" Jim asked.

"Now let's suppose we haven't got one," the officer replied.

"Then you'd be acting illegally," Jim stood his ground.

"And who's to know?" the officer stood his.

"Me!" Amanda screamed. "Now go, and let us clean up this mess."

Amanda had no expectation of being obeyed by a bunch of large men, but they suddenly stopped what they were doing and looked across at her.

"It's her boat alright," Amanda continued, in her normal voice. But we've borrowed it, for a bit of a holiday, well, more of digs really. We start at the University you see, kind of late entrants," she lied convincingly.

"You know what the old bitch does for a living?" the officer growled.

"I'd heard something about her being a retired actress, but I presume she rents boats out," Amanda smiled sweetly, adding. "Now if you can't help us to tidy the mess you have made, would you awfully mind pissing off so that we can."

"You've not heard the last of this! Not by a long shot," the officer said angrily. The threat was probably a real one, but he called his men off and they left.

"Bastards!" Amanda shouted. "Look at it. Bastards! Bastards! Bastards!"

Jim surveyed the scene calmly. "This is what they did to Miranda and

272

Paul.   It's what they always do, but," he breathed out across his teeth. "Everybody has their price."

"I know who's mark is all over this," Amanda replied despondently.

It took the rest of the day, and half the night to tidy the Crimson Lake, and most of the next two to repair the damage the Police had done. All of the time their conversation centred round or returned to the raid, and how best to ensure Vera's continued peaceful existence.   With the "Lake" looking resplendent with new paint and varnish where required, all brass-work polished, and the inside cleaner than Vera kept it (if that were possible to achieve) they sat for a while.

"Gerald!" Jim said.

"Erm.   Have you been drinking from the bilges again," Amanda chirped.   "I was a girl last time I looked. And even if I was a bloke I'd not settle for Gerald as a name."

"Gerald," Jim said.   "The car dealer.   He'd know what to do, or who to do.   I was trying to remember his name.   I'm sure I could get to his car lot."

"We don't want a car Jimbo" Amanda replied.   "Nowhere to park it on the Mayfly."

"Now you are being daft," Jim laughed.   "No, Gerald is one of those dodgy type people, you know, not villains, but in the know.   Him and Vera go back a long way, he told me that when I used the phone there. He'd have a pretty good idea how to fix this.   I mean she could come back but they'd raid her again as sure as, well just as sure as."

It took Jim most of the next morning to find the car lot, and he had to wait another hour for Gerald to come back from the pub.   The man was in his mid fifties, and had known Vera since she was caught pinching cigarettes from his office when she was about twelve.

"A right feisty little cow she was and no mistaking it," he said warmly. "Anyway my lad.   What can I do for you."

Jim related the tale of the raid, and the situation Vera now found herself in over a cup of rather unpalatable instant coffee that was stirred with an old Biro.

"Right bastards some of these new boys," Gerald said.   "I had one go over all of my cars the other month, he never found nothing though.   I made sure of that.   So you want this shite fixing then do you." He spoke as though it was as normal as inviting the vicar to tea.

"The way you say that sounds either painful or terminal," Jim looked

273

worried.

"No," Gerald replied kindly. "You can't kill him, you're right, even though it'd be too good for some of them, but then you'd only get another and you'd have to deal with him. Next thing you know you got a room full of them. No we got to fix the bastard so he stays, but he can't do anything."

"If it costs anything, I'll find a way to pay. I mean I haven't got."

Gerald cut him short.

"Give over. This is Vera Potter we're talking about, a legend in her own, well never mind what she's a legend in. Let me think about it for a day or so. Can you come back at the weekend. I'll have some time on Saturday. I'll tell you what though, this guy is doing a favour for someone too, handshake job, you know?" he frowned.

"I'd been thinking it may be pay back for what she did for us," Jim replied.

"It fits. Now I have to get on." Gerald put his hand out to shake.

The Chysophyllax Diver was about the strangest vessel Vera had seen in her life and it had not occurred to Vanessa to tell her before they arrived what to expect, but it was her temporary home now thanks to the young woman's kindness, and as such to her, now completely normal.   The first day there had been very upsetting, not knowing what on earth was going on in the aftermath of the raid, and it had taken quite a bit of persuasion from Vanessa for Vera to allow Jim and Amanda to sort things out at that end as best they could. She reasoned that it would be best not to make contact for a while, after all Jim and Amanda knew where she was, and could be there by canal inside of a day, or by bus in rather less time, besides which they would be busy enough with the mess that the police had left.   The two women had settled to an easy friendship though, neither finding anything disagreeable in the other, but it was becoming clear after a few days that Vera would not be happy until she knew what was going on back at her proper home. Vanessa had instinctively been careful on the day of the raid to stay out of sight so the police would not associate her with the incident and it had again taken time for Vera to be persuaded to stay on Chrysophyllax Diver whilst Vanessa drove to the basin and back.   The minibus rattled to a halt close to the canal, and Vanessa walked along the towpath to find the Crimson Lake looking much as it did when she had stayed on it a few days previously. Jim and Amanda waved to her from the back of the Mayfly, he was actually about to set off to see Gerald at the car lot, and was just finishing a somewhat late breakfast.

"Hi strangers," she shouted as she crossed from towpath, over the narrowboat and onto Mayfly. "It looks magnificent, did they mess much up on the inside?"

"Not as bad as it could have been," Jim replied. "In all it was pretty careful for a police raid. There were a couple of bits of crockery they broke, but we managed to find identical stuff in the shops so, as soon as we know what Gerald is up to."

"Gerald?" Vanessa looked puzzled. "Who the hell is Gerald?"

"The car dealer that let me phone from his office. He's like, Vera's sort of uncle I guess, like she refers to herself as our auntie. Anyway, he seems to know a lot of people and said he'd think about a way of sorting things," Jim replied.

Vanessa was insistent in her offer of a lift to his car lot as soon as they had tidied up, and it was not long before they were drawing up outside an array of vehicles that all purported to be the best on the planet. As Vanessa stepped out, Gerald instantly homed in on her with charm turned full on.

"Now, what's a stylish young woman like you doing in a thing like that!" He smiled. "Don't worry though I have just the thing for you and it won't cost as much as you think. I'll even do you a trade in on your minibus. I could sell it to some hippies or something."

"Don't believe a word of it!" Amanda called, "He knows about the gold bars you have stashed under the drivers seat!"

"And you have to be a friend of Vera!" Gerald replied with a laugh. "She told me about you and young Jim. Somehow this young lady doesn't fit the description, but hey you can't blame me for trying can you!"

As Jim got out Gerald added, "Right now, into my office, the four of us have some talking to do."

The office, a small shed like structure was next to the workshop in an old corrugated iron building that probably never had looked much better even when new. It was no architectural gem and never had been. The desk was covered in paperwork, and on a small cabinet behind it stood the necessary tackle for brewing coffee or tea plus a half empty bottle of Scotch which Jim later surmised was probably to disinfect the guts after drinking anything brewed there. Above the cabinet was a calendar from a car parts company with a big photo of a woman displaying parts that were

275

decidedly not of vehicular origin.   She was, or had recently been to be more accurate, dressed in a blue overall with the company's logo on it, but it was hard to believe that she had much mechanical knowledge.   Gerald, mindful of the present company made an ineffective attempt to cover the offending item before it was noticed by trying to hang his jacket on the same nail that it hung from, only to lose the garment behind the cabinet.

"It's O.K," Amanda piped up.   "She hasn't got anything we've not got."

Gerald took the calendar down, smiled, and apologised politely, then the four set about the purpose of the visit.

"This copper.   He's a new broom alright," Gerald said.   "And I got a bit of gossip about why they raided our Vera.   I'm not sure quite how to put this though."

"No point in trying to be tactful," Amanda replied,   "Didn't get you too far with Elsie the flasher on the wall there did it."

Gerald laughed as he started to speak, "No, I cocked that up good and proper.   So, straight it is.   Someone with influence tipped him the wink that Vera is undesirable because of the nature of her work, so he had the boat watched, and decided she was trying to recruit you lot.   It's no coincidence about who supplied the information is it."

"Bloody Carver!" Jim said disdainfully.

"It sounds like it might be.   The younger one has a finger in a lot of pies, and even if he is assisting with enquiries, he's the sort to cause trouble where he can.   Vera has always been her own person though, I've known her for years and she wouldn't ever try push people into her line of business, it's not her.   I could get tons of people that'd say the same, but they're all trumped by one funny handshake if you get the drift.   Good job he was too stupid to get a warrant first, too stupid too to think that Vera would have anything on her boat that would interest the law as well.   She knows the ropes, and the coppers that searched know them too.   But this bugger is trying to make a name for himself."   Gerald frowned.

"So," Vanessa spoke as softly as ever.   "What do we do?"

"Well, we can fix him easily, there's a lot of stitch-ups that work, but I have a horrible feeling that you lot think it's all a game of cricket."   Gerald said.

"I said I didn't want him killed," Jim answered.   "I don't want blood on my hands, but police raids are shit, so," his voice tailed off.

"That hit a nerve," Gerald said, sounding slightly surprised.   "Well, a good thing is this guy is going at things like a bull at a gate, he just dives in

276

and he's upset a few people that he shouldn't. People that I wouldn't want to upset, not if I want to play the violin at any time. A repellent little dick he may be, but he's more useful in his job than out of it, so we have to have something on him."

"Blackmail?" Amanda replied. "That's a bit."

"Not cricket?" Gerald's tone was good humoured rather than mocking, and he continued. "Simple blackmail would be pretty easy. Everyone has skeletons in their cupboards, but he'd continually be after the perpetrators. If not him then his friends."

"That's all of what we can't do. And frankly it doesn't help," Vanessa commented quietly.

"That about says it," replied Gerald, "But we can fix him, and as luck would have it, I have a good friend that, well, he sorts paperwork out for me."

"Bloody hell, a forger!" Amanda blurted out.

"If you like, but I haven't said that and you are not here to do anything other than look at cars. How about obtaining the birth certificate of Vera's identical twin sister Millie." Gerald smiled at his suggestion."

"So far as she's aware she's is an only child. She told us!" Amanda said. Jim tapped her ankle with his foot lightly. "Oh! Bloody hell that's brilliant. So it's actually Millie that made those films, not Vera."

"And of course nobody knows where she lives, I think she was last heard of as a stewardess on a cruise ship, I'm sure we can get that circulated as gossip, of course with supporting paperwork. That and a few Polaroids of our friend's little pass-times as insurance, and bingo, everybody is happy. The coppers would probably get that. I mean Vera never uses her real name in the credits, she's not stupid." Gerald frowned again.

"And Carver gets away with something else," Jim interrupted.

"Carver will always get away with things, his sort do. But you just hit the nail on the head there. I wonder, do you have anything that may have Carver's writing on it?" Gerald asked.

"I've got a couple of notes I was supposed to take to the telex room when I sort of worked there," Jim replied.

"So, how do you feel about playing the bugger at his own game. Thing is, we need someone that nobody knows to deliver a letter." Gerald said.

"I'll do it," Vanessa said, enthusiastically. "I owe it to Amanda after," she looked at the floor.

"Don't be stupid," Amanda replied slightly sharply. "You owe me nothing. It was an accident."

"No," Vanessa replied firmly   "It is logical, and I'll do it.   The guy would know you straight away."

"He's gone after Vera so then he will go after you!" Amanda protested.

"Trust me Amanda," Vanessa's voice was more assertive.

Gerald, feeling rather misunderstood, said, "All you need to do is to, well, look the part, and hand the letter over, he doesn't have to see you for long.   Then you disappear at the right time, that's about all of it.".

"It doesn't seem quite right though?" Amanda thought aloud.

"Why ever not?" Gerald replied almost sternly.   "This new copper is a loose canon.   There's people in this town that'll do a lot worse to him if he keeps on like this.   So we fix him before he gets hurt, or worse, and he won't hassle people that live between the lines.   They don't deserve it. This way they'll get a degree more protection than they'd normally expect."

Amanda had the familiar furrow.

"We're a long way from home Mand," Jim said quietly.   "They didn't care about the mess they made when they raided Vera, and the ones that raided the house, didn't give a shit about anything, as long as they found the stuff they'd planted.   Next time they do Vera over, do you really think they'll come empty handed?"

She looked at the floor, then back at the other three in the room.

"O.K," she said.   "Do it.   I just had a moment of convent educated guilt that's all.   When though?"

"You're going to have to give me a few more days to arrange things, I'll drop down to the basin when I'm ready.   This is the best thing all round you know," Gerald directed his last remark to Amanda.   "You've not had a lot of living, neither has our friend the copper or he wouldn't go on the way he has.   Oh yes, he thinks he's tough, but, well perhaps it's best not to know how far some people would go to prove they're tougher.   Not that you want to but, as I said, you will be doing him a favour too.   Now what say we shut up shop here and have some lunch."

Amanda thought about what Gerald had said longer than the other two, not being the sort to be readily pushed into anything she did not think right. The logic that the man had offered seemed watertight, after all the only person that could get into trouble for having false paperwork was Millie, and given that she didn't exist it would be rather hard for anybody to charge her with anything.   Although the letter from Carver would be a fake too, it was hardly likely that the police officer would admit to its existence, or

278

even keep it.   The thought of going outside of the law was abhorrent, but again she could see the reasoning.   If she was reading Gerald right, there were some pretty unpleasant people in the city that didn't take kindly to the new officer, and the people would not be bothered by any form of violence whatever the outcome.   The officer was by no means a saint either, he was busying himself trying to clean up something that he was a part of, and making things much less safe all round by doing so, therefore checking his abuse of power was surely a good thing, but this should be done through the correct channels.   There she could see a problem, and understood how Jim, who probably had the strongest sense of fair play of the four of them, was not bothered by the plan.

"Look where the correct channels got him," she thought, remembering his telling of the police raid that ended one of the best periods of his childhood.   Tangled and distasteful the plan was, but it was a plan and it had a pretty good chance of working, and she couldn't think of anything better.

"Yes," she said, smiling warmly.   "Let's do it, and lets have lunch, I'm starving."

It was Wednesday morning when Gerald turned up at the side of the Crimson Lake and called across to Jim and Amanda who had, in the absence of any immediate plans to move, set about a big spruce up of their own craft.   All of the major work had been finished, and they were now re-stowing the newly painted deed boxes in their original places, having re-varnished and cleaned just about every part of the Mayfly that needed it.

"Now that's a real picture, you've made a good job of that."   Gerald said warmly.   "You can come and do the same to some of my stock any time you want.   You'd double the value of it"

"Want a cup of tea?" Amanda shouted back, beckoning the man to come aboard their home.

The thumbs up from Gerald, set Jim to arranging the gleaming Primus, that would not have looked better had it been made from gold, ready for the job in hand.

"How long have you lived like this?" Gerald asked.   "You've got it all well sorted I'll say that."

"Since I stowed away, or since Jim kidnapped me.   Late spring or very early summer, it's all relative," Amanda replied.

"You're nuts the pair of you, and how is the delightful Vanessa?" he asked.

"Fine, you can ask her yourself when she's back tomorrow afternoon if you want to drop in, she'd be pleased to see you I'm sure," Amanda smiled.

"Good," Gerald replied. "We're about ready. Our mutual friend in blue has a bit of time off, and I'm told the best chance of catching him out will be tomorrow night. I have the paperwork for Millie, all suitably aged and mildly incomplete just as you'd expect. He's done a grand job, even thrown in a few dummy postcards from overseas if you'd be good enough to put them in Vera's boat for her. It'll even have Vera believing she has a sibling if she's not careful. I've got the note from Carver in a bag in my car, just in case the guy thinks it's fake, my friend that does calligraphy has sort of muzzed dust from the inside of the envelope you gave me, so it will have nothing of you on it."

"I can't believe this isn't costing anything," Jim said. "I mean are you absolutely sure?"

"There's no catches my lad," Gerald spoke without the sound of the salesman in his voice. "It is costing, but there are people with bigger fish to fry, and they see it as a good investment. Nothing too sinister you understand, you're not getting yourselves in too deep."

With everything now settled, Gerald set off back to the car lot, to prepare for the next days activity. He'd judged that Amanda Jim and, particularly Vanessa, would not let the side down, but also knew how much her safety mattered to the couple. This was underlined early the next afternoon by Jim's greeting to Gerald.

"Vanessa, she will be O.K. I'm not happy about her taking the risk, even if *she* is," he said.

"I know the people that she will be with, I've sold cars to them and their parents some of them. They'll look after her, and I'll bring her back when she's done her part," Gerald replied firmly. His reassurance was cut short by the sound of Vanessa's aged minibus. He was not, however prepared for the passenger. Vera had decided to return early.

"Yes, I know," she said as she surveyed her home. "If Vanessa here is going to stick her neck out for me, I'm going to see that she looks as she should. It's the least I can do. I know the score, but it's time I got home."

They could all see that she would not budge on the issue, and Gerald didn't seem too worried, so she was soon back aboard the Crimson Lake. The scene that presented its self to her was so much better than she expected. Vanessa had told her that Jim and Amanda were taking care of everything, and she thought they'd do their best, but the place was

280

immaculate even by her standards.   Smiling, she thanked them both warmly for their effort, but there was work to be done.   Vanessa had to undergo a complete change of appearance otherwise, in her opinion, the plot could fail.   In a little over two hours, there emerged a girl with raven black hair, in a short, brightly patterned skirt and a pair of shoes that only the brave would perch on.   On her arm was a matching shoulder bag in which was a small amount of money, and an eight ounce hammer head on a strong loop of white cotton rope, similar to, but slightly thinner than the mooring ropes of the Mayfly.   Vera insisted on this accessory, arguing that, in the event that, anything should go wrong, a well aimed swing would do the trick.

"Call it my lucky charm," she said, adding.   "I've never had to use it, but it's always nice to know it's there."

And so it was time.   Vanessa calmly got into Gerald's old Jaguar, feeling rather less than confident now that the time had come.   Up until this minute, she had seen Jim, Amanda, and Vera in much the same light as she would have looked on characters in a play.   Those people whose normal lives are made artificially interesting by turns of events that just don't happen in real life, but this was real life, she was an event in it and about to influence the outcome.   She nodded as she hardly heard Amanda ask if she was absolutely sure and then the car slowly moved off across the cobbles to take her to an area of life that she had never seen before, but which, if only for a brief time, she was to be a part of.   The caricatures of film and play were, she was sure, not the people she was about to meet, they were as real as the friends she had temporarily parted company with and they may not view her too favourably either.   And why, she thought, should they, here she was the posh bird that was just playing at life, wasting each and every opportunity that came her way.   And the people she was about to meet, why, and how did they get there, what was their world.   Her mind was full of questions.   It wasn't long before she found out.   The Jaguar pulled up outside a rather unprepossessing brick terraced house and Gerald informed her that they had arrived and she was expected.

"Let me do this on my own," Vanessa said softly as Gerald offered to escort her to the door.   "I'll see you later on, when we're all done," she added.

"You're Vanessa," said the young woman that answered the door.   She was not much older, but there was something about her that instilled a feeling of intense respect in Vanessa.

"You'd better come in if you're going to do this, or you can run home to Mummy and Daddy if you want," the girl said.

Vanessa frowned for a moment. "I was going to say that that wasn't necessary, but it absolutely was," she replied. "I've no right to be here but."

"Gerry told us," the girl said. "I just wanted to be sure. That bastard of a copper has been making our lives hell since he arrived. You never know if it's a raid or business."

"Time to fix him," Vanessa added.

The girl fixed her eyes, and looked almost through her. "You do this wrong and you could get hurt, you know that. It's not a game, it could go sour and there's no way out if it does. Vera put that hammer in your bag for a reason, so if you have to use it, don't think, just do," she said flatly.

Vanessa sat silent for a few moments before speaking again.

"It was supposed to be because I owed someone, but it's all shit," she frowned. "How could I have been so stupid to think I was going to change things by pissing my life out of the window."

"Ain't so easy being rich is it," the girl replied, her voice edging to the compassionate. "Sometimes its probably easier to scrape a living and not think. You can't help being born though can you, I mean it's not as if you asked."

Vanessa smiled briefly. "I'll do it right," she said.

"I'm Gemma," the girl said with a smile. "But the punters don't know me as that. Don't take this the wrong way, but you're one of us, no side, just that."

The information given to Gerald was sound, and the offending police officer appeared almost on cue, and was suitably identified. Gemma said it was pretty obvious by his manner that he wasn't on duty, so it was time to move in.

"You want to do some business?" she asked politely, and was replied by a barely perceptible grunt and nod.

"Well, we going to stay here or make a night of it with my pals over there," she waved her hand in the direction of a group of three, one of whom was Vanessa. There was just sufficient light under the street lamp for the transaction to make a decent 35 mm shot, on the fast monochrome film that had been purchased for the occasion. Gerald had mentioned the idea of instant film but it was slow, and would require a flash to be used, which would rather spoil the mood. The officer was in high spirits, having

282

just won a fair sum on the horses and was looking to enjoy the time off. First a few drinks, then a walk to see what could be seen. Gemma and her group of friends had made sure they were a pleasing enough sight, and he soon walked over and joined them, making several more good photographs as he did.

"We going to do this in the street?" Gemma asked, "I've got some paperwork for you if you want it?"

The trap was laid, and he walked right into it, Vanessa's make up and change of hair colour had made it easy to switch her with a lookalike as soon as they got to the house, where drinks were laid on. Vanessa had said that it didn't seem right for her to just leave the dirty work to someone else, but Gemma was quick to set her right.

"You may think you could," she said. "But you can't   Leave the rest to us, it isn't as though he's going to get anything anyway. You've done your bit."

Gerald, as arranged, was waiting in the Jaguar in the back alley, and had gone past the stage of worrying that something may not be right.   He was now beginning to think that something was decidedly wrong.   All he could do was wait, and this was eventually rewarded with the appearance of Vanessa, looking a lot less tidy than she was when she began the evening. She quickly strode over to the car and got into the front passenger seat.

"Let's go," she said. "Now."

The car glided away almost noiselessly, it being one of the perks of the trade to find a good vehicle at a low cost, and Vanessa remained as quiet as it was for some time. Eventually the silence was broken by Gerald.

"You alright?" he asked, somewhat lost for words.

"Gemma was wrong," Vanessa replied. "I didn't give the game away."

Again there was a long silence before she continued.

"So far as virtue is concerned, I'm not as green as I'm cabbage looking. He read the note, and believed it. But I've still got it, I palmed it, so even if he wanted to, he'd have no proof it ever existed.   Now lets get to the rendezvous."

This was to be a phone box about a mile away, down a terrace of empty houses that were scheduled for demolition.

"I'm sorry I ever doubted you," Gerald could say no more.

"Don't be," Vanessa replied.   "I didn't do it for you, or them, or even Amanda for that matter.   It's no game, not for me and definitely not for them."

Gerald drove on, not quite knowing how to react to someone who he had thought was good naturedly ineffective showing her claws for the first time. He parked the car some distance from the phone box, and they waited. It was a while before the officer turned up with a thick looking envelope, which he secreted behind the board that held the phone to the cast iron back of the box. He was surprised on leaving to find Vanessa standing outside. She was out of the car before Gerald had a chance of stopping her and he was left unable to do anything other than watch.

"We all make mistakes," she said firmly. "And you shouldn't have jumped to conclusions."

"You've no proof," the officer said.

"Oh, but I have, plenty, and do you know what, today is your lucky day," Vanessa replied.

"How do you make that out?" the officer asked.

"Because I am giving you the chance to be a better person. And don't try and run, I think you know why," Vanessa said quietly.

"Is this blackmail," the man asked again.

"Not as such. You know your old friend from the lodge, Mr Carver has been leaning on you, and you also know that you could go down with him. Because he's said as much," Vanessa answered.

The officer's expression fell.

"Not for the first time either," he said. "But he's never put it in writing before."

"But it's a measure of how seriously you take it, that you are willing to pay him off. How much was in the envelope?" Vanessa asked.

"Enough. Look what do you want?" the man replied.

"I want you to take a good long look at your actions, and see how easy it is to get things wrong," Vanessa kept calm as she spoke.

"What the hell are you on about?" he said.

"Vera Potter is a good person at heart, no saint, but kind. She helps people out, and never asks for anything back," Vanessa answered.

"But she was recruiting, procuring. I had it on good information," the officer's face fell as he heard his words.

"You had it from Mr Carver Junior I suspect," Vanessa said.

"I can't tell you that," the officer replied.

"But it is true nonetheless. Even the people under you had respect for her, that's why the raid was so neatly done. You usually smash a hell of a lot more if you mean business. I have that on very good authority too."

284

Vanessa frowned.

"Carry on," the officer said.

"Well it looks like you've been had. Carver has got you to do his dirty work, and as you knew you would not get a warrant, you acted outside the law. Then I come along with a letter from the guy, and you follow the orders in it without question. Just where is the justice in that. You know that man is being held on suspicion of a lot of things, including conspiracy to murder, yet you still rough up a law abiding citizen on his behalf," Vanessa replied.

"I never knew it was her sister that was the, actress," the man frowned again.

"Grow up!" Vanessa said sharply. "Just to make it clear. You *have* been had. All of what you have seen this evening is not real, the only thing that is is the blind alley you have driven yourself up. Let me tell you something about me. For a long time I never really thought for myself, now I have done. I can let you off the hook or blackmail you. But I am of a mind to let you off the hook because I don't like blackmail. But that's my choice and nobody else's."

"Am I supposed to have a conversion, see the light or something," the officer almost laughed.

"No, but you should promise to think before you act, and don't let the people with power push you around. We're none of us perfect, but I hope you'll treat the people on the edge of things a bit more decently now. Think about it," Vanessa kept her voice steady despite her nerves.

"You're pretty brainy for a," he cut short the word he was about to use.

"No I am not. I'm pretty dim for a university student if you want the truth. But I'm waking up, and so should you," she said

"So all of this is a set up?" he frowned.

"Yes. You've been had, I told you that earlier," Vanessa smiled.

"I've not been too clever, have I."

"No"

"So, what now." the officer asked.

"Build your bridges, and work by consent. It's a lot easier than using force. Be one of the good guys," Vanessa said.

"I thought I was, but, well. Bang to rights comes to mind," he laughed slightly. "O.K. You win. I'll think on what you've said, and act on it too. You have my word."

"Thank you," Vanessa said warmly. "I'm afraid I have to remind you

285

that there would be consequences if you didn't. Now I must go. I'd stay in the box for about five minutes to let me sort of vanish. I've always wanted to disappear into the night. Oh, and don't forget to take your money."

With that she left and took a roundabout route back to Gerald, who was almost in a state of panic.

"There," she said on entering the car. "I've done my bit, I doubt he'll bother Vera any more. And the paperwork doesn't really matter now either."

"Thanks." Gerald replied. He thought for a moment, wondering if it was better to keep quiet, but he somehow felt that he would be letting the side down if he didn't proffer something more than the one word.

"Not everyone has the chances, so we scratch a living, make do," he thought some more. "For a lot it's not such a bad life, for some it's hell. You have a choice, and even that comes at a price."

"And those girls?" Vanessa replied quietly.

"Of a sort," Gerald answered quickly. "Like me, you either work in a mind numbing nine to five in some awful factory or shop with people pissing on you every day, or you use what you have whilst you have it. Most things turn into shite when you're pushed into doing them, when there's no alternative. Like my national service, I bloody hated that. Some people toed the line and got on, but I was too bloody stupid so I was always in trouble."

"I don't get it?" Vanessa interrupted.

"Them, well, most will have been through school for what? To work in some bicycle factory for a pittance, and then only if they got some kind of good reference. Any that got into trouble with the law, and that's most of them, have no chance, full employment or no, their cards are marked from the start. So it's being a cleaner, or what. There's a lot of villains controlling things, and they're as bad as the bosses, there's villains in my business, in politics too."

"I'm just a spoilt little tart aren't I," Vanessa frowned.

"You have the choice. I'd say you'd best choose before too long," Gerald felt slightly exasperated at having been pushed into thinking. He took life at the pace it offered itself to him, and had given up questioning too much a long time ago. In Vanessa he saw the remnants of the person she was some weeks back. He was unaware of the changes that she had gone through in so short a time, but knew that she would need every bit of her rather limited intelligence to work things out.

As they drew up at the basin, he said, "Look, you've done the right thing, and thanks."

It was towards the end of the following week that he returned with the news that the offending officer had been noticeably better in his dealings, and that the message had got to him that, as long as the man remained in the job, Vera had nothing to worry about and nor did anyone else that lived on the edge of what was acceptable.

"He's going to have to think long and hard before he does anything hasty now," Gerald smiled to be met with a frown from Vanessa.

"And yes, the girls are getting a far better deal out of the coppers too. It's in everyone's interest to keep the real villains out, and that should have been their job in the first place," he said.

Chapter 17

The motor was running as well as ever, and the Mayfly was again looking her best as Jim and Amanda edged slowly out of the basin, having stayed a few days more to make sure that all was well with Vera. Vanessa had left shortly after Gerald's visit, having decided to apply herself to something altogether more useful, as she had put it. She had given no further detail, but promised that she would be in touch somehow. In all they had spent just over two weeks tied up next to the Crimson Lake, and were more than happy to be on the move again, despite the rain and the ever recurrent cash problems. Autumn was beginning to take more of a hold, and was most noticeable on clear nights and bright mornings when the thin plywood shell did not do much of a job of keeping the cold out. Their next main destination was to return the pollution monitor to Clive Prentice. Whilst they were looking forward to seeing him again, it also meant the end of any income from the device, and no further plan other than to deliver two more watches a good deal later in the year. Somehow nothing seemed to bother them, they were on the move again and that was what they did best.

"We ought to phone Marie at some time," Jim suggested, as they passed under a bridge. "See what the state of play is back home."

"This is home," Amanda smiled. "But I know what you mean, but not today, let's have today just for the two of us. There's nobody after us, and that's sort of good I think."

Jim smiled in reply, there was not much to say, their easy going routine had returned and both were savouring it. They decided to stop early in an area of open country and just enjoy the evening, the meal, a long walk under the darkening sky, and the return, lit only by the stars to the warmth of shared closeness in the cabin. Smoothing Amanda's hair gently down her back, and continuing the movement of his hand until it rested neatly on her waist, Jim drew a deep breath and let it out very slowly, happy with the moment. Amanda curled, almost cat-like, relaxed into the bedding, and smiled. More than anywhere, this was where she wanted to be, and as the breeze that had blown up since they retired gently rocked the boat, they both drifted off to sleep, a small parcel of humanness wrapped in a nylon sleeping bag. They would have slept late into the morning had the noise of the breeze, which had now achieved gale force, not woken them at around six o'clock.

"That's going to be a bugger," Amanda said, lazily.

"Bollocks to it," Jim replied as he stretched out. "We're going to get more of this as the year goes on so we may as well get acclimatised."

And more of it they got. Over the next week if it wasn't raining, it was blowing, and often, by way of a change it did both. They started the day damp and finished it soaking, but fuelled by haybox curry, strong tea, and fried bread and marmalade they plugged on forward though progress was very slow, sometimes only a third of their normal daily distance. With covers fully deployed, the wind blown rain still found its target, and what was worse the force of the gusts pushed the boat all over the place. Eventually they put anything that wasn't waterproof in the cabin, and ran without covers, accepting saturation as a fact of life. By the end of each day they were chapped and sore from handling wet rope and windlasses. Also, by the end of the week, Amanda had a bad cold. The weather lacked no energy and continued as wild as it had been.

"Right," Jim said, in a moment of decisiveness. "You stay in the cabin today. There's no way you can work."

Amanda protested, but knew he was right, despite which, she was pretty sure he was probably going to catch the wretched cold and then it'd be her turn. He was right, and so was she. In another day Jim's temperature had risen to what Amanda had decided was probably a dizzying height and she insisted that they both stop until they felt rather better.

"We weren't born to this," she croaked. "And I think even old Lou would let us off for a day or so."

Jim smiled, remembering what seemed like years back.

"I remember," he said. "He didn't want you roughing your hands up."

He'd have said more but the cough he had developed stopped him. The weather continued bad, a mixture of rain, mist and wind making everything in the Mayfly seem damp and cold, mainly on account of the fact that that was exactly what it was. They used the paraffin stoves to provide some heat, but they were noisy, smelly and the instruction booklet that came with one said it should not be used as a heater. The daily walk for provisions and water added to the general state of gloom that suddenly seemed to have settled. As if to add to their problems they were again running short of money, and each day they did not travel, they, due to the need to buy food, literally ate into the budget for fuel. It was the weekend again before either of them felt fit enough to move on, and with the weather only slightly improved, they edged off towards their planned destination, which was the canal bridge near to Clive Prentice's business. They took things easy, thankful that the wind, that had been such a prominent feature of earlier on, had died down, so they could run with the covers up and keep out of the sporadic rain. As the weather gradually cleared, Jim tried a bit of hand towing, to save on petrol, claiming that the exercise would do him some good. With the holiday season being pretty much over they could go on for over a day without seeing another boat on the move which, as Jim pointed out, meant that they avoided daft comments and offers of help, as happened previously, from people thinking they had broken down.

"We're going to have to think of better ways to keep warm once the real cold weather starts," Amanda pointed out, coughing as she did. "Or we'll get something really bad and be found frozen to the marrow in midwinter by one of the lengthmen."

"Best not buy any marrows then," Jim quipped, knowing that his partner was absolutely right. "If we're careful we could get some kind of heater I suppose, I mean it wouldn't take that much to heat the cabin. That's where the real boaters had things right. Those little ranges like the one Vera has, they were a sort of standard fitting. But we've no room for one."

Something of the basic folly of trying to live on such a small vessel was beginning to dawn on Jim. It had been his intention, not Amanda's, to do so and he savoured the moment of consideration of what an ill-prepared fool he had been. He resolved to try and work something out before things got too dire. They had made things worse for themselves by trying to push on against the wind and rain in a boat that was basically arranged for fair weather travel. Since being ill they had decided to be a little more sensible and had reasoned that, by keeping the cabin as dry as possible and not moving in the really bad weather, they could keep themselves drier. Then, by leaving the side screens up if the wind wasn't too high they would be further proofed against the worst of what was thrown at them. They were little trouble to put up and pretty effective considering the lightness of fabric that they were made of.

"Hot water bottles!" Amanda coughed again, as she attempted to shout to Jim who was on the towpath a few yards ahead. He looked round, and caught the relevance of the remark.

"Fire-brick," he replied, smiling.

"Tea," Amanda smiled brightly for the first time in days. "We have to talk inventions!"

Jim let the Mayfly come level with him then tugged the bow rope lightly to bring her towards the towpath, Amanda used what steerage she had from the motor to bring the stern round so that they could tie up. Over tea they worked on the brief ideas they had, and decided to buy some cheap hot water bottles when they next went shopping. This was simple but Jim's mention of fire-brick, had set Amanda thinking.

"We could make something like the hay-box, only sort of backwards," she said.

Jim thought for some moments.

"If we use another deed box," he said slowly. "I mean it's not as if we have one full of watches any more, we only have the two in it and they could easily pack in with our clothes. I hope ordinary brick will do."

"We used bricks round the camp fires when I was at Guides," Amanda replied, "We could go scavenging for some. There was that load of stuff tipped near the canal about a mile ago, if you don't mind doubling back."

"If we gather wood during the day, we could make a small fire wherever we can and heat the bricks on it," Jim thought out loud.

The gloom had gone, and they spent an enjoyable hour going through the rubbish that someone had dumped in the bushes next to the towpath. There was a lot of rubble, an old fridge, an electric cooker that looked like it had been in a somewhat dangerous condition since manufacture, and, the holy grail. Bricks, quite a few of them. They could fit eight of them neatly into the deed box resting on the oven shelves from the old cooker. Satisfied with their find, they decided to stop early for the evening and work on their invention. They needed to dry the bricks out carefully so that they didn't crack when they were heated, and it was a good idea, Amanda thought, to give them a good clean (albeit in canal water) before they actually used them. Once washed, they were carefully arranged around the paraffin stoves so that the heat from cooking would slowly do the job.

"It's going to be O.K. Jim," Amanda smiled. "It's only weather, not the Police, not criminals. We can do this."

The following Monday, they managed to get several cheap hot water bottles from a market. Any left over hot water could be put in to help keep bedding warm during the day as well as at night. They felt that the investment was worth hand towing for another two days, after which they could make it under power to the rendezvous with Clive Prentice. Although this was unnecessary, it was a matter of pride for the two of them to at least look as though they were coping. The weather had brightened a bit, and their colds had just about gone, so the walking along the towpath was pleasant enough, if a bit muddy. They took an hour each, neatly swapping lines under a bridge with no more than a slight check to speed as they performed the change over. Although a somewhat melancholy sight, with little or no traffic, the canal was as reassuring a place as one could wish for. It had been in existence for something close to two hundred years, and could well go on for the same again. This, of course, was only an impression. The two knew well the precariousness of the situation, and were part of the campaigning that was going on to keep the little slice of industrial history that they were occupying alive.

"It's a shame it won't stay like this," Amanda observed, as they sat having lunch. "I mean some of it will, but someone's going to have some grand design for something and ruin bits of it aren't they."

"This was someone's grand design once," Jim replied. "I mean it's not natural whatever it looks like, but it'd be shit if someone changed it radically now. They will though, they always spoil things, but if at least some of it is kept," he smiled briefly and added, "Don't mind me too much, my brain's still full of snot."

"That's something old Lou said wasn't it," Amanda replied.

"What, that his brain was full of snot?" Jim smiled.

"You know what I mean," Amanda went on. "All of this. He reckoned that it didn't do to think about it much, but he liked the men in suits about as much as you do."

Jim smiled as they set to clearing up, ready for another afternoon of towing. It was about another ten or so miles before they decided to tie up for the evening. They had gathered a reasonable amount of wood throughout the day, but the weather was still quite mild, so they added the chore of chopping it into manageable chunks, ready for what was sure to come. When the job was finished, the wood sat in a couple of large wicker baskets that had at one time been used for bread. Amanda had found them in a junk shop when they were looking for hot water bottles. They could sit neatly on the cabin top for the wood to dry, if the weather permitted it, or be stacked on the bunks out of the way in the cabin. The next day would get them to the Clive Prentice's business, and the end of yet another source of income when they handed the electronic box back.

292

"There's going to be a bloody hell of a lot more towing after this," Jim commented matter-of-factly. "We're about skint aren't we?"

"Not as bad as that," Amanda replied. "But not far off. We're going to have to be careful, but we've plenty of time, and the exercise is good for us. Anyway, what I need right now is a bloody good scrub. I'm filthy, and I don't want to turn up smelling worse than the canal at Carver's. We can get a couple of buckets of water from the river and boil them up, it should be clean enough for washing."

"It's that time of year I suppose," Jim replied smiling. "After that cold I feel like I've been stuck together with envelope glue."

Leaving a kettle and a large pan to slowly come to the boil, Jim set off with two big galvanised buckets, and whatever other containers he could find for cold water. Amanda spent the time clearing the cockpit out, and erecting the cover ready for the evening. It took some time for the buckets to heat up, despite the help from the boiling water that Amanda added when Jim returned, and it was dusk before they stood naked on the tarpaulin in the cockpit to clean up. The stoves had warmed the area throughout, and one was now slowly bringing the haybox stew back to boiling point for afterwards.

"It's a sort of odd luxury this," Amanda smiled as they washed themselves and each other. "I mean, I never could reach the middle of my back, it could have been filthy all my life and I'd have never known."

"It's a bit like royalty in the history lessons at school I suppose," Jim replied. "I mean they had servants to do all of that for them. Never lifted a finger."

"Oh! No! I couldn't employ someone to do that. I mean how would you interview them?" She screwed her face up comically.

"They'd have someone to select people I suppose," Jim said dryly. "But that wouldn't be too choice either. This is a hell of a lot nicer," he added, sponging the area of Amanda's back that she had mentioned earlier.

"There," he said firmly. "All those years of muck, all gone."

For his efforts, Amanda rewarded him with a sound slap from a flannel. With the covers up, the warmth of the stove, and the appetising smell of the stew made a relaxing and comfortable atmosphere, one which no holidaymaker would be likely to experience, but which the two lovers almost took for granted.

"I'm bloody starving," Amanda said, as she washed her long, almost black, hair in the last of the hot water. "I know I should leave this until tomorrow, but I just felt so filthy after the colds and all."

"We'll make a late night of it if you like," Jim smiled. "After all it's bad for you to sleep with wet hair. Besides it'll be like sleeping with a sack of damp kittens."

"Pig!" Amanda laughed as she rinsed her hair through into one of the buckets.

"Let's have tea then dress afterwards, we'll be properly dry then," she added. I don't really feel too cold at the moment, with the stoves and everything.

It was about one in the morning that Jim woke to find himself still in the cockpit with the full moon, which had broken through the clouds, illuminating the area through the thin side screen. Although it was colder now, the night was mild, with the broken cloud keeping much of the warmth of the day in. Had it been a clear one, they may well have experienced the first frost of the autumn, but this would not happen for a while yet. On the towpath side of the cockpit, Amanda was still fast asleep on the board that ran between the stern thwart and the centre one. Mayfly was not much more than a large dinghy with a cabin, and the construction must have required the internal bracing of the centre thwart, given the solidity of the piece of wood that it had been made out of. There she slept, as peacefully as if she were on the finest silk sheets of the softest feather bed, and there Jim sat and watched her sleep. There were no thoughts in his head, no words, no plans for the next day, nothing. His mind was filled with the glorious feeling of simply being there. There were no primeval urges stirring, just the peace of the moment, the knowledge that there, opposite him, on a plank of wood, was Amanda, breathing gently. Fast asleep, resting her head on a deed box full of food, and as naked as they day she was born was Amanda. She was there, and he was there. That was all there was and all he wanted. Over half an hour passed before she stirred and, rubbing the sleep from her eyes, saw Jim. She smiled, instinctively noticing his depth of thought.

"Penny for them," she said softly.

"You'd be robbed," he replied, equally softly. "Nothing, absolutely zero."

A couple of minutes passed before he added, "I guess your hair is pretty dry now, so we'd best turn in."

The simple move from cockpit to the warmth of the sleeping bags in the cabin took no more than two minutes, and it was not much more than that before the pair were fast asleep again in each others arms. There was no hurry the following morning, as they had only about half a days running to get to the their tie up, so their waking rather later than usual did not matter. The morning was warm for the time of year, and the sun broke through the cloud making it almost spring like.

"My hair is like a carpet!" Amanda said as she sat up in the sleeping bag and attempted brushing it. "I should have sorted it before I went to sleep."

"Here, let me," Jim replied. "Sit on the thwart and I'll do it for you."

"I can brush my own hair!" Amanda said, rather sharply.

"I know," Jim paused a moment. "But I'd like to, if you don't mind."

She handed the brush to him without saying anything, and relaxed as he started teasing the tangles out gently. Her hair had been rather damp when she slept in the cockpit which, coupled to the difficulty of washing it properly, had made what was normally a bit unruly go into outright rebellion. Jim's patience and gentleness paid off, and the brush eventually glided through with no snagging on tangles. He continued brushing until he was satisfied that he had done a good job, making sure the parting was as Amanda usually had it.

"There," he said.

"You sure you aren't a hairdresser in disguise?" she smiled. "I suppose we'd better get dressed Jimbo," she added, realising that they were still without a stitch of clothing on.

"We said we'd get dressed after tea. I suppose we'd better do it before breakfast," Jim replied, also smiling.

It was early afternoon when they passed under the bridge and turned in to tie up. The weather was reasonable for the time of year, cloudy and with an ever present threat of rain, so they decided to take a walk up to the village and return the little electronic box that had been their companion for quite some time to its rightful owner. The offices of Planetary Electronic Systems were, the last time they visited, as neat and tidy as the owner, and reflected his personality, they thought, rather well. Now however, the appearance was one of total chaos, in the middle of which was a mildly agitated Clive Prentice.

"Well," he smiled at the pair. "Welcome back. I've been right up to my neck in collating all the data you sent me so that I can type up a report. It's all rather exciting you know, but a bit daunting. I may have the biggest order that I've had in my life, and part of that is down to your excellent work. You did a good job to sort the information as far as you have, but there is such a lot, and I have to make it read properly so that the people that may buy the thing can understand its usefulness properly. Now, let's find some space and we can have some tea."

Clive cleared an area amid the disorder and the three sat down around a small table. Once suitably supplied with tea, Clive explained the rather unprecedented success of the little machine. It seemed that there had been a requirement, but nobody could make a working version that was robust enough to stand use in the field. Whilst, on his own admission, the device Clive had invented was not as absolutely precise as could be made, it never seemed to need adjusting, and it could stand long periods of use without failure. It was also small and relatively cheap which meant that, when the necessary paperwork to protect the design was complete, it attracted rather more attention than he had thought it would, and from both sides of the divide on pollution. There were those who had an interest in monitoring to provide proof for an environmental campaign, but rather more from industries who wanted to have data to prove that they did not pollute, or to ensure that they did not. Clive had initially been reluctant to sell to these, but had been encouraged to follow up any interest by an old and trusted friend, who was also a die-hard environmentalist. The reasoning was that the device could influence polluters to change their ways, and that if he was able to sell it in higher volume, the cost to the environmentalists would be less than if it was offered exclusively to them. Things like this would normally happen over a longer period, but the little machine, once publicised had somehow caught its self up in the spirit of the times. Hence the chaos at Planetary Electronic Systems.

"Trouble is," Clive said, in his usual genteel manner. "I haven't the first clue as to how I am going to get any of this done. But it really is too good a chance to miss."

"It is," Jim replied. "I see it can do a lot of good. People may not believe other people, but they can't argue with facts, and that's what this thing gives isn't it."

"To put it in a nutshell, yes. That's exactly what it's meant to do," Clive smiled.

"Then we'd better help you out, if you'll let us," Jim added, noticing Amanda's raised eyebrows as he spoke.

"Yes," he added quickly. "I know we don't know much about the stuff, but we can learn."

"Well," Clive frowned slightly. "It is going to be hard for me to get anybody that is skilled enough to work on this project, apart from the people that I already have, and then there's the issue of trust. At least I can trust you two, so, if you'd be good enough, I'd be glad of the help, and of course, I'll pay. I insist on that."

Though they would not admit it, Jim and Amanda were down to their last five pounds and had been wondering where they would get the money to feed themselves so the offer was gratefully accepted on both sides. Clive had mentioned that he had employees, but they only made the casings and assembled the finished product for him. He built all the electronic parts himself. Amanda, with her knowledge of maths, proved to be very good at sorting the data out whilst Jim, was able to help with manufacture and testing of the first batch of the units. These were destined to be used mainly for demonstration, it being yet to be decided as to how to make a bigger batch of the things.

"It's nice here," Amanda smiled over their evening meal, whilst watching one of the reddest of sunsets.

"But?" Jim knew she was about to go on, but may need the little prompt.

"It could be like a houseboat if we let it," she said, responding to the gentle prod, adding. "This little thing, well, she was made for moving. It's like when we tie up at night, it almost seems like if we didn't, she'd go wandering by herself just for the adventure."

"I felt something like that when I first saw her," Jim replied dreamily. "It was like, well I just thought it was a shame, you know, when you read stories in the papers of people leaving a horse tethered in a field when all it wants to do is gallop around the place. She was drowning and I couldn't let that happen."

"We need the cash though Jimbo, don't we," Amanda frowned slightly. "We'll be on our way soon."

"She'll understand," Jim smiled. "She's one of us you know."

"It's really weird," Amanda continued the thread. "You wouldn't give a sideboard a name, but they are basically the same, made of wood, you know. The little Fly, she is something different though isn't she."

"She really came to life when you added your part," Jim replied. "It's like she was waiting, if that doesn't sound too daft."

"Not with what I was going to say," Amanda smiled. "I kind of thought

297

she'd somehow know that we were working for Clive to get the cash together ready to move on. I know that's stupid, but I can't help thinking it. Thanks by the way, you didn't have to say what you just did."

"Wasn't just the Mayfly if you want the truth," Jim smiled. "It was me too."

"Jimbo, you're an old romantic at heart aren't you," Amanda replied.

It was almost a month before they were under way, and a consignment of four of the devices were entrusted to them to be delivered to a group of environmental campaigners as and when they could. Clive had been more than pleased with their work, and had secured a suitably large, but manageable order which, thanks to a bit of negotiation by Jim, he would be able to service. The idea to use Carver and Green as a contractor for some of the work had at first been a controversial one but, as Jim pointed out, the only bad thing about the company (Mr Carver junior) was no longer involved in the business. Jim also suggested making it a condition of any contract that Ed Donaldson should not be dropped from Carver's board even though he was not in the country. This was not just charity either. Jim reasoned that Amanda's father was an able engineer, who could help in the development of the invention, as well as ensuring fair play from the contractor. That was if he could be tempted to return.

Chapter 18

Amanda cleared her head of all but what she wanted to say, then looked down and shut her eyes. She knew that if she thought too much about anything she would not be able to speak at all and that, although nobody would feel badly of her if she couldn't, it still would not be right. She had made no notes, and was beginning to think that this was a mistake. Still, she was there and there was no other option but to draw breath and speak.

"The last few months have taught me a lot," she began hesitantly. "And one of the greatest things you can learn is how quickly you can have trust in a person. Not so much trust as confidence. Lou expressed that when, after knowing me for only a few hours, he referred to me as a boater. I will remember his words for the rest of my life. That was the best compliment anybody has paid me, and all the better because I know he meant it. He never would say anything he didn't mean and never seemed afraid of speaking his mind. Always to the point, and always sparing with words, generous too and a lot more besides. It takes a very wise person to calmly go about the day without the desire to be noticed. People like that are often the amongst the wisest on the planet, if anything I have read has any truth in it. In fact, it is Lou's wisdom that got to me, and proves the point too. By referring to me as a boater, he made me feel that I wasn't intruding on what was his, and your territory. More than that, he gave me confidence about my life, at a point that I needed it. I'm absolutely sure he knew that too. It doesn't take a long time, or many words exchanged, to know a good person. He's gone from view now, but he'll always be there. In every hedgerow, on every lock-side, pacing the towpath gently for ever. Old Lou was a good man. The best of all."

Amanda looked down and, with tears now running down her cheeks, stepped away from the lectern and returned to sit down with Jim, who put as comforting arm around her. There was nothing he could do or say, but he was there.

The previous week or so had been routine, they had been to the university to talk to Jeremy Simms about his findings and were debating as to whether to use the river or double back on themselves and head for the capital by canal. The news they were about to receive made their minds up for them. As they were sitting with a cup of tea trying to make sense of the meeting with Dr. Simms, a man of about sixty, with a well worn tweed jacket stopped on the towpath near them.

"You're the two kids that are working on the canal?" he stated the truth in a polite, but questioning tone.

"It sort of depends on who you are," Jim replied cautiously.

"I'm no threat, and it is you isn't it? Jim and Amanda?" he smiled.

"Bang to rights," Amanda chipped in.

The man had worked on the canal some years earlier but had taken another job. His departure from the waterway had not been of his own choosing and he had kept in touch with his friends from his old job. Having taken a slightly early retirement, he enjoyed walking the tow-paths, and meeting up with the people he had known, one of whom was old Lou.

"He always spoke well of you, like you was his grandchildren or something. He had a son but he were killed in the war I think," the man frowned, as though he did not want to go on speaking but had to. The next part of his story was almost unbearable for Amanda and Jim to hear. Lou had been found, in one of his favourite spots, leaning over the parapet of a hump backed red brick bridge, one of many that sat on a bend in the canal and afforded a magnificent view of the waterway and countryside that he loved so much. To the passer by in a boat, even on foot, the man looked as though he was in deep thought, looking down, under the wide brim of his hat, at the gently rippled water as the season slowly turned. How many people passed by and thought just that is not known, but he had been dead for almost a whole day before Ruby, his wife went looking for him.

"He was a good man," she said to Jim and Amanda, as they walked down the churchyard. "Good as they come. Married him when I was nowt but a girl and it was best days work I did, even if folks didn't agree at the time."

Amanda looked at the old woman's kind face, but could think of nothing to say.

"An there in't nothin' to say or do is there my love. Nothin'll bring him back, nor should it. I've had many years of his time, an he's always with me, it were his time and that's all there is to it," Ruby said calmly.

"I think he'll always be with us too," Amanda replied softly.

"Aye that too," Ruby smiled. "He were full of you two. Reminded him of him so he said. Took off for the big adventure and found this was

300

his calling. Married me when all said I were too young, and, you knew the man so I don't have to tell." The old lady smiled at the mildly embarrassed look on Amanda's face.

"Aye," she continued. "And he knew that and all. It's not the piece of paper, nor the bell, book an' candle as makes a marriage. 'Tis what's inside as does, an there was more like you than you'd think even then."

Amanda looked down at the ground.

"You said no lie. Lou told as was, and you see if he weren't right about it. Now come back to the cottage and be a part of things my dears, he'd like it if you did, an' so would I."

Old Lou's home was small and built of brick with a slate roof and had been erected by the canal company not long after the waterway had opened. It sat on a lane about half a mile from a narrow waisted bridge of similar build to the one on which Lou had been found. Clearly he had been a well liked person, as the little building was full to overflowing, and these were just the close friends. The thought struck Amanda shortly after it had occurred to Jim that it was very much an honour to have been asked to speak at his funeral, in fact to be one of just two who did speak. Picking up on the look, almost as though she could read their minds, Ruby paused before entering the cottage and said, "He had so many old friends, we'd be there until the good Lord took all of us if they'd all said their piece. No, I thought a lot, and decided his oldest and newest friends could say all that was needed. There's nobody as minded and we'll share enough stories this afternoon to fill more than a pair of boats. Lou said you was both boaters, so you need to be among your own at a time like this."

The afternoon went on into the evening, and then the night. Jim and Amanda heard stories of cold winters, overloaded boats, accidents, marriages births and deaths. They told and retold their story too many times for them to count, and never felt the need to question the fact that, although they knew nobody, everybody seemed to know them. When they eventually had to return to their home, it was a quick goodbye, with the unspoken promise that they would all meet again. The night was cold, with a smell of frost on the air and an almost imperceptible breeze moving the very slight mist rising from the canal towards the pair as they walked along the towpath.

"I'm going to have to see my folks aren't I," Jim quietly dropped the sentence on the night air as though it meant nothing too much. It was enough though to check Amanda as she walked. She stopped so suddenly

301

that Jim took another two steps and only came to a halt when he felt Amanda's hand move in his. He saw her face, wide eyed in the hazy moonlight, framed by her unruly dark hair, almost Pre-Raphaelite in appearance.

"Yours will come home, if not now, then later, like Bo Peep's sheep," he said. "If I leave it, it could be the next world before I see mine, and I don't want that to happen. I know where they are now, but they come and go." He saw Amanda had not moved, or changed her rather startled expression. She had suggested he found his parents, and had no idea that he actually knew where each lived.

"Dave had been on to Marie, that's when we last phoned," he explained. "My cousin, the one that I was staying with." Amanda nodded, and Jim continued. "He knew about the boat, so he contacted Saracen's, and they got in touch with Dave. My folks want to see me. There's a first time for everything I guess. Then all of this happened and I sort of forgot to tell you. Actually that's not true. I mean I thought I didn't give a toss, wasn't going to bother, to be honest, but," his voice tailed off.

"But?" Amanda prodded.

"O.K. But I think Lou would be happier if I did. That's all," Jim said. "I can almost see him telling me it."

"Where do they live?" Amanda asked, not even thinking to question him.

"They'd be about ten or so miles from the canal, about a day or so from the city centre. They're not together, but they're in the same town at the moment," Jim replied.

"Why do they suddenly both want to see you?" Amanda asked, sounding slightly puzzled.

"They're like that. For nearly as long as I can remember, they've been apart, but always keep tabs on each other. It's almost like some kind of competition, so probably only one actually wants to, but the other one won't be out-done," Jim said.

"That's sad," Amanda frowned. "I'm sorry but I have to say it. I can't see why they chose not to look after you. Maybe I'm stupid, or inexperienced, but whatever happened, I hope I'd force myself even if things weren't right at first."

"We'll go and see them if that's O.K. Don't expect too much though," Jim said flatly.

The next morning continued as the previous evening had suggested, the

302

sky remained clear throughout and the temperature fell to well below freezing. They hadn't had time to heat their improvised storage heater the previous night and had relied on hot water bottles, which were now stone cold. Before anything else, Jim set about lighting the Primus, which if nothing else gave an audible hint that at least promised some warmth in the form of a cup of tea. Amanda emerged, dressed in several sweaters, jeans and the thickest pair of socks she could find.

"This is going to start to be a bit of a problem isn't it," she said resignedly.

"Boaters have frozen to death in the past, but it was rare I think," Jim replied. "Let's have a big breakfast and get something good sorted for tea before we move, and we must heat the bricks tonight."

The day stayed cold and, whilst not frozen over, there were bits of ice floating in the canal which made a peculiar sound as they glided through them, not unlike some of the floating debris they had encountered in the city stretches but somehow softer. Progress was not hampered too much, although it all seemed like harder work than it had been. The landscape was now very different to the view that holidaymakers saw. Trees were becoming skeletal objects dusted with frost, the hedgerows were mostly leafless too and the fields devoid of crops. It wasn't unpleasant, just cold, and the two made their way across it to the steady sound of their single cylinder motor. In another three days they would be within a bus-ride of Jim's parents, and about on time for the planned rendezvous.

"What are they like?" Amanda asked, as they made their way across a long pound. The question was more idle curiosity than any desire for insight.

"Jim?" She added, seeing the look on his face. It wasn't anger, nor depression, but she saw an emotion there that she couldn't place.

Jim thought and then drew a deep breath, letting it out slowly as he leant back on the cabin top. He shut his eyes for a moment and then looked about to speak, though it was some time before he did.

"Would it be bad if I said I didn't really know. I mean not the sort of stuff you'd want anyway. I'd like to tell you about the Christmases we had, the summer holidays and all of that. But they weren't there. They may have been but I don't remember them. I've sort of said this before haven't I," he said quietly.

Amanda nodded.

"But, now you've asked, I actually don't know them that well. But I don't want to put you on the spot either. You had all that happy families stuff, and you shouldn't feel bad about it," he added.

"What do you mean?" Amanda asked.

"Well, it's like those people that try and make you feel guilty for what you have so you give to their charity, or support their cause. Why should you though? I mean, it's not your fault that you grew up in a secure home. In any case you'd give, just like I would, but it shouldn't be guilt that drives things, so, well, I just don't know them that's all. Maybe this is the chance, who knows," Jim smiled briefly.

"I won't walk out on you Jim, not ever," Amanda said firmly. "I may not have any experience of life, but I know that much."

Jim smiled again, rather more warmly this time. "They said that to me," he replied. "That was before they split up. And I believed them too, just like I believe you. You're telling the truth though, I know that. And that's the big difference. For what it's worth, you're stuck with me too."

Amanda waited patiently, she could see there was something else in Jim's head that wanted to come out.

"I know I've said this before, but. This is our time Jim," she said quietly. "It's only really just started, and we don't look at when or if it ends."

"I'm made of them though, and it freaks me a bit if you want the truth," he replied.

"I'll take my chance on that one Jimbo. You won't walk, I know it," Amanda looked briefly into Jim's eyes, and then resumed concentration on steering the Mayfly. As short a glance as it was though, Jim was reassured.

"We'll meet them soon enough," he said calmly. "And then you can make your own mind up."

As the day wore on, some cloud drifted in and the temperature slowly rose to that point where it could go any way. Neither person was sure, but there was a strangeness they could sense, almost but not quite a smell on the light breeze. Both Jim and Amanda put it down to the earlier conversation, and both were wrong. Within a half an hour of them noticing the change, the first flakes of snow began to drift across the canal ahead of them. More followed, and before long a steady fall was adhering to anything that would have it. The silence afforded by snow was broken only by the steady pulse of the diminutive black outboard motor that pushed them through the water at or just below the statutory speed limit. As dusk fell, which with the addition of the leaden snow clouds was rather earlier than it should have been, Amanda brought the little boat in towards the towpath to tie up for the night. A fire was lit from their wood store, and the bricks placed on the old oven shelf to heat thoroughly through. As an afterthought, Jim rummaged around in the bag for a couple of reasonable sized potatoes, which he wrapped in a bit of foil and placed close to the edge of the assemblage.

"No harm in a bit of extra energy," he smiled. "I've never cooked spuds like this."

"Nor me," Amanda replied, sitting beside him on the centre thwart. "It's going to be a bugger tomorrow, but lets just enjoy it for the now. I've always liked snow."

Some of the floating ice that had not melted during the day was getting a little covering, and forming miniature islands that slowly drifted round. The trees were picked out sharp relief, the snow adhering, to the upwind side of anything vertical, and sticking by gravity to the rest. The air swirled with the big flakes, and both the lovers took to watching individual ones, or patches as they fell, then glancing up again to a new area until they felt just a little dizzy. After the hay-box stew and potatoes, they set about preparing the vessel for the night, making sure of the tension on the mooring lines, and running the outboard without the tank connected until the carburettor bowl was empty and they could tip the motor to lift the propeller out of the canal. This was not normal practice, but necessary on nights that may go below freezing. The motor was cooled by canal water, which was circulated by a small pump, before being returned to it's rightful owner. If it was left upright, the water inside would not drain away, and could freeze, causing severe damage to the workings of the thing. Whilst tipping the motor up did not fully drain it, it left sufficient air gaps in the system to allow for expansion. The following day was bitterly cold, and the canal had a rather thicker layer of ice across it, not enough to prevent movement, but sufficient to worry Jim just a little. The towpath had a fresh covering of snow which, with nobody having walked on it provided a slip free, if slow, surface. The hot bricks had just about done their job, and they were reheated in the same manner before they set off. It caused more than an hour's delay, but they needed that to prepare for what lay ahead. Exposed areas would have thicker ice and this would need to be dealt with in a way that both Jim and Amanda remembered from old Lou's telling. He had described the work of the ice breaking boats, and commented that, although small, the Mayfly would be good in ice due to the round bilge created by its clinker construction. If they were going to keep the boat rocking, then they would need to secure everything or risk ending the day with it all landing in a big mess in the middle. The bricks, hay-box, and several hot water bottles were stashed in the cabin, which was closed for all but emergencies. A thick blanket covered with a tarpaulin was lashed round the door to keep any draught out in the hopes that it would retain some heat for the evening. Eventually, with a hot breakfast inside them and all Thermos flasks filled with coffee, Jim leant over and pulled the starter cord. The motor was happy to fire up despite the cold, and with Amanda gently rocking her, the Mayfly moved forward. Progress was slow, and fuel consumption higher than normal but they could move and felt that they should, not knowing what the season now had in store for them. Whilst much harder than normal, working the locks did keep them warm, and the regular cups of strong instant coffee kept them alert. More snow followed the previous day's issue, which made it hard to see at times, but despite their protestations, the pair were secretly enjoying the experience even though it was tinged slightly with the knowledge that the situation had proved fatal to boating families with a far greater knowledge than they had, and that, should they for any reason get stuck in the open it would be unlikely that anybody would be alerted to their situation. But they moved forward, hour by hour, until the light began to fade, and they again stopped, rather early by their standards, for the night.

"We're about two days away if this keeps up, day and a half if it clears," Jim said, after looking at the map. The whole boat was well lit with four hurricane lamps, their two spares being pressed into service more for heat than light. Snow still fell in small flurries, but the sky was clearing again meaning there would be another day with ice slowing them down. The fire with the bricks on was looking after itself and glowed red in the dark, Amanda having remembered from her camping trips that you could get a lot more out of fuel if you kept a fire smouldering, so they had piled loose earth up round the sides, and put the bricks in the top with a bit of cover from a piece of sheet metal that they had found when they were foraging.

"We're probably the only boat moving at the moment," Amanda said. "I've kept an eye out for footprints, but there's only been ours."

"Who'd be stupid enough to holiday now!" Jim smiled. "But it's got an atmosphere for sure. All of it's own, and it beats what I had into a hat. Why didn't I tell that to the careers teacher when he asked what I wanted to do!"

306

"Hmm. Yes well Mr. Stratton," Amanda said in a faux schoolmaster's voice. "I fear we may have trouble placing someone whose ambition in life is to be refrigerated in a small wooden box."

They were tied up in open country, and, but for the snow, would be able to see for a long way and, had anyone been looking, would have been visible for a long way too. It was as though, for that night, there was nobody else in the world. There they were, no street lighting visible, all noise attenuated by the covering of snow. They were well fed, had enough fuel, and were even reasonably warm, as long as they kept several layers of clothing on. All things were right and made their world of less than sixteen feet long feel secure. Neither though was stupid enough to let complacency or smugness set in. The line was there and they knew their lives now depended on doing things right. It was no longer a game of evading the authorities, and others who may have meant well, or ill, but whom they simply did not want any dealings with. Even that was no game, but this was nature, more powerful than any petty crook, or government department. There was no appealing or reasoning here, the rules were set and however good or evil a person was, nature would feel no pity in their passing should they set a foot wrong on the ice, or allow hypothermia to take hold of their bodies. It neither mourned old Lou, nor did it celebrate sparing Amanda and Jim on the occasions that it had. It just went on. The next day started much colder than the last, but cloud started to drift in during the morning and there was a noticeable increase in the temperature. Light rain started to fall in the early afternoon, which made the lock-sides and tow-paths treacherous, as the underlying ice became partially exposed, coated elsewhere with a lubricating layer of semi frozen water. Progress was slower than the previous day, as they had to be doubly careful of what they were doing, which coupled to the waterproofs they wore made life very uncomfortable. The cabin was again closed for business, with a newly heated set of bricks and hot water bottles doing their best to keep the cold out. All was going according to plan until some packed ice gave way under Amanda's foot. With nothing to hold onto she was over in less than a second, and had landed in the icy water of the emptying lock. Good swimmer as she was, the layers of clothing and the draw of the water rendered her skill useless. She could not even summon the breath to scream. Jim turned to suggest a cup of tea in the next pound, and saw the Mayfly heading towards the gate, but no Amanda. The feeling of fear that sets all muscles rigid gripped him but it was less than a second,

307

which seemed like hours, before Amanda heard the rasping crash of the paddle gear being dropped in a way that was strictly frowned upon. Moments later she felt Jim's hands grabbing her under the armpits as she surfaced, coughing and shivering. With all the strength he could muster, he heaved his partner up and out of the freezing water, and got her away from the lock-side.

"That's it," he said. "In the cabin and get undressed and dry as quick as you can. We've got to get you warm and there's no time to lose."

"If I do that I'll soak the place, a few seconds isn't going to hurt. Go get some towels please," she smiled though thinned blueish lips.

Jim was gone for less than half a minute and returned to find Amanda standing as she had been, but without her clothes, which lay in a stagnant heap beside her.

"There's nobody except you and you've seen it already. Now give me the towels, I'm bloody freezing," she said through gritted teeth.

Jim bundled Amanda, wrapped in the towels, into the cabin and made the Mayfly properly fast against the lock-side so that he could set about pouring coffee for her from the Thermos. Her hand came out to accept the cup, and it was not long before it was returned empty. The towels soon followed, at which point Jim acting on impulse, took all his sweaters and shirt off as a single garment and threw them into his partner, followed by the rest of what he was wearing. Leaving the waterproofs, which he had discarded after pulling Amanda from the water, in the cockpit to dry.

"Put it on whilst it's still warm, the lot. I'll get something as soon as you're dressed," he began shivering as he spoke.

Without argument, she dressed in his clothes as quickly as he had removed them, almost immediately feeling the benefit of the warmth of Jim's body. There was not much difference in size between Jim and Amanda so with a little belt tightening, and a turn-up on the jeans she looked reasonably well dressed for the task of moving a small boat along a canal in bad weather. Rather less could be said of Jim, who was still stark naked but waiting patiently in the cockpit.

"Hey! You'd better get dressed too," Amanda smiled, sifting through the clothes bag and handing him the necessary. "Thanks pal." She added warmly. She had not thought twice about Jim's action. It was practical, and it worked too. Apart from the feeling that you get when you drink something and it goes down the wrong way, she felt pretty much back to normal. The feel of her partner's clothes gave her more than practical

308

warmth though, and she couldn't quite name how she felt about it. On one hand they were far from clean, Jim had been wearing the sweaters for over a week, and sleeping with them on during the bitterly cold nights they'd had. If they smelt, it was of him, and the warmth they had was generated by him, which to her, at this moment, was better than any warm towels or gowns delivered to any posh hotel room she'd been in when on holiday in, what, to her, were now not better times. This was a luxury that money simply could not pay for.

"Wake up," Jim's voice cut into her thoughts. "You O.K.?" he asked. She nodded and smiled at his concern.

"If I top the lock up again we can head back to that pub we passed. I think it was only a mile or so. They should still be serving food, so we can tie up there and you can get properly warm. Sod the cost!" he said.

There was a firmness in Jim's voice that was totally fake, Amanda knew from the look in his eyes and that he'd been terrified by the incident but didn't want it to show yet. In any case, a hot meal in a warm pub did seem to be a good idea.

"You're the two youngsters on the boat aren't you," the landlady said, rather sternly as she looked the pair up and down. "You'd best come in. I shan't ask your age and you didn't say it. Now what can I do you for?"

"We had a little bit of a bit of a mishap at the lock," Amanda smiled. "I sort of fell in. Stupid of me I know, but I could do with warming up, and a good meal that we don't have to cook would kind of hit the spot. If that's O.K. with you."

"You was the lass that spoke at old Lou's funeral weren't you. I thought I'd seen your face before. I was right at the back of the place, but you did the old man proud you did," the old woman's slightly stern expression was now gone. "You sit yourselves down by the fire and I'll get you something good, and you two don't eat meat if I'm right?"

Jim's eyes widened as she spoke.

"There's a lot more besides I've heard of you two," she added. "Least you're trying to do something about the cut, and that's got to help. There's too many that say a lot and do nothing."

With that she was gone, leaving the couple sitting beside an old fashioned, and totally genuine, log fire. The pub was pretty empty, having dealt with the lunchtime rush from a small industrial estate about a mile down the road. It had clearly been a stop off point for the boats that plied the canal with loads of coal, steel and wood bound for the towns that owed their existence to the industrial revolution that the watercourse helped build. The beam above the fire had initials of long dead lovers carved and burned into it, some being quite artistic in their execution, given the tools and time available. The dates went back well over a century. Amanda had quite recovered from her ordeal when the landlady came back with two plates stacked with whatever could be found that did not contain meat, in the form of a giant mixed grill.

"Now my girl." the landlady said sternly. "You mind you eat up, and I'll bring you some coffee when you're done. That water's awful this time of year, and there's a good few that's perished in it over the years."

"I'm sure there have been. I'm lucky I suppose," Amanda replied.

"You looks out for each other. That's the lucky bit," the landlady smiled. "You look at all them names on there. They all did, had to more like. You didn't get much choice, not like now. Then, if what I've heard is right, you two haven't had much by way of deciding things either."

She was up and gone before either Jim or Amanda could reply, so they set about their rather large lunch not realising at first quite how hungry they both were.

"We'll stop over here, and catch the bus to see my folks tomorrow. The rain should clear the ice away by the time we go. I'm not having you fall in again, and I don't fancy trying it myself either," Jim said, whilst finishing the last of his chips. Amanda half heartedly protested that they should not be wimps, but was cut short by the landlady returning with two mugs of coffee.

"That's for the little lady," she said, handing over something that had a distinct smell of rum about it. "You deserve some too fella, but you need a clearer head for now," she handed him a mug that had a far more authentic smell, and added. "You take a poker and put your mark on the beam, for old Lou if not for yourselves."

Jim looked astounded, as though he had just been told to deface the Mona Lisa with a can of spray paint. The look made Amanda, giggle like the schoolgirl she had been only a few months earlier, having consumed sufficient of her coffee for the large measure of rum in it to have taken some of its effect.

"Now how do you think the beam got like it has young un?" the landlady said. "They make 'em in factories like that now for country pubs that 'aint anything of the sort. This un grew, and if nobody adds it dies the same way as all things do."

She pointed an area that still had some space, and put the poker in the fire to heat up. Jim picked it up and carefully worked away for some time to produce something in a similar style to the more artistic marks made, ending up with his and Amanda's initials entwined with the date and the name of their boat. After he'd finished, Amanda commented that it looked as authentic as the rest.

"It is," Jim replied. "She's right you know. Each one of those were put there by people like us. They had their dreams and we have ours. It's like we really are a part of something bigger."

Amanda, who was a bit drowsy with the food, warmth and rum simply smiled, put her hand in Jim's, laid her head on his shoulder, and fell asleep.

A bus passed close to the pub, but it would be two changes and over an hours journey to meet Jim's parents. Amanda had eventually decided, as Jim had, that it was a lot safer than trying to rush on the icy lock-sides and tow-paths, and the landlady of the pub had also lent her weight to the use of road transport.

"You want to be leaving it a good while yet before you go meeting old Lou," she'd said.

So, as presentable as they could make themselves, they set off with no idea of what to expect. The journey was uneventful, each change took them slowly away from their peaceful mooring, and gradually through urban sprawl to the town centre, and the restaurant where they'd arranged to meet Jim's parents. The place looked reasonably pleasant, and, as they entered they saw someone Jim recognised.

"I thought you knew this was a family matter," his mother spoke first. "But never mind, your dad will be here soon. How are you Jimmy? I hear you've had a little holiday, but you might have told your cousin a bit more beforehand."

"Dad?" thought Jim. It was an incongruous thing to hear, and for him to think. Dad, and it's longer diminutive of Daddy always seemed for other closer family units, not his. He smiled briefly but said nothing. His father then appeared through the door of the restaurant, his raised eyebrows being all the recognition Amanda got before he warmly greeted her partner in a manner that seemed to her just a little forced.

"Now," he said firmly. "Let's order. I'll have a nice juicy steak I think, medium rare, with chips and things."

311

Amanda's face lost a good deal of its colour.

"You joining me in that my lad." he smiled.

Jim's choice of a simple salad, the only thing that he was pretty sure would be free of meat, elicited instant comment.

"You've not gone all *vegetarian* on us have you?" his mother said. The line was spat out by her with a particular tone of disgust. It was met with no reply from Jim, and the menu was taken from his hand before he could manage to pass it to Amanda, who cast a mildly bemused glance his way. The order for two steaks and a salad was taken and again, before Jim had a chance to point anything out his father started speaking.

"You're mum and I have had our differences, you know that lad," he said cheerily. "But we seem to have got over them now, so we thought we'd go for a new start. In New Zealand son! How about that, we all go out there and it's all new to all of us."

Jim opened his mouth but his mother cut in.

"I know it must be a surprise, but it's a marvellous chance. Everything is so good out there, and the weather is like here only better. You'd love it I'm sure. We can leave all our troubles behind us and it'll all be new," she beamed across the table.

Jim frowned. "What if I like the life I have here," he replied flatly.

"What's to keep you here?" his father asked. "I mean really what is?"

"Amanda," Jim answered stonily.

"Now you're just being stupid," his mother chirped. "You're too young for all of that commitment. Trust me I know how easy it is to have a drink too many and next thing you're in the club. Then you're tied down with a mouth to feed that you didn't want. Is that what you want from life.?

"Isn't that up to Jim?" Amanda spoke almost under her breath.

"It's none of your business young lady," Jim's mother cast a withering look her way. "I said this was family business so keep out of it."

"Amanda is my family," Jim replied very calmly.

"That's just nonsense. Someone you knock off a few times isn't anywhere near the same," his father said.

"First off," Jim spoke slowly to keep his mounting anger at bay. "You don't speak like that in front of Amanda. It's not polite. Second, you're damn right, it's no way the same. You have never been there for me. Amanda has, and will be. That makes her a damn sight more like family that you ever have been."

"Look lad, we're talking about a new start, don't let someone like her get

312

in the way," his father said.

"Fuck New Zealand, and fuck you," Jim had a quiet fury in his voice that Amanda recognised, but had never heard in such concentration. "I may not have been that good with school but I can add up. If I'm the mouth you didn't want then, you can do without me now as well."

He got up and left without a further word, followed by Amanda who, taken by surprise, had to run a couple of steps before she caught his elbow.

"Stop, Jim," she said, remarkably calmly under the circumstances. "You can't go without, well, you just can't. Think of Lou!"

She led him back to the table, and both sat down again. She knew Jim's parents were looking straight at her, and looked up.

"What have you done to our son?" Jim's mother piped up. "He's never spoken to us like this."

"Not his fault my love," his father replied. "At his age, a bit of skirt shows you any attention, well, it's a red blooded male we've raised and no mistake. Now, just apologise Jimmy and it'll be fine."

"No," Amanda spoke sharply. "You two start by apologising to Jim."

"Bitch," Jim's mother spat the word at her.

Jim levelled his eyes at his parents, and spoke with the same quiet fury in his voice.

"I came back to the table because Amanda asked me to," he said. "That's her name you know, Amanda. Amanda Josephine Donaldson. If you want this to be family, then you include her and don't think I'm as stupid as you were. You never raised me at all, neither of you did, and you're deluding yourselves to think so. You know where I went, and Amanda has listened to what happened to me. Pretty much all of it. I told her because she listened, and when I knew her better I knew she listened because she cared. It's all about choice in the end. If you'd have wanted to know me, raise me, well, you fill in the blanks. I'm here now and I am happy with the person I am that's all. So far as emigrating goes, well it's all one to me, because I'm not going and, if you want my advice, neither should you. All you'd be doing is running away from your problems, but they can run faster than you. A hell of a lot faster. If you think you can make it together there then do it here and don't pretend on the other side of the world."

He remained silent to the startled stares of his parents for some minutes then continued.

"I said fuck you, earlier on, and I shouldn't have. Even though I appear to be the result of too much alcohol I'm here, and you two brought me into

313

the world, so thanks for that at least. You should apologise to Amanda for what you said to her. I don't have to justify the best friend I've ever had to you, and I won't do. If you can't see what's under your nose then there's an optician across the road," he said, as the food arrived.

"Two steaks with all the trimmings, and a salad," the waiter beamed falsely.

Jim had put a hand in his pocket and found a near empty tube of glue he had been using to do a minor repair at some time. He stood up, and placed it neatly on one of the steaks that the waiter was about to serve.

"There," he said smiling. "We're about done. You take those and glue the cow back together. Oh and you could feed the salad to a rabbit. Mum, Dad, I'll be in touch some time soon, if you're still here."

"No!" Jim's mother said suddenly. "No, you can't leave it like this. It was all supposed to be a new beginning."

"And it *can* be," Amanda seized the chance to speak. "Just not the one you expected that's all. You can't do what you've both done and not expect it to have consequences. I guess I'm one of those."

She looked down at the floor and waited, her sentence was continued by Jim's father.

"And if you had a shred of decency you would go away and and let Jim get his priorities straight. Playing house is different to real life, and playing house is all you are doing," he said.

"And you'd know that I suppose?" Jim's icy voice came in. "You must be prime quality idiots if you think I'd listen for a minute to any of your advice on being a couple," his voice tailed off. "I'm surviving, that's what, just like I've had to since you palmed me off because you couldn't stand the sight of each other. Amanda is right, everything is different, we knew that at some point it all stops being a game, and if you want to take that step you accept what comes at you. Actually, no, I said I was surviving. I was. Now, thanks to Amanda, I'm alive. You asked what Amanda has done to me, I'll tell you. She's loved me, properly. That's all, and it's more than enough, far more than I deserve."

Jim looked at the blank stares from his parents, and then to the slightly watery hazel eyes of Amanda, then closed his own, and said, "Look sorry but fuck New Zealand. Go if you want. You know how to get in touch with us now, but at least bloody think about what you're doing."

"I don't want to speak out of turn," Amanda said hesitantly. "But if I know you at all Jim, I think there's nothing more you'd like in the world than to sort this mess out.   Its eaten bits out of you, I know it has," she paused to gather her thoughts, and started again just as Jim's mother opened her mouth to speak.   "I don't know what happened to you two," she continued, addressing Jim's parents directly.   "I think Jim was too young to know much about it, but I can clearly see you haven't gone back there and sorted that bit out either.   It won't go away you know, Jim's right, but it's the two of you that need to sit and talk, to each other, not us.   You need to talk for a long time too.   There's some of what made Jim who he is in both of you, there has to be, so I can love you for that if nothing else."

"Would sir like to order again?" the waiter asked, having removed the steaks, had returned and was now waiting patiently.   Jim's father ordered coffees for everyone, more to stall for time than the desire to drink it.   His mother sat forming a reply, opening her mouth to start, and then closing it to form a better one, all of which gave her the look of a giant goldfish. Eventually she did speak.

"You're either a clever and manipulative little tart, or there's more to you than meets the eye.   I'm not sure which," she said.

"It's the second one," Jim said firmly.   "Trust me.   Whatever you think, I do know Amanda."

"This was supposed to be so simple son," Jim's father added.

"It is and it isn't," Jim replied calmly.   "Like two sides of a coin.   But it isn't me that has to talk.   Amanda is right, its you that should, both of you. And what's more you've known that since I was about five years old. That's when the rows really started isn't it.   That's the Christmas that never was, I don't really remember much about being four, but I have no memory of anything, well, sorry, but all I can say is that I don't feel I was anything other than something that had to be dealt with."

Amanda laid her right hand on top of Jim's left, and gripped it ever so lightly.   Even his mother, who was doing her best to see Amanda in the worst light possible, could not disregard this simple gesture, nor the effect it had on her son.   A simple flick of a smile, something that Amanda knew meant he was O.K. inside, the recognition between the two spoke more words than had been said since the four had met in the restaurant.

"We've got to go now," Jim's mother said.   "We will be in touch.   Your father will pay the bill before we go."   Looking at his father, she added, "Come on, the girl is right.   We've a lot of talking to do."

They exchanged an embarrassed smile to Jim and Amanda before getting up to leave, and then they were walking between the tables to the

315

door.

"Well. That was all a bit odd," Jim said. "Let's get the washing from the laundrette and go home."

"Yes," Amanda replied, linking her arm in his. "Lets."

The bus journey back was spent mostly in silence. The weather had warmed, but with the milder air came drizzling rain, that was neither a proper precipitation nor a mist. It splattered the windows but the couple were oblivious to it. Amanda again leant her head against her partners shoulder and rested as he slowly stroked her hair. They would have missed their stop had the conductor of the vehicle not prompted them. Smiling, they took their laundry down, past the pub, to the little Mayfly, and put the large bag in the cabin. It was late in the afternoon, and the pub would be opening soon.

"I think we can stand having another meal we don't have to cook," Jim said. "I just realised, we never had lunch."

"They didn't even give me time to bloody well order," Amanda half laughed. "You should have seen the waiter's face when you told him to glue the cow back together!"

Laughing, Jim replied, "It's all I could think of. I mean the poor bugger was dead anyway, but I wasn't having them chew it, half raw, in front of you. It would always turn my stomach even when I was small. I'd forgotten they did that."

About half an hour later, Jim was at the bar, sorting out the order, as Amanda made one of her routine calls to the corner shop.

"There's going to be more music to face when we do land back at the island you know," Amanda said as she sat next to Jim at the same table they had occupied the previous day. "Marie told me that my folks are on their way back."

"That's good," Jim smiled. "Why the face?"

"It's not so much what she said, but what she didn't. I don't get the impression I'm going to be in their good books, something about spending rather a lot of time away from school," she replied.

"It'll come right," Jim smiled. "They can't be arseholes. They're related to you."

Amanda said nothing, but leaned forward and kissed her lover, lingeringly and unashamedly. Her hair still had the slightest smell of frost on it from the fall into the lock, her breath was warm, and the hint of perfume that she had put on that morning emphasised the closeness he felt

316

to her.   As their lips eventually parted company, there was that flick of a smile from each of them.   Amanda caught Jim's eye and he hers, both sets bright and untroubled.

"Sorry to disturb you my dears," the landlady said, as she arrived with their plates.

"Let's eat," Amanda smiled.   "You must be at least as hungry as I am."

Chapter 19

The milder weather had seen most of the snow off, and a good deal of the ice had been replaced by mud which, although disgusting in its composition, was a good deal more predictable. Rain came on and off, but the winds were light so they were able to keep the cover over the back of the Mayfly without being blown all over the canal. Progress was reasonable, as the countryside began to give way to the sprawling housing that surrounded the conurbation of the big city. The pollution monitors had been delivered at an address to the north, leaving the last but one of their Soviet watches which was to go, not as they had thought, to a businessman but some minor and totally undistinguished member of parliament who had an interest in inland waterways. The handover was not to be an event, in fact it sounded almost clandestine in the instructions Dave Harris had left them. But it was a delivery, and they would get paid. The Mayfly was again immaculate, with anything that could be made to shine shining. The motor was running almost better than ever, and the crew had started the morning with a good breakfast. All of these things were the formula for a good day, but there was an almost imperceptible wistfulness about their manner. There were things that they clearly wanted to, but dare not, say. It was eleven o'clock or thereabouts that Amanda turned around from idly leaning on the cabin top and looking forward to leaning back against the closed doors and looking at Jim, who was steering through the long pound between two small flights of locks.

"I know we can't," she said. "But I could go another lap of all of this tomorrow without a thought."

Jim knew what she meant. It was getting very close to the time that their odyssey would draw to a natural close, and there should, they both felt, be some kind of grail at the end of it.

"I really don't feel like being normal again," she continued.

"Were you ever?" Jim smiled.

"Thanks for that Jim! If I had a dish rag I'd throw it," Amanda laughed.

"Normal and you? It doesn't sound right that's all," Jim said. "This, all of it, it was in you like a plant is inside a bulb or a seed. It's daydream

318

stuff I guess, but you went and did it."

"We went and did it, and we still are Jimbo," Amanda replied, smiling now.

"So we keep on, what of it. See what happens. Who knows, we might get sunk when we're doing the tide stuff, then we won't have to face the music," Jim replied.

"Cheery sod!" Amanda laughed and poked her tongue out at her lover.

"At least we have been guaranteed a safe mooring when we get to the city," Jim added. "We'll be able to see the sights if we want to."

The tie up was to be with a small community of boat dwellers who, though of unkempt appearance, were apparently to be trusted. They made fast to a narrowboat, not unlike Vera's but converted in a manner similar to Vanessa's Chrysophyllax Diver. The occupants had gone off for some months to discover themselves, but the protection afforded by the bulk of the vessel was very welcome to Jim and Amanda who, now more than ever, wanted to keep themselves to themselves. It was mid afternoon when they arrived, and the M.P. had sent his secretary to collect the watch which he intended to brandish in front of parliament in a debate on the future of the canal system as proof that trade still existed, and could be made to flourish again. He would have too but for the fact that his party had rather turned against the idea and favoured some kind of regrading exercise that would enable them to appear to be taking decisive action whilst actually doing nothing whatsoever. To wave material evidence that people actually had succeeded in carrying goods by water, and thereby defeat his party's argument that nobody did or even could, may have been detrimental to his career so he put the thing in a drawer and forgot about it, and his principles, for another day. Some of the boat dwellers were going to hit the town and see what was going on, and they offered to take Jim and Amanda with them, but the couple politely declined, preferring to sit and watch the world go by. There was a practical reason as well, as they needed to be up early and have a clear head to catch the tide right for the river.

The following morning was bright but cold, not as bad as to freeze the canal over, but not far off either. The fuel tank and cans were all full, and the motor had been checked over thoroughly whilst they'd waited the previous day for the M.P. to arrive. They had some miles to cover before they got to the tidal river and knew the importance of getting the timing

319

right.   Too late and they would be running against the tide which would slow them down, leaving them with not enough time to get to the island in a single day.   This didn't matter too much, but they wanted to do a good job and finish on a high note as much for their wooden companion as for their own pride.   It seemed all too soon that they were running upriver with the current, and the motor pushing them at a speed that seemed unattainable, and altogether heady, after the months they had spent moving quietly at walking pace.   The wide river was not unlike the run down to the narrow canals in the north, though dirtier but at the same time not as bleak.   As the half tide lock came into view, Jim remembered his first trip to pick up the initial cargo what seemed like years ago.   There was no trouble, or even any shouts this time, and they passed through with their spirits lifting.   The next lock saw them on familiar territory, but with the current now against them.   Melting snow and the days of rain that followed made this something of an adversary, but the little motor was a gem and still managed to keep them moving just faster than canal speed even if it it did need rather more fuel than planned to achieve this.   Jim had wanted to stop briefly at Saracen's to say hello but the yard had been closed for the day for some unknown reason so they continued, which made up for some of the time lost to the water flowing against them.   As the afternoon progressed the speed of flow increased and their forward motion slowed but eventually the island, with it's pretty bridge came into sight.   Jim knew the jetty at the bottom of Dave Harris' garden, and made for it.   It was unusual to come alongside using so much motor power just to stand still, but the little craft was stable, answering her commands with good grace as always she did, and Amanda stepped neatly ashore with the ropes in her hand, to be greeted by the irascible bearded apparition known locally as Dave Harris.

"Bloody hell!" he beamed.   "It's bloody good to see you.   I mean it! Bloody fantastic.   How the hell are the pair of you?"

"Still here," Amanda smiled, giving the man a hug.   "Rumours of my death and all that!" she added laughing.

"And how's your belly off for spots Jimmy my lad," he turned his attention away from Amanda as Jim, having thrown an anchor out as a precaution, came ashore with mooring stakes, two extra ropes and a big hammer.

"Good to see you Dave," Jim said as he bashed the spikes into the ground.   "And on your feet too.   Thanks for all the stuff you did for us."

"Nuffin mate, nuffin!   I'd do it all again.   But there are a few people may want to see you." Dave added.

"Tomorrow," Amanda said firmly. "Today we're here, and that's enough. No offence to you Dave, but I could go and do it all over again right now, I told Jim that several times."

"Nothing but how it should be my love. And I won't breathe a word. I bet the pair of you could kill off a cup of tea," Dave replied.

The Mayfly was now tied with enough slack for her to rise and fall with the river, so Jim got back aboard and disappeared into the cabin, returning with a small box.

"Yours I think," he said, handing it to Dave. "It's done a few miles but it should be O.K."

Happy that the Mayfly was secure, they all went back up the garden to Dave's kitchen where they sat for a long time, filling him in on the details of their voyage around the country, their talk fuelled by regular cups of tea until Dave interrupted them with something altogether more important.

"We need food!" He said. "There's a good curry house opened if you want some takeaway or we could go for a proper sit down. On me of course."

"Bloody hell!" Amanda all but shouted. "I'd forgotten the hay-box! It's been going since about five this morning."

Dave looked nonplussed.

"This, is a must see!" Jim said as Amanda went off in search of the rather battered hat-box that had served them so well over the months. "Amanda was a girl guide you know," he added by way of an explanation, which did nothing to change Dave's confused expression. Amanda returned with the item and, with a flourish that many a magician could not manage, produced a pot of still quite hot vegetable curry.

"There is usually enough for breakfast when we do this. Have you got a pan for the rice?" she said

Still looking somewhat bemused, Dave rummaged around and got the cleanest of his saucepans and handed it over.

"So, how's the bungalow?" Amanda asked as Jim served the aromatic and appetising dish. "Did it ever get new owners, and if so have they ruined it?"

"That's the weirdest thing of all." Dave replied. "Not long after you left, there was a flurry of activity, like they were going to do a quick job to do a holiday let. But nothing was ever done. The vans were there in the morning, and they were carting stuff over the footbridge, signs were down,

321

then some guys turned up in a posh car and everything went in reverse, so now it's just the same as when you left it."

"At least they haven't destroyed it," Amanda sighed.

"I'm a bit out on the edge of things, but you want to see your ex-employer about that," Dave said. "She reckons she has a stack of stuff for you that looks like legal things, you know, solicitors and stuff. She didn't want to send it all on in case it got lost or got you into more hot water."

More stories followed the curry, and the evening ended in the early morning, as Jim and Amanda returned to their home, wondering what the next day would bring. They woke early, and it was turning cold again. Without the bricks to keep them warm, it felt worse than it actually was, and they emerged to a morning that had been frosty, but which was warming, or rather becoming less cold, due to the leaden clouds that had drifted in.

"Looks like we made it just in time," Jim pointed towards the sky. "It's going to snow like buggery today if I'm reading those things right."

"I need a good traditional breakfast before we face the music," Amanda said rather dejectedly. "Get a pan on and we'll do some fried bread and marmalade. It always cheers me up."

Jim smiled as he pushed the pump home, and waited for the familiar sound from the stove. Four more pumps and the burner was running like a small rocket, with the frying pan heating up ready for the first slice. In a few minutes the second stove had been lit for the kettle. Mayfly was still their home, and despite the grey sky, the cold, and the first flakes of what was going to be a lot of snow, they were comfortable in her.

"Better get another cup out," Jim said, as he saw Dave emerging from his bungalow.

"I was going to offer you two breakfast, but you've beaten me to it," he said with a smile on his face. "Weather's going to be crap today, it said on the radio," he added.

Breakfast took longer than planned due to the telling of more stories to Dave, who seemed to want to hear everything they had to say and never looked bored even at the most trivial detail, but Jim and Amanda both knew it was time to walk back to reality. Of course reality for them was their time together on the Mayfly, this was altogether another person or people's reality and both felt unsure of what to expect. First stop was Marie's shop, looking just as it had earlier in the year but for the fresh fall of snow. Marie greeted them and handed Amanda a pile of mail, a lot of which seemed to come from a firm of solicitors that she had never heard of. There followed a phone call that took over half an hour, and left Amanda about as confused at the end as she was at the beginning.

"You two keep an eye on the shop and I'll put some tea on," Marie said calmly. "Then we can talk, and, you're going to have to phone your parents young lady. They arrived back about three days ago, and have badgered me to let them know as soon as I do. But it's better coming from you."

Rather reluctantly Amanda agreed to phone, uncertain as to how things would be. The call was short, she was told to stay with Marie and they would come round.

"Not sure I liked the tone of that though. I've not been told what to do for a long time now, and I cant say I'm too keen any more," she said despondently.

"Let's see how things are before we jump to any conclusions," Jim replied.

It was just over half an hour before a taxi arrived containing Amanda's parents. At the sight of the pair, she couldn't help greeting them in the way any daughter would after a long separation. There were hugs, a few tears, and a long pause.

"This is Jim," Amanda said quietly. "Jim, this is my mum and dad."

Jim politely greeted them but the atmosphere had taken on more of a chill than the snowy air outside.

"I'm sure Jim knows that we have family matters to discuss together," Amanda's mother said. "So if you'll excuse us."

"Jim is family to me now," Amanda protested in the same way Jim had, some days back.

"I know it seems like that dear, but," Jean was cut off by Jim.

"It's O.K. Mand," he said placidly. "You need to talk to your folks. I'm here when you need me," then, turning to Amanda's mother, he added, "We've had a talk like this with my parents, but that's different. I just want to say that, whatever you may think of me, I'm very glad you did come back."

The shop had an old style front with an awning under which Jim sat on an old garden chair, watching the snow. Amanda's parents were deep in discussion in the back kitchen, occasionally dragging Marie in for her contribution. He sat, watched, and waited feeling really rather useless, and just a bit cold. It was nearly an hour before Amanda came back through the door and sat on the step, red faced and silent. She had obviously been crying. Jim raised his eyes from the ground to meet hers,

"There's no talking to them," she said. "I just want to go away again."

"You know that's not possible though don't you," Jim replied. "There isn't really anywhere to run on this one, and I'm not going to be the one that separates you from your family. That wouldn't be right."

"Is this goodbye then?" Amanda's voice was very uneven. "They don't want me seeing you. Not at any cost."

"You've never lied to me Mand. You say I'm family to you," Jim said calmly.

Amanda nodded.

"It's how I've felt for what seems like ever, but well you know all of the details," he added.

Amanda flicked the briefest of smiles on her weary face.

"Your folks weren't there," he continued. "So they don't fully know what we've been through together. Perhaps it's time they should."

With that he got up and walked into the shop, past a bemused looking Marie, and then through to the back kitchen where he found Mr. and Mrs. Donaldson.

"Hello. I'm Jim Stratton, but you already know that." he said calmly and politely. "There isn't much I can say about me, except that my life took a different turn when I walked into this shop a few months ago to get some groceries for Dave Harris. It's all accident and chance that throws things in your face, but it's how you react to it all that can change history I guess."

"What's the point of all this," Edwin said. "We've come to take our daughter to our new home, and that's an end of it."

"So, go and take her. I'm powerless to stop you, and I wouldn't do anyway. But does she want to go?" Jim countered.

"No," Edwin conceded. "And you know that's because she's infatuated with you."

Neither had noticed Amanda's ashen face at the door.

"Do you know what it feels like when someone lays their life on the line for you Dad?" she asked quietly, her speech very uneven.

"I can't really say that I do. But I know your mother would, and so would I for her, and of course we both would for you," Edwin replied. "What are you getting at?"

"I know Jim would, because he already has, and he did it without even

324

thinking about. I know he'd give me the clothes off his back because he's done that too. That's all I came in to say," Amanda said.

"Is this true?" Edwin turned to Jim, who was unable to reply for some moments.

"The guy Carver," he said. "The one that stitched you up. He sent some of his tough guys after us. I sort of got caught by one of them. I think that's what she means."

"I can see her head has been turned by you," Edwin went on, and was cut short by Amanda.

"Is that all you're going to say about it Jim! It was real when I told you about it Dad! You remember, when we phoned from the hotel. They had a knife at Jim's throat, a real sharp hunting knife, and he just told me to keep going. They could and would have killed him! Look at the scar if you don't believe me," she added, pointing to the mark on Jim's chin.

"So," Jim interrupted. "You never listen, you dived off under the bridge and clobbered the git with a windlass. So we're even."

"And you pulled me out of the icy water and gave me the clothes off your back because they were warmer than the ones in the cabin," Amanda retorted.

"And you got me out of jail!" Jim said, beginning to see something of a funny side to the argument.

"Only because you got yourself in there trying to sort things out for my bloody ungrateful parents!" Amanda paused. "Oh shit!" she added. "I'm sorry, to both of you! All three! Shit! Shit! Shit! You know what I mean."

"He was probably only trying to impress you," Jean tried to get the discussion on to some sort of level.

"Do you know what. He bloody well did!" Amanda shouted. "Infatuation is what I felt for George bloody Harrison when I was twelve. I know it's not long after that in the scheme of things, but. Well, bloody but! That's all"

"Jean," Edwin said calmly. "If what Amanda says is true, the boy does rather impress me too, I have to say."

Jean cast a sharp look across to Edwin.

"She befriended Jim, not the other way around," he continued. "He could have just gone away and left our problems for her to sort out. But the lad has stood by her, by all counts they have grown a lot in the last months." Edwin spoke in a softer tone than he had used before. "Amanda

325

had chosen to stay and fight before Jim turned up, we both know that don't we," he added.

"We should never have gone away," Jean frowned. "We should never have worked with Mr Carver."

"Why not? You didn't know he was an arsehole or you'd not have done it," Jim interrupted. "You're back, and you're free of that bastard now."

"Why did you help?" Jean asked.

"Amanda's a friend the best friend I have. We ended up sharing things pretty much by accident, two heads are better than one, you know. I don't really know, it just seemed the right thing to do," Jim meandered. "All of these chances, they just tie my head in knots. Thing is we're here now and you can clear your names if you want to, to be honest if what our friend, Jeremy Simms, at the university says is true they're clear anyway. He's old but as sharp as razor blades. I've met the best person on the planet, and Carver junior is in the nick. I should thank him though because without him I wouldn't have met Amanda. Or maybe I would have because maybe it's all fate."

"Or you could make a shit porridge out of the whole affair," Marie said from the door. "It's in your hands."

"We entrusted Amanda to you," Jean changed her attack. "And you just let her go. Now look what's happened."

"What has?" Marie replied. "Your name has been cleared, there are people that want to work with you. An added bonus is the fact that your daughter appears to have found her soulmate, albeit a little early in her life, but how old were you when you met Edwin?"

Jean blushed, Marie and her had known each other since school, and knew most of each others secrets.

"Things were different then," she said. "We never knew whether the next day would be the last."

"And things are different now?" Marie countered. "Think of what's pointing at this country before you speak. Don't forget too that Amanda had been living on the island for some time before Jim arrived. If you ask me she's done well."

As the argument between Marie and Jean started to heat up, with Edwin adding his bit whenever he could, Jim felt Amanda's hand in his, and followed her slowly out of the room, through the shop, and into the snow.

"I can't do this," she said calmly. "You're not splitting me from Mum and Dad, if that happened it was when they left me on my own. Marie's

326

right.   I was in that bungalow for a good while before you showed up.   I could have run a disorderly house there and they'd not have been able to do much.   Sorry but I really don't care what happens."

"You don't mean that for a minute," Jim replied.   "We have to sort all of this out or it'll blight your life.   I don't know how to do it, but we always sit down with a cup of tea on the Fly and talk.   It's what we do."

They ambled slowly back to the island as the snow silently fell around them.   The Mayfly had a good coating, looking a bit like a celebratory cake in the shape of their home from the distance as it came into view.   It was not long before they were sat in their familiar surroundings with the roar, and   scent of paraffin,   warming their hearts again.   Dave Harris had noticed their arrival, but there was something about their appearance that told him they wanted to be alone together, so he turned the kitchen light off and sat in the late afternoon dusk.   It was some time before Edwin and Jean Donaldson, and to her own personal embarrassment,   Marie too, realised that Amanda and Jim had left.

"I know where they'll be," she said.   "Follow me."

There was really not much need for Marie to point the way as the trail of fresh footprints told their own story.   The heavy, turbulent current of the previous days had gone, and the river was now glass calm in the early evening.   The freshness of the snow picked the trees out in relief making a magical picture, in the centre of which sat two figures in the back of a small boat, illuminated by the amber glow of a hurricane lamp.   The two sat placidly side by side with wisps of steam just visible from the mugs of tea that warmed their hands as they watched the night slowly arrive on the river.   Jean and Edwin Donaldson stood for some time just looking across the water, and did not notice Marie's almost silent departure.   Jean remembered the grey uniform, the skiff, the warm summer evening and the proposal of marriage by the man she saw as a dashing aviator despite Edwin being a ground based engineer who had an almost natural talent for making radar work correctly.   In the normal scheme of things she was too young to make such a decision, but there was a war on and her parents saw the young, clean cut, well spoken man as a good catch and had allowed the marriage to go ahead even if it was slightly against their better judgement. She looked across at her husband, and thought for a long time.

"We can't go back to Spain even if things don't work out here Ed." she said quietly.   "And it would be wrong to force Amanda to do anything against her will."

327

"You know what you are saying." Edwin replied.

"I know," Jean said. "But our parents took a chance on allowing us happiness. I know they're younger than we were, but not by that much. And I can see how unhappy Amanda was this afternoon. She's always had a mind of her own, and been truthful."

"They may not be happy now." Edwin spoke softly. "But I'd say they were contented. You know it's not for us to give our permission. Not any more. But we can be happy for them, and we won't lose anything by that. Amanda never hid anything, and she does wear her heart on her sleeve. I think she is genuine, and from my reading of Jim, I think he is too. That may not be saying much, given the mess I made of the business partnership."

"Jim does seem a good person," Jean replied. "It was just a bit of a shock that's all."

The light form the hurricane lamp flickered with the movement of the boat, and the two figures were now ashore, walking slowly to the bridge to trace their steps back to Marie's shop. In the middle of the footbridge they were met by Edwin and Jean.

"We both knew that life doesn't always go on like it has done," Amanda said, adding, "There's been routine ordinary stuff in that too."

"You said that things can't be the same any more," Jean replied softly. "I should have known that when everything went wrong. I think for a while we all fooled ourselves."

"Mum, Dad. I love you, you both know that, but I love Jim too," Amanda said. "We've been through a lot, and it's the way it is. I know what I'm saying. I was warned not to go lighting fires unless I was sure but I still did it."

"Because you were sure?" Edwin felt he had to say something.

"Yes Dad. I was very sure, and there's been nothing that has made me think differently. Not for a second."

"You've been very quiet, young man," Edwin spoke with a soft voice. "Do you have anything you want to say?"

Jim thought for some moments.

"I know what it's like to be let down," his voice was less than steady.

"Take your time," Jean said quietly.

"I know, and I won't ever let your daughter down. Not ever," he looked at the bridge decking for some time before continuing. "You'll know me better soon I hope, but you may as well know that I have pretty good reasons not to trust people. But I trusted Amanda from the moment I met her. I never even questioned why I did, I just did. I think that's where everything grew from, but I can't say for certain because it grew without ether of us noticing."

"It's cold now," Jean said. "Are you sure you'll be alright on that little boat tonight."

"We've done all kinds of weather, and the Mayfly has been with us all through it. She's a nice little boat if you talk to her right," Amanda said brightly.

"And she does," Jim added. "Not when I'm looking but she does."

"And so, no doubt do you," Jean replied. "And we need to talk to you some more, both of you. Things have changed, I can see that, and I have to accept the way they are. It's unusual, but I think I'd like to get to get to know you Jim, if that's alright by your partner."

"Jean always knows what is in my mind, so count me in on that too," Edwin added. "We have some things to attend to tomorrow, but will be free from about four if we can come and see you again?"

Amanda smiled, a time was set, and the two couples parted for the night. The mood on the Mayfly was somewhat subdued despite the apparent acceptance of Jim by Amanda's parents.

"It's not a battle," Jim said quietly. "There's no winner in this."

"We all do," Amanda spoke firmly but calmly. "They don't change, they're still my mum and dad. It's just the situation. Let's go off tomorrow and you can introduce me to your friends at the boatyard."

There was plenty of time for the round trip so, as soon as it was light enough, they set off to the starting point of the odyssey, the large timber buildings of Saracen Brothers Boat-builders. The company that had been set up in the early years of the twentieth century, and had made a name for itself building day-boats, and neat looking varnished wood cabin cruisers to a very high standard. Without their help it would have been near impossible for Jim to have made such a good job of the Mayfly in the time he did. The yard had been shut when they passed on their return because of the retirement of the oldest member of the family that ran the place. At over seventy, "The Boss," as everybody referred to him, decided that it was time to enjoy his own boat, which was one of the last wooden craft to have been built at the yard some years previously. The trend towards the lower maintenance, and much less interesting, glass fibre boat had reduced demand for their wares drastically so that they now made their money by keeping existing wooden craft in good order. All appeared normal, and Jim was greeted warmly by those that knew him.

"You two have had a grand time of it," the boss's son who, despite now being in charge, did not want to use his father's title said. "Dave's had many a drink on the telling of what you were up to. And you," he addressed the remark to Amanda. "Have by all counts done a really good job of things too. You wouldn't believe what the Mayfly looked like when Jim baled her out, and she was pretty sparse when he left. We gave it about a week," he smiled. "You had the common sense to make the thing habitable. And then you go on to be the other half of a bloody good crew."

"Thanks." Amanda smiled, blushing slightly.

"Now Jim," he moved on quickly. "You can think this one over, but in the new year we'll be looking to hire someone to learn the trade for real. Proper job you understand, college and all. You want it, it's yours. The money won't be great at first but it's more than pocket money. Don't say now, but think on. I'm not advertising until new year, and you'll save me the cash for the ad if you do say yes."

"Bloody hell! I mean thanks!" Jim was wide eyed at the offer. He looked across to his partner and she smiled back.

"Do it, but only if you want," she said. "We have to do something."

"We do," Jim replied. "And if it's O.K. I will."

Hands were shaken, and the two returned to their home, to head back up the river. The run to the island wasn't too long, and although cold, it was pleasant to be about the only boat moving. Dave was at the jetty to greet them and it they were soon sitting in his kitchen with mugs of tea, sharing their news.

"I knew the old guy was planning on retiring, but I never thought he actually would," Dave said with a laugh. "Sort of a bit like me planning the grand voyage. You two little sods went and did it. I might just forgive you for that one day."

"There's time for you too," Jim smiled.

"So what are you doing then?" Dave's attention turned to Amanda.

"I hadn't thought that much," she said, her face clouding over slightly. "But I suppose I'd better conform and finish my exams. It seems so tame though, after."

"We'd better go and see your folks," Jim said, having noticed the time.

"Or they'll think I've kidnapped you again."

The arrangement had been to all meet up at a tea room not far from Marie's shop, and the couple arrived, by bus, with a few minutes to spare. Jean and Edwin Donaldson arrived by taxi, looking somewhat solemn and, after greeting Jim and Amanda, they all went inside and settled at a table by the window.

"There's been rather a lot for us to take in over the last couple of days," Jean said quietly. "And even now I can't say that I'm too happy about the way you two have chosen to live."

"You ran off to Spain," Amanda protested.

"We did, and we thought we were doing the right thing. We also thought you'd take the ticket and follow us there as arranged," Edwin added. "But I don't think that's what your mother means."

"You always taught me to stand up for what I believe in, and that was long before I met Jim," Amanda said sullenly.

"Looks like you believed in your folks if you ask me," Jim said calmly.

Amanda, Edwin and Jean now were all looking at Jim, who sat quietly, having spoken his mind.

"Does he always do that," Jean asked, not expecting an answer.

"Sometimes," said Amanda. "Sometimes he says what I'm thinking, before I think it, which is a bit weird."

"Were you thinking that?" Edwin asked.

"As I said, someone had to stand and fight," Amanda looked intensely at the tablecloth and continued. "You know Jim just turned up at the shop, to do Dave's shopping. And now we're here. It just happened. And, yes, I did believe in you two. Dad, Mum, you'd never do anything dishonest. I know at least that."

"It's more than just being here," Jim said keeping his calm voice. "Amanda has believed in me too," he continued. "And that makes me feel humble in a sort of way."

"And should we believe in you?" Edwin asked.

"Not for me to say," Jim replied quickly. "I never said Amanda should, I said she did."

"Does," Amanda corrected him. "I don't know what comes next, but I want to face it with you Jim. All of it."

"So many people have tried all of these different ways of living." Jean said. "What makes you think you'll succeed where others have not."

"Nothing," Amanda replied. "We didn't choose this, it chose us."

331

"All I was going to do was have a break from real life," said Jim flatly "Only I found it instead."

"Well," Edwin said firmly. "You will die of cold on that little boat. That is what your mother meant before you sidetracked her."

Amanda opened her mouth to speak in defence of their home, but Edwin continued.

"The bungalow was going to be yours anyway," he said. "Held in trust, which is why it could not be sold. They could only stand a chance of doing so if you were declared incapable of making decisions for yourself. And for that they needed to have you assessed."

"The bastards were going to have me sectioned!" Amanda almost squealed, not noticing a large envelope that Edwin had been carrying.

"They seem to have dug some dirt up," Edwin added. "We found that out from your friend Mr Simms. Running away wasn't the best plan, but it was a plan and it appears to have worked for you, and, thanks also to you Jim, for us as well. We are back in the country now for good, and I'll be talking to Clive Prentice in the next few days. Again Jim, that's thanks to you."

"But why should they think I'm nuts?" Amanda continued her protest.

"People can make what they want of just about anything And they didn't think it. It was just more convenient for them to force the pieces to fit," Jim said stonily.

"Yes," Edwin continued, "You're right there, and there seems to be something in the tone of your voice that tells me you have been on the receiving end of such treatment."

Jim nodded.

"I thought so," Edwin said. "And you could of course have ignored all of this."

"Of course he couldn't," Jean interrupted. "He's not the sort. We're the ones that ran away."

"Because at the time it seemed, and probably was, the only option open to you," Jim added flatly.

"We're going to have to get used to the way you make your points aren't we," Jean smiled and went on. "Whatever we say now can't alter the past, and the fact is that you and Amanda are a couple. If you stay as you are, one or both of you could end up unhappy, but if we were to forbid you from seeing each other it would make that a certainty for both of you. We decided that yesterday. Also, for all the hardships of living on such a small

332

boat, I have to say that Amanda, you look very well, and seem to be very happy too."

"We are," Amanda smiled.

"But you must know it can't go on like that."

Amanda's face fell as Jean spoke.

"Your father is right, that is what I meant, you'll freeze to death if you try and see the winter out in that boat, and what's more, both of you probably know it," Jean said.

Amanda stared at the floor, knowing she could not sensibly counter the argument. As she looked gloomily down, Edwin pushed the brown envelope across the table to her. It contained paperwork, and something hard too, though Amanda did not at first see what it was.

"This is held in trust, as I told you. Yours when you come of age. We think you should have it early," Edwin said. "We have rented a house near here, and we have an option to buy it if and when the money that has been taken from us is returned. There's plenty of room in it if."

Edwin stopped mid sentence and looked at the floor himself. Looking back up, he continued, "But things are different now aren't they."

Amanda nodded, with tears forming in her eyes.

"It was going to happen at some time, so don't be sad. And we're only going to be a short way off," Edwin smiled.

"You two have some talking to do," Jean said. "We'd better go now, you do have our blessing though."

Chapter 20

"I'm still not quite sure what happened last night," Jim said, halfway through his fried bread and marmalade.   The two had been rather too tired to talk about the events of the day, and had instead, taken a long walk along the river in intimate silence.   Whilst neither thought in words, they had both thought a lot.

"It's ours Jim, and if we want to take that step, we can take it," Amanda said, staring into mid space.

"We took that step a long time ago, at least I thought we did," Jim replied.   "It wasn't a holiday, and it isn't a holiday romance.   On the boat or somewhere else, the place doesn't really matter."

"I can't believe that someone would have me put away for what is really just a pile of old wood," Amanda continued staring into space.

"People will do anything for money, but I think there was more to it than that.   Carver wanted to humiliate your folks, and you really didn't matter much to him until you stood and fought," Jim replied.

"*We* stood and fought," Amanda corrected Jim.   "And the place is held in trust.   It must have been a special place to the first owner.   Now it comes to us."

"You," Jim pointed out the obvious.

"Us," Amanda insisted.   "You've shared everything with me."

"So why are you sad?" Jim asked gently.

"A house, a couple, back to school, and you probably to work and college, me in the shop.   It's conformity," the familiar furrow between the eyebrows was back.

"Or two idiots in yet another packing case," Jim smiled.   "It's all what we make of it."

A smile flashed across Amanda's troubled expression and Jim continued.

"You know your dad was right, winter hasn't fully hit yet, and a couple of hot bricks won't help much when it does.   Besides the "Fly" will have to come out of the water to be painted and all sorts before long.   And it would be nice to have a bog that you can flush.   We can't crap in the woods here can we."

334

"This was our first home," Amanda replied.

"And the bungalow is sort of like an extension. There's what remains of a jetty at the end of the garden. It won't take much fixing. The "Fly" will sit there nicely. She won't mind having a bit of a rest you know, she's done a lot of work this year." Jim tried to catch his partner's eye.

Their conversation was interrupted by Dave Harris.

"You'll be wanting this," he said, handing them a key. "You left it with me when you had to do a runner."

Startled, Amanda looked up and Dave saw the underlying expression on her face.

"Look," he said. "Most people have to sell their first home when their circumstances change. You can keep yours. You could at least look at the idea."

There was no arguing with the man, so Jim and Amanda walked the short distance to the wooden bungalow, similar in style, but a bit smaller than Dave's. Amanda put the key in the door and turned it.

"Here we go Jimbo," she said.